O GOD OF BATTLES

Harry Homewood

D0039858

BANTAM BOOKS
TORONTO · NEW YORK · LONDON · SYDNEY · AUCKLAND

This low-priced Bantam Book
has been completely reset in a type face
designed for easy reading, and was printed
from new plates. It contains the complete
text of the original hard-cover edition.
NOT ONE WORD HAS BEEN OMITTED.

O GOD OF BATTLES

A Bantam Book / published by arrangement with
William Morrow and Company, Inc.

PRINTING HISTORY

William Morrow edition published June 1983
Bantam edition / September 1984
2nd printing . . . June 1986

O God of Battles *and the characters portrayed therein are wholly
fictional. Any similarity between the characters and actual people,
living or dead, is unintentional.*

Published simultaneously in the United States and Canada

Bantam Books are published by Bantam Books, Inc. Its trademark,
consisting of the words ''Bantam Books'' and the portrayal of a
rooster, is Registered in U.S. Patent and Trademark Office and in
other countries. Marca Registrada. Bantam Books, Inc., 666 Fifth
Avenue, New York, New York 10103.

A MEETING OF WARRIOR BROTHERS

Mike waved his brother to a chair and stretched out on the bed facing Andy. He unfolded the newspaper Andy had brought with him and looked at the picture of Admiral Nimitz draping the Medal of Honor around his neck. He began to read the paper and then sat upright, his face horrified.

"My God, this is just awful!" he sputtered.

"What's awful?" Andy asked.

"Why, this story here about our attack on the convoy. Where did they get this stuff? 'Captain Michael O'Connor, blood pouring from his wounds, raged through the enemy convoy firing torpedoes from both ends of his submarine, his voice roaring Gaelic curses as his torpedoes exploded one ship after another.' That's awful, Andy, it wasn't like that at all."

"What was it like, Mike? Tell me." Andy settled himself in a chair near the bed, his eyes on his older brother. "Start with how you suddenly became the Captain."

O GOD OF BATTLES

Brothers, both bound for heroism
and their own separate destinies.

Bantam Books of related interest
Ask your bookseller for the books you have missed

DARKNESS AT NOON by Arthur Koestler
FINAL HARBOR by Harry Homewood
GOSHAWK SQUADRON by Derek Robinson
THE LORDS OF DISCIPLINE by Pat Conroy
PIECE OF CAKE by Derek Robinson
SILENT SEA by Harry Homewood
THE 13th VALLEY by John DelVecchio

This book is dedicated with respect and affection to Rear Admiral Maurice W. "Mike" Shea, USN (Ret.), a fighting submarine captain who would sail to hell and back and laugh all the way.

Author's
Note

In the predawn darkness of October 25, 1415, King Henry V, the twenty-seven-year-old king of England, came out of his tent. Around him his weary army of five thousand archers and one thousand men at arms were waking. On the far side of a narrow cut between two wooded hills, a French army of twenty-five thousand mounted knights and foot soldiers waited for dawn, when they would attack the small force of invaders.

King Henry, arrayed in his battle armor, knelt to pray in the cold dark. In William Shakespeare's play *King Henry the Fifth* are found the words he is said to have uttered on that chill and dank morning.

> O God of battles! steel my soldiers' hearts;
> Possess them not with fear: take from them now
> The sense of reckoning, if the opposed numbers
> Pluck their hearts from them.

By midafternoon the French dead were piled in heaps, and Henry had won the Battle of Agincourt.

Chapter One

THE HARBOR AIR was cool and damp, not yet warmed by the sun breaking through the clouds rolling in the trade winds above the Waianae and Koolau mountain ranges. A seagull swooped down and perched on a hunk of flotsam floating in the channel. Its arrogant eyes stared unblinkingly as it waited for something edible to be thrown into the water from one of the submarines moored at finger piers. Michael T. O'Connor, Lieutenant Junior Grade, USN, leaned his bulk against the Conning Tower of the U.S.S. *Sea Bass*. He sipped at a cup of coffee, savoring the richness of the liquid and the peace of the early morning. In the distance, across the main channel of Pearl Harbor, he could see the fitful gleam of the sun on the masts of the battleships moored along the south side of Ford Island.

O'Connor drank the last of the coffee, reached up and put the cup on the cigarette deck, the area aft of the bridge on a fleet submarine. He walked forward along the deck toward the gangway, where Pete Savage, Quartermaster First Class, had the deck watch. The enlisted man watched the burly Lieutenant approach. He liked Mister O'Connor, all the crew liked the big man. Since his transfer to the *Sea Bass* from a small submarine in the Asiatic Fleet a few months earlier, O'Connor had won over the crew with his outgoing cheerfulness, his willingness to dirty his hands and uniform when he asked crew members to show him how machinery worked. Captain Barney Saunders, the Commanding Officer of the *Sea Bass*, was famous for the rigorous qualification examinations he gave to newly assigned junior officers and enlisted men. Lieutenant O'Connor had been spending every moment off watch patient-

1

ly tracing each hydraulic and air line in the big fleet submarine, learning the exact location of the hundreds of valves, going over and over the blueprints until he knew the ship thoroughly.

"Mornin', Mister O'Connor," the quartermaster said. "You got everything under control below decks, sir?"

"All copasetic," O'Connor said. "What's new topside?"

"Regular church party shoved off at zero seven-thirty. No one showed up to catch the bus for early mass. Guess we don't have many Catholics aboard, sir."

"We're a minority," O'Connor said. He looked to the northwest across the land spit at the main part of the harbor.

"Lots of planes out there," he said.

"I saw them when you were drinkin' your coffee, sir. Must be the Army holding drills. I went up to the base ship's service after we got in yesterday and run into a guy I know who's stationed here. He said the Army's gone nuts with drills. They think there's gonna be a war with Japan." He looked at his wristwatch as the faint notes of a bugle sounded from the submarine-tender *Pelius*, moored a quarter of a mile away in the backwater of the Southeast Loch.

"That's First Call for Colors," Savage said. He opened a small wooden box that stood on the deck near the Conning Tower and took out a neatly folded American flag. "You mind stayin' here at the gangway while I go back and make Colors, or you want me to get someone from down below, sir?" He looked at his Duty Officer as the ululating wail of a ship's siren sounded across the harbor. The two men saw a column of black smoke rising from the south side of Ford Island. An aircraft, flying low, came rocketing toward them. The plane soared upward in a steep right turn, the red meatballs of its insignia showing plainly on the underside of the plane's wings.

"Is that a Jap?" Savage said. He stood cradling the flag in his arms, his mouth open, his eyes following the aircraft as it raced back toward the harbor. He jumped as the sound of explosions came from the harbor area.

"What the hell is going on?" O'Connor said.

"Damned if I know, sir. I thought that was a Jap plane. It could be one of those Army drills, but I never heard of a drill with all that stuff." He put the folded flag under one arm and pointed at the harbor area. "That's some drill, all that smoke and stuff, sir."

Mike O'Connor stared at the harbor area and saw the rising columns of black smoke shot through with dark red flames. "When in doubt, do something!" his football coach at the Naval Academy had been fond of saying. He turned and ran aft to the deck hatch that led down to the crew's mess compartment, where the in-port duty section was eating breakfast.

"Sound General Quarters!" he yelled down the hatch. "Machine gunners to the bridge with weapons and ammunition! On the double, dammit!" He heard the sudden stillness down below and then the clamor of voices and the rush of feet. He turned and started up the deck, almost colliding with Savage.

"Got to raise the flag," the quartermaster said, his face set and stubborn. O'Connor nodded his approval and ran to the after end of the Conning Tower. He leaped upward and grabbed the top rail around the cigarette deck and hauled himself upward. He squeezed between the rail and the periscope shears and reached the bridge hatch as John Leahy, Gunner's Mate First Class, was struggling up through the hatch with a .50-caliber machine gun in his arms. O'Connor grabbed the barrel of the gun in one big hand and ran aft to the cigarette deck and fitted the gun's spud into a socket on top of a deck-rail stanchion. Leahy and a seaman carrying a box of ammunition followed O'Connor.

"Load and lock," O'Connor ordered. He looked across the pier at the U.S.S. *Narwhal*. There was no sign of activity on the *Narwhal*'s bridge or decks. A cold shiver went through him. He was the only officer aboard the *Sea Bass*. If he had panicked because the Army was holding a realistic drill, he'd be the laughing stock of the submarine force. He chewed at his lower lip, wondering what to do next. From the deck below the bridge Pete Savage raised his voice.

"*Pelius* is making a flag hoist, Mister O'Connor. Signal reads repel enemy attack. This is no drill. You want me to go below and get a signal gun and receipt for the message, sir?"

"Negative," O'Connor answered.

"My fucking oath!" Leahy grunted. He punched Lieutenant O'Connor on the shoulder in his excitement and pointed to the south.

A long line of at least a dozen Japanese Nakajimas—"Kate" torpedo bombers—was turning over Merry Point, heading directly at the submarine piers. The sun, now clear of the

morning clouds, flashed off the long torpedoes slung beneath
the aircraft. The planes began to descend as they neared the
submarines, slowing as they eased down to their torpedo-drop
height of forty to fifty feet. They lumbered toward the moored
submarines, turning, their noses swinging toward the harbor.
O'Connor saw the leather-helmeted head of the pilot in the
lead plane turn toward the submarines as the pilot looked
down at him. A machine gun on the *Pelius* began to hammer
defiantly.

The sight that greeted the pilot of the lead Kate was exactly
what he had expected. He had been to innumerable briefings.
He had waded around in the three-acre model of Pearl Harbor
that had been built in Japan with its ship models of the
American Battle Fleet placed where intelligence reports said
they would be moored. Eight battleships of the U.S. Navy
were moored singly or in pairs along the southeast shore of
Ford Island. Every one of the seventy combat and twenty-four
auxiliary ships that were in harbor seemed to be precisely
where the charts issued to him before he left his aircraft carrier
showed they would be. Those charts had been hastily altered
just before his takeoff after a reconnaissance flight over Pearl
Harbor early that morning revealed that the three U.S. aircraft
carriers that should have been moored on the northwest side
of Ford Island were not in port. The aircraft carriers had been
the primary targets. With the carriers not in port, the
battleships would now be the top-priority targets.

The pilot of the lead Kate completed his turn to his attack
course and looked down to his right at four submarines tied up
alongside piers. Tempting targets, he thought, but not for him.
His objective was Battleship Row, now dead ahead. He passed
over the submarines and the land spit and pulled back on his
throttle a bit, lowering his air speed to just above stalling. He
checked his altimeter reading. Fifty feet. He looked down
quickly; altimeters weren't always accurate this close to the
surface of the water. His altitude looked correct to him. He
hunched forward in his seat, straining against his safety belts.
Ahead of him were the battleships. One single battleship at
anchor and then three groups of two ships each, then a smaller
ship and farther to his left another battleship. His target was
the second group of the double-moored ships.

"Banzai!" he screamed into his microphone and took dead aim at the U.S.S. *West Virginia*.

"Commence firing!" O'Connor bellowed. Leahy swung the .50-caliber machine gun around on its spud and opened fire. The tracers arced toward one of the Kates, missing it well behind.

"Lead those bastards like ducks!" O'Connor roared above the noise of the gun. Leahy crouched behind the machine gun and opened fire again. The tracers arced out ahead of a Kate. The machine-gun bullets and the plane merged. Leahy held the bucking gun steady and the bullets tore into the plane's engine and then stitched back along the fuselage past the cockpit. The plane wobbled, turned its left wing lazily downward and plunged into the water a scant eighty feet off the stern of the *Sea Bass*. A ragged cheer went up from across the pier, and O'Connor saw an officer on the bridge of the old *Narwhal* directing his men as they struggled to mount their machine guns. He felt a sudden stirring of triumph. He, Mike O'Connor, the *Sea Bass,* had opened fire on the enemy and scored a kill before the *Narwhal* had been able to get its guns into action.

The string of Kate torpedo bombers closed formation to take up the space left by the downed plane and passed, flying low and slow, heading toward their targets at Ford Island. O'Connor heard the sullen roar of explosions and saw columns of black smoke and flame erupting in the harbor area.

"The battleships!" he gasped. "Those bastards are after the battleships!"

"Almost out of ammo, sir," Leahy yelled.

"I'll get more," O'Connor said. He started toward the bridge hatch to give the order to pass up more machine-gun ammunition. He stopped as he heard Leahy say, "Ain't no more ammo below, Mr. O'Connor. Three hundred rounds is all they allow us to have on board, sir."

"Christ!" O'Connor muttered. He watched through his binoculars as another flight of Kates came in low over the fuel-oil tank farm on the naval station to the west of the Southeast Loch, dropping lower and slowing as they began their runs at the battleships.

"I don't see how those fuckers can see what the hell they're aimin' at over there," Leahy growled. "Whole damned area is nothing but smoke and fire. Bastards!"

O'Connor heard the squeal of a car's brakes on the pier and saw Captain Barney Saunders, dressed in gray slacks, a T-shirt and tennis shoes, jump out of a Ford driven by a woman who appeared to be dressed in a robe. The car turned, backed up, shot forward and stopped, backed again and then sped off the finger pier. Captain Saunders, his heavy belly bobbing under the T-shirt, ran down the gangway and climbed to the cigarette deck.

"What the hell is going on here, mister?" Captain Saunders yelled at O'Connor.

"We're under attack, Captain," O'Connor said.

"I know that, goddammit! The radio is full of it. They're shooting up the city streets, for chrissake! Who gave the orders to fire? Did we take any hits?"

"We haven't been hit," O'Connor said. "I gave the order to fire, sir." Captain Saunders, his usually pleasant, plump face distorted, stared at him.

"A Jap plane came right over us and then we heard the explosions and saw the smoke. *Pelius* made a flag hoist to repel enemy attack," O'Connor said. "The torpedo planes turned just aft of us and Leahy shot one down. That's the tail out there astern, just about to go under, sir."

Captain Saunders turned and looked aft, his chest heaving. He reached for the binoculars hanging around Mike O'Connor's neck, dropped the strap over his head and focused the glasses on the harbor.

"My God," he muttered. O'Connor could see the tears running down his plump cheeks. "Oh my God!" He let the glasses drop to hang by the leather thong around his neck and wiped his eyes with the back of his hand.

"It looks like the whole of Battleship Row is on fire," he said in a flat voice. "I could see one ship rolling over, a battleship rolling over! Jesus, the men who are dying this morning!" He took a deep breath and turned to O'Connor.

"What's the situation aboard, mister?"

"Crew is at General Quarters. We're almost out of ammunition for the machine gun, sir."

"Where's the other Fifty?" Captain Saunders demanded.

"Been waitin' for a spare part for two months, Captain," Leahy spoke up. "Firing pin, sir."

"Shit!" Captain Saunders said.

"What's happening, sir?" O'Connor said. "I know we're under attack but why?"

"The war that everyone said would happen has started," Captain Saunders said. "All those big-brained Navy strategists who said the Japs wouldn't dare, couldn't take the risk of hitting Pearl Harbor, were wrong." He shook himself like a fighter staggered by a heavy punch.

"Go below, Mike," he said. "Rig ship for dive except for the bridge hatch. I want some line handlers stationed in the Control Room. If they come after us, I'll flood down and put the ship on the bottom."

"Lots of planes out there over the harbor, Captain," Leahy said. "Seven o'clock from the ship's bow, sir. Looks like they're sort of circling around." Captain Saunders raised his binoculars.

"They're circling, all right," Saunders said. "They're dropping bombs, damn them! Where the hell are our planes?"

Down below in the Control Room of the *Sea Bass* Mike O'Connor looked at the "Christmas Tree," the signal board that indicated with red and green lights the open or closed condition of all hull openings. All the lights on the board were green except the one that indicated the condition of the bridge hatch, red for open.

"All compartments report rigged for dive, sir," the telephone talker said.

"Very well," O'Connor said. He climbed halfway up the ladder to the Conning Tower and rested his back against the hatch combing.

"Bridge. Ship rigged for dive except for the bridge hatch, which is open. Line handlers are standing by in the Control Room. Standing by to flood down on order, Captain." He slid back down the ladder to the Control Room as he heard Captain Saunders acknowledge the report.

"Sir," the telephone talker said in a low voice, "everyone, I mean all the telephone talkers in the compartments, is asking what's going on, sir."

"We're being attacked by Japanese planes," O'Connor said. "Pass the word that the Captain is aboard. And you can tell all compartments that Leahy shot down a Jap torpedo plane, shot it down right off our stern."

"Old Gunner got himself one, hey?" Art Apple, Machinist's

Mate First Class, who manned the Trim Manifold at Battle Stations, spoke up. "Shows you that Gunner's Mates are good for something. Jap planes? That means the war is starting and sure as hell that means no liberty tonight and I had myself a standby so I could go ashore." O'Connor started to answer Apple and stopped as he saw a pair of feet in red bedroom slippers coming down the ladder from the Conning Tower. Lieutenant Joe Sibley, the ship's Engineering Officer and Battle Stations Diving Officer, stepped off the bottom rung of the ladder, smoothing down his pajama jacket.

"Heard about this damned mess on the radio. I ran outside to see what was happening and a Jap plane was flying down the street, strafing. Right behind him was one of the *Narwhal* officers, driving his car. I caught a ride with him. Skipper wants you topside, Mike. What's the situation here?"

"Ship's rigged for dive except for the bridge hatch. That's open," O'Connor said. "These extra people in the Control Room are the Forward Room reload crew. Captain wants them to stand by to slack off the mooring lines. He intends to flood down and sit on the bottom if the planes come after us."

"You're relieved, Mike," Lieutenant Sibley said. He tapped the telephone talker on the shoulder. "Would you please ask the steward in the Forward Battery to go into my cabin and get me some clothes?"

Mike O'Connor climbed up to the bridge. Captain Saunders was standing back on the cigarette deck, his belly hanging over the waistband of his trousers. He lowered his binoculars and looked at his wristwatch.

"Did you get a time on when this started, Mike?"

"Yes, sir. We saw a Jap plane that came right over us just after we heard the bugle on the *Pelius* making first call. That would make it zero seven-fifty-five. Almost at the same time we saw the smoke in the harbor and heard the explosions."

Captain Saunders looked at his watch again. "It's zero nine-thirty now. I can't see this thing going on much longer." He put his hands on the cigarette-deck rail and leaned his weight on them.

"Let's figure it out. Those planes have to be from Jap carriers. The carriers have to be two, three hundred miles off Pearl, they wouldn't dare get any closer than that. The planes would take about two hours to get here. So they left their carriers around zero six hundred. I would figure they're using at least three carriers, but that doesn't matter.

"What matters is that those carriers have been stooging around in one part of the ocean for over three hours and they've got to stay there for another two hours to get their planes back aboard. Those carrier skippers have got to be worrying their asses off about getting caught by our planes before they get their own birds back or while they're taking planes aboard." He looked at O'Connor with somber eyes.

"That is, if we know where the Jap carriers are. God knows, I haven't seen any of our planes in the air." He drew a long, shuddering breath and shook his head.

"What a damned Sunday this is," he said in a low voice. "But at least the *Sea Bass* did what she was supposed to do. That's something. You did damned good work, Mike. I'll make a note of that when I make out my ship action report. Not that it's likely to mean much to you for a long time. The brass here and in Washington are going to be too damned busy trying to figure out who to hang for this mess to pay any attention to an officer who did what he was supposed to do when he came under enemy fire.

"God, look at those bastards." He pointed at the sky above the harbor area. Japanese dive bombers were circling, poising like hawks and then shooting down in steep dives and soaring up again in long, graceful arcs, leaving behind them the thundering explosions of heavy bombs.

The attack ended at 0945. From the submarine piers all that could be seen of the harbor was a heavy cloud of smoke that was shot through with the searing flames of explosions and fires. An hour after the attack ended, Captain Saunders decided to secure from General Quarters and let the crew come topside. By noon the men who had been ashore or at church services on the base began to straggle back to the ship. Shortly past midafternoon a car came speeding down the pier. An officer leaned out of the car window and made a trumpet of his hands.

"Commanding Officers will report to Admiral Kimmel's headquarters at sixteen hundred hours. Uniform of the day will be khakis with jackets, black tie and black shoes." The officer pulled his head back into the car and the driver spun the car around and headed off the pier.

"Did you hear that?" Captain Saunders said in an incredulous voice. "Did you hear that? From here it looks like the whole damned harbor is on fire, there's got to be men dying and hurt, ships sinking or sunk, and they're worried about the uniform of the day!" He ground his teeth together. "Dear God," he half-whispered, "no wonder we got creamed." He turned to Joe Sibley and Mike O'Connor.

"The Exec is still ashore. He didn't have wheels yesterday, something is wrong with his car. I gave him a ride home. Until he gets here, Joe, you're SOP. Mike has the duty. I want ammunition issued for the deck-watch sidearm." He paused, thinking.

"Better send Leahy up to the base to see if he can scrounge some ammunition for the Fifty. I don't like the idea of sitting here with nothing but a crate of spuds to throw at those bastards if they come back. And they might do that. No one is to leave the ship except Leahy and one man to help him carry ammunition. No one but ship's company allowed to come on board until I get back. I'm going below and get into uniform for their damned meeting." His rumbling growl died away as he went down the bridge hatch.

The scene at Admiral Kimmel's headquarters was one of orderly confusion. Officers milled about exchanging information with each other. A sturdy Lieutenant Commander, his face a gray mask of soot and dirt, his khaki uniform stained and filthy, stood in front of a dapper young Lieutenant.

"I've been fighting fires and sending my dead and wounded to the hospital all day long," he rasped in a voice made harsh by smoke. "And I'm not changing into any damned uniform of the day, even if I did have any uniforms that aren't burned up, to suit you or anyone else, sonny boy. And if you want to know why I'm here and my Captain isn't, it's because the Captain and the Executive Officer and every other damned officer from the *Arizona* but three or four are dead. You tell me once more that I'm out of uniform and I'll break your fucking neck!" The younger officer backed away, his eyes searching for help but finding none.

The meeting with Admiral Kimmel began on a grim note. A Chief Yeoman read aloud from a sheaf of papers he held in his hand.

The *West Virginia* had taken six torpedo hits, listed heavily and would have capsized if the swell of the ship's port bilge

hadn't hit the bottom and kept the ship from rolling completely over.

The *Tennessee*, moored inboard of the *West Virginia*, had
been saved from torpedo hits by the other ship but had taken
several hits from large aerial bombs and had been set afire by
the bombs and the fires raging aboard the *West Virginia*. As of
1400 hours the fires on the *Tennessee* were under control. *West
Virginia* was still burning.

The *Arizona*, moored just aft of the *West Virginia* and the
Tennessee, took the worst pounding of any of the big ships. A
heavy bomb hit beside one of the ship's forward turrets,
penetrated the decks and exploded in the forward ammunition
storage, sending flames five hundred feet into the air. Rear
Admiral Isaac C. Kidd, who had raced to the signal bridge
when the attack began, was killed by the explosion of this
bomb, as was the ship's Commanding Officer, Captain Frank-
lyn Van Valkenurgh, who had taken his station on the
navigation bridge. Shortly after the first bomb hit the *Arizona*,
a second bomb hit next to a smokestack, penetrated and
exploded in the engineroom spaces and then six heavy aerial
bombs hit the *Arizona*. The ship burst into flames from one
end to the other and settled so rapidly that it did not capsize.
The Chief Yeoman paused and then went on. Best early
estimates were that more than one thousand of the *Arizona*'s
crew had died in the first few minutes of the attack.

The *Oklahoma*, moored astern of the *Arizona* and outboard
of the *Maryland*, took three torpedo hits and began to roll
over. As the ship rolled, two more torpedoes hit it. The
Maryland, protected from torpedoes by the *Oklahoma*, managed to escape significant damage from the dive bombers.

The *California*, moored by itself well astern of the other
battleships, took two torpedo hits and suffered bomb hits that
penetrated the decks and exploded in the ship's ammunition-
storage areas. The ship's crew was fighting extensive fires and
the *California* was believed to be slowly sinking.

Ashore the damage was tremendous. The naval air station
on Ford Island, the heart of the Navy's defense system for
Pearl Harbor itself, had been hit by high-level bombers. One
runway was still usable, but most of the aircraft on the base
had been destroyed. Hickam and Wheeler, the Army's two
major air fields, were a shambles, with most planes destroyed.
Ewa Air Field, the Marine Corps' air base, had also been

smashed up by bombs, and most of its aircraft burned or badly damaged. The Chief Yeoman turned over the last sheet of the papers he held.

"Casualties are very heavy. The last report we have from the hospital at Aiea, the navy yard and the harbor area is that the casualty list may go over three thousand, sir." He turned toward Admiral Kimmel, who nodded his head. The Chief Yeoman sat down at his desk and uncapped a pen, ready to take notes.

"Admiral," a grimy, smoke-stained officer spoke up, "with all due respect sir, why the hell didn't our planes get airborne?"

"Because we had very strong information of planned sabotage, all aircraft were positioned on the runways in close formation with guards around them," a Staff Officer answered. "Apparently the Japs knew about this, and their first attacks were with fighter planes that bombed and strafed the parked planes. Most of our aircraft were put out of commission. Those that could have flown could not take off because of extensive bomb damage to the runways."

"I saw damned little antiaircraft fire from the beach," another officer spoke up. "We got our three-inch batteries going on the *Pennsylvania,* but the bastards hit the *Cassin* and the *Downes,* they were in drydock with us, and cut all the power cables and we had no power, had to sight and train the guns by hand. Where the hell were the shore-based antiaircraft guns?"

"Shore-based antiaircraft batteries are the Army's responsibility," a Staff Officer answered. "The Army requires all live ammunition to be returned to the ammunition-storage areas at sixteen hundred hours on Fridays. It is reissued at zero eight hundred on Monday morning."

"Jesus Christ!" a ship's captain roared. "I suppose the goddam Japs knew that, too!"

"This is not a damned Court of Inquiry!" A four-stripe Staff Captain exploded. "We aren't here to place blame. We're here to get the Admiral's orders!" He turned to Admiral Kimmel.

The Admiral looked up and his eyes went from one man to the other. "I want to give all of you my personal thanks for responding as you did in the face of a sneak attack. A great many brave men died today. I grieve for them." He lowered his head and stared at his desk. Then he raised his head, his face grim.

"We go on from here. We fight! The carriers are at sea and they're now searching to try and find the Jap Fleet. We still have the submarines, most of them are at sea on patrol and those in port were not hit." His eyes looked for Captain Saunders and found him.

"I understand that *Sea Bass* shot down a Jap torpedo plane." Captain Saunders nodded.

"Orders are now being cut to be issued to the submarines at sea and to those of you whose ships are in port to wage unrestricted submarine war against the Empire of Japan." Admiral Kimmel's voice was flat, without emotion. "Submarine commanders will begin making your ships ready for sea at once. You have priority for fuel and stores. Your orders will arrive by messenger. As soon as you are ready for sea in all respects, you will notify ComSubPac for patrol-area orders. I suggest the submariners leave now. The rest of you will please stay."

Captain Saunders walked down the front steps of the headquarters building in company with three other submarine captains. He turned to the other three.

"Unrestricted submarine warfare is what he said," Saunders remarked. "That means we can go after every damned ship except hospital ships."

"Every damned Jap we see," one of the other Captains answered.

Chapter
Two

LIEUTENANT JUNIOR GRADE Andrew T. O'Connor settled himself comfortably in the front seat of his Dauntless dive bomber and looked at the sky above and around him and then at the wine-dark water three thousand feet beneath him. He listened with an attentive ear to the steady roar of the Wright 1,000-hp engine in the plane's nose, checked quickly to each side to make sure he was in the correct place in the formation and sat back. Life was good on this Sunday morning, he thought. He'd be in Pearl Harbor in plenty of time to attend mass. The U.S.S. *Enterprise*, the home of the 6th Squadron, was almost two hundred miles astern, returning from transporting the U.S. Marine Corps' 221st Fighter Squadron to Wake Island. It wouldn't make port before evening. There would be time after mass to go over to the submarine piers and see if his brother Mike's ship had come in. The last letter he had received from Mike was in one of the pockets of his flight suit.

"We'll be back from patrol around the fifth or sixth of December," Mike had written. "We'll probably be in port for three or four weeks. If you get in, come on over and I'll give you a guided tour of the real Navy, a big fleet submarine." Andy had chuckled over that "real Navy" part; Mike had always been the enthusiastic one, ready to throw himself into anything that looked as if it might be fun, urging Andy, the more cautious of the two brothers, to follow him.

"What time we landing, sir?" the voice of Roger Cain, the machine gunner in the rear cockpit of the stubby SBD, sounded loud through the plane's intercom. Andy O'Connor looked at his wristwatch.

"Figure about zero eight-ten, give or take a couple of minutes. What's your hurry? Nice young fella like you hasn't got a girl waiting for you, or have you?"

"Affirmative, sir. Nothing wrong with having a girl, is there, Mr. O'Connor? I mean, it's part of life, isn't it, to have a girl when you're young?"

"Nothing wrong with that at all," Lieutenant O'Connor said. "I hope your intentions are honorable, Roger."

"Well, sir, not too honorable," the rear gunner said.

"I'm going to have to march you up in front of the chaplain when the ship gets in," Andy O'Connor said, trying to make his voice sound stern. "Hold it—" He made a minute adjustment to the radio-receiver knob on his dashboard and cleared the static, hearing the voice of his Squadron Commander in his earphones.

"Now hear this. The *Flag* has just reported on the Command Circuit that Pearl Harbor is under heavy air attack. The Japanese are bombing Pearl Harbor. *Flag* reports many, repeat many Jap planes over Pearl. We are advised of damage to runways at Ford Island.

"We are now under command of the *Flag* at Pearl. We will proceed on the original flight plan. Stay in formation, less chance of us being jumped on if we do that. Approach to Ford Island will be made from the south, over Barbers Point. We'll go in down on the deck, at one hundred feet. All planes acknowledge."

Andy O'Connor waited until his turn came and gave his acknowledgment. The radio crackled. "Permission to shoot some of the bastards down if we get the chance, Skipper?"

"Negative," the Squadron Leader replied. "Unless we come under attack, my orders are to get to Ford Island as fast as we can. Machine gunners can fire clearing rounds as of now. Make sure all test firing is done into an open area."

O'Connor heard the rapping sound of his plane's .30-caliber machine gun as Roger Cain tested his gun. His eyes searched the sky. Did they bomb Mike's ship?

"Plenty of strangers at ten o'clock and high!" The voice of one of the pilots was strained, excited.

"Follow me," the Squadron Commander ordered. He tipped his plane over in a screaming dive, followed by the rest of the formation. The flight leveled out barely 100 feet above the surface of the ocean and roared toward Barbers Point at 220 miles an hour.

"Ford Island bears zero-one-zero from Barbers Point," the Squadron Commander said. "Break formation for landing. Single file. Good God! Look at that!"

Ahead of the low-flying planes there appeared to be a solid wall of smoke over the harbor area, a wall shot through with gouts of flame. The air over the harbor appeared to be filled with darting planes. He saw flashes of gunfire from Hickam Air Field on his right side.

"Those bastards on the ground are shooting at us!" his machine gunner yelled through the intercom. The plane in front of O'Connor suddenly wobbled and fell out of line and O'Connor saw the sudden burst of flame around the plane's engine cowling. The dive bomber slanted off to one side and O'Connor could see the pilot ducking his head to get away from the flames that now enveloped the front of the plane.

"Mary, Mother of Jesus," O'Connor muttered, crossing himself, "it's for real!"

"Don't those bastards know who we are?" his machine gunner wailed.

"I don't know," O'Connor answered. "Hang on, here we go." He was committed now, flying into a wall of smoke, his head swiveling from one side to the other as he looked down, trying to find a familiar landmark to guide him into the runways on Ford Island.

The runway came into view suddenly as the smoke cleared for a moment. The plane ahead of him touched down and then bounced high in the air as its pilot hit the throttle to lift himself over a gaping bomb crater in the runway. O'Connor eased his plane to the left to avoid the crater, gentled it downward and felt the wheels touch. He saw a pile of rubble ahead of him. He touched the throttle with a gentle hand and delicately eased the stick back and lifted his aircraft over the rubble, and then the wheels hit and he stood on his brakes, slowing the plane, steering around the holes in the runway. He saw a Zeke roaring toward him from up ahead, the Zeke's gunfire chewing up the asphalt surface of the runway, stitching its way toward him. He touched the throttle and stamped hard on the right rudder pedal and the SBD shot off to the right as the Zeke's gunfire missed the SBD's tail. He heard Cain's gun hammering in response.

"We're gettin' a wave-in from ten o'clock, sir," Cain yelled.

"Roger," Andy O'Connor said. He ran the plane off the runway, increasing speed as much as he dared as the wheels rumbled over gravel and grass hummocks.

"Whole damned harbor is on fire!" Cain yelled. "Oh, look at that!" His voice rose to a scream as a string of bombs landed on and alongside the *California*, anchored by itself in the gut on the southwest side of Ford Island. A huge column of flame burst out of the battleship as O'Connor steered his plane to where a sailor was frantically waving a pair of orange paddles to guide him. A Chief Petty Officer came running to the side of the plane.

"Get out of that plane and get under cover!" the Chief yelled.

"I can't leave this plane out here in the open!" O'Connor yelled back. "Where's the nearest revetment?"

"Out!" the Chief roared. "Get the hell out of there before they shoot your ass off!"

At 1130 the pilots of the 6th Squadron assembled in a building off the runway. The building's windows had been blown out and there were holes in the roof. A Navy three-striper, his hair singed and his uniform filthy, stood in front of the thirteen pilots. He looked at the clipboard he held in his hand.

"Nobody knows where the Jap carriers were when they launched the attack," he said. "Everyone with more than three stripes says they know but they don't. One theory is they launched from the southwest and are headed back to the Marshall Islands. The *Enterprise*, your ship, has been sent in that direction to try and find them if they're there.

"Admiral Kimmel thinks the attack came from the northwest. I think that myself." He looked at the Squadron Commander of the 6th Squadron.

"I want a sweep made to the northwest, sir. Nine planes. Sweep sector will be from three-three-three to zero-three-zero, true. Sweep range is three hundred miles. I'd advise that you stay together, gentlemen, because if you find the bastards, you're going to find trouble. They've had time enough to get their planes aboard the carriers and refuel and rearm them, and they'll be waiting for you to make a call.

"I want another sweep made to the southwest, to satisfy the

people who think the attack came from that direction. Four planes. Sweep sector is one-five-eight to three-three-three, true. Sweep range is two hundred miles." He ran a smoke-blackened hand through his hair.

"The mission is to find and destroy the Japanese aircraft carriers."

"We return here, right, sir?" the Squadron Commander asked.

"Affirmative, sir. Your carrier is out hunting, and until she gets back, you come under our jurisdiction. Good luck."

The *Enterprise* pilots bunched up around their Squadron Commander at the edge of the runway, where their planes, refueled and fitted with five-hundred-pound bombs, stood in a long row.

"I'll take the sweep to the northwest," the Squadron Commander said. He pointed his finger at one pilot after another until he had the eight men who would go with him. "We'll close up in a tight Vee at fifteen thousand feet. If we assume the Jap carriers were about two hundred miles or so offshore when they launched, and if the attack broke off about two hours ago, they should be taking planes aboard now. We should be there in about ninety minutes, if we can find them." He pointed his finger at Andy O'Connor.

"You take the sweep to the southwest. O'Connor is in charge. Stay in close formation, a Vee with a tail-end Charlie. If you see anything, get off a full report before you attack. Andy, take your people off to one side and work out your search plan. Watch your fuel so you don't run short."

The planes took off a little after noon in what proved to be a fruitless search. The group that searched out to the northwest returned just after dusk, low on fuel. The antiaircraft gunners on Ford Island had been issued ammunition by that time, but communications had not as yet been restored. As the first plane came into sight, a gunner on the northwest side of the island opened fire. The rest of the antiaircraft emplacements followed suit. Four of the planes were shot down before the firing could be stopped.

Andy O'Connor reported at 1700 hours that he had seen nothing. He was ordered to return and land at Hickam Air Field, where work crews had cleared away the wreckage of blasted planes and filled the larger holes in the runways. He let his plane roll up to a shell-riddled hangar where a group of soldiers were repairing a plane.

"Any idea where I can put this bird?" he called out to a sergeant.

"Yes, sir, Navy. Take her down the field until you find an empty revetment." O'Connor nodded and ran his plane down the runway until he could turn into a revetment. He walked back to the hangar as the other planes of his flight moved toward empty revetments. The Army Sergeant spat a long stream of brown tobacco juice on the runway as O'Connor walked up.

"Nice to have you people here instead of the damned Japs," the Sergeant grunted. "My people got one of your pilots out of the water this morning after those trigger-happy gunners shot him up. Sorry about that, Navy."

"How was he?" O'Connor said, trying to keep his voice level.

"Singed a little around the ears, but okay," the Sergeant said. He turned his head and spat again. "We might have been able to do something, but the people who run this Army Air Force ordered all my planes parked out on the runway, wing-to-wing, so they would be safe against sabotage! For the sake of Jesus H. Christ! Damned Japs had a field day for themselves! All them planes lined up full of fuel and bombs. Blooey! Hit one of them and the whole damned row burned!"

"I know how you feel," O'Connor said. "First things first. Can you fuel my planes?"

"I got plenty of fuel, that's about the only thing the Japs didn't hit. But to get fuel you have to have a requisition from the Fuel Officer and it's got to be signed by three officers, and I think all those people are dead, sir." He shrugged his shoulders. "What the hell's the difference? Yeah, I'll fuel your planes. Might take me two, three hours unless they get the electricity back on. If they don't, I'll have to use handy-billy pumps but I'll get you fueled, sir."

"Fine, do the best you can," O'Connor said. "One more thing. Do you have any transportation? I've got to get to the base and report in."

"I've got one Jeep still running," the sergeant said. "If your people can all crowd into it, my corporal can take you wherever you have to go. You'll have to find your own transportation to get back though, sir."

"You people had anything to eat today?" O'Connor asked.
"No, sir."

"I'll see what I can do when we get over to the navy base,"
O'Connor said. "Might be able to rustle up some sandwiches
and coffee and send them back with your driver."

"If you can do that, sir, I'll sign up for the Navy next hitch,"
the Sergeant said. He beckoned to a small Corporal.

"Take these Navy people where they want to go and stick
around while they see if they can big-deal us some chow." He
saluted O'Connor and turned away.

Captain Barney Saunders put the telephone receiver back in
the box that was hung from the rail of the *Sea Bass*.

"Pass the word for Mister O'Connor to lay topside and see
me," he said to the deck watch. Mike O'Connor climbed out of
the Forward Torpedo Room hatch and went aft on the deck to
where Captain Saunders was standing.

"Your brother just called from the BOQ," Captain Saunders
said. "Told me he flew in here yesterday morning in all that
bombing and flew a mission to find the Jap Fleet yesterday
afternoon. I told him he was damned lucky he didn't find
them. How long since you've seen your brother?"

"Three years, sir."

"Hmm. Your work all caught up? No reason you can't go
over and see him. You'll have to walk, there's no transportation. Be back here at fifteen hundred hours." He grinned as
Mike O'Connor started to race up the gangway and then
stopped and carefully saluted the flag that hung at the ship's
stern.

"Mister O'Connor runs like a tank," the deck watch said as
he watched O'Connor run down the pier in the short, choppy
strides of the All-American fullback he had been at the
Academy.

"About as easy to stop as a tank when he had a football under
his arm," Captain Saunders said.

Andrew O'Connor was standing on the lanai of the Bachelor
Officers' Quarters when Mike O'Connor came jogging up to
the steps, blowing hard from the run. The two brothers looked
at each other, smiling. Mike O'Connor, six feet two and 225
pounds of hard muscle. Andrew O'Connor, five feet eight and
160 pounds of equally hard muscle.

"You football players never did learn to run any distance,"

Andy

kill y

"Fi

steps

got t

He

dam

"I

me

acr

bro

bo

M

a

A

"What do you mean?" Andy asked. "Wer

officer aboard?"

"The only officer aboard," Mike said. "

know. Our gunner's mate shot down o

They call them Kates. Shot it dow

"I didn't know you carried AA

said.

"We don't. Just Fifties. Wh

heard the explosions and

General Quarters and ma

ready when the Kate

down."

"They have to f

"Dad will be p

"I think he'

middle of th

Fleet all

"I ha

"H

and

w

and head. His rear g

messed up pretty bad. They said they

don't see how they'll have time. That hospital is so crowd

they've got people out on the lawn in stretchers, there aren't

enough beds. Or doctors or nurses. Do you know how many

people died in that attack? I've heard all sorts of stories here at

the BOQ."

"Our Skipper said about three thousand casualties. He

heard that at Admiral Kimmel's office. But I haven't heard any

figure on how many died. They hit about everything."

"Except the carriers," Andy said. "All three of the carriers

were out at sea. I was told they didn't hit any submarines. That

right?"

Mike nodded.

"Where were you when it started?" Andy asked. He refilled

his brother's glass with cold tea.

"Drinking coffee topside. I saw a lot of planes over the

harbor but we, the deck watch and myself, we figured it was

the Army holding a drill. Then a plane came right over us, real

close, a fighter. A Zeke. I looked it up in the recognition book

yesterday afternoon when I made out my combat report."

e you the ranking

Weekend liberty, you
e of the torpedo planes.
n right off our fantail."
guns on a submarine," Andy

en I saw that Jap plane and then
saw all the smoke, I yelled for
chine guns to the bridge. So we were
came flying right near us, real low

low to drop their torpedoes," Andy said.
oud of that."
be damned proud of you, flying in here in the
at attack and then flying out to try and find the Jap
by yourself."
three other guys with me," Andy said.
ho," Mike said. "Make you a deal. I'll write to the folks
tell them about what you did and you write and tell them
hat I did. Okay?"

"Deal," Andy said with a grin. "Dad might believe it if we do it that way. You remember the time in the All-State high school championship game when you scored the five touchdowns? We were all up in the stands, and every time they gave you the ball, Dad would start yelling in Gaelic."

"Yeah," Mike said. "And when we all got home, he wouldn't let me talk about the game. Said it wasn't fitting to talk about what I had done, that the Irish kings and the Polish heroes never talked about how many men they killed in battle."

"He really believed all that stuff he used to tell us about our being descended from the kings of Ireland and mother coming from a line of Polish heroes," Andy said.

"Because it's true," Mike said. "Don't you believe it?"

"Yes," Andrew O'Connor said softly. "I believe it."

Chapter
Three

THE HOUSE STOOD IN the middle of a block of similar houses. The yard was immaculate, as were the front and back yards of all the other houses in this solidly Polish neighborhood on the west side of Chicago. An iron railing made of gas pipe, painted black, surrounded the tiny lawn. A railing made from the same sort of gas pipe ran from the porch down one side of the steps to the sidewalk.

The arrangement of rooms inside the house was similar to that in most of the other houses on the street. There was a living room, a dining room and a spacious kitchen on the first floor over a small basement containing a coal-burning furnace. On the second floor there were three rather small bedrooms and a bathroom with a large, porcelain-glazed, cast-iron tub that stood on four feet shaped like lion's paws.

The men who lived in the houses on the block were, for the most part, blond, as were their wives. First- and second-generation Poles, hard-working, industrious family men. Except for the newcomer who had recently bought the house in the middle of the block. He was tall, with blue-black hair and powerful, sloping shoulders and a fierce glare from deep-set, piercing dark blue eyes. He spoke to no one as he walked to the corner to get the trolley to work. When he returned home in the late afternoon, the wives of the block watched him, pulling aside the edges of their starched white living room curtains as he walked up to his house and then turned and went to the back door to enter through the kitchen so the dirt on his shoes wouldn't soil the rug in the living room.

The black-haired man was a stranger in the neighborhood. He accepted the role as the price of love. "I love you and I'll

23

marry you," the tall blond girl had said, "but please buy a
house, a nice house, in the right neighborhood, a Polish
neighborhood. I don't want to live among strangers."

"Did you never think," the black-haired man had said in his
soft, lilting brogue, "did you never consider that I might like to
live among my own people?"

"The Irish live in the Patch," she answered. "The Patch has
a saloon on every corner and some in the middle of the blocks.
It's a filthy dirty place with bad women drunk on the streets in
the daytime. It's no place to raise children."

"It's a family you're raisin' already," he said, "and we've not
even seen the priest yet to post the banns."

"Don't change the subject," she said. "Please, my own love,
say you'll buy a house for us, a house not too far from where
my parents live."

The banns were published in the old parish church where
the tall blond girl had taken her communion, and for three
weeks the people of the neighborhood attending mass stopped
and read the banns and puzzled over the name of the intended
bridegroom, moving their lips as they pronounced the odd
name, "Michael Boru O'Connor." What kind of married name
would that be for a good Polish girl?

When the banns came down, Sophia Olszewski went to her
intended, Michael Boru O'Connor. "My mother has heard of a
house for sale near here. The owner is an old man. His wife is
dead more than a year and his children worry about him living
alone. They want him to move in with them, sell his house and
furniture. It's a very good house and nice furniture but the
price is a little high, maybe. Nine hundred dollars." She
looked at him, her eyes pleading.

"I have not that much money," he said.

"My father," she said. "We could borrow what we need from
him."

"I'll not do that," he said stubbornly. " 'Tis no way to start a
marriage, owing money."

The election of that year, 1914, enabled Michael Boru
O'Connor to get the last of the money he needed to buy the
house for Sophia. For the first time in his long political career,
Bathhouse John Coughlin, the alderman of Chicago's infamous
First Ward, was facing a fight for reelection. The struggle
waged by women for the right to vote had been won in Illinois,
and the women, overjoyed at the prospect of not only being

able to vote but also to run for public office, set out programs of reform that swept across the entire state.

Marion Drake, the first president of the Cook County Suffrage Alliance, decided to lead the fight for reform by opposing Bathhouse John Coughlin. Running as the candidate of the Progressive party for Coughlin's seat on the City Council, she began a vigorous campaign against Coughlin and Hinky Dink Kenna, Coughlin's political mentor. The newspapers gleefully ran daily stories of her charges that Coughlin and Kenna were the organizers and sole beneficiaries of a massive vice operation centered in the First Ward, that for all of his eleven terms in the Chicago City Council Coughlin had been the tool of special interests—and that Bathhouse John Coughlin and Hinky Dink Kenna were cheats, thieves and grafters.

Bathhouse John was amused by the charges. Hinky Dink Kenna, a shrewd and calculating politician, was not. All over Illinois women were demanding changes and, in Chicago, the major target was the First Ward, where Coughlin and Kenna had reigned supreme for over twenty years. Hinky Dink Kenna, sitting in his small saloon in the First Ward, knew in his bones that for the first time in twenty years he had to wage an all-out fight to win the election for Bathhouse John Coughlin. He needed help, lots of help. It was time to call in all the political debts owed to him and Bathhouse John. One who owed such a debt was Michael Boru O'Connor.

The idea of an honest election was anathema to Kenna. Only fools believed in honest elections. But this time the women would be out in force to watch and, Kenna was sure, to begin screaming to the newspaper reporters if they saw anything remotely resembling a dishonest election. So Hinky Dink Kenna sat in his saloon and he came up with a plan, a simple plan.

Counterfeit ballots would be printed. Kenna knew a printer who would do that and keep his mouth shut. Each ballot would be marked with a vote for Bathhouse John Coughlin. Prior to election day Kenna's organizers would scour the railroad yards for tramps and hoboes, and the flophouses for derelicts and vagrants. These men would be brought to the First Ward, where Kenna would house them in brothels and the back rooms of saloons, keeping them fed on stew and full of beer until election day.

On election day Michael Boru O'Connor and a few others who owed debts to Hinky Dink Kenna and who could be depended upon to stay sober, would herd the transients to the polls, where some of Kenna's men would hand them the marked counterfeit ballots to hide under their shirts before they went into the polling booths. Once inside they would conceal the genuine ballot given them, deposit the marked counterfeit ballot in the box and come outside and give the genuine ballots to Kenna's men. The genuine ballots would then be marked for Bathhouse John Coughlin and used by others.

The scheme was daring and it had another virtue than providing a continual supply of ballots to be marked for Coughlin. It insured that an actual vote had been cast for Coughlin in return for the fifty cents paid to each voter. Michael O'Connor worked for two days before the election rounding up transients and vagrants. On election day he herded them from one polling place to another to cast votes, making sure that none of them got their fifty-cent piece for a vote until the polls had closed.

When the votes were counted, Bathhouse John Coughlin had won by a margin of three thousand votes, far below his usual eight-thousand margin. Marion Drake and her workers had lost their bid to capture the First Ward and other wards in Chicago, but their first great effort at reform had borne fruit. In almost a thousand political districts in Illinois the women succeeded in banning saloons.

Hinky Dink Kenna, the consummate Chicago politician, took Coughlin to one side during the election victory party that was taking place in Kenna's saloon. Coughlin, a giant of a man physically, leaned down to hear the soft words spoken by the diminutive Kenna. He nodded his great head with its crown of wavy gray hair and grabbed an empty beer stein and banged on the bar for quiet.

"On this great night," he boomed, "I want to extend my wishes for a long and happy married life to our great friend Michael Boru O'Connor, a true son of the Ould Sod who is standing down there at the other end of the bar.

"May you have a dozen sons and everyone of them as fine a man as you are, Michael, my boy. And if you'll do me the honor, I extend to your the invitation to spend your wedding night in the finest hotel in Chicago at my expense."

Michael O'Connor, his shoulders slumping in weariness, raised his stein of beer in salute and nodded his head.

The next day he went to Sophia's house after he had finished work. They sat in her mother's living room and O'Connor detailed the work he had been doing for Hinky Dink Kenna for the past three days.

"It was crooked work, wasn't it?" she asked.

"I am not yet a citizen of this country," he said. "I have not the right to criticize what other men who are citizens do at elections. But it was not honest work. I was payin' back a debt of honor I owed to Mr. Kenna. And in payin' back that debt I earned money, the last of the money I need to buy you the house your heart is so set on, darlin'." He reached in his pocket and pulled out a wad of bills.

"'Tis a fortune, a hundred dollars!" he said in an awed voice. "For three days' work! No man in my position in life has ever been paid more."

Sophia counted the money and tucked it into the bosom of her shirtwaist. "It's dirty money," she said primly, "but the use to which we will put it will clean it up." She listened carefully for a moment and heard her parents' voices in the kitchen. Then she leaned over and kissed him long and passionately. She did not stop him when he wrapped one of his long arms around her, his hand daring to press the solid swell of her breast.

She pulled away from him, her eyes hot and glowing. "Now you had better tell me about this debt of honor you owed, and I hope the debt is over with, because I don't want to be the wife of a man in jail. And tell me of this other thing, the invitation to spend our wedding night in a fine hotel as the guests of Mr. Coughlin and Mr. Kenna. We don't live in their ward, so why should they do this?"

He inhaled gently, savoring the faint scent Sophia's lips had left on his mouth.

"It was this way," he said. "When I stepped off the train with but five cents of the American money in my pocket, a baggage man who had the map of Ireland on his phizog sized me up. He told me if I wanted a job to go and see Bathhouse John Coughlin and Hinky Dink Kenna. They're Irish, you see, and powerful men, and the Irish take care of their own.

"That was four years ago. Alderman Coughlin was running for reelection and Mr. Kenna gave me a place to sleep in the saloon he owns, which is cleaner by far than the other saloons in the ward. He fed me, good food, stew and bread. He gave me jobs, putting up posters and the like of that, before the election. He paid me a dollar a day and I learned something about American elections. Mr. Kenna rounded up men from all over the city, dirty old rapscallions with no homes or anything to their name. He put them up in the back rooms of the poorer saloons and in flophouses he and Mr. Coughlin own, and on election day he marched them to the polls to vote. Mr. Coughlin won the election."

"What debt could you owe?" Sophia asked. "You worked for your money."

"After the election I went to see Mr. Hinky Dink Kenna. He's not the alderman, but anyone with half an eye could see that while Mr. Coughlin is a great, huge man with a grand mustache, who dresses like a grand duke and has a trumpet for a voice—anyone could see that Mr. Kenna, who is a tiny elf of a man who speaks so softly you must pay attention to hear him— anyone could see that it is Mr. Kenna who is the real boss of the First Ward.

"I went to him and said I'd work for him every election if he'd help me find a job, a decent job with a future for me. Mr. Kenna put a word in for me with Mr. Patrick Nash. He's a big contractor and he has the ear of all the politicians. Mr. Nash put me to work digging sewers. When I was promoted to be the foreman of my own sewer gang, I began looking for a girl." He smiled guilelessly.

"She didn't have to be a beauty, you understand. Just a girl. Someone who knew how to cook and take care of a house. Somehow or other I found you, and now I'm stuck with you."

"It was not 'somehow or other,' and you're not stuck with me," she said. "If the priest of your church didn't know the priest of my church, you never would have known I was alive. And when your priest brought you around to introduce you to my father and mother, they couldn't understand why he brought a stranger instead of a Pole."

"Priests are wise men," he said with a grin. "Both the good fathers knew that you scared away all the young men who knew you because you're too hard to handle, darlin'."

"And do you think you can handle me?"

"Ah, darlin'," he said, his dark blue eyes crinkling with

humor. "The Irish have a way with them that is more than a
match for a feisty Polish girl."

"They do?" she chided him. "Well, we'll find out how well
you can handle this Polish girl once we're married." She
smiled at him and he thought he detected just a trace of
licentiousness.

"You'd better eat a lot of my mother's cooking before the
wedding, Irishman, you're going to need all the strength
you've got."

Michael Boru O'Connor took his snow shovel around to the
back of the house and got a broom to sweep the sidewalk.
When he came out to the front of the house, there were four
men standing on his newly shoveled sidewalk. In front of the
men stood Stanislav Brzinski, a giant of a man who handled the
long puddling iron at the steel mill.

"And a good day to you, gentlemen," O'Connor said.
"What's your pleasure with me on this cold morning? Is it a
fight you've come for or friendship? You'll find the O'Connor is
your man for either one."

"We do not come to fight," the giant said. "We have come to
ask why it is now three weeks since you married and moved
here and you have invited no one to your house to meet you."

"In Ireland, where I was born and raised," O'Connor said,
"in Ireland good neighbors didn't have to be invited to visit.
When a new man moved into their neighborhood, they came
to call on him and welcome him. No one has welcomed the
O'Connor to this neighborhood."

"The Irish must be a strange people," John Polkowski, a
meat cutter in the slaughterhouse spoke up. "The Polish
people respect good manners. It is not good manners to go to a
stranger's house without an invitation. That is our way."

"Ach, so it's a difference of customs, is it?" O'Connor said.
"Then let me conform to the custom of the neighborhood. I
welcome you to my house. Come inside out of this bitter cold.
My wife bought some drink she says her people like, although
it tastes nothing like whiskey. Come inside and I'll serve you
some as friendly as ever you could wish."

The men sat around the scrubbed kitchen table while
Sophia poured liquor into the clean jelly glasses she took out of
the cupboard. She put the bottle in the center of the table and
busied herself making a pot of coffee.

"Slivovitz, Irishman," the giant said, raising his glass. "Plum brandy. Let this be a welcome to our neighborhood. You are among friends." The four men raised their glasses and then drank.

"It is said among our people, your wife would know this," the giant said, "if a bride and groom each drink a full glass of slivovitz every night before bed that in good time a fine baby boy will be born." He winked ponderously at Michael O'Connor. Sophia turned from the stove.

"Is that why, when I see you at church, you have four daughters with you?" she asked. The giant roared with laughter and slapped O'Connor on the knee.

"You will learn, Irishman," he boomed, "Polish women cannot be beaten. When you think you have done so, they knock you down. You will learn, my new friend."

The ladies of the neighborhood came to call on Sophia the following afternoon. They trooped through the house, their sharp eyes looking for signs of careless housekeeping. Sophia served coffee and a platter of home-made cookies.

"I know your aunt Stella," Mrs. Polkowski said. "She told me you could have had your pick of good Polish boys. Why did you choose a stranger with a funny name?"

"He's different," Sophia said.

"All men are different and all men are the same," one of the ladies said. "How is this one different?"

"He's Irish," Sophia said. "He has dreams about our future. He talks of them. When he talks, it's like it was when I was in high school and a young Jesuit priest we had used to read poetry to us. It makes me shiver all over to hear Michael talk."

"He talks much?" Mrs. Polkowski said around a mouthful of cookie.

Sophia smiled. "All the time. He says it's what the Irish do best, talk. But it isn't." She saw the women look at each other, saw the small sly smiles that were erased as soon as they formed.

Michael Turloch O'Connor was born on a blustery, bitter-cold day early in February of 1916. The midwife who delivered him was awed by his size and by the roar of protest that erupted out of his throat when she held him by the heels and spanked his rump. Michael Boru O'Connor, waiting in the kitchen with the men of the neighborhood, half-rose from his chair at the table when Mrs. Polkowski came scuttling down the stairs to announce that Sophia had been delivered of a boy, weight twelve and a half pounds, and both the baby and Sophia were fine. O'Connor raised his glass of Irish whiskey as the men around the table stood and held their glasses of slivovitz aloft.

" 'Tis the union of two bloods," O'Connor said. "The Irish and the Polish. Two great races of men, and this boy of mine will be a man worthy of his heritage."

"To the Poles and the Irish," Stanislav Brzinski roared in his great voice. "Men who fight to the death against all enemies. Men who love Mother Church. Men of honor and the women who are fit companions for such men!"

Andrew Turloch O'Connor was born in late December of the same year. Unlike his brother, he was a small baby, and the midwife let it be known around the neighborhood that strong as she was, Sophia had not had the strength to produce another big, strong baby in such a short time between births.

The two boys grew up, constant companions in every boyhood adventure. Michael, stronger and larger than others his age, was a natural leader. Andrew, smaller and agile of mind, was the thinker and the planner of the two.

When the O'Connor boys started school, the routine was set by their father. They went to early mass and then to the parochial school that stood next to the church. After school they went straight home, did the chores assigned them and went out to play only after they had finished their homework. During the winter, when it turned dark early, the family assembled in the living room, where Michael Boru O'Connor read to the family in American history and from Shakespeare ("an Englishman, more's the pity, but a grand writer nevertheless") and of the great men in Irish and Polish history. Stories about Boleslaw I, who was called Boleslaw the Brave; of hard-fighting Wladyslaw Lokietek, who fought successfully to reunite a divided Poland in the fourteenth century. He went over the recent history of the great Polish revolutionary Josef Pilsudski, who had helped to organize the 1905 revolution and after the end of World War I had restored Poland as a sovereign nation among the nations of the world.

But most of all Michael Boru O'Connor told his two growing boys of his own Irish heritage and history.

"My own middle name," he said one winter evening. " 'Tis

Boru, after the Brian Boru. A king of Ireland, he was, in the long ago.

"The Vikings had conquered Ireland at the time when the Brian Boru grew to manhood. He fought them because they were invaders of his land. And it came to pass that when he was a grown man, he built a fleet of ships and gave battle to the Vikings on the River Shannon.

"Now this was an uncommon thing to do, because the Vikings were great warriors on the sea and no one dared fight them in their ships. But the Brian Boru defeated them and drove them from Ireland. And in time, because of this great victory, he won control of all of the southern half of Ireland and in the year One Thousand and Two he became the king of Ireland.

"All of those who are named O'Brien today are descendants of the Brian Boru, as are all the O'Connors. You are the descendants of kings on your father's side and of great heroes on your mother's side, my sons. As such you must behave as the descendants of kings and heroes should behave. You must honor God and the Church. You will be gentle with women and stand ready to protect their honor. You must protect the weak and feed the hungry, going without food yourselves if need be. That is my heritage. It is yours. I am a man of honor. My word is my bond. You will honor the Church, your country and your family name. Always."

"The Brian Boru, Father," Andrew said, "was he king for a long time?"

"It came to pass," his father said, "that Brian Boru's rule as the king was challenged. That is always the fate of those who lead, to be challenged by the unworthy.

"The challenge came from the north, from up Dublin way. The people of that area, jealous of the Brian Boru and coveting his lands to the south of the River Shannon, made an alliance with two other groups. One of the groups was led by the earl of Orkney, who was beholden to the king of Norway, a Viking, of course. The earl of Orkney ruled over the Orkney Islands, which lie to the north of Scotland. The other group was from the Isle of Man, which is in the sea between Ireland and Scotland.

"By that time the Boru was too old to fight, almost seventy-three years he had at that time. That was a very great age to be when most men of that time died before they were forty of diseases or wounds in war.

"The Boru put his son Murchad in command of his army. They marched north and met the enemy in a great battle fought at a place called Clontarf, near to Dublin. That was in the year One Thousand and Fourteen.

"The battle went on all day, the men fighting each other with swords and maces and other weapons that cut and smashed. And the men of Boru, led by Murchad, put the enemy to rout.

"And then a sad thing happened. The Boru, old as he was, had marched with his army to the battle, to give them encouragement. The men of Dublin, fleeing the battlefield and Murchad's men, came across the tent of the old king in their flight and hacked him to death with swords. The Boru is buried in Saint Patrick's Church in Armagh. My own father took me to visit his tomb when I was but a boy. I remember it well."

The faces of the two boys were grave. "Tell us again, Father," Michael said. "Why do we have the same middle name, Turloch?"

"Ah, he was a king of Ireland as well. A great warrior. Many years after the death of Brian Boru the Turloch came to be king. The Turloch was descended from the Tara Dynasty, from which sprang the Brian Boru and all the kings of Ireland. Your mother and I had many talks about your middle names."

"Your father won those arguments," Sophia said with a soft smile.

"Didn't you mind losing?" Andrew said quickly.

"No," she said. "I won in other ways, and when you're old enough, you'll learn about such things as compromise."

On this teaching at home, and under the supervision of the priests in the parish school, the two boys grew into their teens. Michael played football in high school and was named All-State fullback three years in a row. Andrew, smaller but muscular and agile, distinguished himself in baseball and track. A brilliant student, he skipped his junior year of high school and caught up with Michael.

By that time the elder O'Connor had made a point of ignoring his promise to work in elections for Hinky Dink Kenna. The growing alliance between Kenna and Coughlin and the rising star of Al Capone had soured Michael B. O'Connor. He had become the general superintendent of the cluster of contracting companies owned by Patrick Nash. As

Nash, now half of the Kelly-Nash political machine that ruled Chicago, spent more and more of his time administering his political fiefdom, O'Connor assumed greater control of the contracting business. Just before his two sons were due to graduate from high school, O'Connor went to Patrick Nash.

"These are hard times, Pat, hard times indeed, although the companies do well enough, I think."

"They do, Michael," Patrick Nash said. "We make a good team. I get the contracts and you produce the work on time and below the estimates. What's troubling you this day?"

"'Tis my two boys, sir."

"Your boys? They're fine fellows, never give anyone any trouble. What's wrong?"

"Nothing is wrong and it's good of you to speak well of them, Pat. It's this Depression. I'm hard put to figure out what field either of them could go into in college. I have been thinking that the military would be a good place for them to go for an education and a career. Both of them have good marks in school, although I think the priests could have been a bit more generous with Michael, he gave so much time to making the school famous in football." He drew a deep breath.

"I've heard it said that you have a bit of influence with United States Senator James Hamilton Fish, him who wears the pink whiskers."

"I don't have any influence with Senator Fish," Patrick Nash said with a grin. "I own the man lock, stock and barrel."

"Well, then," O'Connor said, returning the grin, "do you think you could see your way clear to asking the senator to propose my two boys for West Point?"

"I can and will," Pat Nash said. "We Irish have to stick together. That's the secret of politics and business, sticking together."

A week later Michael O'Connor was summoned to the mayor's office. Patrick Nash was sitting in the chair behind the mayor's desk.

"His Honor is out making a speech, Michael," Nash said. "About your two boys. Senator Fish told me he has already filled his quota for West Point. He showed me the names of the boys. I could strike one off but not both, one has a powerful father." He watched O'Connor's face closely and saw no change of expression.

"But all isn't lost," Nash continued. "Senator Fish tells me that members of the House of Representatives appoint candidates to the Naval Academy. I know of one such representative who owes me a favor. That man is willing to sponsor the appointment of both your sons to the Naval Academy, if that's to your liking, Michael."

"It is," Michael O'Connor said. "My boys will pray for you, Patrick, they'll be that pleased. And they'll make you proud, I guarantee it. I owe you a lot, Pat."

"That you do, Michael," Patrick Nash said with a grin.

"Will there be a bit of the Irish corned beef to go with all the fancy things you do with cabbage in this feast you're making for the boys' going-away party?" Michael O'Connor asked Sophia. "Or will it all be those dishes you cook that a man can't get his tongue around the names of, although I'll admit they're tasty and stick to the ribs?"

Sophia O'Connor patted her apron down. "The Irish know only corned beef, wet cabbage leaves and boiled potatoes. Our two boys got their strength from good Polish food. But for you, my only love, there will be corned beef and plain boiled cabbage even if it makes every neighbor on the street sick. They'll be sure to eat the strange food anyway to do you honor as the father of two sailors who will one day be Admirals."

Michael and Andrew O'Connor joined the class of 1933, Naval Academy. The curriculum was difficult for Michael. He spent long night hours in his dormitory shower room, his head shrouded in a towel to conceal the gleam of the flashlight he used to study. Andrew had little difficulty, but was reluctant to offer help to his older brother. He was mindful, as was Michael, of their father's orders to make it on their own.

Michael's marks improved enough in his second year to allow him to go out for football. After the third game of the season he was offered lots of help by upperclassmen who gloried in the big man's ability to score touchdowns. Andrew, too light for football, made the track team as a cross-country runner.

At graduation, in 1937, Michael and Sophia O'Connor sat in the front row at the graduation exercises, their faces flushed with pride. After the ceremony the two new Ensigns joined their parents.

"And what now?" Michael B. O'Connor asked. "Do you both become regular sailors and go to sea?"

"Not right away," Andrew said. "Michael has been asked to go to submarine school, the submarine people always reach out for football players. And I have been accepted for flying school."

Sophia O'Connor crossed herself. "Dear God," she murmured, "one of my sons under the water and the other above it. Watch over them, Lord."

The two brothers met a year after graduation in New York City. "You have your wings now, do you?" Michael asked.

"Yes," Andrew said. "They want me to stay on as an instructor but I want to go to sea, to a carrier. How was submarine school?"

"No sweat," Michael said. "I like small ships, submarines."

"Small ships," Andrew said with a grin. "You're not so dumb, brother. Command comes faster in small ships. What submarine will you be going to?"

"Thought you'd never ask," Michael said happily. "I'm going to an S-boat, a small submarine in the Asiatic Fleet. We'll summer in northern China and winter in the Philippines. Some life, huh?"

"Told the folks yet?" Andrew asked.

"I wrote them yesterday," Michael said. "I have to leave in four days by train to go to Goat Island, in 'Frisco. I catch the *Chaumont* there, she's a transport, and ride her out to China. I'll have a five-hour layover in Chicago and I'll take the folks to lunch. How about you, any idea of what carrier you'll get?"

"Thought you'd never ask," Andrew mocked. "I'm getting the *Ranger*. She's not even four years old, she's the first ship ever built as an aircraft carrier. The *Saratoga* and the other big ones were converted from heavy battle cruisers to carriers. All I have to do is learn to fly off her and land on her."

The two Ensigns turned into a restaurant and made their way to a table. They ordered, and as they waited for their meal, Michael looked at his brother.

"I was thinking about Dad the other day," he said. "Thinking about how it must have been to land in Chicago with a nickel in your pocket. A foreigner, even if he did speak the language. He found a job, and in twenty years or so he's the head of the biggest contracting business in the whole country. And he never fooled around with any funny stuff, never gave bribes or took them. When you come to think about it, he's one hell of a man. I've known a lot of people in the Academy and sub school who couldn't have cut the mustard in his house, they just couldn't have made it. Sometimes I wonder how I did."

"I know," Andrew said. "If we ever turn out to be half the man Dad is, we should both wind up as Admirals."

"Wouldn't that be something!" Michael said, a wide smile splitting his face. "Wouldn't that just be something? The Admirals O'Connor!"

Chapter
Four

THE HANDLERS PULLED in the mooring lines and coiled them down on the finger pier as the U.S.S. *Sea Bass* backed away from the pier and began to make the turn to leave the Southeast Loch and begin the slow trip through Pearl Harbor itself and to the sea. On the submarine's black, wooden-slatted deck Chief Joseph O'Brien, the Chief of the Boat, lined up the off-watch crew, facing them to starboard. He walked down the line, checking to make sure dungarees were clean, shirtsleeves rolled down and buttoned at the cuff, white hats clean and squared on the sailors' heads. He looked aft where a seaman was standing by the flagstaff to dip the Colors in honor of those who had died in the sunken ships along Battleship Row.

"Now hear me," Chief O'Brien rumbled, "we'll stand easy until we begin to clear the loch, until we can see Battleship Row. When I tell you to come to attention, I don't want to hear any talking or see anyone pointing." He raised his voice and reported to the Bridge that the deck party was in formation and standing easy.

"Very well, Chief," Captain Saunders answered. He looked around, his seaman's eyes assessing his ship's position.

"Better change course a bit to starboard, Mike," he said to O'Connor, who had the Officer of the Deck duty. "We have to make a ninety degree turn to port when Pier Ten-ten bears dead abeam to port. After we make the turn, have Chief O'Brien about-face the men on deck so they can see the drydock as we go by."

The sailors drawn up in formation on the deck of the *Sea Bass* came to attention at Chief O'Brien's command and stared in awe at the incredible wreckage of Battleship Row. Although the crew had been given liberty two days after the attack, the navy yard and Ford Island were off-limits to everyone not engaged in rescue or repair work. Now they saw the huge battleships that had been the pride of the U.S. Navy's Pacific Battle Fleet, shattered hulks resting on the harbor bottom, their fire-scorched upper works dull in the morning sunshine. Navy yard workers were swarming over the hull of the overturned U.S.S. *Oklahoma*, their acetylene torches winking in the sun as they cut their way through the ship's double-bottom and ballast tanks in an effort to gain access to the interior of the capsized ship. The hope that some of the *Oklahoma*'s crew might still be alive, existing within air pockets in the overturned hull, was almost gone, but the effort went on. If no one was left alive, at least the dead would be brought out for burial.

The *Sea Bass* completed its turn around Pier 10-10 and passed slowly down the north side of the navy yard. As the submarine passed the drydock, the crewmen in ranks could see the bulk of the U.S.S. *Pennsylvania*, the flagship of the Pacific Battle Fleet. In the drydock, ahead of the battleship, was the wreckage of the U.S.S. *Cassin* and the U.S.S. *Downes*, two destroyers that had been drydocked when the attack began. The *Pennsylvania* had opened fire on the Japanese planes with its 3.50-inch antiaircraft guns within five minutes after the first bombs hit Ford Island. The destroyer sailors responded with machine guns while their shipmates ran to the Navy Yard Ordnance Shop to retrieve parts for their antiaircraft guns that had been removed days earlier. The destroyer sailors, ignoring bomb blasts and dodging the fire of strafing Japanese planes, had found their gun parts, raced back to their ships and had their guns in action twenty minutes after the attack began.

"Hell of a thing those people did," Captain Saunders said to the men on his ship's bridge. "The old *Nevada* was the only battlewagon to get underway after the attack started. She sortied right about where we are now, off the drydock, and she opened fire on the Jap planes. The Jap dive bombers went after her and then realized they had bigger game sitting there in the drydock, three ships that couldn't move. They purely beat the hell out of those two destroyers, hit them with incendiary bombs.

"The skipper of the *Pennsy* ordered the drydock flooded to

try and douse the fires the bombs started but he goofed; the oil tanks on the two destroyers had ruptured and the leaking oil caught fire, and as the water rose in the drydock, the fires rose with it. Then the depth charges on the destroyers began to explode in the fires and one of the destroyers just up and rolled right over on the other one." He leaned over the bridge rail.

"Chief, clear the deck and rig topside for sea."

The *Sea Bass* eased around the end of the land and began the passage past Hickam Field to the mouth of the harbor. Two tugs that were waiting for the arrival of the submarine began to pull aside the submarine net that guarded the harbor entrance. Outside the harbor an old destroyer, too sea-weary for combat against the Japanese Fleet, cruised slowly back and forth, listening for enemy submarines while it waited for the *Sea Bass*. The submarine cleared the harbor net and picked up speed as it fell in behind the destroyer. A half-hour later the destroyer turned away, its whistle blasting a farewell. *Sea Bass* was on her own, lifting to the swell of the open sea, alone. Mission: Proceed to the Marshall Islands, reconnoiter the islands, intercept, attack and sink any and all Japanese ships sighted.

The ship's cook drew a cup of coffee and sat down on a mess bench beside Pete Savage. "How the hell long is it goin' to take to get to those Marshalls?" he asked.

"Figure about fifteen days," Savage answered. "It's about two thousand miles from Pearl. The Old Man is chewing his fingernails down to his knuckles, he wants to run on the surface day and night on four engines until we get close. Pearl Harbor says we got to run submerged in the day and on one engine at night to conserve fuel oil."

"Conserve fuel oil?" a seaman sitting at a mess table with a big ham sandwich and a cup of coffee in front of him spoke up. "Hell, about the only thing those Japs didn't hit at Pearl was the fuel tanks. Pearl's got plenty of fuel, so why this conserve shit?"

The alarm bell in the compartment began to clang and the Officer of the Deck's voice sounded over the loudspeakers.

"Fire! Fire in the Forward Battery! Rig ship for fire."

"Shit," the seaman said. "Another damned drill. This Old Man's drill-happy, lemme clue you." He picked up his sandwich and his cup of coffee and began to move slowly toward his fire-drill station in the crew's berthing compartment. The sandwich and coffee cup went flying as Chief O'Brien's heavy hand smacked against the seaman's back.

"You don't carry chow to your fire station," O'Brien growled. "You move your button ass and you move it fast. And when they secure from the drill, you get your ass back in here and clean up the mess you made on deck." The seaman fled aft.

"Those damned NQPs give me a pain," O'Brien said to the ship's cook, whose fire-drill station was manning the telephones in the crew's mess.

"That's a new one on me, Chief," the cook said. "Never heard of a NQP."

"Non-Qualified Punk," O'Brien said. "They're aboard a couple of months and the only thing they know is where to sleep, where to eat and where to take a crap, and they think when they've learned all that they're a submarine man." He hunched his heavy shoulders and went forward, ducking his six-foot frame to go through the watertight door between the crew's mess compartment and the Control Room. Lieutenant Henry Baker, the ship's Executive Officer and navigator, was standing by the gyrocompass table, a stopwatch in his hand.

"One minute and four seconds," Lieutenant Baker said. "Awfully slow, Chief. Skipper's not going to like it."

The big Chief Torpedoman looked at his Executive Officer. "They aren't slow, sir. They're tired. Damned tired. We had that long patrol off Midway before the war started and we drilled day and night all during that patrol.

"We got into Pearl with a lot of the ship's gear broken down, and then the attack came. Most of the gear is still not working right, and the people are working extra watches to try to keep the ship running, sir. I think you'd better tell the Captain that the drill times are going to get slower and slower, sir. The people are just plain worn out."

"We were scheduled for a lot of navy yard time if it hadn't been for the attack," Lieutenant Baker said. "I'll tell the Captain what you said, Chief." He watched the Chief of the Boat go forward into the Forward Battery Compartment, where the Chief Petty Officers had a tiny cabin that slept four men, just aft of the Captain's cabin.

The *Sea Bass* reached the Marshall Islands and began a periscope survey of the harbors of Bikini, Bat, Wotho, Bokar, Kwajalein and Tsongi. A week after the submarine had arrived

on station, Captain Saunders sat in the Wardroom with
Lieutenant Baker, a chart of the area spread out on the
Wardroom table.

"These charts are just about useless," Baker grumbled.
"God Himself only knows when they were made. There's no
information on any of them about harbor entrances, reefs,
tides, depths of water."

"Japan took these islands away from the Germans in 1914,"
Captain Saunders said. "Not putting out any updated charts
might have been deliberate. I was up in the chart room at
Pearl before we left, and the cartographers there told me that
Japan hasn't updated a chart on their own harbors for over
twenty years; that is, they haven't put out updates on old
charts to the other seagoing nations of the world. That's got to
be deliberate."

"You mean they were thinking about war with us that long
ago?" Baker asked.

"No, I think it was the traditional Japanese distrust of all
foreigners," Captain Saunders said. "But that doesn't solve our
problems. We've had a quick look at the islands they want us to
look at. Tomorrow we start trying to get as much information as
we can get on those islands. I want the height of mountain
peaks, location of reefs if we can spot them, accurate locations
of headlands, depths of water at harbor entrances." He sighed
and reached for a cup of coffee. "It's a hell of a way to fight a
war. First we have to do an oceanographic survey of the
damned enemy islands, and then, if we see something, we can
attack it."

"Getting water depths means using the fathometer, sir,"
Baker said. "That thing starts clanging away and someone in
those harbors will know we're out here."

"Good," Captain Saunders said. "They might come out to
find out who's making all the noise. If they don't come out, I
intend to go right into the harbor entrances to chart them."

"You don't mind if I cross my fingers a lot, do you?" Baker
said.

The *Sea Bass* prowled around Bikini Island. Lieutenant
Baker spent most of the daylight hours taking periscope
bearings, using the fathometer to find out the depth of the
water on the approaches to the island's harbor and then
painstakingly entering his findings on the chart. The same
routine was followed at the islands of Bat and Botho. Navigat-

ing by the seat of his pants and with an immense faith in God, as Captain Saunders wrote in his ship's log, the *Sea Bass* turned south to explore Kwajalein Island.

Lieutenant Joe Sibley, manning the periscope just after the *Sea Bass* had made its usual predawn dive, turned to the quartermaster of the watch.

"Make an entry in the log that there are a lot of heavy rain squalls sweeping across the island," he said. He suddenly stiffened.

"Contact! Call the Captain. I've got three Jap submarines up here!"

Captain Saunders scrambled up the ladder to the Conning Tower as the General Quarters alarm began its muted clanging in response to his order. Sibley stepped aside as Captain Saunders put his eye to the periscope.

"Hot damn!" Saunders said. "Three of the bastards! Open torpedo-tube outer doors. Set torpedo depth four feet, all tubes."

"Plotting Party is ready," Lieutenant Baker's voice floated up the hatch from the Control Room. "Can you give us a bearing and range, Captain?"

"Torpedo-tube outer doors all open. Depth set four feet all tubes, sir," Chief O'Brien's deep bass voice said from the Control Room.

"Dammit," Captain Saunders said. "We're in a damned thunderstorm. I can't see a damned thing. Henry, give me some idea how far we are from the harbor mouth. When I saw them, they were broadside to us, their port side to us."

"We're about six thousand yards from the harbor, Captain. If they were port side to us, they were heading for the harbor. Does Joe have any idea at all about how far they were from us?"

"I'd say about four thousand yards. That's a guess," Joe Sibley said.

"That would put them on a course for the harbor mouth. We charted that harbor entrance yesterday, Captain," Baker said.

"Dollar to a doughnut we've lost them," Captain Saunders said. "Henry, put me on a patrol course back and forth across this damned harbor mouth. Secure from General Quarters. Close outer torpedo-tube doors. When this damned rain stops, we'll take a look at things, go in close and see if there's a submarine-tender in that harbor. There's room enough in there for lots of ships. That harbor inside the atoll is over seventy miles long."

The rain squalls eased and became sporadic as the day wore on. Late in the afternoon Lieutenant Baker was at the periscope, taking bearings of the distinctive features of the atoll of Kwajalein. He turned the periscope.

"Ship standing out of the harbor!" he yelled. "Sound General Quarters!" The crew rushed to their battle stations as Captain Saunders climbed the ladder to the Conning Tower. The Plotting Party assembled around the table over the gyrocompass in the Control Room, their plotting and maneuvering boards ready.

"Open all torpedo-tube outer doors. Set torpedo depth eight feet on all torpedoes," the Captain snapped. "Target is a Jap destroyer. Target bears three-five-seven." He twisted the range-finder knob on the right side of the periscope.

"Range is twelve hundred yards. Angle on the bow is eighty starboard."

Ensign Robert Hall, his young face flushed with excitement, spun the small cranks on the Torpedo Data Computer in the after end of the Conning Tower.

"You have a solution, sir," he said, trying to control the excitement in his voice. "You can shoot, Captain."

"Stand by Forward," Captain Saunders said. He kept his eye to the periscope eyepiece, watching his target. "Stand by . . ."

"FIRE ONE!" He counted down from seven to one.

"FIRE TWO!"

"FIRE THREE!"

"All torpedoes running hot, straight and normal, sir," the sound man reported from the Control Room.

"Torpedo run is forty-two seconds, Captain," Henry Baker called out.

"Very well," Captain Saunders said. He watched through the periscope lens, listening to Lieutenant Baker toll off the seconds at five-second intervals. Baker continued calling out the intervals until he had reached one minute, and then he stopped.

"Dammit to hell!" Captain Saunders' voice was questioning. "How could I miss at that range? He's turning! He's seen the torpedoes or heard us! He's coming! Take me down . . . two hundred feet . . . fast! Close outer torpedo-tube doors. Stand by for depth charges!"

The *Sea Bass* plunged downward, seeking the safety of deep water as the Japanese destroyer raced toward the submarine. The sound man turned on his stool.

"Twin screws coming real fast. Bearing is three-five-eight, sir."

"Right full rudder," Captain Saunders ordered. The sound of the destroyer's twin propellers filled the interior of the submarine's hull and the crew members stared upward, as if they could see the enemy ship racing over them.

There was a sharp cracking sound, and then, a few seconds later, a roaring explosion that lifted the submarine and shook it violently. The *Sea Bass* rolled heavily to one side as light bulbs broke and bits of cork hull insulation rained down. The submarine rolled back sluggishly to an even keel and the sound man turned to report.

"He's turning, sir, coming back!"

The sound of the destroyer's propellers rang through the interior of the *Sea Bass*, and then the depth charges began exploding, four this attack, each one of them close enough to twist the long, slim submarine in a vise of turbulent water and sound.

"Two hundred fifty feet. Meet your helm there." Captain Saunders had come down the ladder from the Conning Tower and was standing back of the bow and stern planesmen. "Henry, keep plotting that bastard's movements and the charges he drops. What the hell is that?"

The interior of the *Sea Bass* was filled with a sharp, ringing sound that submarine crews would hear and dread for the remainder of the war in the Pacific—the sound of a Japanese destroyer's sonar search beam hitting the submarine and bouncing back to the destroyer's receivers to pinpoint the position of the submarine.

"He's pinging on us, sir," the sound man said.

The attack lasted for more than four hours before the Japanese destroyer gave up the hunt. An hour later the *Sea Bass* slid upward to sixty-five feet, periscope depth, and Captain Saunders ordered the periscope raised. He put his eye to the big rubber eyepiece.

"Can't see anything," he said. "Everything's foggy. Down this 'scope. Raise the search 'scope."

The quartermaster lowered the battle periscope and raised the big-lensed search periscope. "This one is foggy, too," Captain Saunders said. "Joe. Joe Sibley. Get up here and take a look."

Joe Sibley looked through one periscope and then the other. "Looks to me as if the depth charging might have damaged the periscopes, sir."

"That ever happen before, you know?"

"No, sir," Sibley said. "But I don't know of any submarine that ever took depth charges going off right above them, Captain. Everything that happens out here is the first time. One thing is dead sure, you can't use either periscope. It's like looking into a gray wool blanket."

The officers of the *Sea Bass* seated themselves around the Wardroom table, waiting for Captain Saunders to take his place at the head of the table. He came into the Wardroom and nodded briefly at his officers. He put a pad of paper on the table in front of his place.

"I called this meeting to get an assessment of our material damage," he said. "We'll begin with you, Joe." He took a pencil out of his pocket and wrote "Engineering" at the top of the page on the pad.

"Briefly," Joe Sibley said, "engineering isn't in too good a shape, sir. We have both periscopes out of commission. Art Apple, the machinist's mate in the Forward Engine Room, spent a few months working with periscopes some time ago. He thinks we've got a nitrogen leak in the periscopes. They're filled with nitrogen, you know, so they won't fog. Apple says the only cure is pulling the periscopes and finding the leaks and recharging them.

"The port evaporator isn't working and the starboard evaporator is about to quit for good. Which means no fresh water, other than what we have in our tanks. I recommend we go on strict water rationing as of now.

"Numbers One and Four main engines can't be run at more than fifty percent of normal cruising speed. Numbers Two and Three main engines are a little better, we can run them at about sixty-five percent of normal cruising speed. All the main engines need new bearings. And the forward battery won't take a full charge anymore. The after battery is even worse.

"That's the worst stuff, Captain. I've got a laundry list as long as my arm of minor stuff, but most of it can wait."

Captain Saunders nodded and turned to Mike O'Connor.

"No damage at all, sir," O'Connor said.

"What about those torpedoes?" Captain Saunders said. "I just won't accept the fact that I missed a straight-on shot with the target damned near broadside and only twelve hundred yards away. The sound man tracked all three torpedoes into the target bearing and heard them running after they had passed the target."

"I don't know, Captain," Mike O'Connor said. "I sat down with Miller and Chief O'Brien. They're both marvelous torpedomen, as you know, sir. They did all the preliminary and final work on every torpedo up in the shop on the base before we took the fish aboard. They say the fish were as perfect as they could make them.

"Chief O'Brien says the only thing he can think of is that the torpedoes ran a lot deeper than the eight feet they were set. Just to make sure they had the depth setting right, they pulled the fish out of the other tubes and checked them. They were all set at eight feet so we figured the ones you fired were set at eight feet, sir." He stopped and looked at Captain Saunders.

"There's another thing, sir. Even if the fish ran deeper than what they were set, there's the Mark Six exploder; that exploder is supposed to go off when the torpedo goes underneath the target. If the torpedoes ran under the target and didn't explode like they're supposed to, we might have two big problems. Torpedoes that are running too deep and an exploder that doesn't work."

Captain Saunders turned to Henry Baker. "Dammit, Henry, I'm not going to ask to go back to port. Draft a message to Pearl. Tell them the extent of our damage. Don't elaborate. Tell them we'll continue on patrol. Tell the Chief of the Boat to secure the showers and washing machine. Joe, see what your people can do to keep the engines running."

Henry Baker looked at his Commanding Officer. "Captain, what in the hell are you going to do with no periscopes? We're blind when we're submerged, sir."

"We'll do the best we can," Captain Saunders said.

Chapter
Five

THE *Sea Bass* HAD ONLY twenty-four hours to wait for a response to its bare recital of materiel failures. The submarine command ordered the submarine back to port at once, and Captain Saunders, not reluctantly, turned toward his home port. Pete Savage finished helping Lieutenant Baker lay out the course for Pearl Harbor and then drew two cups of coffee from the galley and went up to the Forward Torpedo Room, where he lived. He handed one cup to Dandy Don Miller.

"When we gettin' back to Pearl?" Miller asked Savage.

"Figure about two weeks," the quartermaster said. "The Old Man will run on the surface as much as he can. He was pretty cute, the Old Man; he sort of kissed off the way the engines ain't workin' so good and the fact that we haven't got any periscopes we can use and told Pearl he would continue on patrol.

"Pearl Harbor comes back with a pat on the back for him and the ship and orders us home."

"Can't be too quick for me," Miller said. "I just hope the damned engines don't break down and they have to send someone out to tow us home."

"What's the big hurry to get back to Pearl, Dandy?"

"Well, for one thing, I heard before we left that they're gonna put submarine crews coming in offa patrol in the Royal Hawaiian Hotel for two weeks of rest and relaxation," Miller said. "I always wanted to go in the bar at that joint, but I never figured I could afford to do more than buy one beer there, I heard it costs an arm and a leg. Another thing, I don't think they'd let an enlisted man in the gate of that damned hotel. If the scuttlebutt is right, we'll live there for a couple of weeks."

"I don't suppose that tall ol' blonde we saw you with the day before we left on patrol has got anything to do with you wantin' to get back there in a hurry, has it?" Savage asked.

Dandy Don grinned over the edge of his coffee cup.

"Where'd you meet that piece of gear?" Savage asked. "The way things are in Pearl there's about a thousand men for every woman and you come up with a blonde that's built like a brick shithouse."

"I was in the commissary buyin' some Tabasco sauce, I like to put a little of the hot sauce in my beer," Miller said. "She was ahead of me in the line and she looked kinda down in the mouth. So I put my bottle of Tabasco in my pocket and offered to carry her grocery bags to her car.

"Now you got to get the whole picture. This is a tall broad with a lot out in front, and walkin' behind her is like watchin' two small boys fightin' under a blanket. I mean, that woman has got some kind of ass!

"I stowed the grocery bags in the trunk of her car and she kinda looked me up and down and asked me if I'd like to volunteer to carry her groceries into her house on account of her garage was kinda far from the kitchen door and the bags were heavy.

"She lives up in the hills, nice house. I mule-packed the grocery bags into the kitchen and helped her stow the chow away and she made me a cup of coffee. Now it don't take any kind of genius to figure out what's on her mind.

"So we drink the coffee and I figure nothing tried, nothing lost. So I come right out and tell her she's got the finest ass I ever walked behind. I figure it was maybe two minutes later and we were in her sack. And I mean to tell you, Pete, that was prime stuff! I mean prime! She like to wore me down to a frazzle but I stayed with it until she asked me to stop and we both went to sleep. She woke me up about three hours later and we went at it again. It was better the second time around, because by then I knew exactly what the lady wanted."

"Don't lay it on too thick, Dandy," Savage scoffed. "I seen you in the shower. You ain't hung heavy enough to scare anyone."

"It's called 'technique,' old buddy," Miller said. He sat back in his folding canvas chair, aware that a half-dozen heads had appeared over the edges of the bunks in the torpedo room.

"Technique is when I see some Third Class up here in the

room going out of his everlovin' mind tryin' to thread the connection to the combustion pot and not bein' able to get the threads to catch just right. I tell him to get out of the way and I slide my hand inside the afterbody of the fish and take hold of the connection real gentle like and imagine that I'm the connection and I want to get hooked up to the combustion pot. I use the technique I learned when I was a Third Class. Makin' a combustion-pot connection by feel and makin' a broad is all the same—technique."

"She's got to be married if she was in the commissary," Savage said. "Where's her old man?"

"He's a Marine pilot stationed on Wake Island."

"Japs took Wake," Savage said. "Maybe the dude flew his plane off before they got there and landed on some carrier or something. If I was you, I'd have the yeoman run a check on the Wake Island personnel list, make sure he's a prisoner. If he got off the island some way or another, could be trouble for you. Officers don't like enlisted men plowin' their fields." He picked up Miller's empty coffee cup and turned to go.

"Old Man's sweatin' a little blood. They's some kind of order out he should shoot only one fish at a target. He fired three and missed with all of them. He figures he's gonna get his ass chewed off at his chest. Mr. Baker thinks if they come down too hard on the Old Man, he'll start hollerin' for an investigation of the torpedoes. How'd that strike you, Dandy Don, they begin investigatin' your torpedoes?"

"Suits me," the lanky torpedoman said. "They can start with the fish we got left. Every damned one of them is as good as we can make them. All the rudder throws check out to a gnat's ass. Air flasks are up to three thousand pounds. Water and alcohol compartments full. They were about as good as me and Chief O'Brien could make them when we did the preliminary and finals on them in the shop. We've kept them that way. We did our part. It's up to the Old Man to get the hits. He's been a damned good shot with exercise fish, so somethin' must be wrong with these fish that I don't know about." Pete Savage nodded and went aft.

The *Sea Bass* limped into Pearl Harbor and moored alongside the submarine-tender *Pelius*. A swarm of artificers waited while the staff officers of the Pacific Fleet Submarine Command welcomed Captain Saunders. When the brief welcoming was over, Saunders walked aft down the deck to where Lieutenant Baker was talking with the officer in charge of the repair crew.

"I've got to go up to Admiral Withers's office," Saunders said. "You take over until I get back, Henry. The buses to take the crew to the Royal Hawaiian will be here at eleven hundred thirty hours. Noon chow in the hotel for the crew. Uniform of the day will be whites. Tell the Chief of the Boat to have everyone ready to go by eleven-thirty and to make sure everyone has enough gear for two weeks in the hotel."

Baker and the repair-crew officer watched Captain Saunders plod up the steep gangway and disappear through a big square hatch in the side of the submarine-tender.

"You'd better have your Pharmacist's Mate standing by with a blood transfusion when he gets back," the repair-crew officer said. "I heard you people shot three torpedoes at one target and missed with all three. The Admiral blows his cork when you people shoot more than one fish at a target. Especially when you miss, and everyone's been missing. I heard the Squadron Gunnery Officer say the other day that if this keeps up, there won't be a torpedo left in Pearl by July."

Lieutenant Baker's eyes hardened. "If you ask me, there's something wrong with those torpedoes. The Old Man had a dead setup on a target at twelve hundred yards, broadside shot, and nothing happened. The sound man heard the torpedoes run right through the target bearing and keep on going. The magnetic exploder didn't work."

"I heard all that before, too," the repair officer said.

Lieutenant Joe Sibley was sitting in the Wardroom drinking coffee when Henry Baker came in and sat down.

"The Old Man's been gone for over two hours," Baker said. "Sure hope they didn't come down too heavy on him. He's the sort of man who will stand up on his hind legs and fight back, and he's getting too close to three stripes to lose any points. What's the dope on our repairs?"

"We go into the navy yard day after tomorrow," Sibley said. "Complete overhaul of all four main engines and the auxiliary. New periscopes. New evaporators. They're going to give us new cells to replace the bad ones in the two batteries and that's a hell of a big job, they have to pull the hull patches off to do that. Looks like we'll be in the yard for a long time, maybe a month."

"Don't count on a month," Baker said. "I heard the yard people are working around the clock, going twenty-four hours a day seven days a week." He half-turned in his chair as the loudspeaker on the bulkhead crackled and the voice of the deck watch echoed tinnily.

"Captain is returning to the ship."

Captain Barney Saunders had waited for twenty minutes outside Admiral Withers's office before the Admiral's Chief Yeoman opened the door and asked him to come in. The Admiral waved him to a chair in front of his desk. Saunders recognized the folder on the desk. It was the war-patrol report he had handed to the Admiral's aide when the *Sea Bass* had tied up alongside the *Pelius*.

"The navigational information you put together on the Marshalls, Captain—simply magnificent. What did you do, go right into the harbor mouths? You have channel depths, bearings from mountain peaks. A wonderful job, Barney."

"Thank you, sir," Barney Saunders said. "Yes, we did go into harbor mouths when I was sure we couldn't be trapped there by ships coming out of the harbor. I used the fathometer every time I could risk it to get channel depths. I'm sorry we couldn't do a better job on plotting in reefs. They're pretty hard to see from the vantage point of our bridge, we're too low down, sir." He straightened in his chair, conscious of the pot belly that hung over his belt, making a mental vow to go on a diet as soon as he went back to sea.

Admiral Withers nodded, his eyes on the patrol report. He turned several pages and looked up.

"You fired three torpedoes at the destroyer." The Admiral's normally kind voice was suddenly sharp, crisp. "You know the orders: one torpedo to a target unless it's a major target. The Mark Six exploder makes it unnecessary to fire more than one torpedo at any ordinary target. Not that a destroyer is an ordinary target in that sense. The orders forbid you to attack destroyers except in self-defense, Captain, the risk of losing your ship is too great."

"Yes, sir," Captain Saunders said. He stared at the wall behind the Admiral's head.

"You missed with all three torpedoes." The words dropped like stones in a pond.

"I had a perfect setup, Admiral. I've gone over the plot of the firing a dozen times on the way back to Pearl, sir. I had a straight shot, no gyro angles on the torpedoes. Range was just under twelve hundred yards. Target's angle on the bow was eighty starboard. Target speed was fifteen knots, its course steady.

"The sound man reported all three torpedoes ran hot, straight and normal. He tracked each torpedo into the target bearing and beyond, sir."

Admiral Withers touched a page of the patrol report. "You set torpedo depth at eight feet. Your orders are to set torpedo depth at ten to twelve feet beneath the keel of the target. In this case you should have set the torpedo depths at least twenty feet. Why didn't you?"

"I wanted to make sure of a hit, sir. We've never fired a torpedo with a Mark Six exploder in its warhead. I know the exploder is supposed to explode as the torpedo passes under the target—"

"And break the target's back, its keel, Captain. Which is why you only need one torpedo for each ordinary target."

"Yes, sir," Captain Saunders said. His pleasant face set in determined lines. "Admiral, with all due respect, sir; I know from my sound man's report that those three torpedoes ran through the target bearing. Which to me means they ran under the target. But they didn't explode. The Mark Six exploder didn't work, sir."

"Your sound man probably made an error, Captain," the Admiral said. "We'll let that pass for the moment. The Chief of Staff will have something to say to you about torpedo depths and you can discuss it with him.

"Now, about the depth charging you underwent, which you seem to have weathered by good seamanship—you say in your report that you distinctly heard the Japanese destroyer echo-ranging on you with sonar gear. Our information is that the Japanese do not have sonar echo-ranging gear."

"Sir," Captain Saunders said, "every man in the crew heard them pinging on us with their sonar. We know the sound, we've heard our own destroyers ping on us in practice, sir. The only difference between the sound of echo-ranging from our destroyers and what we heard is that the Japanese sonar seemed to be much more powerful than our own, Admiral."

"That information might just be worth more than the three torpedoes you wasted," Admiral Withers said. He pressed a button on his desk and his Chief Yeoman opened the door and came in.

"Get the photographer, Chief," the Admiral said, "and then take Captain Saunders to the Flag Office, please."

The buses carrying the crew of the *Sea Bass* pulled up to the gate of the Royal Hawaiian Hotel. Dandy Don Miller, sitting in a window seat in the lead bus, nudged Pete Savage. "Look over there, across the street. The convertible. That's her." He waved a hand out of the bus window and the woman sitting in the convertible waved back at him.

"Got to hand it to you, Dandy," Savage said. "One of these days when I'm off watch, I'll get you to fill me in on that technique of yours."

"It's never how much money you got, old buddy," Dandy Don said. "It's how you spend your money."

"I still think you ought to have the yeoman check out that guy she's married to," Pete Savage said. "Hate to have a buddy get shot in the ass with a forty-five by some Marine officer dude."

"I already asked the yeoman to do that," Miller said. "He knows a Chief in the base personnel office who can get the dope on her old man." He waved again at the woman as the bus ground into gear and began the curving trip through the hotel gardens to the hotel entrance.

The crew saw little of Dandy Don Miller during the next twelve days. He appeared infrequently, and when he did, there were deep circles under his eyes and he walked slowly, as if he were afraid that if he moved with his usual bouncing stride something would break. Two days before the end of the Rest and Recreation period the Staff Command had reasoned would be sufficient time for a submarine crew to unwind from a rigorous war patrol, Miller met briefly with the ship's yeoman and left, walking slowly to the gate where the woman in the convertible waited for him. He said little on the ride to her house. When she had parked the car, he walked into the kitchen, and with the familiarity of a man who was living there, he made a pot of coffee and poured a cup for the woman and for himself.

"Let's take the coffee into the bedroom, Don," she said. "We've only got today and tonight before you have to go back. I need you."

"Ain't studyin' none on going to bed with you," Dandy Don said.

She grinned lasciviously. "I can get it up for you if you're tired."

"Ain't tired," he said. He rinsed his cup in the sink and put it on the sideboard and went into the bedroom and began to pack his belongings into the small suitcase he had brought to the house the first day of the R & R period.

"What are you doing?" she said.

"Goin' back to the hotel while I'm still in one piece," he said.

"I love you!" she said. "You told me you loved me!"

"Well, I did say that, I guess," Miller said. "But lemme tell you something, Betty Lou. I read once in a book when I was on watch in the torpedo room that love was the same as trust. You lied to me and I don't trust you."

"I never lied to you," she snapped. "I told you I love you and I do."

"You lied," he said flatly. "You told me your husband was a Marine Corps pilot and that he was on Wake Island. Fella I know checked the personnel records for Wake Island. Ain't nobody with your name on that list, and they're damned sure of those names because all the people on Wake Island are in some Jap prison camp.

"The fella did find your husband's name. He's a Marine. That was the truth. He flies an airplane. That was the truth. But he wasn't never on Wake Island. He was at Ewa, right here on Oahu, and right now he's in the hospital all shredded to shit by shrapnel from a Jap bomb. I guess that means he ain't gonna be a regular man anymore, least not the kind of man you need."

She stared at him.

"Maybe I'm kind of old-fashioned," Miller said, "but I think you're a cheap sort of broad, husband right here in the hospital and you're romping around in bed with someone who ain't been shot up. If you had the guts to get a divorce, I might listen to you when you say you love me, but I doubt it." He closed the lid of the suitcase and snapped the locks shut.

"You know what I can do to you, don't you?" she snapped. "I can report you for trying to rape me, for raping me. How much chance do you think you'd have, the word of an enlisted man against a Major's wife?"

"Not very much," Miller said. "But I'll take the chance. I got a lot of shipmates saw you waitin' for me the day the bus pulled up to the gate at the hotel. Lots of shipmates saw you eating lunch with me at the Wagon Wheel. Lots of shipmates saw you waitin' for me at the gate every time I came back to get a change of skivvies. You're gonna have one hell of a time provin' rape, and if you try, your old man will probably kick your ass out. He might do that anyway, if I tell him what kind of a miserable broad you really are." He picked up the suitcase. "It's been nice, real nice, Betty Lou. See you around." He opened the screen door and walked down the sidewalk to the road.

Captain Saunders sat down heavily in his chair at the head of the Wardroom table. He put a manila folder on the table in front of him. The officers of the Sea Bass filed in and took their seats, their faces carefully impassive.

"You're not going to believe this," Captain Saunders said. He fumbled in his shirt pocket and pulled out a medal. He laid the medal on the green baize cloth of the table. The officers stared at the Maltese Cross and the dark blue ribbon with a white stripe running from top to bottom up the center of the ribbon.

"That's a Navy Cross!" Henry Baker said in an awed voice. "First one I ever saw other than in a picture."

"They gave one of these to every one of the skippers who made a war patrol to the Marshalls," Captain Saunders said. "Everyone except poor Rainier in the Dolphin. That damned ship was in no condition to go to sea and they knew it but they sent the Dolphin out anyway. Trying to keep his ship operating got to Captain Rainier and he collapsed. I doubt he'll ever go to sea again. But the rest of us got these things. Hell of a thing. Admiral Withers gave me this and there was a photographer there to take a picture of him pinning this thing on my shirt and then he sent me in to the Chief of Staff and that man chewed my ass out until hell wouldn't have it. I haven't been talked to like that since I left the farm in Iowa." He sighed and put the medal in his shirt pocket.

"Were they upset because you fired three fish at one target?" Baker asked.

"That was part of it," Captain Saunders answered. "I got chewed out for firing three fish. I got chewed out for attacking a destroyer. I got chewed out for missing with the torpedoes and I got chewed out for running submerged all day and on one engine at night on our way to the patrol area."

"Those were our orders!" Henry Baker protested.

"There's a whole new command outlook here," Captain Saunders said. "Admiral Nimitz is running the whole show. He's thrown away the book. We aren't going to fight this war the way we thought we would. The way it was, the submarines were supposed to be a scouting force operating out ahead of the Battle Fleet. If we got lucky, if we could shoot submerged, we'd shoot.

"Now there isn't any Battle Fleet to scout ahead of. The battleships are sitting on the bottom at Ford Island. We're the Battle Fleet now. Nimitz is going to carry the fight to the Japanese with submarines. After we've softened up the Japs enough, he'll move in with the carriers and mop them up." He stopped and looked around the table at his officers.

"That means submarines are going to have to be aggressive. It means that any submarine captains who aren't aggressive will lose command. That's started already, they're shifting captains who haven't demonstrated aggressiveness to desk jobs here in Pearl until they grow some backbone." He stopped and opened the folder he had laid on the table.

"Let's get down to business. Sea Bass is going into the yard for an overhaul, and God knows we need it. I'm being relieved as of today." He half-smiled. "I'm not being relieved because of a lack of aggressiveness, shooting at that destroyer saved my skin on that score.

"I'm going to new construction. East Coast. I don't even know what ship I'm getting, all I know is that she's almost ready for sea trials, so I should be back out here in a couple of months."

"I guess we should be congratulating you, Captain," Henry Baker said, "but, dammit, I hate to see you leave. I think I speak for all of us here and for the crew as well when I say that."

"Well, that's nice of you, Henry," Captain Saunders said. "I wish I could take this entire Wardroom with me to the new boat but I can't."

"Who's your relief, sir?" Sibley asked.

"I don't know that, either," Saunders said. "All I know is they told me they'd give *Sea Bass* a good man. I may know who he is after I come back from a meeting with the Chief of Staff." He looked at the clock on the bulkhead. "I have to get moving. They said they'd send a car for me to take me to the meeting and it's due on the pier in ten minutes. All of you stay close aboard. Don't mention to anyone that I'm leaving. I'll fill you in when I get back."

Two hours later Captain Saunders returned and the officers assembled in the Wardroom. Saunders sat down at the head of the table, opened a manila envelope, pulled the contents out and put them in front of him.

"They've got about twenty yeomen up there on the base who are doing nothing but cutting new orders for officers and men," he began, "and what I've got here are orders for some of you.

"Henry, you're being sent to the *Pompano* as Executive Officer. That doesn't sound much like a step in the right direction, but it is. *Pompano* had a hell of a good war patrol under Dave Parks, and Dave is slated for new construction after a couple more patrols. If you watch yourself, you could step up into his shoes. I told the Chief of Staff you're fully qualified for command." He pushed a set of orders across the table to Henry Baker and then he looked around the table, his face grim.

"I don't like what I'm going to say now, but it has to be said. It goes no farther than this Wardroom.

"The *Tigerfish* came in from her first war patrol this morning. She's one of our sister ships, same class, as you know. Her Captain made a night attack, submerged, on an oil tanker. The tanker was so far away that he had almost no chance of getting a hit." Captain Saunders closed his eyes and then opened them.

"He ordered his torpedoes set in low speed. He fired one torpedo at seven thousand yards, and went down to two hundred fifty feet, rigged for depth charge and silent running. He spent the next twenty-four hours down there at two hundred fifty feet.

"His Executive Officer wrote a report that said his Captain was a coward. He might be right, but you can't do that and expect to stay aboard the ship. He's been transferred as of this noon. The Captain has been relieved of command.

"I was told the *Tigerfish* is filthy dirty, the morale of the crew is shot all to hell. Admiral Nimitz is boiling. He's giving *Tigerfish* a new Captain, new Exec, new Engineering Officer, new Chief of the Boat and God only knows what else. He's going to send her to the hottest area in the Pacific and find out if he's got a fighting submarine or if he has to transfer the whole crew." Captain Saunders leaned back and lit a cigarette.

"They're giving the *Tigerfish* to Hugh Foster. I know him, he was two classes ahead of me at the Academy. He's a damned good man. We had a talk and I made some suggestions to him and he accepted them. I know I should have talked with the people I suggested that he take but I just didn't have the time.

"We both agreed he needed a hard case for a Chief of the Boat to whip that crew into shape. I suggested he take Chief O'Brien and he agreed. I made some other suggestions to him and he took those, too.

"Joe, you're going to *Tigerfish* as the Executive Officer. You've earned it and you'll learn a hell of a lot under Hugh Foster.

"Mike O'Connor goes to *Tigerfish* as Engineering Officer. That's a big step up for you, Mike. You've been a damned good gunnery officer for me and I told Foster you've got the savvy to handle engineering." There was a dead silence around the Wardroom table.

"That doesn't mean the rest of you aren't good enough to go to *Tigerfish*," Captain Saunders continued. "*Sea Bass* is a fine ship. The crew is excellent. The new CO is going to need a good Wardroom, and I'm leaving him the nucleus of that. Most of you will move up into different jobs under the new captain and you'll be getting some youngsters to train.

"That's about it. I'd like to say that serving with all of you has been a great experience for me. Henry, Joe, Mike, I congratulate you. If you don't do a good job for Hugh Foster, I'll see to it you're transferred back to me, and believe me, I'll make your asses ring like a big Chinese gong." He grinned.

"Captain," Joe Sibley's normally deep voice dropped a tone, "sir, it's been our privilege to serve under you. And if the chance ever comes, I think I speak for all of us in saying we'd

jump at the chance to serve under you again." The officers
tapped their spoons against their coffee cups in approval.
Captain Saunders smiled and left the Wardroom.

The buses pulled up on the submarine pier and the crew of
the *Tigerfish* spilled out and made their way down the
gangway, shoving and pushing. Chief O'Brien, dressed in a
crisp khaki uniform, stood on the afterdeck of the submarine,
his eyes narrowed, watching the crew come aboard.

"Fall in!" O'Brien roared as the crew began to cluster on the
deck. He waited until the men had formed into two ragged
lines.

"Now hear me," O'Brien said. "My name is Joseph O'Brien,
Chief Torpedoman's Mate. I'm the Chief of the Boat of this
submarine as of now.

"I went through this pigpen you call a submarine after you
people went to the hotel. In the eighteen years I've been in
this man's Navy, I never saw how pigs lived before. You people
are pigs. PIGS!

"I know how to handle pigs." He stopped and his hard eyes
bored into the assembled crew.

"The relief crew cleaned this ship and painted it, inside and
out. It will be kept clean or you'll answer to me. If I find one
piece of clothing adrift, I will personally stuff that piece of
clothing up the man's ass who owns it. If that isn't clear, if any
of you people think I'm blowing wind, you march right up that
gangway and out on the pier and I will personally whip your
ass in front of all hands."

The crew stood silent, awed by the intensity in the big Chief
Petty Officer's voice. O'Brien took two steps forward and
stopped a pace from the front row of men. He walked slowly
from one end of the line to the other, staring each man in the
eye.

"We understand each other," he said. "You're in the
submarine Navy. My kind of submarine Navy. You have a
choice. You do things my way or I'll break you.

"There will be a change-of-command ceremony on this deck
in one hour. All hands will be topside in clean whites, clean
white hats and shined black shoes. Chief Hahn will stand fast.
The rest of you lay below and get ready for the change of
command."

O'Brien waited until the crew had gone below and then

walked over to Chief Electrician's Mate Harold Hahn. He eyed the tall, rangy man and grinned.

"Long time no see, Hal." Hahn reached out a hand and shook O'Brien's big paw.

"Heard in the hotel you were coming aboard. We need you, Joe. Damned ship's been run like a kindygarten school."

"Where are the other Chiefs?" O'Brien asked.

"Chief of the Boat was transferred the day after we got to the hotel. That's when I got an idea that they might be shaking up the boat. Then we heard you were coming aboard. The two Chiefs we had in the engine rooms put in for transfer to the relief crew and got it." He shrugged his wide, bony shoulders.

"Can't say I'll miss either one of them, they were sorry excuses for Chief Petty Officers. What's bugging me is who are we getting for an Engineering Officer? The one we had didn't know his ass from a cylinder head."

"Your new boss is up forward of the Conning Tower. He wanted to stay out of sight while I was introducing myself to the crew. Might as well go forward and meet him."

Lieutenant O'Connor was sitting in the pointer's seat of the 5.50-inch deck gun, working the gear train and making the gun barrel move up and down. He stood up as the two Chiefs approached.

"This thing was frozen solid when we looked at it ten days ago, Chief," he said to O'Brien. "Works fine now."

"All it needed was some lubrication," O'Brien said. "I want you to meet an old shipmate of mine, Chief Harold Hahn. He runs the electrical gang and you'll remember that his gear was the only gear aboard that was clean and in four-oh shape when we looked at the ship last week."

"I remember," O'Connor said. The two men eyed each other and then O'Connor stuck out his hand.

"I'm damned glad to meet you, Chief. I'm going to have to depend on you for a lot of help."

"We've got ourselves a little problem, Mister O'Conner," O'Brien said. "The Chief here tells me that both Chiefs in the engine rooms bailed out, got themselves transfers to the relief crew. We're going to have to get two men to replace them."

"I'd like to promote someone from the ship's company if I can," O'Connor said. "That would be good for morale." He turned to Chief Hahn. "Is there anyone aboard who's qualified for a Chief's hat?"

"The First Class in the Forward Room, dude named Bill Joy, is a damned good man," Chief Hahn said. "He's been carrying the load for the two Chiefs who left. Kind of a quiet guy but he knows his job. He's never been allowed to do the job the way he wants to do it. He's qualified for Chief."

"Okay, we'll promote him to Chief Machinist Mate," Mike O'Connor said. "Anyone else qualified?"

Chief Hahn shook his head. "Not in my book, sir. You'll have to look somewhere else."

"How about Art Apple on the *Sea Bass*?" Chief O'Brien said. "He's a hell of a good man, you know that, sir. He's due to make Chief anytime now, and maybe we could get him over here." Mike O'Connor nodded his approval and O'Brien turned to Hahn.

"Who's the yeoman on this bucket? Is he a good man? This is going to take some hustle to get everything typed up and cleared."

"No sweat," Chief Hahn said. "The yeoman's name is Ken Harrington. Damned good man. Little dude. Skinny. Goes around with a chip on his shoulder. Every time he goes ashore, he picks a fight with some guy twice as big as he is. Hasn't won a fight yet, I know of, but he keeps trying. He used to pick on the Chief of the Boat we had in front of the crew. I heard him tell the Chief that he was the poorest excuse for a Chief of the Boat he'd seen in fifteen years in submarines. Chief used to walk away from him."

"Why?" O'Brien said flatly.

"He was old, Joe. He's got twenty-five years in the Navy. First time we went to Battle Stations, the only time, he like to shit his pants." Hahn looked at Mike O'Connor. "Excuse the language, sir."

"It's okay," O'Connor said with a grin. "Plain talk never hurt anyone, especially an officer. I take it you like Harrington?"

"Everyone likes the little bastard, Mister O'Connor. He knows his job, he's a damned good submarine man and he's a damned good bow planesman on battle stations. He's kind of like one of those little dogs, a Pekingese? Yaps a lot but when the chips are down, he's there and ready to go." He stopped and looked at his new Engineering Officer.

"Do you know the new skipper we're getting, sir?"

"No, I don't," Mike O'Connor said. "All I know is that

Admiral Nimitz is high on him and the Admiral is a hard man to please."

"While we're talking and waiting for the change of command," O'Brien said, "Hal, who's the torpedoman in charge of both the torpedo rooms?"

"A First Class named Dick Smith," Chief Hahn answered. "A real left-hander. I don't think the man can walk across the deck and chew gum at the same time. He and the Chief of the Boat were buddies."

"Mister O'Connor and I came over and looked at the ship after you people had gone to the hotel," O'Brien said. "Mister O'Connor was Gunnery Officer on the Sea Bass. We figured whoever had charge of the torpedo rooms was a deadhead." He turned to O'Connor. "I don't want this man Smith aboard, sir. How about you talking to Mister Sibley about geting rid of him?"

"I'll do that," Mike O'Connor said. "But I should have someone's name to give to him to take his place."

"How about Dandy Don Miller? I trained Miller myself. You know he's a good man. He ran both rooms on the Sea Bass to suit you and me."

"He's a damned good man," O'Connor said. "But would it be wise? Some of the crew might think you're putting your own people in key jobs. Might make your job a lot harder."

"Ain't nothing going to make this job easier," O'Brien said.

The change-of-command ceremony was brief. Admiral Chester Nimitz walked down the gangway followed by his staff and took his position across the deck from the two rigid lines of the ship's crew. Lieutenant Commander Hugh Foster came down the gangway and saluted the Admiral and his staff and stood to one side. The Admiral's Chief of Staff, a burly four-stripe Captain, stepped forward and handed Commander Foster a sealed envelope. Foster ran a thumb under the flap of the envelope and broke the heavy wax seal. He took out the single sheet of paper, cleared his throat and began a ceremony that was as old as the Navy itself, the reading aloud of the ship's company of the orders that made him the Commanding Officer of a man-of-war. He finished reading, folded the paper and turned to the Admiral and saluted him.

"Sir," he said in a ringing voice. "I accept command of the

U.S.S. *Tigerfish* and I will carry out my duties to the best of my ability."

Admiral Nimitz saluted him, stepped forward and shook Hugh Foster's hand. "We are confident you will do that, Captain," he said. He stood to one side as his staff stepped forward in turn to shake Captain Foster's hand. When the congratulations were over, Admiral Nimitz walked to the gangway and turned.

"Carry on, Captain," he said and left the ship, followed by his staff. Captain Foster waited until the Admiral's party had departed and turned to his crew.

"At ease," he said in a crisp voice. The crew obeyed the order, spreading their feet slightly apart and clasping their hands together behind their backs. To a man they studied their new Commanding Officer.

What they saw was a tall man with heavy shoulders and a wide chest. His khaki uniform was immaculate. His eyes, the calm eyes of a seaman, were studying the crew as they studied him.

"I will introduce the new officers of the ship," Captain Foster said. He made the introductions and nodded his head briefly toward Chief O'Brien.

"You've met the Chief of the Boat. He is *my* Chief of the Boat. I back him to the hilt.

"This is not my first submarine command. I know how I want things done. The officers of the ship know how I want things done. Chief O'Brien knows how I want things done.

"I am proud to command the *Tigerfish*. I am proud to serve with all of you. If you don't share that pride with me, you can see the yeoman and ask for a transfer. That transfer will be granted without prejudice." He stopped, his eyes searching the faces of the crew.

"Very well. I assume that all hands are willing to serve aboard the *Tigerfish*. We start even, with a clean slate. We go to sea in six days. Admiral Nimitz has assured me we will be given a good patrol area. We are going to prove that the *Tigerfish* is a fighting ship, a ship all of us can be proud to serve on. That's all. Dismissed."

Late that afternoon Mike O'Connor climbed out of the After Engine Room hatch and walked aft and sat on the capstan head. Bill Joy followed him and squatted on the deck in front of his Engineering Officer.

"First thing tomorrow morning you get yourself up to the ship's service and get yourself some khakis and a Chief's hat," O'Connor said.

"Yessir," Billy Joy said. "I want to thank you, sir, for thinking I can do the job for you."

"What about your people?" O'Connor asked. "If you've got any deadheads, now's the time to get rid of them."

"I think they'll be okay, Mister O'Connor. There's a few been riding the vents. Mostly what they need is someone to show them how to get on the ball. That new Chief, Art Apple, we'll get along fine. He thinks like me; that is, he likes machinery and he likes to keep it running the way it was made to do." He looked at O'Connor.

"The new Chief of the Boat, you hear what he said to the crew this morning when we came back from the hotel? Sure shook everyone up, sir."

O'Connor smiled widely, showing two rows of solid white teeth.

"I heard. I was with him on the *Sea Bass*. Work with him and he'll back you to hell and back. Work against him and you'll wish your mother had stayed a virgin."

"Everyone sort of got that feeling this morning," Bill Joy said. "What you just said about working with him—he said just about the same thing about you, sir." The two men grinned at each other and Bill Joy took a clean rag out of his back pocket and handed it to Mike O'Connor, who used it to wipe a glob of grease from his bare forearm.

Chapter
Six

THE LONG, SMOOTH SWELLS of the Pacific broke into white foam as the bridge structure of the *Tigerfish* emerged, streaming water. The submarine remained partially submerged, its decks still under water, as the lens of the thick-necked search periscope swept twice around the horizon. Then the sea parted as the submarine rose until its decks were above water. The Officer of the Deck climbed up through the hatch, followed by the quartermaster of the watch and three lookouts who scrambled aloft to their perches in the steel webbing of the periscope shears. A plume of water spray shot out each of the four exhaust ports of the submarine's diesel engines. Mike O'Connor squinted into the last rays of the sun dead ahead of the bow and raised his binoculars to his eyes and searched the sea and the sky. Pete Savage, the quartermaster, took his station on the port side of the bridge. A pair of dolphins arched out of the water on either side of the *Tigerfish*'s bow and then plunged back in, playing their incomprehensible sea games with the ship.

"Nice evening," Pete Savage said as he polished the lens of his binoculars with a handkerchief. "Hardly any wind. No sea. Nice. Hard to realize that Japan is only forty miles out ahead of us, sir."

"We should be able to see Japan when we surface tomorrow evening," Mike O'Connor said. "How do you like being aboard with the other guys from the *Sea Bass*? It happened so damned fast I didn't think we'd get you aboard before we sailed."

"Oh, I like it fine," Savage said. "I lived in Miller's torpedo room on the *Sea Bass* and I'm living in his torpedo room here. He runs a good room, nice and clean. I kind of figured I'd get a

66

call. Mister Sibley never was a navigator before, and that dude they had on here as the leading quartermaster doesn't know his ankle from his elbow, so I thought he'd holler for me. I was all packed, ready to come." He searched the horizon with his binoculars and then turned to O'Connor.

"I know where Bungo Strait is, sir," he said, "but I don't know why it's so important. Mister Sibley said it would be a good patrol area."

"Bungo Strait is the eastern entrance to the Sea of Japan," O'Connor said. "The Inland Sea is a major staging area for Japanese warships."

"That ain't such good news," Savage said.

Below decks Chief O'Brien was making his daily tour of inspection. His face wore its usual dour look. O'Brien was hard to please. He could find dirt where people were sure there was no dirt. His eyes never missed brightwork that didn't gleam as brightly as it could. As he worked his way aft, he grudgingly admitted to himself that the people of the *Tigerfish* were better, much better, than they had been when he took over as Chief of the Boat. The *Tigerfish* was clean, almost clean enough to suit him.

The crew had changed. The pride that came with being clean, with caring for the ship, with knowing their jobs, was evident in the way they bore themselves. He stopped in the crew's mess and drew a cup of coffee from the urn, then sat down at a mess table.

The idea Lieutenant O'Connor had come up with had worked out pretty well, he thought. O'Connor had suggested that while he wouldn't think of telling the Chief of the Boat how to do his job, he knew that O'Brien was going to have to be hard on the crew and that it might be a good idea if he, O'Connor, were to occasionally walk through the ship and compliment the crew on the way the ship looked.

"Sort of after you hit them with the hammer I come along with the powder puff," O'Connor had said. "Providing you agree, Chief."

"This bucket isn't like the ship we came off of, sir," O'Brien had said. "These people haven't been in the real Navy for a long time. They've been riding the vents, taking things easy. What makes you think if you pat a few people on the back they'd work harder? If you want to tell me, sir."

"When I played football at the Academy," O'Connor said,

"we had a coach who used to scream at the linemen to block, block, block. Screamed at them all the time. He was right, of course. Linemen have to block. But I found that when I'd made a few yards on an off-tackle play, if I came back into the huddle and thanked them for opening the hole for me, they'd block even harder the next time I carried the ball. Coach never told them they did a good job but I let them know I appreciated what they did and it worked.

"Not that I think you won't tell them when they've done what you want them to do but maybe coming from an officer it might make a little difference."

It had worked, O'Brien mused to himself. Every other day or so O'Connor would check with him to find out which part of the ship was improving and then he'd casually walk into that compartment, look around and congratulate the people who worked there. It was also making O'Connor the most popular officer on the ship. O'Brien sipped at his coffee, his eyes distant. Not that O'Connor was hard to like. The big, burly Lieutenant was as friendly as a puppy without ever breaching the invisible barrier that existed between an officer and an enlisted man. He spent most of his off-watch hours with Chief Hahn and his electricians, soaking up information about the complicated diesel-electric propulsion system that powered the *Tigerfish* on the surface and submerged. When he wasn't with Chief Hahn, he was with the two engine-room Chiefs, Art Apple and Bill Joy, learning the intricacies of the four big main diesel engines and the auxiliary machinery. All three Chief Petty Officers reported to Chief O'Brien on Mike O'Connor's activities.

"The man is sharp and getting sharper all the time," Chief Apple said. "He gets his teeth into something and he doesn't let go until he's chewed it up and swallowed it and digested it. He wants to know what the guy operating the gear has to know and what he has to do in an emergency."

"He spent all yesterday afternoon crawling around on top of the battery cells when we were watering batteries," Chief Hahn said. "Awful cramped space for a man that big. He must've sweat off ten pounds, but he didn't complain. Like Art says, he wants to know and he keeps nagging at you until he's got it straight in his mind. I get the feeling that once he knows something he'll never forget it."

"He was that way when he took over as Gunnery Officer on the *Sea Bass*," O'Brien said.

"The people in the Black Gang, they think the sun rises and sets on his ass," Bill Joy said. "The dude we had for an Engineering Officer last run, he didn't know anything. And you couldn't tell him anything if your gold stripe was in the seat of your skivvies. He only listened to people who had their gold stripe on their sleeve."

O'Brien finished his coffee, rinsed the cup in the sink, put it back in the rack and plodded aft. The ship's cook waited until he had passed the enlisted men's head and washroom, picked up the telephone and dialed the Maneuvering Room.

"Chief of the Boat's in the engine rooms and heading aft. Pass the word."

Mike O'Connor made his report on the condition of the ship to his supper relief and took one last look around at the dark sea. He went below into the Wardroom for his evening meal. Captain Foster was sitting at the table and O'Connor noted with some surprise that all the off-duty officers were still at table.

"Before you eat, Mike," Captain Foster said, "there's something you should have." He took a small white box and a radio-message flimsy out of his shirt pocket and laid them on the table in front of him.

"As of yesterday, Mike, you are now a full Lieutenant. I agreed fully with Captain Saunders's recommendation that you be promoted and I congratulate you." He opened the small white box and took two sets of Lieutenant's collar bars out of the box and handed them to Joe Sibley, who passed the bars on down to the table to O'Connor.

O'Connor took the two sets of bars. "Well, Captain, I thank you, sir. I thank you a whole lot. I never expected this so soon. I mean, I'm only the class of thirty-seven, sir."

"And we're at war," Captain Foster said. "Promotions come fast in war time. We've only been at war for a few months and already they've made something like eight new admirals. I think it fitting they should make a few lieutenants."

"Yes, sir," O'Connor said. His face flushed slightly. "I think it was awful nice of you to give me the collar bars, sir."

"I knew the promotion was coming," Captain Foster said with a grin. He rose and left the Wardroom, followed by the rest of the officers. Mike O'Connor sat looking first at the shiny collar bars and then at the plate heaped with slices of rare roast beef and small, white, canned potatoes. He put a piece of beef in his mouth and chewed slowly, wondering if his brother Andy had been promoted to full Lieutenant or whether only submarine officers were benefiting from an accelerated promotion program. He swallowed and wondered where the *Enterprise* and Andy were at this moment.

Andrew O'Connor was sitting in the junior officers' Wardroom of the Big E, playing acey-deucey with Orville Masters, who flew as Andy's starboard-hand wingman. Like Andy O'Connor, Orville Masters wore shiny new full Lieutenant's bars on his collar tabs.

"Bombing Wake Island might not be a piece of cake," Masters said in a low voice. "The Japs have had the time to reinforce it since they took the island. You scared at all, Andy?"

Andy carefully moved two of his men on the board. "Yes," he said quietly. "I was scared when we flew into Pearl Harbor that morning. I was scared when we bombed the Marshalls.

"I used to be scared when my brother and I got into fights when we were kids. My dad said it was normal to be scared. He told both of us that if you weren't scared when you had to fight, if you fought just for the sake of fighting, then you lost your right to be a member of the human race, that you were an animal."

Lieutenant Masters dropped the leather dice box on the playing board and stood up. "I'm sorry, Andy, I just can't concentrate." Andy watched him walk away. He knew that Masters was a solid, dependable man but like most of the squadron he was still feeling the shock of the loss of their squadron leader, his gunner and three other dive-bomber pilots and gunners in the attack on the Marshall Islands little more than two weeks earlier. He collected the large brass and white-metal washers used for playing pieces in the game and put them into a small box with the dice and folded up the playing board, his mind going back to the raid on the Marshalls that had been hailed as a great victory. A raid that the newspaper stories that were reprinted on the ship's newspaper from radio dispatches said had produced the first great hero of the war, Vice Admiral William F. "Bull" Halsey.

The U.S.S. *Enterprise* had been designated as the flagship

of Task Force 8 to cover the arrival at Samoa from San Diego of a task force made up of four troop transports and the aircraft carrier *Yorktown*. The Marines aboard the transports were needed to beef up the skimpy defenses of Samoa. Once the Marines had been landed, everyone assumed Task Force 8 would return to Pearl Harbor.

Admiral Halsey had other ideas. He had a strong force; Rear Admiral Raymond A. Spruance's flag was in the heavy cruiser *Northhampton*. The rest of Task Force 8 was made up of the cruisers *Salt Lake City* and *Chester,* six destroyers and three fast fleet-oilers. Admiral Halsey sent off an urgent radio message to Pearl Harbor requesting permission to make a detour on his way from Samoa to Pearl Harbor so he could launch an air raid and a gunnery attack from the sea against the Japanese forces in the Marshall Islands.

The message caused some dispute in Pearl Harbor. By prewar standards Task Force 8 was not a strong force. To be a strong force, the "big gun" Admirals reasoned, required the presence of at least one and preferably two battleships. Halsey had no battleships. Before the war had ever started, pro-battleship naval strategists had argued for hours with Admiral Halsey that an enemy battleship could hammer any task force that did not have a battleship into rubble. Admiral Halsey had argued just as strenuously that a carrier task force was fast, that its aircraft could scout out ahead and locate the enemy battleships, that a fast carrier task force could stay out of reach of a battleship's heavy guns and while it was doing so the carrier's planes could seriously damage the enemy battleship.

That latter argument had been received with amused smiles. No aircraft could seriously damage a battleship. Those smiles had disappeared after the Japanese attack on Pearl Harbor, although some of the "big gun" advocates continued to argue that sinking battleships at anchor and trying to do that to a battleship at sea, with all its antiaircraft batteries in action, was another thing entirely. The Japanese aircraft torpedo and dive-bombing attacks that sank the British capital ships *Repulse* and *Prince of Wales* off Singapore reinforced Admiral Halsey's arguments. After some discussion Admiral Halsey's request for the detour to attack the Marshall Islands was given grudging approval.

Steaming north from Samoa on a course to the Marshall Islands, Admiral Halsey issued his orders. Task Force 8 would split into three parts. Rear Admiral Spruance in *Northhampton*, in company with the cruiser *Salt Lake City* and one destroyer, would break off from the main task force during the night hours before the dawn attack and prepare to bombard Wotje Island. Captain Thomas M. Shock, in the cruiser *Chester* with two destroyers, would split off at the same time to stand by to bombard the island of Maloelap. The *Enterprise* with the remaining three destroyers operating as an antisubmarine screen would attack Wotje and Maloelap islands at dawn from the air and also smash at Kwajalein.

The flight deck of the *Enterprise*, blacked out for security, swarmed with sailors during the night hours before the attack. The flight-deck sailors, called "airdales" in the carrier Navy, worked by the light of a full tropic moon to fuel their planes and arm them with machine-gun ammunition, torpedoes and heavy bombs.

The Big E began launching her planes just before 0500. Commander Howard L. Young led thirty-seven dive bombers and nine torpedo planes into the dark sky. At launch point the *Enterprise* was only 36 miles from Wotje Island, 106 miles from Maloelap and 155 miles from Kwajalein, the prime target of the raid.

At 0700, fifteen minutes short of full sunrise, twenty-seven of the dive bombers split off from the formation and headed for Roi Air Field on the northern end of the seventy-mile long Kwajalein Atoll. The remaining ten dive bombers and all nine torpedo planes stayed on course for Kwajalein itself, forty-four miles across the atoll's lagoon.

Roi Air Field was shrouded in a heavy ground mist as the force of twenty-seven dive bombers arrived. Andy O'Connor squinted at the chart clipped to his right thigh and shook his head. The chart was a copy of a chart drawn in the mid-nineteenth century. It showed no details of the atoll that might guide a pilot to the location of the area where the air field was known to be located. The dive bombers droned over their target, passed the area where Commander Young believed the air field might be located and reformed. On the ground below, the Japanese, alerted by the sound of the aircraft above the ground mist, opened fire with their antiaircraft guns, shooting at planes they could not see.

The morning sun began to burn off the canopy of mist. Lieutenant Commander H. L. Hopping, the squadron leader, caught sight of a runway through a hole in the mist and waggled his plane's wings as a signal to attack. He led the way in a screaming, almost vertical dive. Behind him Andy O'Connor saw his squadron leader's signal and waggled his own wings to signal his wingmen and the planes behind him. O'Connor extended his dive brakes and tipped over into his bombing run, his eyes on the squadron leader's plane diving through a morning sky suddenly pockmarked with black and white bursts of AA fire. He saw the dark shape of a bomb drop clear of the squadron leader's plane before the plane itself turned into an exploding ball of fire.

"Dear Lord, have mercy on his soul," Andy O'Connor grated as he rocketed downward. He picked his target, an aircraft hangar with a plane being rolled out of the hangar's big doors, and adjusted his course slightly. He pulled his bomb release and felt his plane suddenly lighten as the bomb dropped away and hauled his dive bomber up and around in a long, curling zoom. He looked quickly to the right and saw Orv Masters a few yards away from his wing tip. As he turned his head to search for Red Olsen, his other wingman, his gunner's voice screamed over the intercom.

"Jap! Seven o'clock!"

O'Connor turned his head and saw the faster Japanese Zeke overshoot Red Olsen's plane. Instinctively he slammed his throttle to the firewall and took out after the Zeke. It was an unequal chase. The Zeke, faster and more maneuverable, outran the stubby dive bombers. The Zeke's pilot, apparently deciding the odds were too great, tore off to one side and disappeared. O'Connor dropped down as low as he dared and raced across the air field, hearing his gunner's machine gun stutter as Roger Cain strafed a truck speeding down one side of a runway. He looked around and raised his right fist in salute as he saw Olsen and Masters close aboard. The three planes, led by O'Connor, pulled up at the end of the air field, strafing hangars, trucks and parked planes. After three strafing runs O'Connor set a course for the Big E.

At 0935 that morning he took off again with eight other dive bombers for a second attack against Roi Air Field. The strike was virtually unopposed, except for sporadic AA fire and machine-gun fire. O'Connor planted his five-hundred-pound bomb next to an antiaircraft emplacement and his rear gunner reported seeing the two guns flying through the air after the bomb exploded.

At 1300 hours Vice Admiral Halsey decided he had pressed his luck to the limit. For almost nine hours the Commanding Officer of the *Enterprise* had been maneuvering his big aircraft carrier in company with the three destroyers in a rectangle of sea that measured only five miles wide and twenty miles long. During most of those nine hours the ships had been within sight of Wotje Island and its airstrip. The threat of Japanese submarines that might have been within reach of Kwajalein was in the forefront of Admiral Halsey's mind. He gave the order for Task Force 8 to end the attack and haul off at high speed.

There was no air of victory aboard the *Enterprise* as she raced away from the Marshalls. Four dive bombers with their pilots and gunners had been lost to enemy action. The fact that the *Enterprise* planes had sunk one large Japanese transport ship, a submarine chaser and heavily damaged a number of other ships including a large submarine-tender in the harbor at Kwajalein, and destroyed eighteen planes on the ground, was almost forgotten as the flight maintenance crews of the lost planes stood in small groups, mourning their dead.

"Aircraft! Dead ahead!" The starboard lookout on the *Tigerfish* yelled the sighting. Captain Hugh Foster, pacing the cigarette deck aft of the bridge, raced forward to the bridge area.

"I saw him cut across the stars, Bridge," the lookout called down from his perch in the periscope shears. "Heading from starboard to port, sir. Low down on the horizon, kind of."

"Clear the bridge!" Captain Foster shouted. He stood to one side as the lookouts came plunging down from their lookout stands, their hands and feet finding the hand and footholds made familiar by hours of practice in drills. As the last lookout went down the hatch, Captain Foster punched the diving alarm.

"Dive! Dive! Dive!" he called out. He waited until the quartermaster and the Officer of the Deck had gone down the hatch and then he followed them, his feet searching for the ladder rungs. He reached upward and grabbed the toggle on a short bronze cable that hung from the underside of the hatch. He yanked on the cable and pulled down with all his strength.

The quartermaster squirmed up on the ladder beside him and spun the dogging wheel tight to secure the hatch. The bridge hatch light on the Christmas Tree showed green, and a machinist's mate in the Control Room released a blast of compressed air into the submarine.

"Green board. Pressure in the boat, sir," Mike O'Connor reported from the Control Room. "Down angle is ten degrees. Passing sixty feet, Captain."

"Very well," Captain Foster answered as he slid down the ladder from the Conning Tower. "Make depth one hundred feet. Come right to course zero-one-zero."

"Make depth one hundred feet. Come right to course zero-one-zero, sir," O'Connor said. Hugh Foster looked at his watch. He'd give the aircraft fifteen minutes. If it didn't drop a bomb by then, he'd assume the *Tigerfish* hadn't been seen.

What concerned Captain Foster was, why there was an aircraft out there at all? The *Tigerfish* was a good forty miles away from Bungo Strait. The plane had to be no more than five miles distant from the submarine to be seen at night, even by a sharp-eyed lookout who knew enough to realize that the sudden blotting out of a few stars for seconds could only mean an aircraft was flying by. Was the plane making a routine patrol, or was it scouting out ahead for something that might be coming out of the Inland Sea? He decided to extend his waiting time to twenty minutes and then go up and take a good look through the search periscope. He acknowledged Chief O'Brien's report that all Battle Stations were manned, all outer torpedo-tube doors closed. He leaned against the gyrocompass table and waited. The constant drills, the repeated crash dives he had ordered while on the way west from Pearl Harbor, had had some benefit, he thought. The *Tigerfish* had gone from running on the surface on four diesel engines with six people on the bridge to periscope depth within forty-five seconds. It could be done more quickly and it would be, once the crew had heard aircraft bombs hitting above them. He looked at his watch.

"Sixty feet, Mike," he ordered. He climbed up the ladder to the Conning Tower as the submarine slanted upward. He moved to the periscope well and nodded at Pete Savage, who was holding the periscope control box in his hand.

"Up periscope," he said quietly. He waited until the bottom of the periscope cleared the deck well and leaned down and snapped the periscope handles out in the open position. He acknowledged O'Connor's report that the *Tigerfish* was at sixty feet and began to search the horizon and the sky through the lens of the search periscope. He walked the periscope around the full 360 degrees twice.

"Stand by to surface," he ordered. "I want a shot of high-pressure air and then switch to the low-pressure blowers."

"Surface!"

The klaxon horn blared and the *Tigerfish* shuddered as a machinist's mate opened valves that sent a blast of high-pressure air into the water-filled ballast tanks. The machinist's mate shut the valves and the submarine was filled with the hum of the low-pressure blowers forcing the remaining water out of the ballast tanks, bringing the submarine to the surface. The *Tigerfish* broke water, rolling slightly, and Captain Foster spun the hatch wheel and pushed the hatch open, snorting as a gush of residual water from the bridge doused his head. The lookouts clambered up to their perches and began to search the sea, horizon and sky with their binoculars.

"Contact!" the starboard lookout yelled. "Bearing is zero-six-zero, Bridge! I can see masts!"

Captain Foster grunted as he hauled himself upward into the periscope shears and squeezed in beside the lookout. "Show me, son," he said in a quite voice. He trained his binoculars on a line indicated by the lookout's pointing arm. He stared through the binoculars and then clambered down to the bridge deck. He bent his head to a microphone located just beneath the rail of the bridge.

"This is the Captain," he said. "We have a convoy in sight, Mister Sibley to the Conning Tower to take periscope bearings and ranges. Plotting Party stand by to begin the plot. Maintain present course and speed."

Joe Sibley climbed halfway up the ladder from the Conning Tower to the Bridge. "Can you give me any idea of what you've got, sir?"

"Looks like three or four ships bearing about zero-six-zero, Joe. I want Plot to put me on a course to intercept." He looked around at the black sea.

"No moon, Joe. We should be able to go right into them on the surface. That's what we'll do if we can."

"On the surface. Yes, sir," Joe Sibley said. His voice choked a little as he repeated the orders to the Plotting Party in the Control Room.

Down in the Control Room Chief Yeoman Harrington, sitting on his padded bench in front of the bow-plane controls, heard the Executive Officer repeat what Captain Foster had said. He looked over at Chief O'Brien.

"You hear that, Chief? Go into the convoy on the surface? What's he think we are, a battleship?"

"Maybe," Chief O'Brien said. "Maybe he's a different breed of tiger than most." O'Brien looked over at Mike O'Connor, standing back of Harrington, and saw that O'Connor was grinning broadly. "The man wants to fight," O'Brien said to himself, and found himself returning O'Connor's smile.

Chapter
Seven

THE CLOUDS THAT had been forming on the eastern horizon during the night had massed and covered all the sky astern of the *Tigerfish*. Captain Hugh Foster looked aft and smiled grimly. The conditions favored a surface attack; there was no horizon against which the steel webbing of the submarine's periscope shears could be seen, there was little starlight to give away the presence of the *Tigerfish*. He glanced upward as he heard Joe Sibley's feet scraping on the deck plates of the Conning Tower. The big lens of the search periscope manned by Sibley was steadying on the ships out ahead. He heard Sibley's crisp reports of the bearings of the ships and the acknowledgment from the Plotting Party down in the Control Room.

"I've got three ships, Captain," Sibley's voice floated up through the bridge hatch. "Two fairly large ships, one astern of the other. From their upper works and booms they look like big freighters. One other ship, a smaller one, is now dropping astern of the two bigger ships. I make him to be a destroyer or a destroyer escort, can't tell. From here it looks as if he's going to let his two sheep go on ahead of him and then reform on their starboard hand, sir."

"Very well," Captain Foster said. He braced his elbows on the teak bridge rail and held his binoculars to his eyes. He could see the smaller ship Sibley had mentioned, it was astern of the two larger ships, and as he watched he could see it turning to starboard. He let his binoculars hang from the leather strap around his neck. He bent his head to the microphone below the bridge rail.

"What are you people in Plot doing, dammit! I want a course

to intercept. I want to shoot at one thousand yards. Give me some information."

"Target course is one-seven-zero," the bridge speaker rasped. "We make the convoy speed to be fifteen knots, Captain.

"At our present speed of ten knots we'll be four hundred yards from the target track when he crosses our bow. Target will bear zero-zero-zero in four and one-half minutes. Recommend we slow to five knots, Captain."

"Make turns for five knots," Captain Foster ordered. "Open all torpedo-tube outer doors. Set depth thirty, repeat, thirty feet on all torpedoes. Plot, I want to shoot two fish at the lead ship and then two at the second ship." He waited a few seconds and then bent his head to the bridge microphone.

"Now hear this. This is the Captain speaking. We've got two big targets up here and only one destroyer to guard them. We're going to attack on the surface, and if the tin can comes after us, we'll go after him. Let's be sharp as hell. Here we go!"

In the Forward and After Torpedo Rooms the leading torpedomen went between the torpedo tubes and engaged the depth spindles and cranked in the ordered depth of thirty feet and then disengaged the depth spindles.

"All torpedoes set at thirty feet. Depth spindles are disengaged, Bridge," Chief O'Brien called out.

"Very well," Captain Foster replied.

"We've got a shooting solution, sir," Joe Sibley yelled up the hatch. "Torpedo track to the first target is now fifteen hundred yards, Captain."

"Make turns for ten knots. Put all four engines on the line. Stand by Forward to shoot!" Captain Foster felt the vibration under his feet as the *Tigerfish* surged ahead to ten-knot speed.

"Constant solution, Captain. Gyro angle is two degrees left and opening slightly. Range is now eleven hundred yards."

"Torpedo run will be thirty-four seconds, Captain," the Plotting Party reported.

"Stand by!" Captain Foster's voice was like a whip in the darkness of the bridge.

"FIRE ONE!" He counted down slowly from seven to one.

"FIRE TWO! Shift target to the second ship in the line!"

"You have a solution on the second target, sir."

"FIRE THREE!"

"FIRE FOUR!"

The people standing in the bridge could feel the jolts in

their feet and legs as a fist of compressed air at six hundred
pounds to the square inch hurled each of the torpedoes out of
their tubes, their steam engines screaming into life as they left
the torpedo tubes. Captain Foster put his binoculars to his
eyes, watching the black shapes of the ships ahead of him,
waiting for the explosions of the torpedoes he had fired.
Judging from the size of the ship's outlines, he was confident he
had ordered the correct depth set on the torpedoes. Each ship
should draw about twenty feet, he estimated. The torpedoes,
running ten feet beneath the ships' keels, would explode as
they passed under the ships. The explosive force of the six-
hundred-pound warheads would be diverted upward through
the air-filled hulls of the ships, breaking their keels. That was
the principle of the highly secret Mark VI exploder device that
had been installed in the warheads of the torpedoes.

"All torpedoes running hot, straight and normal, Bridge,"
the sound man reported in his boyish voice, and for a fleeting
instant Captain Foster saw in his mind's eye the young face of
his Battle Station sonar operator. He turned his head toward
the hatch that led down to the Conning Tower, listening to the
Plotting Party counting down the seconds of the torpedo run in
five-second increments. He heard the count reach forty
seconds and then sixty seconds and then the counting stopped.

"Torpedoes are still running, Bridge," the sound operator
reported.

"Dammit all," Captain Foster snapped, "I missed! Give me
another setup on the second ship. Sibley, make damned sure
your bearings are right this time!"

"Range is nine hundred yards," Sibley yelled out. "You have
a solution, Captain."

"Range is closing, Captain. Eight hundred yards and
closing, sir."

"Stand by Forward," Captain Foster said.

"FIRE FIVE!"

"FIRE SIX!"

"Torpedo run is twenty-four seconds, sir."

Captain Foster braced his legs and raised his binoculars. He
counted the seconds down in his head. He reached twenty-
four and then thirty and then a full minute. Out ahead of him
his targets plowed onward, undisturbed.

"What the hell is going on?" he said to himself. He looked
upward as the port lookout yelled.

"Destroyer standing this way bearing three-five-zero!"

"Right full rudder. Clear the bridge. Dive! Dive! Dive!" He hit the bridge diving-alarm button with his hand and jumped to one side as the lookouts and the quartermaster went plunging down the hatch. He followed them, closing the hatch as the *Tigerfish* slid downward into the sea.

"Two hundred feet. Make course zero-nine-zero," Foster snapped as he slid down the ladder from the Conning Tower to the Control Room.

"Make depth two hundred feet. Rudder is full right, coming to course zero-nine-zero, sir," Mike O'Connor reported. "Passing one hundred feet, sir." O'Connor leaned over the shoulders of his bow and stern planesmen. "Ease your bubble at one hundred sixty-five feet, men."

Captain Foster looked around the Control Room and then down at the plotting board on the gyrocompass table.

"There was no way in the world we could miss at that range," he said. "No way we could miss." He looked toward the sound operator.

"What do you hear, son?"

"I've got a twin screw, sir, bearing one-seven-zero. He's not making any speed at all, medium turns. He's going away from us, sir."

"Secure from General Quarters," Captain Foster said. He looked at the clock on the forward bulkhead of the Control Room. "It's zero four hundred hours. We'll stay down until dusk this evening. Set regular sea watches. I want the Plotting Party and Mr. Sibley in the Wardroom. I'm going to find out what the hell went wrong."

The officers of the Plotting Party sat around the Wardroom table, their faces carefully impassive, as Captain Foster studied the plot of the two attacks. He pushed the plots over to Joe Sibley.

"I can't see one damned thing wrong, Joe. You look at it. Maybe you'll see something I didn't." Sibley examined the two plots and sat back in his chair.

"They look like something we'd get as a problem in attack school, sir. It's all there. You couldn't miss."

"But we missed," Captain Foster said. "Missed with six torpedoes fired at almost point-blank range. The only thing I can think of is that the fish didn't run right."

"Sonar man reported all fish running hot, straight and normal, sir," Lieutenant Hank Copper, the ship's Gunnery Officer, spoke up.

"Ask him to come in here," Captain Foster ordered.

The sonar man, a nineteen-year-old youngster named Amos Stuckey, stood at attention just inside the green cloth curtain that served as a door to the Wardroom.

"At ease, son," Captain Foster said. "You tracked the torpedoes we fired, all of them?"

"Yes, sir," Stuckey said. "All the torpedoes ran hot, straight and normal. I tracked each one into the target bearing and I heard them running long after they went through the target bearings, sir."

"Let me get this straight," Hugh Foster said. "You heard them run into the target bearing. You heard them run through the target bearing. And then you heard them keep on running, is that right?"

"Yes, sir, that's right. That's what I heard, sir."

"Thank you, Amos," Captain Foster said. He waited until the enlisted man had left and turned to the officers around the table.

"I'd appreciate your thoughts, gentleman."

Joe Sibley doodled with a pencil on a pad of paper. "Sir," he said in his deep voice, "you set torpedo depth at thirty feet. I know that's what the orders say we should do, set depth at least ten feet beneath the estimated draft of the target ship. They were pretty good-sized ships, so it's reasonable to assume they'd draw twenty feet or close to it.

"Captain Saunders, on our first war patrol on the *Sea Bass*, set his torpedoes to run at eight feet when he shot at a destroyer at twelve hundred yards. He missed. The sonar operator on the *Sea Bass* heard the torpedoes run into the target bearing and keep going, sir. I believe you were there when the Chief of Staff reamed out Captain Saunders for setting his torpedoes at eight feet, weren't you, sir?"

"I was," Captain Foster said. "Captain Saunders had a copy of his patrol report and the Chief of Staff went over it with him. I went over it with him. We agreed there was no way he should have missed the destroyer. No way he could have missed, unless he had changed his plot of the firing when he made out his patrol report so it would look as if the torpedoes had malfunctioned.

"That's a terrible thing to say and I just couldn't believe that Captain Saunders would do something like that. But something definitely was wrong. The conclusion reached was that the bearings of the target had been wrong or had been misread or that the angle of the bow of the target was misjudged. Barney Saunders got pretty sarcastic about that one point. He pointed out that he had judged the angle of the bow of his target, a destroyer, was eighty degrees starboard and it didn't make a damned bit of difference if it was seventy or ninety degrees at that range.

"The upshot of the whole thing was that we sent the periscope repair shop Chief down to the *Sea Bass* to check the alignment of the periscope and we found it was out by about three degrees." He looked around the table. "I had the alignment of our periscopes checked before I took command. They're right on the nose."

"What was the final decision on Captain Saunders?" Joe Sibley asked.

"After a long consultation with the torpedo experts it was decided that Captain Saunders had missed, no matter what his plots said." He smiled wryly. "I can understand, now, why he was so angry. Using the same procedures as we used with Barney, it would be ruled that I out-and-out made mistakes and that's why we missed our targets. And I don't believe we made any mistakes." He signaled to the Officers' Cook in the Wardroom galley.

"Ask the Chief of the Boat to come in, please."

Chief O'Brien walked into the Wardroom and Captain Foster motioned to him to sit down.

"Chief," the Captain began, "we have a problem. The plots for the torpedo firing seem to be almost perfect. We were firing at close range. Stuckey says he heard the torpedoes run into the target bearing and keep going. Have you any ideas you'd like to contribute?"

"Yes, sir," Chief O'Brien said. "I've got a couple of ideas. After we missed a destroyer on *Sea Bass*—Captain Saunders had a perfect setup, too—I talked with Miller in the Forward Room, trying to figure out if the fish ran poorly. But the sonar operator on the *Sea Bass* said the fish ran right through the target bearing and beyond.

"When we got back to Pearl, I went to see a couple of Chief Torpedomen I've known for years. They work in the shop at the base. They told me that very few ships were getting hits and almost every ship was reporting they had a perfect setup for a shot. But they missed.

"What they think, what I think, Captain, is that the torpedoes are running a lot deeper than the depth setting. It's the only thing that could be happening. The Chiefs in the Torpedo Shop think that and they asked for some tests, they want to fire some fish with practice heads on them through a net and see if they're running deeper than they're set to run.

"The officers who are supposed to be torpedo experts won't do that, sir. They say the torpedoes will run at the depth they're set to run.

"There's another thing, sir, as long as you're asking my opinion. That Mark Six exploder. It's supposed to explode the warhead when it gets under the target. I don't think it's worth a damn, sir."

"I don't know the principle back of that exploder, Chief, how it knows when to explode the warhead. I asked, but I was told it was top secret. Do you know?" Captain Foster looked at O'Brien.

"Yes, sir, I know how it's supposed to work," the Chief Torpedoman said. "I ain't supposed to know but the Chief in charge of the exploders at Pearl is a guy I had when he was Second and First class. I got him his promotions. When a steel or iron-hulled ship goes through the water, Captain, it sets up a magnetic field around it. There's an antenna in the exploder that picks up the electromagnetic field. The impeller, that little propeller in the nose of the warhead that arms the exploder, also runs a little generator that stores up electrical current in a thyraton tube. When the antenna picks up the target ship's electromagnetic field, it trips a circuit that lets the juice stored up in the thyraton tube activate the electrical firing mechanism in the exploder. There's enough delay built into the process so the exploder won't go off until the torpedo has run far enough after picking up the electromagnetic field to be under the keel of the target, sir. At least that's how I understand it.

"That's all supposed to be top secret, sir. But some of the Chiefs I know on the boats are going to deactivate that magnetic feature and convert the exploder into a simple contact exploder, an exploder that will go off when it hits the side of the target ship, if they can talk their Captains into doing that, sir."

"Could you do that, Chief?" Captain Foster asked.

"I've never seen what the inside of that exploder looks like, sir. The experts from the exploder shop come down to install the exploders and they make ship's company leave the torpedo room when they do that. But what some other torpedoman can do I can do, no matter what it is. I would ask, sir, that you back me up if I get a court martial for touching one of those exploders because there's a strict order out that we can't touch them."

"How would it be if I worked with you to do whatever you have to do?" Captain Foster asked in a soft voice.

"I'd be proud to work with you, Captain," O'Brien replied.

"Let me know when you're ready to start," Captain Foster said. "We'll change all the exploders, and if we get another target, we'll set depth at two feet. The torpedoes won't broach at that depth, will they?"

"Not if they're running deep, and I figure they sure as hell are running deeper than they're set, sir."

"We'll do the Forward Room first," Foster said. "Let me know when you're ready to start."

Dandy Don Miller sprawled in a folding canvas-back chair that the torpedoman on watch sat in, a cup of coffee in his hands.

"First time I ever had a Captain for a tool passer," he said to the people who lived in the Forward Torpedo Room. "That man catches on a lot quicker than some torpedomen I've tried to train."

Amos Stuckey sipped at his coffee. "What did he do up here when you were working on the torpedoes?"

"First think I told the Old Man to do was to turn the torpedo one hundred eighty degrees, because the exploder is on the bottom of the warhead. So he takes the slewing bar and strap and he puts the strap around the fish and hooks it on the slewing bar and he gives a heave so hard he like to give himself a hernia because my stupid Third Class didn't take off the belly band that holds the fish in the reload rack."

"Nobody told me to take it off," a voice said from one of the bunks up near the overhead.

"Once the belly band was offa the fish, the Old Man gave another heave and he spun that fish in the rack like it was a pool ball. That man's got a pair of arms and shoulders on him, lemme tell you.

"Once we got the first exploder out, me and Chief O'Brien figured out how to deactivate the electrical circuits. Then we split the people working into two groups and we had all those damned exploders out, modified them and got them back in and reloaded the tubes in five hours. Then the Old Man and the Chief and me went back aft and we did all their exploders. The Old Man turned to like some striker trying to make Third Class. He's a good man. I wish I had a couple of him working for me up here in this Forward Room."

"But can he shoot torpedos straight enough to hit anything?" a voice came from a bunk.

"We'll find out next time we see a target," Miller said.

The *Tigerfish* surfaced just as full dark was setting in. The lookouts, warned by Joe Sibley that the submarine was only a few miles off the coast of Japan and there might be fishing boats around, swarmed up into the periscope shears and began to search the sea and sky for the enemy. Lieutenant Henry Copper, the Officer of the Deck, acknowledged reports from the lookouts of land in sight. On the cigarette deck aft of the bridge Captain Foster used his binoculars to study the land mass of Cape Ashizuri at the southeastern tip of Shikoku Island. Somewhere up Bungo Strait, to the west and north in Japan's Inland Sea, there were concentrations of Japanese warships and merchantmen. There was plenty of water in the strait to make a submerged entrance into the Inland Sea, but once there, the charts, old and not at all accurate, showed water depths of up to three hundred feet—deep enough to submerge in but not deep enough to offer safety to a submarine under attack. Captain Foster looked upward as he heard a periscope being raised. Joe Sibley was taking bearings on the cape to pinpoint the ship's position.

The lookout on the starboard side of the periscope shears scraped his feet and Captain Foster tensed, sensing that the man wasn't just changing his position as he searched his area, that the man had seen something. He waited, his head turned upward toward the lookout who was studying something through his binoculars.

"I've got something bearing zero-one-five, Bridge," the starboard lookout said.

Lieutenant Copper acknowledged the report and raised his binoculars.

"That's a ship!" the starboard lookout said suddenly. "Ship bearing zero-one-five, Bridge." Captain Foster went forward to the bridge area.

"Joe," he called down the hatch. "There's something out there bearing zero-one-five. See if you can see it through the search 'scope."

"There's a big destroyer out there, Captain. Two big

destroyers. And back of them I can see two, no, three ships coming down the channel, sir."

"Sound General Quarters," Captain Foster ordered. "Lookouts, get below." He waited until Chief O'Brien's voice came up the hatch telling him that all hands were at Battle Stations and the Plotting Party was standing by.

"Rig ship for dive," Captain Foster said into the bridge microphone. "Mike, as soon as I close the hatch, I want to flood down to decks awash." He went down the hatch and pulled it shut and dogged it down.

"Ship rigged for dive. Pressure in the boat. Flooding down to decks awash, Captain," Mike O'Connor reported.

"Very well," Captain Foster said. Joe Sibley moved away from the search periscope to let the captain look through it. He steadied the cross hairs of the lens on the targets.

"Stand by for bearings, Plot," Captain Foster said. He steadied the cross hairs on the nearest destroyer. "Mark," he sang out. Joe Sibley read the bearing from the azimuth circle and called it down to the Plotting Party. He called down each bearing as Captain Foster identified a second destroyer and three large freighters coming out of Bungo Strait.

"They're beginning a turn to their starboard," Foster said. "Come left to course two-zero-five. Those freighters look like they're low in the water. Probably loaded. They look like they've finally lined up on their course. Plot, stand by for another set of bearings and then give me their course and speed." Joe Sibley called the bearings down to the Plotting Party around the gyrocompass table.

"Target course is two-two-zero, Captain. We make their speed to be ten knots from the last set of bearings, sir. Can we have a range, sir?"

"I'll give you another set of bearings and ranges on all targets and then give me a parallel course to the targets." He steadied the periscope on the targets. When he had finished giving the bearings, he focused on the last ship in the line.

"Range to the tail-end Charlie is six thousand yards."

"Targets are on a base course of two-two-zero," Hank Copper called out. "Recommend we come to that course, sir."

"Make course two-two-zero," Captain Foster ordered. "I don't think they've got a chance in hell of seeing us at this range. Let's get up on the surface. Make turns for full speed." He climbed the ladder to the bridge hatch and opened the hatch and climbed out into the bridge. He could barely see the targets, dark shapes against the blackness of the land. The *Tigerfish* trembled as the four big diesel engines rumbled into life and began to drive the submarine at twenty knots.

"Mister Sibley to the bridge," Captain Foster called out. Joe Sibley climbed out of the hatch and breathed deeply, relishing the cool night air.

"We've got the advantage of no horizon back of us," the Captain said. "What I want to do is this; I want to get up ahead of the targets before morning and then submerge on their course line. When they come to us, we can get at least two of the freighters, maybe all three."

"Supposing they put on too much speed for that, sir?" Sibley said in a low voice. "I mean, they looked like pretty big ships. They might make as much speed as we can make."

"I don't think so," Foster said. "They looked like they were low down in the water, looked like they were down to their Plimsoll marks or even lower. I'd figure them for maybe ten or twelve knots. But if I'm wrong, if we can't make an end-run on them, we'll go after whatever we can get.

"I want you on the search 'scope, Joe. Feed Plot every bearing you can get. I'll keep the deck watch myself. This might be a long chase, so see to it that the relief lookouts are in red goggles for at least fifteen minutes before they relieve the watch." Sibley nodded and dropped down the ladder and raised the search periscope. The line of ships leaped into view. He took the bearings and Pete Savage relayed them to the Plotting Party in the Control Room.

The hours ground by as the *Tigerfish* raced at twenty knots on a parallel course three miles to the east of the convoy. Shortly after midnight Captain Foster ordered Sibley to take the bridge watch while he went below to look at the plot.

"It doesn't look too good," he said to Hank Copper. "We don't seem to be pulling ahead fast enough."

"That's correct, sir," Lieutenant Copper said. "As we reported an hour ago, the convoy has increased speed to seventeen knots. Even if they don't put on any more turns, it's going to be touch and go to get ahead of them before we have to dive, sir."

Captain Foster studied the plot. He raised his wrist to his mouth and bit a hair off with his teeth and then spat it out.

"Assume that I want to attack in three hours," he said. "Assume I want to shoot at a range of one thousand yards. Give me a course that will let us close to that range and tell me if we can make the intercept." He stood back to give the Plotting Party room to work. Hank Copper straightened up and pushed the plot toward his Captain.

"If we begin the intercept right now, sir, we could be in position to bore in at a ninety-degree angle to the convoy track at zero three-thirty. That assumes you would be content to take the middle ship of the convoy as your first target. The targets are spaced out at thousand-yard intervals. One destroyer has been ranging ahead of the convoy. The other destroyer is covering the stern of the convoy. That's been the destroyer dispositions since we began watching them. We could make the intercept on the middle ship of the three. There's no way we can get far enough down their track to intercept the lead ship. Right now we're six thousand yards off the convoy's port hand. I don't know how close you can go in before we're seen."

"There's no moon and no horizon to the east," Captain Foster said. "I think we can attack on the surface." He turned to Mike O'Connor.

"Can you get any more out of those engines?"

"We can maybe squeeze out another knot if we strain, Captain."

"Then strain," Captain Foster said. He took off his hat and put on a pair of red goggles and snugged the rubber eyepieces down against his cheeks. He smoothed his hair and put on his cap, turned and fumbled for the ladder that led up to the Conning Tower. He stopped and turned toward where Chief O'Brien was standing.

"Chief, I want all torpedo depth set at two feet. I want that done now and I want it double-checked. I'll slow down before I give the order to open the outer doors.

"Hank, I want the word passed that I want everyone on their toes. I know it's been a long night and we've got three hours or so before we go into action but I want everyone sharp. Tell the galley to serve coffee and whatever they've got handy, sandwiches, doughnuts, sweet rolls.

"You can pass the word about the targets and what we intend to do. We're going to attack on the surface, run through the convoy if we have to, and then turn and come back and hit the bastards again. After that we'll just see what happens." He climbed up the ladder into the Conning Tower.

Harrington swiveled around on his paddled bench in front of the bow-plane handwheel and faced the people in the Control Room.

"I'll clue you in to what happens after that," he said. "What happens after that is that the shit hits the fucking fan."

Less than a thousand miles to the north and east, Task Force 16 under the flag of Vice Admiral "Bull" Halsey in the aircraft carrier *Saratoga*, was steaming toward Tokyo. The fleet-oilers *Sabine* and *Cimarron* had finished refueling the four cruisers that were accompanying the three aircraft carriers and turned to the east to run for Pearl Harbor, accompanied by the 12th and 22nd Destroyer Divisions. The three aircraft carriers and four cruisers constituted what Vice Admiral Halsey called a "fast carrier strike force."

The flight deck of the *Hornet* was crowded with sixteen Army Mitchell bombers—B-25s—under the command of Lieutenant Colonel James A. Doolittle. The *Hornet* plowed forward into steadily rising seas. The mission of the task force was breathtaking at this stage of the war with Japan.

Bomb Japan. Bomb Japan in a night raid.

None of the B-25 pilots had ever flown his aircraft from the deck of an aircraft carrier. They had been trained on a runway on which the outline of a carrier deck had been painted. The training period had lasted long enough to assure Colonel Doolittle that the B-25s could indeed take of after such a short run.

The bombers were to be launched when the task force was five hundred miles from Tokyo. Each plane was armed with four five-hundred-pound bombs. Each plane had been loaded with its maximum quantity of gasoline, 1,141 gallons. After flying the five hundred miles to Tokyo and unloading their bombs on the city, the planes would fly another 1,093 nautical miles from Tokyo to air fields in China where Generalissimo Chiang Kai-shek had promised the fliers would be safe and would be transported back to the United States.

Andy O'Connor lifted his dive bomber off the deck of the *Enterprise* at dawn on April 18, 1942, to make a search out ahead of the task force. Radar operators had reported one, possibly two, distant contacts. The search flight of eight dive bombers swept out in a fan to search for the contacts. They found them, forty-two miles ahead of the task force. A short time later another small ship was sighted and radio operators in the task force heard messages being transmitted.

The task force was 150 miles short of its launch point, but Halsey reasoned that if he waited until the task force reached the launch point—another six to seven hours in worsening weather—the Japanese would have had time to concentrate scores of fighter planes to defend against the air raid. The decision was made: Rather than abort the entire mission, he would launch now and trust to luck that the bombers could still reach friendly Chinese air fields despite the extra 150 miles they would have to travel.

At 0824 the last of the clumsy bombers fought its way into the sky from the deck of the *Hornet* and the task force swept around in a long curve and set a course for Pearl Harbor.

Andy O'Connor, standing beside his dive bomber with Alabama Jones, his crew chief, watched the Army bombers struggle into the air from the *Hornet's* flight deck.

"Hell of a thing," Jones drawled. "I woulda bet that half of those Army people woulda got their asses wet but ever' one of them got offa the deck." He took a package of gum from his pocket and offered it to O'Connor, who took a stick, peeled the paper off and put the gum in his mouth.

"Funny thing I noticed when we went past the stern of the *Hornet* yesterday," Alabama Jones said. "I was over to Hickam a couple of days after the big raid, scrounging for whatever was worth taking, and I looked at some of them wrecked Mitchells. When we went past the stern of the *Hornet* yesterday, I noticed that all them Mitchells now got tail guns, twin Fifties looked like. Must have been one hell of a hurry-up job, modifying them planes because none of them Mitchells I saw at Hickam had any tail guns."

"They don't have any tail guns now," Andy O'Connor said. "Those are dummy guns to scare the Jap fighters off their tails. They won't be over the target area until some time after noon today, and then they've got to fly over a thousand miles to get to China."

"Hell of a thing," Alabama Jones said. "Bombing Tokyo in the daylight with dummy guns in the tail and cold rice when you finally get to China. If you ever get there." He stripped the foil from another piece of gum and put it in his mouth.

"This is one hell of a war, Mister O'Connor. Just one hell of a screwed-up war."

Chapter Eight

THE NIGHT SKY was as dark as the inside of a pocket. The sea was calm except for a long, rolling swell that occasionally cast a shower of white spray to either side of the bow of the *Tigerfish* as the big fleet submarine raced on a converging course toward its targets.

The lookouts manning the port and starboard sides of the periscope shears had sighted the outlines of the targets some time earlier. Lieutenant Joe Sibley had briefed the six lookouts who came on watch at midnight to alternate hour-on and hour-off for four hours. They were to pay no attention to the targets out ahead. They were to watch for the destroyers that were guarding the convoy and, particularly, watch for aircraft. Joe Sibley, manning the search periscope in the Conning Tower, would also keep watch on the destroyers as well as feed bearings and ranges to the Plotting Party in the Control Room.

The plot was already well along. On the plotting board Hank Copper had drawn in the base course of the convoy and the course *Tigerfish* was on. As the bearings and ranges came down from Joe Sibley, Copper made little "X" marks on the *Tigerfish* course line. Mike O'Connor, standing easy as the Battle Stations Diving Officer, watched the Plotting Party do its work, absorbing each detail, committing as much to memory as he could of the intricacies of the problem of getting into position to make an attack on a target. He turned his head upward as he heard Joe Sibley make a report to the Captain on the bridge.

"Captain, the second ship in the line bears zero-one-five. Range is now two thousand, repeat, two thousand yards. The lead destroyer has done a right turn and is now on the other

92

side of the convoy. The destroyer patrolling astern is well back. The range to that destroyer is eight thousand yards and opening slightly, sir."

"Very well," Captain Foster replied. "Reduce speed to five knots. Open all torpedo-tube outer doors. Resume speed as soon as the doors are open. Pass the word to all hands: We'll be shooting in a few minutes." He waited until he heard the word from the Control Room that all torpedo-tube outer doors were open. Depth set on all torpedoes, two feet. He felt the vibration in his feet as the *Tigerfish* resumed speed and rushed toward the targets.

"You have a constant shooting solution, Captain," Joe Sibley's voice came up through the hatch. "Range to the second ship in the line is now sixteen hundred yards, sir."

The telephone talkers in each compartment passed the word to the crew at their Battle Stations that the Old Man had a shooting solution and the action was about to begin. In the Forward Torpedo Room Dandy Don Miller took his station between the torpedo tubes, his hands resting lightly on the brass metal guards over the manual firing keys on Numbers One and Two torpedo tubes. His eyes glittered as he looked down the length of the room at his reload crew.

"They're only two people who talk in this room from now on," Miller said. "That's me and the telephone talker, and he don't talk unless he gets an order for me or from me. This Old Man is gonna do something submarines ain't supposed to do, he's gonna go in on the surface and shoot the living shit out of them Japs. And that means they're gonna shoot back. I don't want no yelling or no panic if the shit hits the fan. You keep your ears open for my orders and your assholes tight, that clear to everybody?" He stared at the set faces of the men.

In the Conning Tower Pete Savage stood by the periscope control box as Lieutenant Joe Sibley watched the enemy convoy and fed a steady stream of bearings and ranges to Hank Copper and the bridge. Lieutenant Wayne Raleigh, USNR, the Assistant Engineering Officer who manned the TDC, the Torpedo Data Computer, which was located in the after end of the Conning Tower, fed the ranges, bearings and the angle on the bow of the first target into his machine, cranking each piece of data into the TDC with the small hand cranks that studded its face. He watched the arrows on the dials intently.

"Constant solution, arrows match," Raleigh said. "Torpedo

track is thirteen hundred yards and closing." Sibley repeated the information to the Captain, and down in the Control Room Hank Copper double-checked to make sure the TDC was working correctly. Wayne Raleigh positioned his hand over the electrical firing keys for the Forward Torpedo Room tubes, his eyes questioning.

"He wants to shoot at a thousand yards or closer, Wayne," Sibley said in a low voice. "He'll let you know when to shoot. Don't worry." He put his face against the rubber eyepiece of the periscope and sharpened the focus on the second ship in the line of three ships.

"Target bears zero-one-zero. Angle on the bow is one-three-zero port." He twisted the range-finder knob on the right side of the periscope. "Range to the target is eleven hundred yards, Captain."

"Very well." Captain Foster's voice was calm. "I confirm the angle on the bow from here. We'll shoot if we're seen but if they don't see us, we'll go in to eight hundred yards and then shoot. Shooting order will be One, Two and then Three. Plot, if I have to, I'll go behind the target, make a left turn and then take the third ship with the after tubes. If the destroyers don't react too quickly, I might be able to take both targets from this side of the convoy."

"Range is now nine hundred yards, Captain," Joe Sibley called out. He half-turned as Wayne Raleigh muttered something about the Captain ramming the convoy.

"Range is eight hundred yards, Captain," Sibley called out. "You have a constant solution, sir."

"Stand by Forward," Captain Foster barked. Wayne Raleigh locked the transmitter button on the telephone set hanging around his neck in the "talk" position and positioned his hand over the electrical firing button console.

"FIRE ONE!" Captain Foster yelled. Raleigh repeated the order into his telephone mouthpiece and pressed the firing button for Number One tube at the same time. In the Forward Torpedo Room the telephone talker yelled out the order and Miller jammed his fingers down on the manual firing key a split-second after the firing light flared on the firing console.

"Number One fired electrically," Miller's telephone talker said into his mouthpiece.

"FIRE TWO!" Captain Foster counted down slowly.

"FIRE THREE!"

"Torpedoes running hot, straight and normal," Amos Stuckey reported from the sound gear.

"Torpedo run, Number One, ten more seconds, Bridge," Hank Copper yelled up the hatch.

On the bridge Captain Foster stared at the second ship in the line of three ships. There had been no indication the *Tigerfish* had been seen. He counted down the seconds to himself. As he reached the figure two, he saw a huge gout of flame erupt just forward of the bridge of his target.

"HIT!" He yelled as a dull roar echoed across the water. "Plot! Give me a setup on the next ship in the line!"

The night was suddenly filled with light as the torpedoed ship exploded in a thunderous roar. A rain of burning debris splattered across the water, reaching for the *Tigerfish*. As Hugh Foster watched, he saw dozens of fiery trails reach up into the sky from the ship he had torpedoed.

"My God!" he yelled. "She must have been an ammunition ship!" He caught at the bridge rail as the *Tigerfish* heeled suddenly in a change of course.

"Coming to course two-nine-five, Bridge," Hank Copper called out from the Control Room.

"Range to the second target is twelve hundred yards, Captain," Joe Sibley yelled. "We have a constant shooting solution, sir."

"Stand by Forward," Captain Foster said. "Shooting order will be Four and Five. We'll save Six in case that destroyer aft comes after us. Stand by . . ." He waited, listening to Joe Sibley chant the decrease in range.

"Destroyer bearing two-seven-zero, Bridge," the stern lookout reported.

"FIRE FOUR!" Captain Foster raised his binoculars and looked at his target, counting down softly to himself.

"FIRE FIVE! Joe, get on that destroyer aft. Keep me informed."

"Torpedoes running hot, straight and normal." Amos Stuckey's voice had risen a full octave above his normal speaking voice.

"How far away is that destroyer?" Captain Foster bellowed.

"Range to the destroyer is four thousand yards, Captain. He's got to swing out to his starboard to get clear of that first target."

A dull boom echoed across the water and Captain Foster

saw a blossom of flame appear near the bow of the second target. The blossom suddenly flared into a giant red flower and then a second burst of flame appeared in the midsection of the ship followed by a tremendous roar and a geyser of white steam.

"HIT! Second target took two hits! She's breaking apart! Let's get the hell out of here! All-ahead flank! Right full rudder! Hank, put me on a course to show our tail to that damned destroyer aft!"

In the Forward Torpedo Room Dandy Don Miller was in a crouch between his torpedo tubes, his right hand hovering above the firing key guard for Number Six torpedo tube.

"Man, this dude can shoot fish!" he said in an awestruck voice. "I mean this Old Man can shoot!"

Captain Foster looked around him. Off to the port side his first target was still exploding, sending long fingers of flame high into the sky. His second target had broken in two pieces, and in the light from the burning first target he could see the big three-bladed propeller of the second ship sticking out of the water, still turning lazily. He bent to the bridge microphone.

"Close outer torpedo-tube doors." He straightened up and took one last look around.

"Clear the bridge!" he yelled. "Dive! Dive! Dive!" His hand hit the diving alarm as the last of the three lookouts, followed by the quartermaster, went down the hatch. He dropped down the ladder, grabbing the hatch as he did so and pulling it shut. Pete Savage struggled up the ladder beside Foster and dogged the hatch down tight.

"Two hundred and fifty feet, Mike," Captain Foster called down the hatch. "Fifteen-degree down bubble, all-ahead full, we've got two tin cans up there and they're both coming after us."

The *Tigerfish* slanted downward at a steep angle, her crew grabbing for handholds as the deck suddenly tipped downward. Captain Foster half-slid, half-climbed down the ladder from the Conning Tower and grabbed at the gyrocompass table. Hank Copper shoved the plot across the table toward him.

Captain Foster looked at the plot. "Let's turn back toward the destroyer that was coming up from aft," he said. "They won't expect us to do that. Joe, will you please come down here?" He waited until Sibley had climbed down the ladder from the Conning Tower.

"You had a better look with the periscope than I did on the bridge. What exactly did you see?"

"First ship you hit was an ammunition ship, Captain. No doubt about that. She put on a regular Fourth of July show when she went up. The second ship was a troop transport, I think. I saw lots of people going over the side when she broke apart. I was watching when the first torpedo hit her. Caught her forward and stopped her dead. The second torpedo must have hit her engine rooms, because she exploded amidships and I saw a lot of steam and then she broke in two. The stern section tipped up, I saw the screw in the air. The forward section stayed on an even keel and I saw the people jumping over the side and I saw at least one lifeboat being lowered before I swung around to look for the destroyer. I saw so many people that maybe it was a troop ship."

"Two hundred and fifty feet, Captain," Mike O'Connor said.

"Very well," Captain Foster said. "Stuckey, give us everything you hear. Rig ship for depth charge. Rig ship for silent running." He waited until the reports came in from all compartments.

"We're going to catch it, I think," the Captain said to the people in the Control Room. "How much water does the chart show here?"

"It doesn't," Sibley answered. "The charts we're using are copied from old official Japanese charts, sir. They don't show any water depths."

"We had one hundred fathoms when you fired at the second target, sir," Mike O'Connor spoke up. "I ordered a fathometer sounding just after you fired Number Four tube, sir. Knew we didn't have any water depths on the chart. Didn't think it would hurt to know, sir."

Captain Foster looked up from the plotting board and stared at O'Connor. "No," he said slowly. "It doesn't hurt to know." He turned back to the plot.

"I've got twin screws bearing three-four-zero, Captain," Amos Stuckey said. "He's pinging but he hasn't found us yet." A sharp ringing sound echoed through the length of the *Tigerfish*.

"He's found us," Stuckey said.

"Three hundred feet, Mike," Captain Foster ordered. "Pass the word, silence throughout the ship."

The bow and stern planesmen strained at the big brass handwheels, tilting the bow and stern planes downward by hand, sending the *Tigerfish* deeper into the sea.

"I've got another set of twin screws, Captain," Stuckey said. "These bear zero-five-zero, sir." He pulled the mufflike earphones off his ears and settled them on his temples as the hull of the *Tigerfish* rang with the hammer blows of a searching sonar beam finding its target.

"We're at three hundred feet, sir," Mike O'Connor reported. "Zero bubble, sir."

"Very well," Captain Foster said. "You pretty sure, Joe, that the second target might have been a troop ship?"

"I'm not sure, sir." Sibley winced as the searching sonar beams hammered at the hull of the submarine. "I saw so many people going over the side, it had to be something like that. Way too many for ship's company."

Captain Foster put his finger on the plot. "Put me on a course back there, Hank. That's where we hit that second target. If there are people in the water, they might think twice about depth charging us. They'd be killing their own people if they did."

"I've got a set of twin screws picking up speed, sir," Stuckey said. "Bearing is two-one-eight, sir." Stuckey was sitting on a stool in front of his sound gear, his eyes closed, his entire being intent on what was coming through his earphones. "He's picking up speed, sir, coming fast! I think he's going to drop depth charges, Captain."

Captain Foster stood at the gyrocompass table, his hands gripping the edge of the table. He had never been depth charged. Except for the few men aboard who came from the *Sea Bass*, none of the rest of the crew had been depth charged. Now he was faced with meeting a situation that had never been truly considered in the prewar peacetime Navy—how to elude two enemy destroyers bent on smashing the submarine below them into a crushed length of metal full of dead men.

The book on submarine operations said that when faced with a depth-charge attack, "The Commanding Officer of the submarine will evade, changing depth, course and speed. These measures, with astute seamanship, should bring the submarine safely through the attack."

The book also said that by using the bathythermograph the submarine could find and safely lie beneath a layer of saltier, and thus denser, water. The enemy destroyer above would not be able to hear the submarine hiding beneath the layer of saltier water. Captain Foster glanced at the bathythermograph mounted above the gyrocompass table. The crude instrument, which measured the temperature of the water and the depth of the submarine with a stylus that drew a thin line on a smoked card, failed to show any indication of a temperature change that would indicate a layer of saltier water.

The book also said the Japanese Navy did not have sonar transmitters which could find an enemy submarine.

"Here he comes!" Amos Stuckey said in a thin voice.

The sound of the destroyer's propellers could be heard clearly through the thin hull of the *Tigerfish*. Captain Foster gripped the edge of the gyrocompass table tightly. He looked down at the plot. Hank Copper put the point of his pencil on the plot. The *Tigerfish* was very near to where the second target had been hit, should be almost under where the survivors were floating in the water or on their life rafts. Would the Japanese drop depth charges? He felt his stomach muscles tighten as the thunder of the destroyer's screws filled the interior of the submarine.

"Four hundred feet, Mike," he said. "Left full rudder."

A sharp banging sound echoed through the hull of the *Tigerfish*.

"That's the depth-charge pistol going off, sir," Joe Sibley said.

The first two depth charges exploded with a roar. The painted cork insulation that lined the interior of the submarine's hull rained down in a shower of small bits. Light bulbs popped with tiny sounds. In the Forward Torpedo Room a member of the reload crew was thrown against a reload torpedo. His face hit the torpedo. He reeled back, his eyes uncomprehending as blood gushed down over his mouth and chin. Dandy Don Miller snatched a towel from a bunk and pushed it against the man's face.

"Ain't nothin'," he growled. "You don't get a Purple Heart for a bloody nose, fella."

The second depth-charge attack twisted the *Tigerfish* in a tumbling vortex of water, racking the thin hull until it creaked. The *Tigerfish* rolled heavily to port and then sluggishly righted itself as two more depth charges exploded just above the submarine, driving it deeper into the sea.

"Four hundred and seventy-five feet, Captain!" Mike O'Connor reported.

"Very well," Captain Foster said. "Let her stay there. Rudder amidships."

"I've got screws bearing . . ." Stuckey's voice was blotted out by the thunder of the destroyer's screws, followed by the explosions of four depth charges. The force of the explosions tore Captain Foster's hands from the gyrocompass table and hurled him across the Control Room. The machinist's mate at the high-pressure air manifold braced himself and caught his Commanding Officer as he slammed into him. The machinist's mate grunted loudly as the weight of Captain Foster's body crushed him back into the valve studs of the high-pressure manifold.

"All compartments report damage," Captain Foster said as he struggled back to the gyro table. The auxiliary electrician grabbed a towel and began to dab at the blood on the machinist mate's back where the valve studs had cut into his flesh.

"Get the pharmacist's mate in here to take care of that man," Captain Foster ordered.

"No serious damage, Captain," Sibley said. "The electrician's mates are replacing the broken light bulbs."

"Belay that," Captain Foster said. "They'll only break again." He looked around the Control Room, dim now in the light of the heavy-lensed battle lanterns.

"Those people up there are dropping charges on us and we're right under where their people are in the water. They're killing their own people. Pass the word, all hands not needed on their feet, get into bunks. We might be down here a long time and we'll have to conserve oxygen."

On the surface one of the Japanese destroyers heeled sharply to port, its knife-edged bow slicing through a crowded life raft. The screaming soldiers on the life raft pitched into the water. As the destroyer continued on its course, a floundering soldier was sucked into the spinning propellers, to surface a moment later as a bloody froth of foam studded with bits of flesh that spread around the other swimmers.

The attack went on. First one destroyer would echo-range on the submarine and pinpoint its position and the other destroyer would make its depth-charge run. Then the second destroyer would repeat the process as soon as the thunder of he other destroyer's depth charges had died away. Down below, the *Tigerfish* twisted and turned at 475 feet, seeking a layer of saltier water to hide under. The temperature within he submarine reached 120 degrees Fahrenheit, and the needle of the humidity gauge was steady against its peg—100 percent humidity.

Captain Foster stood braced at the gyrocompass table, a towel around his neck to absorb the steady flow of sweat from his face and neck. He squinted at his wristwatch in the gloom.

"Four hours," he said.

"Here he comes again," Amos Stuckey called out as the thunder of twin screws filled the hull.

The attack was by far the most accurate and savage of the entire four hours. The *Tigerfish* was caught up in a series of explosions that violently twisted the long, slim submarine's hull. As the explosions died away, Stuckey reported that the other destroyer was beginning its attack run. The second destroyer, determined to be as effective as its mate, rolled four depth charges off its racks while its Y-guns fired two more charges out to either side.

"Those damned people up there are getting too much practice," Captain Foster muttered. "They're getting too damned good at their trade. Get me damage reports, please, all compartments. I want a complete report of all damage."

"Forward and After Engine Rooms report the welds around the engine-exhaust lines overboard have been broken, Captain," Sibley said. "They're taking some water, but Chief Apple says he can handle it. The bolts on the flanges for the engine-circulating water have been stretched and they're taking water there but not too serious."

"The bolts lengthened?" Captain Foster said, his voice incredulous. "My God! What else?"

"Lot of small leaks, sir, but nothing the people in the areas can't handle."

There was a fetid smell of fear in the ship. The abysmal terror of a depth-charge attack, an attack in which the submarine is powerless to do anything except try to evade, had set in. All through the ship men fought the terror they felt, trying their best to conceal their own fear, instinctively aware that any display of open fear might trigger an outbreak by another man, equally terrified. Some, those who were in bunks, curled into the fetal position, their hands protecting their genitals. Others wrapped their arms around their chests, clutching tighter as the depth charges thundered and the ship twisted and shuddered. In the Forward Torpedo Room Dandy Don Miller was braced between his beloved torpedo tubes, his hands gripping the inner-door handles of the two top tubes in the six-tube nest, baring his teeth as the charges threatened to tear the *Tigerfish* apart, muttering over and over, "Bastards! Bastards! Bastards!" as he fought for breath in the thick, oxygen-depleted air.

Captain Foster tapped Mike O'Connor on the shoulder. "Five hundred feet, Mike. Make it fast, fast as you can."

"Five hundred feet, sir," O'Connor answered. He shook his heavy mane of black hair. The *Tigerfish* was rated for safe cruising at a depth of two hundred feet with a 50 percent safety factor. He gently eased Harrington's thin body away from the big brass handwheel and used his powerful arms and shoulders to spin the bow planes into hard dive. Harrington, his bony chest heaving under the hours-long exertion of handling the bow planes in handpower, relaxed on the sweat-slippery leather seat in front of the bow planes, nodding his appreciation to O'Connor.

"Here they come!" Stuckey called out, and the thunder began again, this time closer, the crashing explosions smashing against the submarine's thin hull. Captain Foster's eyes widened in disbelief as he saw a thick cable that went through the hull suddenly push inward, exposing four inches of unpainted metal sheathing around the cable.

A sudden wailing sound filled the dimness of the Control Room. The Battle Stations messenger, a gaunt nineteen-year-old named John Ribbon from the ghettos of New York City, was standing rigid near the radio shack, his eyes closed. His open mouth emitted a high, ululating sound. Ribbon's arms began to jerk as his head rolled from side to side.

Mike O'Connor spun away from the bow-plane wheel and reached for the man. His big hands clamped tight on the sailor's thin upper arms.

"Shut up!" he hissed. "You shut up!"

Ribbon's eyes opened, and with some effort he focused on Mike O'Connor's harsh face.

"I can't take it!" Ribbon screamed.

"You'll take it!" O'Connor rasped into the man's face. "You'll take it because the Captain is taking it and I'm taking it and every damned man on this ship is taking it and you're no damned better than we are. Now shut UP!" His muscular hands clamped on the sailor's arms until the pain of the grip penetrated the man's mind. Ribbon shook his head back and forth.

"You're hurting me, Mister O'Connor," he gasped. "Stop hurting me."

"I'm sorry, son," Mike O'Connor said in a soft voice. He released his grip and his big, blunt fingers began to massage the bruised flesh. "Captain wants to know if there're any leaks down in the Pump Room. You'd better go down and take a look, the Captain's depending on you." He nudged John Ribbon toward the deck hatch that led down to the Pump Room. Ribbon nodded and knelt and opened the hatch and put one leg down into it, feeling with his foot for the ladder rung. He climbed down and disappeared. There was a silence in the Control Room and then Ribbon's voice came up through the hatch.

"We've got a pretty bad leak down here from one of the overboard discharge line flanges," Ribbon called out. "Pretty bad, Captain."

"Very well, John," Captain Foster called down the hatch. He nodded his head at an auxiliary man in the Control Room. The auxiliary machinist's mate went down into the Pump Room as the thunder of the destroyer screws filled the hull.

The two men came up out of the Pump Room after the attack. Ribbon pointed at the machinist's mate. "He stopped most of the leak after I showed him where it was, Captain."

"Good work, John," Captain Foster said. He turned his head suddenly as Joe Sibley blurted out, "Layer! We're in a layer, sir!"

"About time something good happened," Foster said. He moved around the gyrocompass table until he could see the slim stylus tracing a sudden jagged course down the smoked card of the bathythermograph, an indication that the submarine was now surrounded by water colder than the rest of the ocean, a "heavy layer."

"Lost contact with the destroyers, sir," Amos Stuckey said suddenly.

"Damned thing really works," Captain Foster said in a

wondering voice. "Now all we have to do is stay in this colder water."

For the next three hours he maneuvered the *Tigerfish* with a delicate hand, keeping the ship beneath and inside the protective clot of saltier, colder water, using the tiny movements of the bathythermograph needle as a guide. The heavy layer blotted out the propeller sounds of the *Tigerfish* and caused the destroyer sonar search beams to bounce harmlessly off at an angle that indicated to the sonar operator on the destroyer that his sonar beam had not contacted anything.

"I'm losing the damned layer," Foster suddenly grunted. "Oh, dammit all, I've lost it! Stuckey, give me a search all around."

Up in the Forward Torpedo Room Miller had organized his reload crew, all muscular men, into four groups to turn the sound heads that stuck down beneath the keel of the *Tigerfish*. The deck around the sound heads was slippery with water squeezed out of the humidity inside the submarine and the sweat that poured from the dripping bodies of the men. Stuckey's request for two full turns of each sound head brought groans from the reload crew.

"Strain your balls, you bastards," Miller said. "This fuckin' war is just beginnin' and there's lots more where this came from before you get back to Pearl and a cold beer."

"Shut your fuckin' mouth up," a beefy fireman said. Miller grinned and pushed in beside the fireman to help.

"I can't hear anything, Captain," Stuckey said. "I mean, I can hear the normal things, water moving alongside the hull, that sort of thing. No screws at all, sir."

"Very well," Captain Foster said. He turned to the telephone talker. "Pass the word we think we've shaken the destroyers. But just to be sure, we're going to stay where we are for another half-hour." He thought for a moment.

"Ask Miller in the Forward Room how his people are holding up on the sound heads. If he needs help, we'll get some for him."

The telephone talker relayed the order and listened for a moment.

"Forward Room says they don't need any help, sir."

"Didn't think they would," Foster said. He turned to Joe Sibley and smiled. "We've got ourselves a submarine crew here, Joe. A damned good submarine crew."

"Yes, sir," Joe Sibley said, and Chief O'Brien, standing near the Christmas Tree board, grinned to himself.

A half-hour later Captain Foster ordered hydraulic power restored to the bow and stern planes, the helm and the sound headgear. The men who had been manning the gear in handpower slumped in relief, satisfied they had done their jobs.

After dark had fallen, the *Tigerfish* crept cautiously toward the surface. The search periscope was raised and Captain Foster made three complete inspections of the sea and sky around the ship. Satisfied there was no enemy in sight, he gave the order to surface, and as the four big diesels coughed into life, a windstorm of cool, fresh air swept down the bridge hatch and roared aft through the ship. The air-conditioning plants were started to pull the humidity out of the forward area of the ship, and the cooks began frying steaks in the galley.

Captain Foster and Joe Sibley climbed up to the bridge. Foster leaned over the wide teak rail and stared down at the forward deck. There was no forward deck. The black, slatted wooden deck had disappeared, leaving behind only the twisted metal struts that had supported it. The deck aft of the Conning Tower was not as badly wrecked, only two large holes had been torn in it.

"I want a complete damage report prepared, Joe," Captain Foster said. "Take O'Connor through the ship with you. Whatever we can fix I want fixed. This is a damned good area and I don't want to be ordered home for damage that isn't important."

The damage report filled two pages. Foster looked at it and shook his head. "No way they're going to let me stay out here. Damn, Damn, DAMN!" He looked down the Wardroom table at Mike O'Connor, who had written the report.

"Half of this stuff you know damned well you can't fix," he said. "But thanks for trying to make us look good. I want you to know I appreciate the way you handled John Ribbon. You've got a nice touch with the men. I've made a note of that in my contact report."

Just before the *Tigerfish* dove two mornings later, the message from Pearl Harbor came in over the radio. "The staff extends its heartiest congratulations to Captain Foster and the crew of *Tigerfish* for a determined and successful attack. Intelligence reports credit *Tigerfish* with sinking an ammunition ship, six thousand tons, and a troop transport, eight thousand tons, with heavy loss of life among the troops. ComSubPac commends Captain Foster and his crew for sterling performance of duty while under heavy enemy attack. *Tigerfish* is ordered home at once for repairs."

The *Tigerfish* surfaced that night and began running the long sea miles toward Pearl Harbor. Captain Foster walked through the ship as the submarine cruised submerged on its first day of the trip home, congratulating each man on his performance of duty. When he came to John Ribbon, the sailor hung his head until Captain Foster suddenly put his arm around the young man's bony shoulders.

"Every man has to find himself, John," he said in a low voice. "You found yourself. I want you to stay aboard with me, if you will." Ribbon nodded, turning his head away so his Captain wouldn't see the tears in his eyes.

Chapter
Nine

COLONEL DOOLITTLE'S BOLD raid against Tokyo, four months after the Japanese strike against Pearl Harbor, did little real damage to the Japanese war machine. The very audacity of the raid raised American spirits and stiffened the resolve of Admiral Yamamoto that Pearl Harbor had to be neutralized, sealed off until Japan had accomplished its primary objective: to expand its military power into Southeast Asia to insure an ample supply of oil, rubber, ore and food for Japan. The raid on Pearl Harbor had been expected to so cripple the U.S. Battle Fleet that it would be out of action for at least a year. But the American carriers had not been in port on the morning of December 7, 1941, and the submarines had not been damaged. So long as those two arms of the American naval force in the Pacific were able to operate out of Pearl Harbor, the Japanese plans were in hazard. Admiral Yamamoto gathered his staff and began to plan how to neutralize Pearl Harbor.

A week after the Doolittle raid Naval Intelligence experts working at Pearl Harbor knew that something was afoot. Japanese radio traffic increased tenfold. The cryptanalysts intercepted and decoded hundreds of Japanese radio messages. The work began to show a pattern as one piece after another of the jigsaw puzzle began to drop into place. It was evident that Admiral Yamamoto was planning another major naval strike.

The questions that could not be answered were—where and when?

Admiral Ernest Joseph King, Jr., who carried the dual load of Commander in Chief of the U.S. Fleet and the Chief of Naval Operations, argued from his office in Washington that

Yamamoto would launch another strike at Pearl Harbor and that this time the Japanese would invade, rather than strike and withdraw.

The ranking generals of the U.S. Army were equally certain the Japanese would bypass Pearl Harbor and invade the continental United States, striking at key areas along the West Coast.

Admiral Nimitz did not wholly share either view. Nimitz thought that a naval and air strike against Pearl Harbor, followed by a massive invasion attempt, was a possibility, but that the more probable target would be the Aleutian Islands. He requested an update from his intelligence office on the latest information on Japanese warship movements. The report he received was devastating.

Yamamoto had issued orders to assemble a massive Battle Fleet. The fleet was divided into three sections: a main body, a carrier strike force and an invasion and occupation force.

The main body of the force under the command of Admiral Yamamoto was made up of seven battleships, a small aircraft carrier, two seaplane carriers, a cruiser, thirteen destroyers and four fleet-oilers.

The carrier strike force consisted of four big aircraft carriers, two older battleships, two cruisers, twelve destroyers and five fleet-oilers.

The invasion and occupation force was massive. Two of Japan's older battleships were assigned to this force for shore bombardment prior to the invasion. It also included a small aircraft carrier, eight cruisers, twenty-one destroyers, a fleet-oiler and twelve transports carrying the invasion force of five thousand battle-tested troops, plus minesweepers and cargo vessels that carried the supplies needed to support the invasion force once it had gone ashore.

As Admiral Nimitz studied the report, he ran over in his mind what force he had to combat the Japanese. It was woefully weak. He had three big aircraft carriers, eight cruisers, seventeen destroyers and nineteen submarines. Not enough, by any measure. But if the Japanese attacked, he had to counter. If he knew where the attack would come, he could gain some slight advantage to offset his lack of ships. But no one knew where the Japanese would strike.

Commander Joseph Rochefort, a strange, nonconformist naval officer whose usual daily uniform was a worn smoking jacket and carpet slippers, headed the group of cryptanalysts who worked in a secret basement room in the supply depot area of the naval base at Pearl Harbor. Drawing on all his experience in divining the workings of the Japanese military mind—and particularly his knoweldge of how Admiral Yamamoto's mind worked—the dour intelligence expert came to the conclusion that a pair of initials, "AF," that appeared constantly in the Japanese radio traffic stood for Midway Island. Others in his group argued the initials could stand for Pearl Harbor, the Aleutians or, as the Army believed, the West Coast of the United States.

Trusting his instincts, Commander Rochefort laid a trap for the Japanese. Without informing Admiral Nimitz, he ordered the Commanding Officer at Midway to send a radio message in plain language to the effect that Midway was woefully short of fresh water, due to a breakdown in the island's distilling plant. In a matter of hours after the message was sent by Midway, Rochefort's radio operators intercepted a message addressed to Admiral Yamamoto that "AF was short of fresh water." Commander Rochefort put on a clean shirt and tie and black shoes and hand-carried the information to Admiral Nimitz.

Admiral Yamamoto's decision to strike at Midway was based on sound strategy. Most naval strategists considered the tiny atoll called Midway, 1,135 miles WNW of Pearl Harbor to be the gateway to the Hawaiian Islands. The atoll, a mere dot on the charts, was only six miles across. Within a barrier reef there were two islands above water; Easter Island, barely two miles long and the site of a commercial cable station, and Sand Island, one mile long, where Pan-American Airways had built an airport in 1935 for its trans-Pacific clippers. Naval strategists agreed that if Midway fell to the Japanese and the enemy invaded the Aleutians at the same time, the cork would be driven into the bottle—the United States would effectively be bottled up in Pearl Harbor, unable to move out of the port for fear of being destroyed by enemy aircraft from Midway or the Aleutians. With Pearl Harbor neutralized, the Japanese could conquer Southeast Asia and then assemble the force needed to capture the Hawaiian Islands and force the Americans back to their own West Coast.

On May 5, 1942, the cryptanalysts in Pearl Harbor intercepted and decoded a radio message from the Japanese Imperial Headquarters in Tokyo. The message, coded in the most secret of the Japanese codes, read "Commander in Chief of the Combined Fleet will, in cooperation with the Imperial Army, invade and occupy strategic points in the Western Aleutians and Midway Island."

Admiral Nimitz was certain that Midway would be Yamamoto's primary target. Nimitz and his staff knew they had to strike first, strike hard and then hope for the best. Nimitz ordered Midway to be reinforced with all the aircraft available; thirty-two PBY Catalinas, lumbering amphibious planes; fifty-four Marine Corps fighters and dive-bomber aircraft, four B-26 and nineteen B-17 bombers from the U.S. Army Air Force.

On May 28, Task Force 16 under the flag of Rear Admiral Raymond A. Spruance left Pearl Harbor. The task force was made up of the carriers *Enterprise* and *Hornet*, six cruisers, eleven destroyers and two fleet-oilers. The orders issued by Admiral Nimitz were succinct: "Hold Midway and inflict maximum damage on the enemy by means of strong attrition tactics."

On May 30, Task Force 17 under command of Rear Admiral Jack Fletcher left Pearl Harbor to rendezvous with Task Force 16. This smaller task force consisted of the carrier *Yorktown*, two cruisers and six destroyers. The nineteen submarines available, some hastily summoned back from war patrols, took position in a semicircle around Midway.

The Japanese Fleet sailed eastward, hidden behind a weather front that was moving ahead of the ships. The strike date for Midway was to be June 4, 1942.

The U.S.S. *Enterprise* ploughed through the night seas, sailing westward. On the carrier's bridge the Officer of the Deck listened to the brief reports from the radar operators on watch. Below decks the men in the engine rooms, those on the hangar decks who were fueling the planes and arming them with bombs and machine-gun ammunition, the cooks in the galleys—all shared one common feeling. With the dawn would come the launch of the aircraft and the search for the enemy fleet and the battle for supremacy.

The ringing tones of a bugle sounded reveille over the loudspeakers of the *Enterprise* two hours before dawn. Sailors fumbled their way into their clothes, carefully buttoning their dungaree shirts at the wrist as protection against flash burns, and made their way to the chow lines. A gunner's mate nudged the man standing ahead of him in the chow line.

"Hey," he said, "today we get the big chow." He reached a serving station and a mess cook plopped a steak on his tray. Another mess cook put two fried eggs on top of the steak. Fried potatoes and green beans were added to the tray. As the gunner's mate made his way to his mess table, he passed a table where a group of dive-bomber machine gunners were eating and he wondered to himself how many of those men would be at that table for breakfast tomorrow morning.

In the flight-ready rooms the pilots were restless. They had eaten their breakfast at 0130 and had twice been ordered to man their planes and then sent back to wait in the ready rooms.

At 0430 Admiral Yamamoto's carrier force was 215 miles from Midway. He ordered his carriers to launch planes and attack Midway. Before the planes had reached Midway, a patrolling PBY sighted the Japanese Fleet and radioed the alarm. As the first bombs struck Midway, other patrolling planes from Midway found the Japanese Fleet and radioed its precise location to Pearl Harbor.

The radio messages were picked up by the radiomen on the *Enterprise* and the navigators and Air Group Commanders clustered around a chart on the bridge. The navigator finished drawing his lines on the chart and carefully pricked off the distance between the *Enterprise* and the enemy's position— two hundred miles WSW.

On the flight deck of the *Enterprise* the plane-tenders moved among the parked planes, surefooted in the darkness of the early dawn. The blue-shirted plane-handlers pulled and pushed aircraft into position for takeoff. The fighter aircraft would leave the carrier first, followed by the dive bombers and the torpedo planes. The purple-shirted chockmen slid wooden chocks in front of plane wheels while red-jerseyed gasoline crews topped off fuel tanks and ordnance men slipped fuses into bombs and made a last check to see that all the machine guns had maximum ammunition.

In his flight-ready room Lieutenant Andrew O'Connor double-checked his equipment. Parachute harness, gun belt and pistol, life jacket were in place. His shoes were tightly laced. He picked up his navigational clipboard as he heard the bullhorn rasp and then bellow, "Pilots man your planes!" He raced up the ladder to the flight deck and trotted down the deck to his plane. Roger Cain, his radioman-gunner, was already in the rear seat of the SBD-2 dive bomber. Alabama Jones, the crew chief, his cheek bulging with a chew of tobacco, followed O'Connor up the short boarding ladder and leaned into the cockpit, helping his pilot fasten his safety belt.

"Y'all come back safe, now, Lieutenant," Jones said softly. He patted O'Connor on the shoulder and went back down the ladder, unhooked it and gave it to one of his crew. O'Connor sat in his cockpit and crossed himself and prayed in a low voice. He heard the bullhorn give the order to start engines and he fired up his engine, hearing the steady roar of the perfectly tuned machinery. He looked upward and to one side at a yardarm above the ship's bridge. A small bundle soared upward to the yardarm on a billowing signal halyard and then opened in the brisk wind to show the red and white colors of the Fox flag. As the flag snapped open in the wind created by the carriers' speed, O'Connor heard the scream of a fighter plane's engine as the first Wildcat F4F took off, to be followed by the rest of the fighters.

Then it was the turn of the dive bombers. O'Connor eased his plane into position, his eyes on the flight-deck officer standing near the bridge structure. The officer raised his left arm and rotated his left hand rapidly. O'Connor pushed both feet against his brake pedals and shoved the throttle forward. The SBD shook violently as its powerful engine roared, and then the fight-deck officer waved his black-and-white checkered flag downward and O'Connor released the brakes. The dive bomber raced down the flight deck, its tail lifting as O'Connor gentled the stick and then he lifted the plane off the deck and made a climbing turn to take position over the carrier until his air group had formed up.

O'Connor led his squadron up to fifteen thousand feet and set a course to intercept the enemy fleet. He looked around him and marveled at the beauty of the morning. The sky was clear except for a few fluffy cumulus clouds. Below him the sea was flat, a soft delft blue in color. Visibility, he estimated, was at least thirty miles at this altitude. He looked to his right, and Orv Masters, flying as his right wingman, raised a fist in salute. When he looked to his left, Red Olsen, his other wingman, returned his salute of a clenched fist and grinned widely. O'Connor wondered, hoped, that all three of them would survive this day.

There was cause to wonder. The radio reports in the ready

room had been full of the tremendous damage done by the Japanese air strikes at Midway. There had been other reports from the scouting PBY pilots of the great size of the Japanese Battle Fleet. O'Connor stared out ahead of his plane's nose, looking for the enemy fleet.

Suddenly they were there, the twisting white wakes of ships. He saw three aircraft carriers close together, a fourth some distance ahead of the three.

"Sir," Roger Cain's voice came over the intercom from the rear cockpit. "I've got binoculars and I can see torpedo planes attacking those ships out ahead. Lots of planes going after the torpedo planes, sir."

"Thanks, Rog," O'Connor said. "I see them now. One of their planes just splashed. There goes another one into the water. See it?"

"Ours, sir, not theirs." Cain's voice was subdued.

The order from the Air Group Commander was terse. O'Connor's squadron would follow him down to attack the carrier on the far left side of the group of three carriers that were bunched up. Lieutenant Best would lead his squadron in an attack on the carrier in the center of the three.

Andy O'Connor tipped his dive bomber over in a seventy-degree dive. He glanced at his air speed gauge; 280 knots. Then his whole being was centered on, consumed with, the problem at hand: to center the target in his sight, to release his bomb at precisely the right second to insure a hit and then to pull out of his almost vertical dive and get away before the Zeke fighters he could see circling below him jumped him.

"Bogeys ahead to starboard!" Roger Cain yelled. O'Connor ignored the information. The flight deck of the enemy carrier was growing larger with frightening speed. His eyes flicked to his altimeter, twenty-five hundred feet. He took a deep breath and held it and then he released one of his five-hundred-pound bombs and hauled back on the stick, pushing hard on his left rudder pedal, rolling the plane into a steep, climbing turn. In the rear seat Roger Cain twisted around in his seat.

"Hit!" Cain yelled. "We hit the bastard right on the flight deck!"

The Japanese carrier *Akagi* took three hammer blows in that attack. The first was a near-miss that exploded only yards from the carrier's hull, dishing in the ship's hull plates and causing flooding. Before the damage crews could respond to that crisis, a bomb plunged through the flight deck and exploded on the hangar deck. The bomb's blast exploded all the torpedoes stored on the hangar deck and started immense fires. The third bomb slammed into the planes on the afterdeck of the carrier that were being refueled and rearmed with torpedoes intended for the American carriers. As O'Connor climbed, he saw the carrier below him engulfed in flames.

"Second target is the carrier in the middle," the Air Group Commander ordered. "Attack!"

O'Connor checked his altimeter and decided he had enough altitude and saw the carrier ahead of him, a long, twisting wake curling out behind it as the carrier's Captain turned from left to right and left again to confuse the attacking planes. O'Connor saw fires on the after end of the carrier's flight deck, where at least one bomb had hit, and he tipped his plane over into a dive and went hurtling downward, aiming his plane at the flight-deck area just ahead of the fires. He released his remaining five-hundred-pound bomb and fought the plane into a steep climbing turn and heard Cain's shout that he had scored a bull's-eye on the carrier's flight deck.

"Bogeys!" Cain screamed into the intercom. "Bogeys dead astern and coming fast!" O'Connor heard the stammering chatter of Cain's machine gun. He knew he couldn't compete against the deadly Zekes, the Japanese Zero-3 fighters. The Zekes were much faster and more maneuverable than his stubby dive bomber. He pushed his stick forward and went shooting down toward the placid surface of the ocean. He leveled off a scant twenty feet above the water and set a course for where the Big E should be waiting on the featureless surface of the ocean.

"Two bogeys still coming!" Cain yelled. O'Connor gritted his teeth and began delicately changing course, first to the left and then to the right, dipping down to within ten feet of the water and then easing up a few feet and then down again.

"Hold me steady, sir," Cain yelled through the intercom. "I've got me a bastard back here got more guts than sense." O'Connor steadied the plane on course and heard the hammering of Cain's .30-caliber machine gun and the machine gunner's ecstatic yell. He twisted his head and saw a Zeke, its wing enveloped in flames, smash into the water off to his left and then cartwheel along the surface.

"Other bastard's gone home, Lieutenant," Cain said. "Let's us do that, sir."

"Will do," O'Connor said. "Nice shooting, my friend. Keep your eyes peeled. I'm going to go upstairs so we can see where Mother is." He eased the stick back and began a slow climb to gain altitude.

O'Connor entered the landing circle of planes around the Big E and was waved off as he neared the carrier to let an SBD, its right wing sagging dangerously, make its approach and land. The plane landed far forward of the stretched cables that should have caught its landing hook and slammed into the wire cable barrier farther up the deck. O'Connor saw the "Hot Papas," the fire and rescue crew in their bulky asbestos suits, running toward the plane. He checked his fuel gauge and relaxed. He had enough fuel for another thirty minutes. He could wait.

Alabama Jones helped him out of the plane and down the ladder. He watched as the lanky crew chief and his crew went over the plane, checking every inch of the wings, tail and fuselage.

"The Man up there likes you, Lieutenant," Jones said. "You got six or seven holes through the fuselage but nothing that matters. We'll have you refueled and rearmed and ready to go in a little while."

"Go where?" O'Connor said. "I know we hit two carriers, I got a hit in each of them. What's left?"

"You people flying around up there in the sunshine don't get the word, sir," Jones said. "Word we get here is that the whole damned Jap Navy is out there. Lots of battlewagons, carriers, cruisers and destroyers up your giggy, sir. I sent one of my people to get you and Cain something to drink and some sandwiches. This here is one hell of a battle and it's gonna go on all day, from what they say."

In midafternoon O'Connor raced down the deck of the Big E and was airborne. Around him as he flew westward there were twenty-three other dive bombers. An hour and a half later the dive bombers found the Japanese carrier *Horyu* fleeing from the battle at thirty knots. O'Connor took station behind his Air Group Commander and then he was in his attack dive, his bomb sight steady on the after end of the carrier's flight deck. He plunged downward through a curtain of black antiaircraft bursts, holding his plane steady on target. At 1,750 feet he released his bomb and pulled up in a curling climb. Below him and to one side the *Horyu*, fatally wounded by the Air Group Commander's bomb, staggered under the impact of O'Connor's bomb and then began to list as another bomb plunged through its flight deck and exploded in the engine-room spaces.

O'Connor landed on the *Enterprise* and climbed down to the flight deck, feeling an overpowering weariness in his legs. He looked at his wristwatch. It was past four P.M. reveille; the pilots had been called at four in the morning. The hours of waiting to be called, the intense, nerve-racking tension of battle, was taking its toll. He nodded his thanks to Alabama Jones, who somehow had procured a canteen of scalding tea.

"We hit another carrier," O'Connor said. "I saw it listing and on fire."

"Makes four of their carriers hit and either sunk or burning so bad they ain't gonna make it," Jones said. "You hear about the *Yorktown*, sir?"

O'Connor shook his head.

"She bought the farm," Jones said. "Jap planes got her and then a Jap sub came in and nailed her. The sub got one of the tin cans that was standing by to pick up people in the water."

"What about her planes, what about our people?" O'Connor asked.

"Don't know how many of her planes set down on the *Hornet*," Jones said. "Ain't seen any of them come aboard us. The people who keep score tell me we're missing fourteen of our SBDs. Only four of the torpedo planes made it back. Could we be lost the other ten, sir." He looked away as Andy O'Connor crossed himself and began to pray.

Just before dark the radio crackled with disturbing news. Army B-17 bombers sent from Midway to attack the burning carrier *Horyu* were jumped by the *Horyu*'s fighter pilots, who had no friendly flight deck to land on. The news bothered Admiral Spruance, who could not be sure the Zekes that attacked the B-17s were from the *Horyu* or if they had flown off the flight deck of a fifth carrier that had not as yet been seen. He ordered the *Enterprise* and *Hornet* and their escorting vessels to turn to the east. At midnight he ordered the task force to reverse course and head for the enemy out to the west.

The *Enterprise* launched her fighters and dive bombers into increasingly bad weather at midafternoon the next day. The overcast thickened and lowered by the minute, and after three hours of fruitless search the Air Group Commander ordered the planes to return to the carrier. Early the next morning two search planes launched by the *Enterprise* found the Japanese cruisers *Mogami* and *Mikuma*, part of the invasion task force. During the night hours the *Mogami* had rammed the *Mikuma*, damaging its bow and rupturing fuel tanks in the *Mikuma*. Admiral Spruance ordered the dive bombers to the attack. The *Mogami* managed to escape the attack, but the dive bombers left the *Mikuma* a smoking wreck.

Admiral Yamamoto had suffered heavy losses, losses that he reasoned he could not afford. Admiral Spruance had outmaneuvered him at every turn. His capital ships had not fired a shot against an American ship. As the reports came in, he summed them up. All four of his big fleet aircraft carriers had been sunk by American aircraft. He had lost a heavy cruiser and another was so badly damaged it would require a year to repair it. More than 250 of his carrier aircraft had been lost, and the death toll of sailors, officers, pilots and aircraft gunners and radiomen was at least three thousand, including Rear Admiral Yamaguchi, a brilliant officer who was rumored to be in line to succeed Admiral Yamamoto. No coward, Yamamoto wanted to fight, but he was getting reports of as many as "six American carriers" to the east of his fleet. He realized that if he steamed toward the enemy, he might be the target of a massive dawn air attack. Shortly before 0300 on June 5, Admiral Yamamoto ordered the rest of his Combined Fleet to reverse course to the west, rendezvous for refueling and set a course for Japan.

The losses on the American side had not been inconsequential. The carrier *Yorktown* and the destroyer *Hammann* had been sunk with a loss of hundreds of lives. The price paid in lost aircraft, their pilots and radio gunners had been staggering. The torpedo bombers had taken the worst beating. The plots of those slow, lumbering planes had pressed home their suicidal attacks through withering antiaircraft fire and the determined attacks of the deadly Zeke fighters. The stoical courage of the torpedo-plane pilots had been responsible for the success of the dive bombers attacking the Japanese carriers; the Zekes, preoccupied with defending their carriers from torpedo attacks, could not prevent the American dive bombers from getting into position for their deadly bombing dives.

The *Yorktown* had lost ten of its twenty-five fighters, twelve of its thirty-seven dive bombers and all but one of its thirteen torpedo planes before it was sunk. The *Enterprise* had lost only one of its twenty-seven fighters but eleven of its fourteen

torpedo planes were missing as were twenty of its thirty-eight
dive bombers. The *Hornet* lost twelve of its twenty-seven
fighters, five of its thirty-seven dive bombers and all fifteen of
its torpedo planes. The price paid had been high, but as the
naval historians were to later sum up, the Battle of Midway
was the turning point in the war on the sea in the Pacific. It
soundly proved that carrier airpower, if used boldly and
intelligently, would be a decisive weapon in future battles.

The noise in the Officers' Club on the naval base at Pearl
Harbor was deafening. The din from the bar where pilots stood
four deep drowned out the music of an orchestra that valiantly
played dance music to an empty dance floor. Andy O'Connor
moved through the crowd, buying a round of drinks here,
buying another round there. He held a half-full glass of tonic in
one hand and from time to time he'd sip at the tonic to give the
appearance that he was drinking. Finally, when he thought he
had made a show of celebrating the victory at Midway
sufficiently so there would be no comment later on, he eased
out of the crowd and found a table near the dance band. A
waiter brought him a roast beef sandwich and a bottle of milk.

Andy O'Connor didn't feel like celebrating. He had known
every one of the thirty-two pilots and their gunners who were
missing from the *Enterprise*. He had gone to mass three times,
pouring out his silent grief as he prayed for their souls. He ate
his sandwich slowly, wondering if his father had been right in
teaching that it was foolish to drink alcohol, wondering if his
own way of grieving was better than letting go and drowning
the sorrow he knew all of them felt.

He sat at the table, enduring the noise and the frantic
merriment. Everyone was calling the Battle of Midway a great
victory. Too many died, he thought to himself, too many who
were so young. He looked up, his face somber, as a Lieutenant
holding the arm of a tall, slim, dark-haired girl came weaving
across the dance floor to his table.

"Andy, ol' buddy, this here pretty thang knows Ah got a wife
back home in Houston because Ah tole her so and Ah tole her
Ah'd find her a nice pilot who ain't married up to anyone and
her name is—" He stopped and looked owlishly at the
embarrassed girl.

"What's yore name again, pretty thang?"

"Carol Oster," the girl said in a low voice.

"Meet Andy O'Connor who is a good Irishman which ain't as

good as a good Texan but it'll have to do because Ah don't know any other single dudes." The Lieutenant bowed unsteadily and lurched away as Andy stood up.

"I'm sorry, Miss Oster," Andy said. "Tex is, well, Tex is just Tex. He doesn't mean any harm. Won't you sit down? Can I get you something to drink?"

"No thanks, to the drink, I mean," the girl said. She sat down at the table and looked at the empty milk bottle. "You don't drink?"

"I never learned how," Andy said. "Can I get you something? Coffee, a soft drink?"

"That would be nice," she said. "A Coke, if it isn't too much trouble." Andy pushed his way through a crowd at the end of the bar and managed to get two paper cups filled with ice and Coca-Cola. He brought them back to the table.

"I'd ask you to dance," he said, "but I don't think we could even hear the music. Why don't we go outside, if you don't mind. It's got to be quieter." She nodded and he followed her around one edge of the empty dance floor. She found a bench under some large oleander bushes and they sat down.

"What on earth were you doing in that mob?" Andy asked.

"The club asked all the single women to come tonight," she said. "I don't think the club realized the carrier officers wouldn't be interested in dancing. I was getting ready to leave when that nice Tex found me and said he would be a committee of one to find me a single man, 'dude' he called him, for me to dance with. I'm sorry if I spoiled your evening."

"Just the opposite," he said slowly. He looked at her profile.

"Is your father in the Navy?" he asked. "I mean, if the O-Club asked you to muster around tonight, you must be Navy?"

"My father was in the Navy," she said. "He was a Captain in the Supply Corps. We were eating breakfast when the attack came. He went back to the base. He was killed by a bomb." She said the words quietly, looking away from O'Connor. He put his soft drink on the bench and stood.

"I apologize," he said in a low voice. "I've forgotten my manners. I should not have asked you about your personal affairs. My father, bless his Irish heart, would give me a taste of his belt if he knew how I'd forgotten the manners he and my mother taught me. I'll see you to your car. You said you were about to leave when Tex grabbed you. Please accept my apologies."

She looked at him as he stood in front of her, taking in the solid muscularity of his compact body, the face that was young but yet no longer young, marked with a grief she had seen in so many other faces earlier in the evening. She felt a sudden wave of compassion for the young man standing before her.

"Sit down, Lieutenant O'Connor," she said. "I have no car, I came in a bus with the other girls. Sit down and tell me about yourself, about your Irish father and your mother and all your brothers and sisters if you have them, and I would guess you do if you're Irish."

"You're sure?" he asked.

"I'm sure," she said. "Please sit down."

He sat and told Carol Oster about his Irish father and his Polish mother and the great love between them; about his older brother Mike, who was at sea somewhere on a submarine, about their growing up and the Naval Academy. He talked and she listened, interrupting only occasionally until a Marine Corps First Sergeant wearing the brassard of the Shore Patrol on his sleeve coughed discreetly from a few feet away.

"Begging your pardon, ma'am, Lieutenant," the Sergeant said. "The party in the O-Club is about over, and if you were one of the people who came in the bus, ma'am, it's time to go."

"Thank you, Sergeant," O'Connor said. He rose and put his hand under Carol's elbow, helping her to stand. "I'll walk the lady over to the bus."

As they walked, he suddenly turned toward her, his face earnest in the moonlight. "If I may," he said, "I'd like to ask you out to dinner."

"I'd like that," she said.

"Tomorrow?"

"That would be fine," she said. "I live with my mother, but we're still listed under my father's name. Look under Oster, Captain Frank Oster." She stopped as they neared the bus.

"You've been at sea," she said. "They have a very strict curfew now. If we go to dinner, it will have to be early so you can get back to the base. If I may, I'd suggest you come to the house about midafternoon. My mother will want to meet you." She smiled at him and climbed into the bus. He waved at her and she waved back, and as the bus drove away she thought about the man she had just met and wondered if he had a girl back in Chicago.

Chapter
Ten

THE *Tigerfish* RECEIVED orders to return to Pearl Harbor on the seventh of May. The crew, disappointed because there had been no targets the *Tigerfish* could close with and attack, welcomed the order to return to base.

The promised two weeks of R & R had been cut short, however, to one week, when all available submarines were ordered to be made ready for sea to repel the expected attack on Midway. *Tigerfish* had taken station as one of nine submarines deployed in an arc two hundred miles west and southwest of Midway, cruising on the surface, its search periscope extended in a hunt for the Japanese Fleet.

Although the air was full of radio messages telling of contacts by aircraft with Japanese ships, hours went by before the submarine command in Pearl Harbor issued orders for the patrolling submarines to pursue and attack. When the orders to pursue and attack did come, no enemy was found; either the enemy had moved or the coordinates given had been in error. Captain Foster divided his time between the search periscope in the Conning Tower and the radio shack where the radiomen were busy copying the scores of messages filling the airways.

"There is no damned logic to this," Captain Foster griped to Joe Sibley. He held up a small bundle of radio-message flimsies. "Two hours ago we intercepted messages from a half-dozen pilots. They were giving the position of a Jap aircraft carrier they were attacking. We're no more than thirty miles away from that carrier, if the pilots have the position nailed down accurately, and I can't go over there and help out because our orders say we don't move off station until Pearl tells us to move. This is no way to fight a damned war."

"Keep a diary, Captain," Sibley said with a grin. "When you get to be an Admiral, you'll be able to show them how to do it."

News of the victory in the Battle of Midway came to the *Tigerfish* in orders to report back into Midway, top off with fuel and stand by to receive patrol orders coming by plane from Pearl Harbor. Captain Foster eased the *Tigerfish* into the narrow ship canal at the south end of Midway Atoll and cautiously made his way between Easter and Sand islands and anchored in the small lagoon in the center of the atoll. Standing on the bridge of his submarine, Captain Foster studied the two islands through his binoculars.

"Looks like they took a pretty good beating," he said to Joe Sibley. "Lots of wrecked aircraft over there on Sand Island. Looks like the buildings on Easter got a working over, too." He lowered his binoculars as the deck watch reported a small boat standing toward the *Tigerfish*.

"Patrol orders," Captain Foster said as he ripped open the manila envelope the boat coxswain had delivered to the deck watch. He read rapidly through the orders and turned to Sibley.

"Maybe we didn't get to do anything the last week or so, but we should be busy where we're going. They've given us a patrol area off the east coast of Honshu Island, the big island of Japan. Our area is just north of Tokyo Harbor. Let's get ready for sea, Joe."

The *Tigerfish* was running submerged, one hundred feet below the surface on a course that led to the east coast of Honshu, now eighty miles dead ahead. The Officer's Cook cleared away the plates from the noon meal and Captain Foster sent word to the Officer of the Deck to turn the dive over to Chief O'Brien and come to the Wardroom.

He spread a chart of the island of Honshu out on the table. "Joe has penciled in our patrol area," he said, pointing at the chart. "I value your opinions, so I'm asking you to give me your ideas of how we might patrol the area.

"The patrol orders say we should expect plenty of enemy shipping in this area, most of it going from north to south. Our area ends just north of Tokyo Harbor, but the submarine south of us has an area that ends just south of the harbor." He grinned. "Her skipper is junior to me, so that sort of leaves it up to me to scout the harbor if I think it will pay off. But what I want right now is your opinion. How would you patrol this area?" He waited as the chart was passed from hand to hand down the table.

"Hank?" Captain Foster said.

"Well, sir," Hank Copper said. "I think I'd patrol north and south up the very center of the rectangle as Joe has laid it out. At night we could zig and zag to increase our area of visibility. Before I submerged, I'd try to be at the south end of the area and close in to the land, as near to Tokyo Harbor as I could get, sir."

"That's sound thinking," Hugh Foster said. "Mike? You were a football player. How would you try to score from this position?"

Mike O'Connor hunched his big shoulders and stared at the chart on the table in front of Captain Foster.

"The patrol area's western boundary is the land mass of the island," he said slowly. "If I were the coach on the other side, I'd send my ships down the coast as close as they could sail. They'd be safer from attack if they were close to the coast."

"Why?" Hugh Foster said.

"It figures," O'Connor answered. "My ships would be harder to see at night against the land mass of the island. I'd only need half as many escort ships because I'd only have to guard the east side of the convoy, the side where the open sea is, sir."

"So how would you set up a patrol?" Captain Foster asked.

"I'd go in as close as I could to the beach," O'Connor answered. "Patrol on a north and south line. They wouldn't be expecting me to be there. It would be a sort of surprise if we hit them from there. Something like letting a defensive tackle come into your backfield without blocking him in the line and then nailing him with a blind-side block when he got into the backfield. It would be something the tackle didn't expect."

"I don't think a whole lot of your analogy but I see your point, Mike," Captain Foster said. He stood up. "Thank you. Joe. I want to see you in my cabin."

Hugh Foster sat on the chair in the cabin. Joe Sibley squatted on the edge of the lower bunk.

"O'Connor has the right instincts," Foster said. "We talked about that very way of patrolling yesterday. He couldn't know that. Don't say anything to him, but lay out the patrol area in that way. We'll go in tonight and submerge just off the coast."

"Yes, sir," Sibley said. He stood up and rubbed the lower area of his back. "I agree with you, O'Connor has the instincts. If he ever gets command, he'll make one hell of a record. If he lives, that is."

"He'll live," Captain Foster said. "He's got the killer instinct but he's not self-destructive."

The *Tigerfish* reached the coast of Honshu that night and submerged just before dawn barely a mile off the rugged coast of the island. The day order book read "Periscope observations will be made on the quarter-hour. All contacts, no matter how small, will be reported to the Captain."

Three small fishing vessels were seen during the day. A half-hour after full dark the *Tigerfish* surfaced, water streaming from her superstructure. Captain Foster went to the cigarette deck aft of the bridge and took up his usual night station. He would stay on the cigarette deck all night. Up above him the lookouts began scanning the horizon and the sky.

The contact came on the third night on station. The *Tigerfish* was running on a southerly course, the land mass less than two thousand yards off her starboard side. The after lookout grunted aloud and Captain Foster tensed on the cigarette deck below the lookout.

"Got me something out there bearing one-nine-zero, Bridge," the after lookout reported. "Can't quite make it out, sir." He moved to one side as Captain Foster climbed up to the lookout perch and squeezed in beside him.

"There's something out there, but it's damned hard to make it out," Captain Foster said. "Good work, son." He dropped down to the cigarette deck and went forward to the bridge.

"I'm going to run up the search periscope and take a look," he said. He went down the ladder to the Conning Tower, and Hank Copper, who had the deck watch, heard the hum of the periscope motor and saw the big-lensed search periscope steady on the bearing the after lookout had given. Captain Foster climbed back up the ladder.

"I'll take the deck, Hank," he said in a quiet voice. "Go below and sound General Quarters. We've got a convoy coming over the hill back there. I want Joe Sibley on the search periscope." Copper slid down the ladder to the Conning Tower and Hugh Foster heard the muted clanging of the General Quarters alarm and the quick rush of footsteps as the crew raced to their Battle Stations.

In the Forward Torpedo Room Dandy Don Miller surveyed his reload crew from his station between the torpedo tubes.

"You people up here, most of you, have been through this on the last patrol," he said. "You know how I want things done. When the Old Man gets close to shootin', I don't want to hear no talkin' except when the telephone talker gives me an order or takes an order from me. Clear?"

An engine-room fireman with a massive chest and shoulders, the reason he had been picked for the heavy work of reloading torpedoes, tied a sweat rag around his bull-like neck.

"A lookout told me we're running so close to the beach you could throw a baseball over there and hit sand," he rumbled. "I got the opinion this Old Man is a little nuts. Fuckin' O'Connor comes back in the engine rooms and tells us the Old Man asked for all the gold braid to give him an idea of how to patrol this here area and O'Connor suggests we go in on top of the beach and attack from there. I got the opinion that O'Connor is nuts, too."

"Why don't you tell O'Connor that?" a Third Class Torpedoman asked. "I'll clue you why you don't. You ain't big enough to take on that man if he takes off his gold and lets you go at him man-to-man. O'Connor would break your fucking back for you. He's such a four-oh dude he'd even give you first punch."

"Bein' a four-oh dude ain't got nothin' to do with him bein' a little nuts," the fireman said. "I've been in this submarine navy for three years and he's about the best Engineering Officer I ever saw. But he's still a litte nutty. I think he must of made All-American playin' without his fuckin' helmet."

"Knock it off," Miller said. "I had Mike O'Connor on the *Sea Bass*. Taught him how to be a torpedo officer. Ain't nothing wrong with his smarts. Now pipe down and stand easy. Talker, lemme know what they're saying on the bridge."

The telephone talker put his hand over the mouthpiece of the telephone set that hung around his neck as added insurance he couldn't be heard on the circuit.

"Mister Sibley is giving bearings on some ships," he said in a voice just loud enough to be heard by the men in the after end of the room. "The Old Man is telling the Plotting Party to put him on a course to intercept." The men in the Forward Torpedo Room felt the ship vibrate slightly as all of the ship's four main diesel engines suddenly coughed into life and began to roar.

"Old Man's on a course to intercept," the talker said. "Sibley says he's got four ships in sight. They're in a line. He can see two destroyers on the other side of the line of ships."

"He didn't say nothin' about any destroyers bein' between us and the ships, did he?" Miller asked. The talker shook his head.

"Maybe Mike O'Connor ain't so dumb, shithead," Miller said to the fireman. "We're between the ships and the land, and the destroyers are outboard of the ships." He left his station between the tubes and checked the impulse air gauges. "Six hundred pounds on the nose," he said. "If the Old Man says shoot, they'll go out of the tubes."

Captain Foster rested his elbows on the rail of the bridge and steadied the binoculars against his eyes. The Japanese ships were visible now, three big ships in a line led by a smaller ship. Above him the search periscope turned and then stopped.

"I have a positive ID on two destroyers outboard of the ships," Joe Sibley called up the hatch. "I make distance between the ships in line to be about one thousand yards. I make the angle on the bow of the lead ship to be fifteen degrees starboard, Bridge."

"Very well," Captain Foster said. "Plot, give me a time of intercept."

"Recommend we come right to course one-one-zero, Captain," Hank Copper called out from the Control Room. "Recommend we continue making turns for twenty knots for eight more minutes. At that time we should be one thousand yards from the target track and the first ship in the line should be seventeen hundred fifty yards up the track, sir."

"Come right to course one-one-zero," Captain Foster said. He bent his head to the microphone below the bridge rail. "This is the Captain," he said. "We have four enemy ships coming right to us. We'll be shooting in a few minutes. I want everyone on their toes. God bless." He straightened up and looked at the ships on the horizon for a moment, and then he lowered his head and directed his voice down the hatch.

"Plot. We'll attack on the surface. That first ship in the line looks pretty small, smaller than the others. We'll let it go by. First shooting target will be the second ship in the line. Second target will be the third ship in the line. After that it depends on which way the last ship of the line turns and what the destroyers decide to do.

"Shooting order will be tubes One through Six Forward. Set depth two feet on all torpedoes. I'll slow down to let the Forward Room open the outer-tube doors when the time comes."

"Set depth two feet on all torpedoes," the telephone talkers in the two torpedo rooms repeated. They told the Control Room that depth was set at two feet on all torpedoes and Chief O'Brien relayed that information to the Captain.

"Old Man's going to attack on the surface," the talker in the Forward Room said. "He wants to hit the second ship in the line of four ships because the first ship is too small. Then he'll go after the other two big ships."

Dandy Don Miller stood between his torpedo tubes, his left hand resting lightly on the brass safety guard over the manual firing key of Number One tube.

"He likes to attack on the surface at night," Miller said. "That's his technique, and when you got a technique that works, that's what you use. Know what I mean?" He grinned at the men in the room.

"Yeah," a voice came from one of the reload crew. "But when *you* talk about technique, you're talkin' about screwin' some broad, and what I want to know is who's goin' to get screwed this time, us or the Japs?"

The minutes ticked by slowly. Captain Foster looked at his wristwarch and then turned his face upward toward the lookouts.

"Keep a sharp lookout, men," he called out. "Keep your ears open. If you hear me yell to clear the bridge, don't waste a second getting down below." He looked at his watch and spoke down the hatch.

"Slow down and open the torpedo-tube outer doors." The *Tigerfish* slowed abruptly as the Maneuvering Room electricians cut back on the ship's speed, and then, as the two torpedo rooms reported all torpedo-tube outer doors open, the submarine picked up speed again and began rushing toward an unmarked place on the sea where the course of the enemy ships and that of the torpedoes of the *Tigerfish* would merge.

"Range to the first ship is three thousand yards, repeat, three thousand yards," Sibley said.

"Very well," Captain Foster said. "Start the shooting problem."

Lieutenant Wayne Raleigh cranked the data being fed to him by Joe Sibley into the TDC and watched the dials spin around.

"Solution, Bridge," he called out.

"Distance to the target track is now one thousand yards," Hank Copper reported.

"Range to the first ship is seventeen hundred yards, Bridge," Sibley said.

"Slow me down," Captain Foster snapped. "I don't want that first ship to see us."

"Aye, aye, sir," Hank Copper called out. "Making turns for ten knots, Captain. The first ship should pass ahead of us in one minute and forty-five seconds, sir. Second ship should bear zero-zero-zero in three and a half minutes at this speed."

"Very well," Captain Foster said. "We'll let the first ship pass." He stood in the center of the small bridge area, feeling strangely exposed. It seemed to him that someone, some lookout on the first ship, must surely see the *Tigerfish*. He turned and looked astern at the black bulk of the land and relaxed. It would be very hard to see something as small as the *Tigerfish* against that background.

"First ship is passing ahead," he said. "Give me a solution on the second ship as soon as you have it."

"Solution!" Wayne Raleigh sang out. "Torpedo track is eleven hundred yards. Closing to one thousand fifty yards . . . closing steadily, Captain . . . one thousand yards . . . nine hundred fifty yards . . . nine hundred yards . . . constant shooting solution, Captain."

"Stand by," Captain Foster said. He leaned his elbows on the bridge rail, his binoculars steady on the second ship in the line.

"FIRE ONE!" he yelled. He felt the shock in his feet and legs as a fist of compressed air hurled the torpedo out of the tube. He counted down from seven to one and drew a deep breath.

"FIRE TWO!"

"FIRE THREE! Shift target to the third ship!"

"All torpedoes running hot, straight and normal," Amos Stuckey's voice floated up through the hatch.

Captain Foster heard Joe Sibley calling out the bearing and the angle on the bow of the third ship in the line to Wayne Raleigh at the TDC and to Hank Copper in the Control Room, the frantic yet ordered haste to switch targets. He jumped suddenly as a booming roar echoed across the water and he saw a gout of flame soar skyward from the second ship in the line. A siren on one of the Japanese ships began screaming as a second explosion echoed in the night and a burst of flame enveloped the waist of the target.

"HIT! Two hits in the first target!" Captain Foster yelled. "Give me a solution on the next target, dammit!"

"Solution!" Wayne Raleigh yelled in the Conning Tower and then he flushed as Joe Sibley took his face away from the periscope and scowled at him for shouting.

"Stand by . . . Stand by . . ."

"FIRE FOUR!"

"FIRE FIVE!"

"Torpedoes running hot, straight and normal," the sound man reported.

"Lookouts! Joe! Watch for those destroyers!" Captain Foster yelled. "All-ahead full. Left fifteen degrees rudder." The *Tigerfish* heeled under the drive of her big twin screws as the rudder was put over.

"I'm going to run down their starboard side," Foster called out. A tremendous roar bellowed across the water.

"HIT! Hit in the second target!" Foster shouted. "My God! He's blowing apart. Oh, my God! Look at that!" The third ship in the line, hit in its engine rooms, was disintegrating, hurling great pieces of the ship high into the air as its boilers exploded.

"Destroyer standing this way between the first ship and the first target!" Joe Sibley yelled out.

"Very well," Captain Foster said. He was gripping the edge of the bridge rail, his feet seeming to dig for purchase through his shoes. He looked at the last ship in the line. It was turning to starboard, running for the land, trying to get close to the beach for safety.

"Give me a range on that fourth ship in the line," Foster yelled down the Conning Tower hatch. "Give me a range on that destroyer."

"Range to the fourth ship is four thousand yards. Range to the destroyer is four thousand yards. Angle on the bow is zero. Destroyer bears two-seven-zero, Captain. The other destroyer bears one-seven-zero. Range is five thousand yards. Angle on the bow is ten port, Captain."

"Clear the bridge!" Captain Foster shouted. "Dive! Dive! Dive!" He punched the diving alarm and followed the lookouts down the hatch. Pete Savage pushed by him on the bridge ladder and dogged down the hatch. Captain Foster squatted by the hatch to the Control Room.

"Rudder amidships. Two hundred and fifty feet. Close outer tube doors. When we pass one hundred feet, Mike, I want full left rudder. Rig ship for depth charge. Rig ship for silent running."

The *Tigerfish* slanted downward through the sea. As the long black needles on the depth gauges touched the figure 100, Mike O'Connor snapped out the order for full left rudder and the *Tigerfish* began turning toward her enemy.

On the bridge of one of the Japanese destroyers Captain Hiroaki Yamaguchi snapped out his orders. The Captain's face wore a perpetually bitter expression. Not only had the Japanese Navy suffered a humiliating defeat at Midway, but his father, Rear Admiral Tamon Yamaguchi, had gone down with his ship, the carrier *Horyu*. Captain Yamaguchi had sworn on his father's memory to have revenge on the Americans and now he had his chance. The American submarine that had torpedoed two of the ships he was escorting was in plain sight, dead ahead of him. On the destroyer's fantail sailors pulled the safety pin from the depth charges in the racks and Y-guns, grabbing for handholds as the destroyer's squat stern dug into the ocean in response to his order for full speed.

"The submarine is submerging, Captain," the Japanese Officer of the Deck reported. "Range to the submarine is three thousand yards, sir."

"Left five degrees rudder," Captain Yamaguchi snapped. "Is the attack problem running?"

"Yes, Captain," a voice behind Yamaguchi spoke. "We should slow speed and begin a sonar search in two minutes, sir."

"He attacked from the land side of the convoy," the Captain said. "He will think that we will assume he will run for the safety of the open sea. So he will turn the other way, head toward the shore. He has lots of water all the way in close to the beach. Where is the *Kazagumo*?"

"*Kazagumo* bears zero-three-zero, sir. Range is three thousand yards, sir."

"Signal the *Kazagumo*. The submarine dove one minute ago, three thousand yards dead ahead of our position. Begin box formation attack. We will locate and attack first." A searchlight began to clatter above Captain Yamaguchi's head as a signal rating sent the message to the *Kazagumo*.

"Slowing now for sonar search, Captain," the Officer of the Deck reported. Captain Yamaguchi nodded and walked to the starboard wing of the bridge and looked out over the black water. The lookout stationed in that wing of the bridge tried to make himself smaller so as not to touch his august Commanding Officer. The destroyer's Captain stared out over the black water toward the first ship the submarine had torpedoed. The ship had rolled over, its rusty hull shining wetly in the dim starlight. Somewhere out on the blackness of the water a man was screaming for help. Captain Yamaguchi's lip curled in disgust. It was a sign of weakness to cry for help. He despised weakness. He whirled around as he heard the word.

"Contact!"

Amos Stuckey, his mufflike earphones covering his ears, looked up with a mournful expression on his face.

"The twin screws that were turning up fast have slowed, sir. Bearing on that ship is zero-one-zero. There's another set of twin screws bearing one-seven-five. Both ships are echo-ranging, but they haven't found us yet." He winced as a ringing sound echoed through the hull of the *Tigerfish*.

"They just found us," he said. "Screws bearing zero-one-zero are picking up speed, Captain."

"Make depth three hundred feet," Captain Foster ordered. "Fifteen-degree down bubble." He cocked his head and listened to the increasing thunder of the destroyer's propellers. "Right fifteen degrees rudder." Mike O'Connor leaned over Harrington's shoulder and head and added his powerful arms to Harrington's effort to spin the big brass wheel to tip the bow planes to hard dive.

"Here he comes!" Stuckey said suddenly. Throughout the *Tigerfish* the crew instinctively turned their eyes upward as the sound of the destroyer's propellers pierced through the submarine's thin hull. A series of sharp cracks were heard.

"Man, this is it," Miller said as he took hold of the handles on the front of torpedo tubes One and Two. "The shit is right now hittin' the fan!"

The *Tigerfish* shuddered in the violent explosions of four depth charges that burst above the ship. Two more depth charges, flung out to either side of the destroyer by its Y-guns, twisted the *Tigerfish* in their explosions. Captain Foster, standing beside the gyrocompass table, was driven to his knees by the force of the explosions. Mike O'Connor, off-balance as he tried to help Harrington with the bow-plane wheel, sat down hard, bouncing as he landed on the deck. He scrambled to his feet, rubbing his rear end.

"Bastard knows how to drop charges, Captain," he said with a grin.

Hank Copper was busy erasing a long mark on the plot that had been made when he sprawled across the gyrocompass table, pencil in hand. He looked up as the ringing sound of a destroyer's sonar search beam echoed in the ship.

"The other destroyer bears one-six-five and he's speeding up, Captain," Stuckey reported. Captain Foster nodded his head and gripped the edge of the gyrocompass table and waited.

The attack ground on hour after hour. The destroyers, working as a practiced team, alternated their attacks. As dawn broke, Captain Yamaguchi accepted a bowl of hot rice gruel from a cook.

"That man down there is good at his trade," he said to the Officer of the Deck. "But we are better." He ate the rice gruel hungrily, wondering if other men felt as famished as he always felt when he went into action.

"Give me a triangulation," he snapped as he handed the empty bowl to a seaman. "I want to know how deep he is."

"Target bears zero-five-five and is four hundred feet deep, sir."

"That's as deep as we can set our depth-charge pistols," Captain Yamaguchi said. "Signal the *Kazagumo* and tell him how deep he is. Order them to set their depth charges to maximum depth."

The Gunnery Officer standing on the port wing of the bridge, his eyes half-closed as he concentrated on the bearings coming from his sonar operators, raised his right arm and then brought it down in a chopping motion. Four depth charges rolled off the stern of the destroyer and the Y-guns boomed as their explosive charges hoisted two heavy depth charges outward through the air.

"What time is it?" Captain Foster said. Chief O'Brien, standing by his battle station at the Christmas Tree, the flood and vent manifold, peered at the face of his wristwatch in the gloom of the Control Room battle lanterns.

"Just past zero seven hundred, Captain."

"Eight hours," Captain Foster said. "Long time. They're persistent." He looked over at Mike O'Connor. "How are your people doing on the planes?"

"We'll make it," O'Connor said. "I was thinking, sir."

"Go ahead," Captain Foster said.

"I noticed that when we went to four hundred feet, they didn't drop as many charges. That last time when they did drop four or five of them and we were driven down to almost five hundred feet, they didn't drop another charge until we came up to just above four hundred feet. We didn't leak when we were real deep. Maybe if we went down to about four hundred seventy-five feet and could stay there . . ."

"Make it four hundred seventy-five feet," Captain Foster said. "Let's find out if they'll drop when we're that deep."

The depth charging stopped abruptly as the *Tigerfish* reached 475 feet. The two destroyers on the surface kept up their sonar search, the sonar search beams ringing constantly through the submarine's hull. Captain Foster looked around the dim Control Room.

"Your point is made, Mike. They don't waste charges on us when we're this deep. But that doesn't solve our problem. There's almost twelve hours of daylight left up there and I don't want to take this beating all day long." He turned to the telephone talker. "Ask the Chiefs in the engine rooms how their bilges are, if there's any oil in them, please."

The talker relayed the request and waited. He turned to Captain Foster.

"Chief Apple says he's got about a hundred fifty gallons in each engine-room bilge, sir, mostly oil."

"Thank you," Captain Foster said. "Tell the Forward Torpedo Room I want them to drain Number One tube to WRT and vent it as gently as they can. I want two mattresses loaded into the tube." He turned to Mike O'Connor and Hank Copper.

"How much impulse air do you think we'll need to shove those mattresses well clear of the ship?"

O'Connor took a small leather-covered notebook he used to figure the submarine's trim out of his sweat-soaked shirt pocket. Copper handed him a pencil.

"What depth sir?"

"Say three hundred fifty feet."

O'Connor figured rapidly. "Water pressure at three hundred

fifty feet would be a little over one hundred fifty-five pounds to the square inch, sir." He looked at Hank Copper. "What do you think, about four hundred pounds of impulse air would give two mattresses a good shove out of the tube?" Copper nodded.

Captain Foster stared at the plot. He pulled the towel from around his neck and carefully wiped up the drops of sweat that had fallen from his face to the table.

"Make a note of the temperature and humidity for the log," he said.

"Temperature is one hundred twenty degrees. Humidity needle is on the peg at one hundred percent, Captain," Hank Copper said.

"Very well," Hugh Foster said. "Here's what I'm going to do. "They're triangulating us constantly. They know how deep we are. They aren't dropping any charges on us because we're down here at four hundred seventy-five feet. I'm going to suck them into making another depth charge attack, and when they do that, we'll go up and get them.

"So here's what we'll do. We'll ease up to about three hundred fifty feet. If they come in for an attack, we'll weather it, and while they're dropping charges, we'll pump the engine-room bilges overboard and fire the two mattresses out of Number One tube. We'll keep coming up and hope that when they see the oil and the mattresses they'll think they sunk us, and we'll nail them while they're slapping each other on the back. What do you think?" He looked around the Control Room.

"Might be a good idea to take the heavy mattress covers off those two mattresses and rip them up the middle with a knife," Hank Copper said. "I mean, if they see the mattresses and see them all torn up, it might be more realistic."

"Tell that to Miller in the Forward Room," Captain Foster said to the telephone talker. He turned to O'Connor.

"I want the engine-room bilges put on the drain line, Mike. As soon as he begins dropping charges, I want the bilges pumped overboard." He touched the telephone talker on the shoulder.

"Tell Miller to open his outer door on Number One tube as soon as the depth charging begins. Pass the word to both torpedo rooms to open all tube outer doors when we pass one hundred feet. Zero gyro angle on all tubes. Depth set two feet on all torpedoes.

"Mike, put the planes on one degree up and let her ease up to three hundred fifty feet. If he takes the bait and begins a run to depth charge, stand by to hit all the ballast tanks with one shot of high-pressure air and then shut it down. Go to hydraulic power on the planes and steering at the same time. Don't let me get above sixty feet, no matter what happens. Stand by to go deep in a hell of a hurry." He turned and began to climb up into the Conning Tower. Halfway up the ladder he looked down at O'Connor's big Irish face, split from side to side in a wide grin.

"I do believe you like this sort of thing, Mike," he said, and went up the ladder.

On the destroyer's bridge Captain Yamaguchi whirled around as his Gunnery Officer reported that the triangulation showed that the submarine was now at 375 feet and slowly rising.

"We must have hurt him," the destroyer Captain said. "He must have been leaking badly when he was down deep and now he thinks he can sneak away. Signal *Kazagumo* we will make a joint attack. *Kazagumo* will lead." He shrugged his shoulders as the Officer of the Deck raised an eyebrow a fraction of an inch.

"He has been number two on every attack," Captain Yamaguchi said. "Don't worry, we will get the kill. You'll see."

"We have the traget pinpointed, sir," the Gunnery Officer reported.

"Stand by for the attack run," Captain Yamaguchi said. "This will be the death blow. His luck has run out, I feel that in my bones." He raised his right arm and a sailor at the flag hoist yanked on a halyard and the attack flag, freed of its slip knot, snapped out in the morning wind. The destroyer heeled over as it fell in behind the *Kazagumo* to begin the depth-charging run.

The ocean erupted with explosions and giant gouts of white water. On the starboard wing of the bridge a sharp-eyed lookout cried out.

"There's a mattress! It's all torn up! Now I see oil, lots of oil!"

"We got him!" Captain Yamaguchi said calmly. "We got him! Sound, what do you hear from the target?"

"Sound hears rumbling noises from the target area, Captain!" The Gunnery Officer's voice was loud, almost a shout. He was laughing and slapping his knee. "Ayee! What a beautiful attack, Captain!"

*   *   *

Down below the surface the *Tigerfish* was slanting upward toward periscope depth. Mike O'Connor, juggling the trim figures in his head, was mentally figuring out how much water he would have to transfer to keep an even trim if one torpedo were fired or if two were fired at the destroyers. He looked over at Chief O'Brien.

"Stand by to flood Negative and Safety on my order," he said. He watched the depth needles carefully, calling off the depths as the *Tigerfish* rose steadily toward the surface.

"One hundred feet," he called out.

"Open all torpedo-tube outer doors. I'll shot from the After Room if I can. Don't let me broach." Captain Foster was squatting at the periscope well in the Conning Tower. He made a small motion with his right hand and Pete Savage pressed the UP button on the periscope control box. Captain Foster grabbed the handles of the periscope as it rose out of the well and snapped them outward and let the rising periscope pull him erect. He swung the periscope in a half-circle.

"Mark!" He twisted the range-finder knob on the right side of the periscope.

"Range is seven hundred yards. Angle on the bow is eighty starboard. He's dead in the water! Hard left rudder! I'm going to shoot as we swing by . . . stand by . . ."

"FIRE SEVEN!"

"FIRE EIGHT!"

The lookout on the Japanese destroyer saw the submarine's periscope at the same time the destroyer's sonar operator screamed out a warning that a torpedo had been fired from the bearing of the submarine. On the destroyer's bridge Captain Yamaguchi stared in disbelief at two white streaks in the water arrowing toward his ship.

"Right full rudder! All-ahead emergency!"

The destroyer's knifelike bow reared in response to the sudden surge of power to its screws as the first torpedo slammed home just below the destroyer's bridge. Captain Yamaguchi was blown into the air, his legs sheared off at his trunk by the explosion. As his body whirled through the air, he thought he saw his father's face, smiling in welcome.

"Don't let me broach!" Captain Foster yelled as the *Tigerfish* rolled violently in the explosion of the torpedo that had blown the Japanese destroyer into two parts. He yanked the heavy periscope around. "Mark! Range to the second destroyer is, oh, dammit! The sonofabitch is running away. Got his tail to us. Oh, damn, damn, damn!" He swung the periscope back to the bearing where he had last seen the destroyer he had fired at.

"He's broken in two. Joe, get up here and confirm this." He stepped aside and let Joe Sibley look through the periscope.

"I can see his bow and his screws, Captain," Sibley said. "You must have hit him dead amidships. He's busted right in two." He stepped back from the periscope and Captain Foster swiveled the scope around. "That other bastard is still going all-out. All I can see is his stern. Range is . . . six thousand yards and he's going like a bat out of hell." He motioned to Pete Savage to lower the periscope.

"Mike, take me down to one hundred feet. Forward and After Torpedo Rooms will begin a reload. I want fast work but I want safe work. Galley can serve coffee and sandwiches or whatever they've got available."

In the Forward Torpedo Room Dandy Don Miller surveyed his reload crew. He noted the heaving chests as the men fought for breath in the humid, oxygen-depleted air.

"Okay," Miller said. "We'll take this one tube at a time. Everyone take their time. Listen to me and don't do nothin' before I give the word." A Third Class Torpedoman laid out the block and tackle to pull the torpedoes into the tubes.

"That was my mattress you cut up and fired out the tube with Stuckey's mattress, Dandy," he complained. "What do I sleep on now?"

"You don't think I was going to fire my mattress, do you?" Miller answered. "You can hot-bunk with the Officer's Cook or you can volunteer to stand double watches. That way you'll be so crapped out you can sleep on your feet." His eyes found the muscular fireman who had earlier given his opinion about Captain Foster and Lieutenant O'Connor.

"The Old Man might be a little nutty, like you think," Miller said. "But I'll bet you a ten-spot that when you're an old dude, you'll be tellin' your grandchildren how you helped to cut up a couple of mattresses and fired them out a torpedo tube and fooled a Jap destroyer and then sank it."

Chapter
Eleven

LIEUTENANT ANDREW O'CONNOR climbed out of the Jeep he had requisitioned at the naval base and smoothed down his uniform shirt. He flicked some dust from his shoes with his handkerchief, squared his uniform hat on his head and marched up the sidewalk to the Oster house. He rang the bell and heard footsteps approaching, solid-sounding footsteps. A woman, tall and matronly, appeared on the other side of the screen door. He took off his uniform cap and tucked it under his left arm.

"Lieutenant Andrew O'Connor, ma'am," he said politely. He smiled tentatively. The woman opened the screen door and smiled back at him.

"I'm Caroline Oster, Lieutenant. Come in. Carol will be ready in a moment." He scuffed his shoe soles across a mat outside the door and walked into the house, his eyes taking in the spotless housekeeping. A Regular Navy household, he thought to himself. No dust anywhere. The furniture waxed and polished. A place for everything and everything in its proper place. Mrs. Oster led the way into the living room.

"Would you like something to drink, Lieutenant?"

"Andy, if you don't mind, Mrs. Oster. No thank you, I don't drink."

"Nothing? Not even water?" He could see the glint of amusement in her eyes.

"Yes, I do. I mean, I drink water, milk, coffee once in a while. I just don't drink liquor."

"Why?" she asked. "Every officer I've ever known likes a cocktail or a martini before dinner. And most of them like a lot of cocktails after dinner."

"Well, Mrs. Oster," he drew a long breath, "my father, who was born in Ireland, told me the Irish can't handle hard liquor and that it harms the body."

"And now that you're a grown man and a pilot you still obey your father?"

"I wouldn't dare disobey him if I thought he'd find out," he said with a grin. "I did try some whiskey once and it tasted to me like fuel oil smells. I tried wine once or twice but it gives me heartburn."

"Do you smoke?"

He shook his head. "My brother Mike and I were both in sports in high school and the Academy, and smoking doesn't go with sports. Mike was an All-American fullback at the Academy."

"I know," Mrs. Oster said. "My late husband, Captain Oster, was a great football fan. I remember the O'Connor name." She turned as her daughter came into the room.

"Very well," she said, her voice amused. "You may take my daughter to dinner, Lieutenant O'Connor. Have her back in quarters in time so you can get back to the base before curfew. It's exactly a twenty-minute drive from here to the main gate if you don't break the speed limit. Carol, this young Lieutenant doesn't drink or smoke, so don't try to teach him any bad habits."

"Mother likes to joke a lot," Carol Oster said as she waited while Andy spread a clean white towel over the seat of the Jeep so she wouldn't soil her dress.

"I think that's great," Andy said as he climbed back of the wheel. "A good sense of humor must be a salvation after you've lost your husband."

"She took it very well. Better than I did, I think. Daddy was never a combat man like you are. He used to say he was a CPA in uniform. But he loved the Navy very much, and he died, I guess you could say he died in battle."

"I think you'd have to say that," Andy said. "I'm showing my bad manners again, talking about sad things. Where would you like to go for dinner? I don't know this town at all."

"We could go to the Wagon Wheel. It's not far from here and the food is supposed to be quite good."

"You haven't eaten there?"

"No," she said. "Mother kids a lot but I haven't dated very

much since I came back from college. Not at all since the attack."

"That was over six months ago," he said as he pulled to a stop for a traffic light. "You're a very lovely girl, I'd think your date book would be full."

"I went out with a lot of boys when I was in California, in school. I graduated two years ago and came back home and I did date quite a bit after that. But not usually twice with the same man."

"Why not?" He grinned. "What did you do, what *do* you do, to frighten them away from asking for a second date?"

"You might as well know right now," she said. "I'm a person, not just a woman. I have a mind. I use it. I don't think I have to sit as quiet as a mouse just because I'm a woman when a man is talking. If I think he's talking nonsense, I say so and if he wants to argue about it, I'm ready. I've learned that most men don't like that in a woman."

"I think it's wonderful," Andy said. "My father and mother used to talk and argue politics and world affairs and about literature and all sorts of things. They did that all the time. Most of the time Mother used to win."

"That didn't make your father angry, to lose to a woman?"

"Great heavens, no! He loved it when she could argue him down. When I got older, I realized that lots of times he'd say something at the dinner table that he knew was wrong, just to get her started. They'd be arguing all through washing the dishes.

"But on serious things, like ethics and literature and things like that, one or the other of them would start a discussion going at the dinner table and my brother and I, he's ten months older than I am, we were expected to get into the discussion and we were listened to as if we were adults."

"My father was something like that," she said. "There's the restaurant over there on the right."

They lingered over after-dinner coffee, talking about their childhoods, their hopes and dreams. Andy finally looked at his watch and then rose and walked around the table to pull out Carol's chair. As he drove out of the restaurant parking lot, she half-turned in the Jeep's hard front seat.

"There's one other thing I didn't tell you about why I seldom dated the same boy twice. I don't believe in a lot of kissing and petting on a first date."

"You're a tough customer," he said in a solemn voice. "I was planning on doing just that but if you say no, then I guess I'll have to wait until tomorrow. If you'll see me tomorrow, that is."

"Are you asking me for another date?"

"Something like that," he said. "I guess I don't do it very well because there's something I haven't told you. You're the first girl I ever took out on a date."

"Oh, come on!" she said. "I remember you asking me if I wanted to dance when I was introduced to you at the O-Club. Then you decided there was too much noise to hear the music. If you know how to dance, you must have had dates."

"The Naval Academy tries to turn out officers who are gentlemen," he said in a solemn voice. "Dancing was required. The daughters of the officers who were instructors and the town girls would come to the dances and we were required to dance with them and make small talk. I wouldn't call that dating. It wasn't like what we did today, which was very nice."

"What did you have in mind for tomorrow?" she said.

"I don't know," he said. "Maybe we could take your mother somewhere, out to eat or for a drive, if I can get a better vehicle than this one and I think I can."

She burst into laughter, rocking from side to side. He pulled the Jeep over to the side of the road and turned in his seat and looked at her.

"Did I say something wrong?" he asked, his face concerned.

"You just proved that you never dated any girls," she said. "No boy I ever dated wanted my mother along. But I think it's a good idea. She hasn't been out anywhere except with me since the attack. I think it's a lovely idea. She'll be delighted."

He pulled into the driveway of her house, hopped out of the Jeep and trotted around to her side and helped her down. They walked to the front door hand in hand. At the screen door she stopped and turned to face him. She put her hands on his upper arms and lifted her face and kissed him, her lips soft and gentle on his face.

"I never kissed a boy on a first date in my life but I wanted to kiss you. You're a very sweet man and I like you."

He stood very still, his dark blue eyes studying her. "I like you, too," he said softly. "I like you an awful lot."

"Come by a little earlier tomorrow," she said. "Mother likes

to talk and she hasn't had anyone new to talk to for a long
time."

The midafternoon dinner date with the Osters, mother and
daughter, was pleasant, Andy thought as he drove back to the
base. Mrs. Oster had a deep, sly sense of humor that bubbled
over all during the meal. Carol, for the most part, had been
quiet, laughing at her mother's sallies and Andy's good-natured
attempts to reply. Mrs. Oster had gone into the house when
they arrived, leaving Andy and Carol on the porch. Carol had
walked him to the end of the porch where they could stand
behind a large bush that grew high enough to shield that area
of the porch from the street. She moved into his arms and held
him close and kissed him, this time with a firmness that he
suddenly wanted to match and did. As he drove away from the
house, he could still smell the faint scent she had left on his
lips. If he grew a mustache, he wondered, would her scent
stay longer? That evening, sitting in his small cabin aboard the
Enterprise, he wrote a letter to his parents and told them he
had met a girl that he wanted to marry, if she would have him.

The next day Andy took Carol to lunch at the Officers' Club
and on a tour of the *Enterprise*. They played tennis and had
soft drinks on the lanai of the O-Club and he took her home.
She turned at the door of her home and looked at him for a
long moment.

"Tomorrow, if you like," she said, "we could go on a picnic."

"That would be great," he said. "I haven't been on a picnic
since, oh, since I was in grade school. We, my family, used to
go out to the forest preserves, those are parks around Chicago.
It was like being in the countryside. In the spring of the year
you can go out there. My father used to drive us, and we'd see
the older Polish people, other Slavic people, the old-timers,
out picking the fresh mushrooms. Each group of people
seemed to have its own private place where they got the
mushrooms they liked. Yes, I'd like to go on a picnic. I can get
the cooks on the ship to fix up a pinic basket." He waited for
her to kiss him.

She opened the screen door. "I'll take care of the picnic
lunch," she said. "If you can be here about eleven? And thank
you for a wonderful day." He drove away, wondering if he had
done something to offend her, and reasoned that he had not or
she wouldn't have suggested going on a picnic tomorrow.

Carol watched him drive away and turned as she felt her

mother's hand on her shoulder. "He's a very sweet young man,"
Caroline Oster said.

"Yes," she answered. She gave her mother a quick hug and
went to her room to change her clothes, remembering the
astonishing musculature of his powerful legs in his white
tennis shorts. She couldn't remember seeing any man's legs on
a tennis court or in a swimming pool that were as powerful
looking as Andrew O'Connor's.

Andy O'Connor pulled his Jeep into the Oster driveway at
1100 hours the next day. Caroline Oster was sweeping the
front porch as he drove up. She put her broom against the wall
and walked down the steps.

"I like a man who's on time," she said with a grin. "Carol
should be out in a minute or two, if you don't mind talking to a
lady who's going to holler her head off at the city government
for not sweeping the streets. This dust and dirt is getting my
cork, as Frank used to say."

"I don't mind at all," Andy said, and turned as Carol came
out of the house with a wicker basket on her arm. He ran to
take the basket and put it in the back of the Jeep while Carol
kissed her mother good-bye.

"I'd better drive," she said. "I know where we're going and
you don't."

"Where are we going?" he asked as she backed the Jeep
expertly out into the street, shifted gears and began driving
away from the house.

"There aren't too many places to go to, nowadays," she said.
"All the good places we used to go to up in the mountains are
off-limits now because of military security. But I know a place I
went to once with Mom and Dad, up in the foothills of the
Koolau Range. It's nice up there at the edge of the rain forest.
The view is wonderful."

They followed a secondary road up into the foothills. The
road ended and she drove the Jeep across a flat meadow and
parked it behind a stand of trees. He got the picnic basket out
of the back of the Jeep and followed her, admiring her tanned,
slim legs. She took a blanket out of the wicker basket and
spread it on the ground.

"If you were with my brother Mike, he'd have a football and
he'd run those pretty legs of yours right off going out for
passes."

"Mother told me that your brother was a famous football player at the Academy," she said. "Did you play football?"

"I was too smart to poach on Mike's sport," he said. "I went out for track. I wasn't fast enough for the dash events, but I did fairly well in cross-country. And I wrestled some as a middle-weight."

"What weight is that?"

"A hundred and sixty-five pounds, tops. One hundred and sixty is my normal weight. I'm a shrimp compared to Mike. He's over six feet tall and weighs about two hundred twenty-five. He's as strong as an ox."

She sat down and smoothed her dark blue dress down over her thighs and stretched her long, tanned legs out in front of her. "You love your brother a lot, don't you?"

"Of course," he said. "He's my brother. He loves me. We're a very close family, the O'Connors." He sat on the blanket, his arms around his drawn-up knees and looked at her shyly.

"I wrote my parents after our first date. About meeting you."

"Oh," she said. She looked at him, her clear green eyes steady.

"I told them I had kissed you."

"I kissed you," she said, smiling. "You were too shy. And I had warned you I didn't kiss anyone on the first date."

"It would mean something to my mother, that I kissed you," he said in a low voice. "She knows I'm not good with girls. It used to worry her that I didn't have dates when I was at the Academy, and when she and my father came to the graduation, Mike had a half-dozen girls trying to kiss him after the graduation was over and I had no one. Mother is Polish, I told you that, and very beautiful, and I think she wants Mike and me to get married so she can spoil her grandchildren."

"That's a very normal thing for a mother to want," Carol said. "I think my mother would like me to be married and have children."

"This an odd thing to be talking about," he said suddenly. "I mean, talking about being married, having children for our mothers to spoil.

"Maybe it's the war. Everything seems to be speeded up, like seeing one of those old movies where they ran the camera real fast or something and everything is happening four times as fast as normal.

"It's as if we, everyone, were living at top speed. So many guys I knew, guys I flew with and ate with, are dead. Sometimes I think there's nothing left to hold onto." He hung his head, his eyes on the blanket.

"I told my parents that if you thought I was worthy of you, if you'd have me, I was going to ask you to marry me." He raised his head and looked at her. She returned his look with a steady gaze, her eyes calm and serene.

"My mother asked me this morning if I were in love with you," she said. He looked at her.

"I told her I loved you," she said. "I told her I had kissed you and it made my stomach feel like it did when I was a little girl and ate too much and wanted to upchuck and couldn't."

"You're a real romantic girl," he said, smiling. She laughed and laid back on the blanket looking at the leaves above her head. He sat looking at her, marveling at the long, sweet length of her legs, the elegance of her feet, the softly rounded mounds of her breasts. He put a hand on the blanket beside her.

"May I lie down beside you?"

"You'd better or I'll open the basket and begin eating everything in it." He stretched out beside her and tentatively put his arm above her head. She shifted and put her head on his arm and then she rolled on her side and put an arm around his neck. He moved against her and they stayed there for a long, long moment, and then his mouth searched for hers and found it.

"If you want to, you can. I love you," she said in a muffled voice. "But I don't know what to do next. I'm a virgin."

"So am I."

She sat up suddenly, grinning impishly. "This is a fine state of affairs, Andrew O'Connor! I've offered you my fair body and you've refused me. You're going to have to make an honest woman out of me if this thing is going to go any further."

"Very well, madam," he said. He sat up, crossed his legs and rose in a fluid motion and extended his hand down to her. "Please stand up, Miss Oster." He pulled her erect and then dropped to one knee in front of her.

"Miss Carol, I love you with all my heart. Will you marry me?"

"Proposal accepted," she said. "Let's eat." He looked up at her, his face crinkling in a grin.

"Like mother, like daughter," he said. "My folks are going to love you."

"When I was a little girl," she said, "my father used to kid me. He'd tell me that when I grew up and found a man I wanted to marry, I'd have to bring the man to see him and ask him for my hand. Now he's gone, so I guess I'll have to take you home and you'll have to ask my mother for my hand."

"Which I will do this very afternoon, my lady," Andy O'Connor said. "But after lunch, if you don't mind."

"Carol is twenty-three years old," Mrs. Oster said as she looked at the two young people standing in front of her, hand in hand. "She has the right to do as she wishes. But her father would be happy to know that you have observed the amenities, Andrew, old-fashioned though they might be." She smiled broadly.

"Your argument that the war seems to have speeded everything up," she continued, "makes me think back. Frank graduated from the Naval Academy in the class of 1916. There was a war in Europe, if you remember your history. We made the same arguments to our parents, that even though we had only known each other a few months, we felt we should be married, that we wanted as much happiness as we could have in case war came to the United States. In those days a newly graduated Ensign wasn't paid enough to support a pet cat. I went to work to pay for the apartment we rented. Frank was sent to sea a few weeks later and I didn't see him for six months. But we were happy, and when you came along, Carol, it made everything worthwhile. But that's neither here nor there. What we have to do now is get things started, make plans for the wedding." She looked at Andy, her eyes smiling.

"If I remember my Navy Regs, and I think I do, you'd better get back to your ship and inform your Squadron Commander of your intention to marry, see the Pay Officer about an allotment and arrange for some leave, if you can."

"Mother is practical," Carol said. "You'll have to get used to that."

Andy smiled. "As my father would say, you can't dig a ditch until you pick up the shovel. He got his start in this country digging sewers."

"And what does he do now?" Caroline Oster said.

"He's the general superintendent of the biggest contracting company in Chicago," Andy said proudly.

"So now he has others to dig his ditches?"

"He makes sure they have the shovel and pick it up. You're going to like my folks, ma'am and they'll like you. You're the same kind of people."

"I may never get to meet them if you don't stop calling me 'ma'am'," Mrs. Oster said. "My name is Caroline and see to it that you call me that, Lieutenant."

"Yes, ma'am," Andy said. He got into the Jeep and drove away, uttering a silent prayer of thanks that he had not taken advantage of Carol's offer when they were lying on the blanket, that he had not committed a carnal sin.

Andrew O'Connor and Carol Oster were joined in marriage in the chapel on the base. They walked out the door of the chapel under the traditional arch of swords held aloft by the pilots of his squadron. After a wedding reception in the Officers' Club the newlyweds left for Carol's house. Mrs. Oster had made arrangements to stay with friends for the next week, until the *Enterprise* went back to sea.

The fumbling uncertainties of the first two nights of the marriage turned into a blazing passion on Carol's part that Andy O'Connor strove manfully to meet. The days and nights blurred into one as the week passed.

"Will you be on the pier when we sail this afternoon?" Andy asked as he packed his bag.

"Of course," she said. "And I'll be waiting there when the ship returns. I'll always be waiting for you." She walked to the door with him, hugged him and pushed him through the open screen door.

"Go," she urged. "Go before I start blubbering."

The *Tigerfish* swept into the entrance to Pearl Harbor. On the sides of her Conning Tower she bore the evidence of her work. To the two white flags with a red ball in the center of each that stood for the two merchant ships she had sunk on her previous patrol had been added a Rising Sun flag to denote the destroyer she had blasted, and four merchant flags. Two stood for the freighters the *Tigerfish* had sunk in the attack on the convoy. The other two stood for two smaller freighters that had run afoul of the *Tigerfish* during the rest of the war patrol.

Lieutenant Sibley leaned over the side of the Conning Tower and looked at the painted flags.

"Would have been more of those if they hadn't taken us out of our patrol area," he grumbled to Captain Foster. "They must have been out of their minds, shifting us to the north. There was nothing to shoot at except those two small ships we got up there."

"Not out of their minds, Joe," Captain Foster said in a low voice. "Politics is the name of the game. If you're the Operations Officer and you've got a classmate in command out there and you want to help him out, you transfer him to a patrol area where there's something to shoot at. I didn't think they'd leave us in that area once we'd established there was a lot of traffic there."

"All I've read in the radio messages from the guy who took over our patrol area is that he saw a lot of ships but they were always too far away. The thing he did best was to tell the skipper of some other boat that traffic was coming his way. Far as I know he hasn't fired a single fish at anything. That's a hell of a way to fight this war, Captain."

"Let's forget it, Joe," Hugh Foster said. "Did you pass the word to the crew to clam up about the torpedo depths we used?"

"Yes, sir," Sibley answered. "They know the score. But I just don't see the sense of doing it this way. Every skipper who's fired at targets and set the torpedo depths where they're supposed to set them misses. There's something damned wrong with the torpedoes to make them run deeper than their settings.

"Saying that you set the torpedoes to run at thirty feet and got hits when they were really set to run at two feet—it seems to me that all you and anyone else who does this are doing is to reinforce those people who say there's nothing wrong with the torpedoes. Sooner or later someone is going to have to tell the truth."

"Whoever does that might find himself in front of a board of inquiry," Captain Foster said. "I've thought a lot about what you just said, because it's true. I intend to talk to some of the Captains who've been sinking ships and find out if they're doing the same thing we did. I'm sure they are, so maybe we can go in a group and make an appeal to test the torpedoes, fire some torpedoes with dummy warheads through a net and find out what's wrong. Maybe if four or five of us go together, they'd think twice about giving anyone a court martial." He walked forward to the bridge area where Hank Copper had the deck watch.

"I want you to make the docking, Hank," Captain Foster said. "Be on your toes. There's likely to be a big reception party waiting for us to tie up."

"Aye, aye, sir," Copper said. He wet his lips. The last thing I need, he thought, is to make a clumsy landing with a lot of admirals standing there watching me.

The reception party on the pier was large and loaded with high-ranking officers of the Pacific Submarine Command. A four-stripe Captain, the Staff Ordnance Officer, looked at the flags painted on the Conning Tower of the *Tigerfish*.

"By God, Hugh," he said, "you're one of the few damned skippers we've got who can shoot and hit anything. Most of the skippers complain about the torpedoes running deep or the exploders being defective. From now on I'm going to refer them to you, maybe you can teach them how to hit the targets. Getting that damned Jap destroyer the way you did, that was a hell of a thing, Hugh!"

"Thank you, sir," Captain Foster said. He saw Joe Sibley standing off to one side, a sour smile on his face.

Mike O'Connor read his brother's letter, his eyes widening. "Hey, Joe," he said to Joe Sibley, who was munching on an apple. "My little brother's got himself married to some girl here in Pearl!"

"He's a fly-boy, isn't he?" Sibley asked. "Fly-boys get the shore leave, and them on shore leave get the girls. You must have been the dumb brother to put in for submarines, Mike. You should have been a fly-boy, like your brother."

"I'm too big," Mike said. "I don't fit into the cockpit of a fighter or a dive bomber. Andy is only about five nine, weighs maybe one-sixty soaking wet. He fits into a dive-bomber seat."

"Been fitting somewhere else if he just got married," Sibley said. "No offense, Irish, just my weird sense of humor."

Driving out to the Oster home, Mike wondered why Andy had been in such a hurry to marry someone who wasn't Catholic. In such a hurry that he had not written to Mike to talk about his plans, hadn't, apparently, even told their parents until he had taken the marriage vows. He rejected the thought that perhaps Andy had had to get married because the girl was pregnant. Andy wouldn't get into that sort of mess, he reasoned. As close as they were as brothers Mike couldn't recall Andy ever going on a date with a girl. He grinned, remembering some of his own escapades at the Academy and how Andy had lectured him about carnal sin and the necessity of going to confession and making an act of contrition.

Maybe the girl was just looking for a husband, looking for a fat pay allotment and the insurance and the pension that would come to her if Andy should be killed. In his letter Andy had mentioned that her father had been a four-striper who had been killed by a bomb during the raid on Pearl Harbor. Her mother would be getting a pension, Mike thought, maybe the daughter was looking out for her future. Andy was such an innocent that he wouldn't think of anything like that. Although Mrs. Oster had seemed very nice when he had called to ask if he could pay a visit. He turned the car into the street where his new sister-in-law lived with her mother. He'd keep an open mind, he decided.

Mrs. Oster met him at the door. She stepped back and measured him from head to feet with her eyes, smiling. "You're much, much larger than Andrew," she said. "But you both have the same eyes. Please come in, Carol should be out in a few minutes." She led him into the living room and he sat down carefully on the sofa and then rose quickly as Carol walked in. She came up to him, her hand out, and then moved past his own extended hand and kissed him on the cheek.

"I would have known you anywhere, Michael," she said. "Andy talked about you so much, about how you grew up together, about your parents. He adores you, do you know that?"

"Andy's a good guy," he said awkwardly.

"Sit down," she said. "The coffee should be ready. I'll get it." She served the coffee Navy-style, with canned evaporated milk in a small pitcher.

"You didn't see Andy after you got in?" she asked. He shook his head.

"I haven't seen Andy since before the Battle of Midway. We went west after the battle and just now got back. We'll be going back to sea in about three weeks."

She looked at the red-and-white striped ribbon below the

gold dolphin pin he wore above his left shirt pocket. "Did you know that Andy has the Silver Star also?" Mike shook his head.

"He got it for the Battle of Midway," she said. "I asked him what he did and he said he did what everyone else was doing. He dive-bombed ships. That's all he'd say about it. There must have been more to it, mustn't there?"

"I'd think so," Mike said slowly. "But Andy was never one to talk much about what he did. Our father used to tell us never to boast because there might be someone within hearing who had done more than we did." He looked at each of the two women.

"Andy's a very good pilot, a really crack pilot."

"He said the same thing about you, that you were one of the very best submarine men," Carol said with a smile. Mrs. Oster finished her coffee and stood up, waving at Mike to remain seated as he began to struggle up out of the depths of the sofa.

"I've got to walk down to the store," she said. "You two have a lot to talk about." She picked up her purse and left. The silence in the living room hung in the air.

"I guess you want to know, your parents would want to know, why we married after knowing each other only a week," Carol said. Her voice held an undercurrent of defiance that Mike could sense.

"It's none of my business," he said.

"I think it is."

"Really, it's not. It's Andy's business. Your business."

"I think it is," she said firmly. "Maybe I wouldn't think that but one of my girl friends shocked me after Andy went to sea after the marriage. She asked me why I didn't marry an older man, someone with a higher rank so I'd get a bigger pension if he got killed." She was looking squarely at Mike O'Connor, her green eyes boring into his blue ones.

"I couldn't imagine anyone would think something like that," she said. "I'll tell you why I married your brother, Michael.

"I fell in love with him when one of his friends introduced us at a party that was given for the *Enterprise* pilots. The O-Club had asked all the single girls and women to go to the party. Everyone was drinking or drunk. Andy was sitting by himself. He wasn't drinking. One of his friends introduced us and we went outside and talked and drank Coke. I fell in love with him that night.

"I love him. He loves me. It's that simple. And I'm not pregnant. He didn't have to marry me. When I wrote to your parents, I told them that."

"That was thoughtful of you," Mike said slowly. "Although I don't think my father or mother would think Andy would get any girl in trouble."

"And I'm not one of those girls who follow the fleet," she continued. "I've forgotten what they call them."

"Seagulls," he said. "They call them seagulls, the girls who do that." He grinned at her. "I know Andy too well to think that he'd marry anyone he wouldn't be proud to take to our house in Chicago."

She let her breath out in a long sigh and relaxed against the cushions of the armchair she was sitting in.

"I believe you," she said. "I think I'd love your mother and father as much as I love my own."

"I'm damned, excuse me, darned sure they'll love you," Mike said. He looked at his wristwatch. "I asked my skipper for time enough to drive over here and meet you and your mother and I've got to get back. I want you to know something Andy asked me to do in the letter he wrote to me.

"He asked me to take care of you and your mother if anything happened. So I'm telling you that if you need anything, anything at all, and Andy is at sea and you can't reach him or anything, I'm standing by to help."

She rose from the chair as he stood and went to him and hugged him tightly and then kissed him on the cheek.

"Okay, big brother. I'll tell Mother that neither of us has to worry about anything. And I'll write to your mother this afternoon and tell her you came to visit us and what a bear of a man you are with your little-boy manners."

"Don't you dare," he growled.

Driving back to the Royal Hawaiian Hotel he thought about the meeting. Carol was a beauty, no doubt of that. She had that straightforward honesty that was such a big part of his parents' characters. To tell him about the girl who had given her the needle about marrying Andy, the defiance in her face when she had said she wasn't pregnant. That took guts, he concluded. He returned the salute of the marine sentry at the entrance gate of the hotel, parked the car and went to his room. He lay on the bed for a long time, thinking.

Chapter
Twelve

THE DAWN CAME SWIFTLY four hundred miles southeast of the Fiji Islands. A breeze kicked up small whitecaps and relieved the humidity of the night. Scattered over the ocean was a sight to make a seaman's heart pound: an Allied Battle Fleet of eighty-five warships and auxiliaries maneuvering, vigilant against attack from above or beneath the sea.

The fleet, which contained three Australian cruisers, was led by the battleship *North Carolina*, its upper works bristling with newly installed antiaircraft guns to complement its mighty sixteen-inch batteries. Three aircraft carriers, the *Enterprise*, the *Hornet* and the *Saratoga*, were making speed into the wind to launch and receive planes. The carriers' screening cruisers and destroyers maneuvered smartly to keep station on their carriers, changing course in response to the brightly colored signal flags that snapped in the wind from the carrier yardarms.

In the center of the Battle Fleet a line of troop transports zigged and zagged, their upper decks crowded with Marines—more than nineteen thousand fighting men and their officers. The air cover from the carriers droned overhead. In less than two weeks the fleet would strike.

The objective: Invade and capture Guadalcanal.

Lieutenant Andrew O'Connor sat in his squadron's ready room, his face somber. The losses from the Battle of Midway had been made up, but the replacement pilots were raw, untested in battle. Expecting savage opposition from enemy dive and torpedo bombers escorted by the fast, maneuverable Zeke fighters, the carrier Air Group Commanders shifted some of their best dive-bomber pilots into fighters, where

their experience could best be used to combat the Zekes.
Andy O'Connor, in company with his wingmates Red Olser
and Orv Masters, was assigned to fly Wildcat F4F-4s. Lieutenant O'Connor was named squadron leader of the thirty-six
Wildcats of the *Enterprise*.

O'Connor welcomed the responsibility. But flying alone ir
the Wildcat, he missed the presence of Roger Cain, his gunner
and radioman, missed Cain's cheerful voice on the intercom
missed his sharp eyes and his gunnery. Cain had asked to see
Andy shortly after the reassignment of pilots was made.

"You see, Mr. O'Connor, the way it is, the new Lieutenant
who's flying your old plane, he's fresh out of flight school and
he, well, he's pretty all-Navy. He doesn't talk to me wher
we're flying. I can't talk to him. I just don't like it much, sir.'
He smiled slyly. "Old Alabama Jones don't like him either
Alabama ain't happy even though you made him a Chief, sir."

O'Connor managed the transfer of Cain to another veterar
pilot and asked for and got Alabama as his crew chief. The
lanky Chief Aviation Machinist's Mate grinned when the
Division Yeoman told him of his new assignment.

"I kep' that little ole Lieutenant alive up to now and I guess
can keep doing that."

What was bothering Lieutenant Andrew O'Connor on thi:
bright, sunny morning was something he felt he couldn't tall
about with anyone, except the ship's chaplain. As a bomber
pilot he had been trained to attack targets. Ships. Shore
installations. Fuel-tank farms. He attacked targets, not people
He knew there would be people on the ships, around shore
installations, but they were removed, distant.

As a fighter pilot he would be engaged in one-on-one
combat. He would see his enemy. If he won his duel with the
other man, he would see that man die. Andy O'Connor didn'
think much about dying. He thought a lot about how it woulc
be to kill another man, and see the other pilot's plane ge
crashing downward into the sea. He sat in the ready room, hi:
head lowered, and prayed for guidance.

Lieutenant Orv Masters sauntered into the ready room anc
plopped down in a chair next to O'Connor. He peeled the
paper from a Baby Ruth candy bar. "Want some pogey bait.
Andy?" O'Connor shook his head.

"You ever hear of this place Guadalcanal?" Masters asked.
"Not before we started getting ready to invade it," O'Con-

nor said. "I talked with one of the Chiefs in the intelligence
section and he told me it's a bad place. Covered with heavy
jungle. The Marines are going to have to land there and fight
some pretty good troops, troops who threw the British out of
Singapore and our own Army out of the Philippines."

"Sounds scary," Masters said.

"It is. What could be real hairy is that this is an amphibious
operation and we haven't done anything like that in this
century. I think the last one was in 1898."

"Can't learn much from that one, I guess," Masters said. He
chewed reflectively. "But it should be a piece of cake. Did you
see that fleet out there? With all those ships, those Marines in
the transports, how can we lose?"

"Maybe that's what the Jap pilots thought when they formed
up over their fleet before they attacked Midway," O'Connor
said. "Maybe they thought they couldn't lose, they had us
outnumbered and outgunned. But they lost."

"You're too gloomy, old buddy," Masters said. "You're
supposed to set the example for us ordinary people, you're the
squadron leader, you're the happy bridegroom, remember?"

At 0300 on the morning of August 7, the invasion fleet
transports separated as they reached a point ten miles
northwest of Guadalcanal. Transport Group X-Ray split off to
head for Red Beach on Guadalcanal. Transport Group Yoke
veered north to attack Tulagi on the southeast coast of Florida
Island, twenty miles north and across the channel from Beach
Red. Flying high above the transports, Andy O'Connor saw
the cruiser *Quincy* splinter the predawn darkness with broad-
sides from her heavy guns. The shore bombardment was
backed up by the carrier dive bombers, stopping like predator
hawks before hurtling downward to release their bombs out in
front of the Marines landing on Red Beach.

At 0700 O'Connor's squadron was recalled. He passed the
relief squadron of fighters from the *Saratoga* and waggled his
wings in salute. When he climbed out of the cockpit, Alabama
Jones grabbed him by one arm.

"They want you all for an intelligence briefing like right
now," Jones yelled above the noise of the flight deck. "I'll
refuel the plane. You do any shooting? I'll have the belt feeds
checked anyway."

The Intelligence Briefing Officer, a pointer tucked under his arm, was pacing back and forth in front of an easel that held a large chart of the invasion area. He waited until O'Connor's pilots were seated.

"We expect strong counterattacks as soon as the Jap can get himself organized," he began. He tapped the chart with his pointer.

"The attacks will come from Rabaul, if our intelligence information is correct, from the west."

"What kind of planes, sir?" O'Connor asked.

"We assume the Jap will respond as we would in this case. He'll throw his dive bombers and torpedo planes against the invasion transports and supply ships. You can expect plenty of Zeke fighters. I can't tell you the caliber of the pilots you'll be facing because we don't know what squadrons the Jap has assigned to this area. He's been shifting aircraft squadrons around as if he were playing checkers."

"Go," Orv Masters muttered.

"I beg pardon?" the briefing officer said.

"Go," Masters repeated. "The Japanese play Go. They don't play checkers." The briefing officer raised an eyebrow and cleared his throat.

"The odds are pretty strong that you'll be running into fighter pilots who were blooded at Singapore and in the Philippines. The word we had from the British at Singapore is that the Zeke pilots look for single planes, so don't get separated from your wingmen.

"The Jap pilot in the Zeke is using a seven-millimeter machine gun with tracers to get his line of aim, and once he has that nailed down, he opens up with his big guns, twin twenty-millimeter stuff. He can't carry a lot of ammo for the Twenties, so he tries to get his point of aim with the small stuff and tracers. Keep your eyes open for the tracer fire. Orders are you stay here. Chow will be served, and if you have to go to the head, make it as fast as possible. That's all."

At 1315 that afternoon radar operators on the cruiser *Chicago* picked up enemy planes coming in from the west. Andy O'Connor and fifteen of his squadron roared off the deck of the *Enterprise* and headed for the area the *Chicago's* flight director gave as the location of the enemy planes. O'Connor and his flight circled the area for two hours without seeing anything. Back in the ready room he complained bitterly to the Air Intelligence Officer.

"Sorry about that foul-up," the Intelligence Officer said. "The radar operator on the *Chicago* obviously gave us a reciprocal bearing, read the bearing from the opposite side of the azimuth circle. That can happen. The flight director on the *Chicago* never had to work with more than two planes at one time, so don't blame him or his people.

"What I want to get across to all of you right now is the old lesson that we all should know. Don't get caught flying low. *Saratoga's* fighters saw a flight of Jap torpedo bombers and went after them. They went in low. They were jumped by the Zekes waiting up above. The *Sara* lost five Wildcats in twenty seconds." He drew a deep breath.

"The last word we have from the beachhead is that the operation on Guadalcanal is going well. The Marines on Tulagi are in a donnybrook, fighting for their lives. They'll be reinforced tonight."

"Will we be flying cover for the reinforcement operation, sir?" O'Connor asked.

"No need for that," the briefing officer said. "The Jap doesn't like to fight at night. That's all, gentlemen. Get a good night's sleep."

The American Admirals responsible for protecting the Marines from attack by sea and air were faced with a critical problem. There was no doubt that the Japanese would respond to the invasions of Guadacanal and Tulagi with everything they had. If the Americans could hold Guadacanal and Tulagi, they would have a base in the Solomon Islands, and from that base they could move west and threaten the Japanese bases at Rabaul and New Britain. The question was where would the retaliatory attacks come from? Would the Japanese attack from the west, where they had strong bases, or would they come from the heavily fortified stronghold of Truk, to the northeast? When would they attack? The three carriers with the invasion fleet were low on fuel. Fearing a concentrated torpedo and dive-bombing attack, the carriers were ordered to withdraw from the invasion area to refuel.

The news of the invasion of Guadalcanal and Tulagi struck Vice Admiral Gunichi Mikawa, the Commander, Eighth Fleet and Outer South Seas Force, like a blow to the pit of the stomach. Japanese intelligence had not detected the massive buildup of the invasion fleet. Mikawa called his operations staff into consultation aboard his flagship, the heavy cruiser *Chokai*. Standing in front of his staff, he read aloud a message from the Japanese force at Tulagi which promised resistance to the last man and asked for prayers for the enduring fortunes of war.

"We will answer the prayers of our brothers on Tulagi and Guadalcanal," the Vice Admiral said. "We will answer them with reinforcements, guns and torpedoes." He issued orders in a rapid monotone. The troops at Rabaul would be loaded aboard six transports and would reinforce Guadalcanal and Tulagi at once. All available capital ships would be assembled. The transports would leave for Guadalcanal as soon as the troops were aboard. The task force of warships would overtake the slower transports and protect them while disembarking the troops.

The transports steamed out of Rabaul and into trouble. The S-38, a small submarine, a nineteen-year veteran of service in the U.S. Navy's Asiatic Fleet, saw the transports leave harbor and got into position. Two torpedoes from the old submarine smashed into the *Meiyo Maru*, the leading transport, and blew it apart. Admiral Mikawa, afraid that his unguarded transports would run into more submarines, recalled them with orders to stand by until the force assembled.

By late afternoon on D-Day Admiral Mikawa had a force of five heavy cruisers, two light cruisers and one destroyer. He wanted to strike the Americans at night. His own gunners and torpedomen were highly trained in night fighting. A night strike would lessen the chance of American aircraft response to his attack. Japanese intelligence reports indicated that American carrier pilots had little or no night-flying training. The major problem that faced Vice Admiral Mikawa as he bent over his charts was that in order to hit the American invasion forces at night, he would have to make his approach to the channel that led to the invasion fleet during daylight. He decided to take the risk.

The S-38 spotted Mikawa's task force at 2000 hours that night, but the submarine was far too slow to get into position for an attack. The submarine radioed the location of Mikawa's force and its base course, but the American strategists did not consider the presence of a Japanese cruiser force so close to its own bases to be of any importance.

At 1026 the next morning, as Admiral Mikawa's force steamed on a course for Guadalcanal, the Admiral's fears of being sighted were realized. An Australian long-range patrol plane circled the Japanese force, now only 350 miles from Guadalcanal. Admiral Mikawa's luck held; the pilot of the patrol plane did not report the sighting until after he had landed at his base in New Guinea, and then not until he had enjoyed his post-flight tea.

The weather turned foul on the night of August 8. Rain squalls burst out of low clouds that shrouded Savo Island to the north of the western end of Guadalcanal. Walking the bridge of his flagship as his fleet raced at twenty-six knots through the rain squalls, Vice Admiral Mikawa rubbed his hands together in satisfaction. The dirty weather was to his advantage. He had no radar, but he had lookouts who had eyes like cats. He sent his attack order by blinker signal; the task force would proceed in single file, thirteen hundred yards apart. The cruisers would launch torpedoes at the invasion transports and supply ships and take all enemy ships under fire at Guadalcanal. The task force would then smash the invasion ships at Tulagi and retire at high speed to be out of range of the American carrier planes by dawn.

The Japanese force continued at high speed, running undetected through the rainy night. At 0130 the lookouts picked up the dark shapes of American ships patrolling southeast of Savo Island. The Japanese cruisers launched their float planes to drop high-intensity flares over the targets. As the flares burst into light, the Japanese cruisers wheeled and launched a broadside of torpedoes. The Australian cruiser *Canberra* took two torpedo hits and in the space of seconds was hit by twenty-four shells from the enemy guns. The *Canberra*, afire, its communications systems and engines dead, was out of the battle that was shaping up.

The U.S.S. *Chicago*, patrolling in company with the *Canberra*, took a torpedo that tore off part of the ship's bow. Despite the damage, the *Chicago* increased speed and headed for the only enemy ship its lookouts could see—Mikawa's lone destroyer that had been ordered to leave the formation and blockade the south passage past Savo Island. Unknowingly the *Chicago's* Captain was taking his ship out of the battle area and for some reason he did not notify his fellow cruiser Captains patrolling north of Savo Island that an enemy force was in the area.

Mikawa's lynx-eyed lookouts picked up the American cruisers patrolling north of Savo, and Mikawa turned his force in that direction. The cruiser *Astoria* was bracketed by a salvo of Japanese shells and her Officer of the Deck gave the order to return the fire. The *Astoria's* commanding officer, asleep in his cabin, was awakened by the gunfire and rushed to the bridge. Fearing that his ship was firing on a friendly ship, he ordered a cease-fire. The debate between the *Astoria's* Captain and the Officer of the Deck gave the Japanese gunners the time they needed to find the range. *Astoria* was crushed by a salvo of eight-inch shells and became a burning wreck.

The heavy cruiser *Quincy*, steaming ahead of the *Astoria*, was the next target. The Japanese cruisers illuminated the *Quincy* with searchlights and saw the *Quincy's* guns were not trained out to fire. Finally the *Quincy's* guns did train out and begin to bark as shells began to hit her. As in the case of the *Astoria*, the *Quincy's* Commanding Officer, summoned to the bridge from sleep, decided his ship was firing on a friendly ship and ordered his guns to cease fire. The cease-fire gave the Japanese the edge they needed; the *Quincy* was caught in the cross-fire from two cruisers and sunk.

The heavy cruiser *Vincennes* was the next victim of Vice Admiral Mikawa's deadly gunners. Caught in the nerve-racking glare of the Japanese searchlights, the *Vincennes* reeled under the blows of dozens of shells and torpedoes. Gutted by roaring fires, smashed by shells and holed by torpedoes, she slowed and then stopped dead in the water. The *Vincennes* sank at 0250.

In less than an hour of fighting, Mikawa's force had smashed and sunk four enemy cruisers. His own ships had taken only a few hits. At this point, victorious in a night battle, Mikawa hesitated. He didn't know where the Americn carriers were. He was certain the American forces had been alerted by the battle. He decided to withdraw rather than risk a counterattack.

The American destroyer *Ralph Talbot*, assigned to picket duty near Savo Island, saw the battle develop. Her Captain headed for the battle at full speed. The lone destroyer met three of Mikawa's heavy cruisers and took on all three at one time, opening fire with its deck guns and launching torpedoes. The Japanese cruisers returned the fire. Hit, on fire, listing badly, the *Ralph Talbot's* Captain conned his ship into a rain squall that hid it from the enemy gunners. The bold assault by

he *Ralph Talbot* convinced Vice Admiral Mikawa that a large
American force must be close by and that his decision to
withdraw was a sound one.

The Battle of Savo Island soured the success of the initial
stages of the invasion of Guadalcanal. In a space of less than
sixty minutes the Japanese Navy had inflicted the worst defeat
he U.S. Navy had ever suffered in battle on the high seas.
Four heavy cruisers, one of them Australian, had gone to the
bottom with a loss of over one thousand men. At least another
thousand men had been wounded or suffered severe burns.
The Japanese had demonstrated beyond argument that they
could and would fight at night and that their gunners and
torpedomen were superior to the American gunners in night
fighting, a bitter pill for the U.S. Navy to swallow.

Intelligence reports poured into the strategists aboard the
American carriers. A Japanese task force had formed up off
Truk. The force consisted of three battleships, three aircraft
carriers, five cruisers, eight destroyers and auxiliary ships to
supply the task force with fuel and ammunition. There were
reports that the Eleventh Japanese Air Force had been flown
into the airport at Rabaul with at least one hundred combat
aircraft. Admiral Mikawa's cruisers, now en route to Rabaul,
were also a force to be reckoned with in the strategists'
planning.

The victory in the Battle of Savo Island gave the Japanese
strategists confidence. Vice Admiral Mikawa had demonstrated that swift, bold action could insure that the seas around
the Solomon Islands could be controlled. With that control the
U.S. Marines on Guadalcanal and Tulagi would, in time, rot on
the vine. In the meantime the planes of the Eleventh Air
Force would hammer the Marines by day and warships would
steam down and bombard them by night.

The codebreakers working in their hidden quarters in Pearl
Harbor sifted through a mass of Japanese radio traffic and
discovered "Operation KA," a plan designed to push the
American forces out of the South Pacific. The codebreakers
pinpointed the movements of warships and planes toward Truk
Atoll and Rabaul and warned the American strategists that a
major move by the Japanese was pending. The carrier *Hornet*
was loaded with planes and left Pearl Harbor for the Solomons
on August 17. Two battleships, the *Washington* and the *South
Dakota*, were ordered to leave the East Coast and, in company

with several destroyers and cruisers, transit the Panama Cana
and make all possible speed to the Solomons.

Andy O'Connor gathered his pilots around him in thei
ready room on the *Enterprise*.

"We all know it's coming," he said, his face grim. "So I wan
to discuss some things I've been thinking about with you.

"The way I see fighter combat is this: It consists of three
elements. The first one is observation. The second is analysis
The third is action. Now let me take each one in order.

"By observation I mean—what do you see? Where is the
enemy? What is he doing? How many of them are there
Observation means seeing, and that means that you must
constantly, be turning your head, be looking. Even when
you're sure nothing is there to be seen. Keep looking.

"What I mean by analysis is—what is the relationship of the
enemy plane or planes to your plane? What is he doing and
how will that affect you? I think that here you have to do a lo
of planning when there is no enemy around, when you have
time to do it. It's like playing shortstop in baseball. Say there'r
men on first and third. If there's no one out and a ground ball i
hit to you, what do you do? Do you cut the runner on third
down at the plate? Do you bluff him back and then make the
force at second? If you have an idea ahead of time what you ca
do in any given situation, the odds are you can do it.

"The last thing is action. By that I mean what action is open
to you? What action is dictated by what you've seen and wha
your analysis of the situation is?" He sat back in his chair, hi
face intent.

"Those three elements if you link them together will,
believe, determine whether you win or lose. If you are quicke
to see what the situation is; if you are quicker to analyze the
situation; if you take action faster than the enemy, you have the
upper hand.

"Once you've taken action, you've come full circle and you
start over. Now what do you see? What does it mean? Wha
should you do? The cycle never stops.

"I think that if you consistently do this quicker than the
other guy, he has to be put in a worse and worse position and
he can't survive. You win."

"Sounds reasonable," Red Olsen said. "I think most of us d

something along those lines, Andy, but I never thought it out before. Should work."

"I think it's vital to survival," Andy said slowly. "And since six eyes are better than two, we stay together, we don't go off by ourselves in the middle of a fight. We fight as one unit."

The weather favored the Japanese for a reinforcement of their troops on Guadalcanal. It was typical mid-August weather for the region, low clouds, intermittent rain squalls, an uneasy, heaving ocean. Japanese transports accompanied by cruisers and destroyers were sighted by a patrol plane at 0850. *Saratoga's* dive bombers and torpedo planes took to the air. They were joined by a flight of Marine fighters and dive bombers from Henderson Air Field on Guadalcanal, but they found no targets. The Japanese patrol planes spotted the Americans and the transports pulled back out of range of air attack.

The weather continued foul the next day. By noon so many reports of Japanese ships had been received from search planes that the flight directors on the American carriers were confused. Fighter patrols ranged high above the *Enterprise* and the *Saratoga* to protect the carriers while the flight directors tried to figure out the location of the main body of the Japanese Fleet. Other fighter aircraft were poised on the flight decks, fuel tanks full, engines warm, ready to take off.

Sitting in the cockpit, Andy O'Connor listened to the constant flow of radio traffic, relaying the information to Alabama Jones, who was hanging over the cockpit rim, his feet braced on the boarding ladder. Jones passed the information from O'Connor to others in his crew, who relayed it to the Airdales on the flight deck.

The reports came in a steady stream. Five torpedo planes from the Big E had made contact. Two had launched torpedoes that missed and the others were driven off by Zekes. Two *Enterprise* dive bombers had found the carrier *Shokaku* and launched an attack, getting one near-miss. Two torpedo planes going in for an attack on the cruiser *Tone* were jumped by Zekes. One torpedo plane managed to escape the attack. The other was shot down.

In midafternoon the *Saratoga's* attack force of dive bombers and torpedo planes found the carrier *Ryujo* turning into the wind to launch planes. The dive bombers screamed down from fourteen thousand feet, releasing their thousand-pound bombs and then rocketing up through clots of antiaircraft fire, dodging the greedy Zekes that swarmed after them. The *Saratoga's* torpedo-plane pilots, heeding the brutal lessons of what happened at Midway, delayed their attack until the dive bombers were attacking and then they came in, flying low, attacking both bows of the carrier so that no matter which way the carrier turned, its hull was exposed to attack.

The carrier, mortally wounded by bombs and torpedoes, steamed in a circle, smoke gushing from the fires started by the bombs. A search plane from the *Saratoga*, dodging in and out of cloud cover, saw the carrier's crew abandon ship just before dusk. At 2200 hours that evening the *Ryujo* turned turtle and sank.

The attack on the *Ryujo* was confirmation that the battle was about to begin. The *Enterprise* formed up with her protective screen and headed for the enemy. The carrier took the center of the formation with two cruisers and six destroyers arranged in a circle around it and maintaining a distance of two thousand yards from the big carrier. The battleship *North Carolina* steamed twenty-five hundred yards astern of the carrier formation. Ten miles to the east the *Saratoga* was in the same sort of formation.

The weather favored the pilots of both sides. Towering cumulus clouds reached upward for thousands of feet and gave the attacking planes plenty of cover. But the glare of the lowering sun worried the American antiaircraft gunners most. They knew, as certainly as they knew they were breathing, that the attacks would come out of the sun.

At just past 1600 the radar operators on the *Enterprise* reported enemy blips on the radar screens bearing 320 degrees, distance 86 miles. Alabama Jones leaned over the rim of the cockpit and helped Andy O'Connor fasten his safety belts.

"Y'all come back safe, y'hear me?" Jones said, and punched his pilot gently on his shoulder. O'Connor nodded, crossed himself and lowered his head as he prayed. Then he raised his head as Jones unhooked the boarding ladder, maneuvered his fighter into position for takeoff.

At 1615 a fighter pilot to the northwest of the carriers yelled a warning over his radio. "Lots of enemy bombers at twelve thousand feet, with fighters above and below!"

Flying at eighteen thousand feet and six miles northwest of e Big E, Andy O'Connor sighted a flight of Japanese Aichi 9-I dive bombers, called "Vals" by the American pilots. He w the distinctive "pants" that partially covered the Vals' heels as he made his contact report. Then he tipped his Wildcat over in a screaming dive, coming almost straight down ut of the sun at the unsuspecting Japanese dive bombers. He oked quickly to both sides and saw Red Olsen and Orv Masters diving with him.

He centered his gun sight on the Val directly below him and ently squeezed the gun triggers on the joystick. A stream of ncendiary .50-caliber shells poured out of his machine guns. he plane exploded and he saw a large dark object blown out f the plane cartwheel in the air and realized, with a sickening eeling, that the object was either the pilot or the rear gunner. He shuddered, breathed a prayer for the man's soul, and hipped his fighter up and around in a tight circle to put the un at his back. Again he rocketed down at the dive bombers. he pilot of the Val in front of him suddenly realized he was nder attack and turned off to the right. O'Connor turned side him and opened fire, watching his incendiaries tear into is target's cockpit. The Val nosed over and began a long, creaming dive toward the sea.

O'Connor hauled his fighter upward, fighting for altitude, urning so the sun was again at his back. Suddenly he heard a ud banging sound, and with a sense of surprise that he later emembered as being almost indignation, realized that he was nder fire. He pulled the stick back into his belly. At the top of he loop he rolled over to his right and saw the Zeke that had ttacked him down below with Orv Masters's plane behind it. he Zeke staggered in flight as huge chunks of its right wing pped off and fluttered away, followed by the fuselage, artwheeling wing over shattered wing, down to the sea. He ashed by Masters, raising his right fist in salute, and bore in n the Japanese dive bombers. He opened fire on the tail of a al and delicately gentled stick and rudder to line up his sights n the other plane. He shook his head in disgust as he saw his acers flash by above the Val's fuselage and then the enemy lane jinked wildly to the left, downward and out of range.

"Left! Andy! Turn left!" Red Olsen's voice in O'Connor's arphones was almost a scream. Instinctively he kicked his left udder and slammed the stick over, rolling the plane into a

sharp diving turn. He heard Olsen's exultant "Gotcha, yo
bastard!" He whipsawed his plane and saw Olsen behin
another Zeke, his gunfire tearing the Zeke's tail into shreds
O'Connor swiveled his head around, remembering his ow
advice to see, analyze and act.

Down below him the two remaining Vals of the flight wer
diving toward the surface of the sea, turning away from thei
targets, heading for the safety of their carrier to the north
O'Connor looked around for his squadron. Olsen had followe
his target down until it had splashed and was climbing back u
to rejoin Andy. Orv Masters was steady on Andy's right wing
The rest of the squadron was scattered.

"Belay any chases to the north," Andy barked into hi
microphone. "Squadron will form on me above Mother."

The *Enterprise* waited for the attack that was certain t
come. The frustrated radar operators searched their screens
trying to identify friend from foe. All the blips on the screen
looked alike. All hands were under orders to be alert for low
flying torpedo planes, so on the flight deck and in the gun tub
along each side of the flight deck, and across the ship's stern
hundreds of pairs of eyes were straining in search of th
enemy.

High above the *Enterprise*, cruising at nineteen thousan
feet, a flight of Vals circled, their camouflaged underbellie
blending perfectly with the sky. At just past four in th
afternoon their flight commander sighted the torpedo bomber
from the *Shokaku*, tiny specks flying just above the waves
streaking toward the *Enterprise*. He waited, judging thei
distance, planning his attack so that the carrier's gunners, an
the protective fighter screen he could see below him, would b
preoccupied with his dive bombers. He judged the torped
planes were close enough, waggled his wings as a signal an
tipped his plane over in a dive toward the *Enterprise* belo
him.

A sharp-eyed sailor on the Big E saw a sudden glint c
sunlight on metal high above him as the lead dive bombe
went into its dive and yelled a warning. A battery of 20-mr
guns steadied on the diving planes and sent a stream c
sparking tracers toward the plane. The gunners on the five
inch batteries, using the tracers as an aiming point, opened fir
in company with all the other ships in the circle around th

Enterprise. Bright signal flags snapped out from the carrier's yardarms as the big ship heeled over in a sharp turn. The moment dreaded by the Commanding Officer of every aircraft carrier had arrived.

The Captain of the *Enterprise* raised his binoculars and stared out to starboard. "Here they come!" he snapped. "Torpedo planes bearing zero-six-zero. Right full rudder. Repel torpedo plane attack!"

Designated five-inch gun batteries on the Big E swung their gun muzzles downward and leveled at the incoming torpedo planes. Then the gun muzzles depressed even further and the gun captains began firing, aiming at the surface of the ocean ahead of the incoming planes. Great gouts of water rose as the shells exploded. The lead torpedo-plane pilot, realizing too late what was happening, flew into one of the water spouts and sheared off his right wing. The plane behind him jinked violently to the right and lost its left wing against the fifty-foot column of solid water thrown upward by an exploding shell.

The Vals' flight leader shot down through a curtain of antiaircraft fire, his flight following him. The gunners on the *Enterprise* could see him clearly now, could see the dark mass of the heavy bomb slung beneath the Val's belly. All over the ship, as the guns roared, men sucked in their breath, waiting for the Val to release its bomb.

"Sonofabitch!" Alabama Jones yelled from his 20-mm gun mount. "They's some of our damned Wildcats right in with them Japs! Fucking bastards get themselves shot down by us. If that damned pilot of mine gets my plane shot up, I'll purely kick his Irish ass!" He pointed upward at three Wildcats chasing the Vals downward, plunging through the same maelstrom of gunfire that was reaching for the Japanese planes.

The Japanese flight leader released his bomb and pulled his plane up out of its dive. As the plane hung for long seconds in the climbing turn, a five-inch shell smashed into its underbelly. Its bomb plunged into the water alongside the carrier and exploded, shaking the ship violently.

The Vals kept coming, one every ten seconds, down through a curtain of exploding antiaircraft fire. Three were blown out of the sky before they reached their drop point. Two others, their wings shredded with shrapnel, tried to crash their planes and bombs on the carrier's flight deck but failed.

The *Enterprise* took her first wound before the last of the twenty-four dive bombers had made its attack. A dive bomber, staggering as it came through the curtain of gunfire, released its bomb and scored a hit near the after flight-deck elevator. The bomb plunged downward through the flight deck, through the hangar deck, and then exploded, killing dozens of sailors and starting a huge fire. Less than thirty seconds later another bomb hit near where the first bomb had struck and shot downward through three decks before its delayed-action fuse exploded it in an ammunition-storage magazine. The resultant explosion ripped upward through the carrier, wiping out an entire five-inch gun battery of forty men and starting several more fires.

The battleship *North Carolina*, unable to match the thirty-knot speed of the *Enterprise* and her escorts, had fallen behind. A flight of sixteen Vals spotted the big battleship and zeroed in on it. But the Val pilots were unaware of the massive array of antiaircraft guns that had recently been installed on the *North Carolina*. None survived.

By 1700 hours the attack was over. The *Enterprise*, her steering gear damaged, steamed in a big circle, a great column of smoke rising from her deck as damage-control crews fought the fires and made emergency repairs. Fire fighters, dressed in their bulky asbestos suits, dragged sheet-metal plates over the holes in the flight deck that were gushing hot smoke, and the ship's artificers riveted the plates in place. Before dusk the *Enterprise* had repaired its steering gear and was steaming at twenty-five knots into the wind to take her planes aboard, despite fires still raging below decks.

Alabama Jones hooked the boarding ladder over the edge of the cockpit and climbed swiftly upward. He peered into the cockpit.

"You okay, sir?" He saw Andy O'Connor nod his head, and then Jones roared.

"What the hell you done to my plane? Look at this damned canopy, all full of holes back of your head!"

"I'm sorry about that," Andy said as he squirmed out of the plane. He climbed down the ladder and did a deep knee bend to relieve the cramps in his legs. Orv Masters and Red Olser came across the deck.

"How many you get, Mr. O'Connor?" Jones asked. O'Con-

nor lowered his head, thinking of the man he had seen thrown
out of his first target.

"I fired at three Vals in the first attack," O'Connor said. "I
saw two of them blow up. The third went down and crashed.
On the way back from that we ran into some Kates. I saw Red
and Orv get one each and I took a crack at another. I saw him
jettison his torpedo and turn away, but I don't know if I got
him."

"I saw him go in," Red Olsen said. "You got that one Zeke,
too, right after Orv and I got us a Zeke. I saw yours go in the
drink."

"Makes five," Alabama Jones said. "Makes us an ace,
Lieutenant. I'll have the flags painted on the fuselage after we
fix the canopy."

"Shouldn't be hard to fix," one of Jones's crew said.

"Then why ain't you fixin' it?" Jones growled.

The Battle of the Eastern Solomons was not as decisive as
the Battle of Midway. But it made its mark on history. The
main objective of the Japanese, to defeat the Americans on the
sea and in the air and thus facilitate the reinforcement of
Guadalcanal, had been foiled. The Japanese would continue
their efforts to retake the island in the months ahead, and
there was much bloody fighting to be done. But for the
moment the Japanese had been halted. The *Enterprise,*
heavily damaged by the two bombs that had hit and penetrated its flight deck, was ordered back to Pearl Harbor for
repairs.

Chapter
Thirteen

THE *Tigerfish* MADE the turn from the ship channel and began traversing the length of Pearl Harbor. Mike O'Connor, standing on the cigarette deck, raised his binoculars and studied the upper works of the ships on the far side of Ford Island. His heart jumped a little. The big flattop, could it be the *Enterprise*? If it was, it meant Andy was in port. He smiled to himself and then he felt a sudden wave of fearful doubt. Suppose Andy had been hurt or even killed? The nightly news bulletins that came in over the radio had mentioned a big air battle near the eastern end of the Solomon Islands. Had the *Enterprise* been in that battle? He didn't know, the news bulletins never mentioned the names of ships for security reasons. He lowered the binoculars and said a silent prayer for Andy's safety, a prayer he said every night he was on patrol.

The patrol had been successful. The *Tigerfish* had sunk four medium-sized ships in the area outside Manila Harbor and had missed two others. The retaliation by the Japanese destroyers had not been too severe. *Tigerfish* had suffered only minor damage from the depth charging.

Chief of the Boat Joseph O'Brien walked past the Conning Tower, grabbing at the hand rail to make sure he didn't fall over the side. Submarines on war patrol removed their deck stanchions and lifelines because they rattled when submerged. O'Brien looked up at the splashes of color on the dull gray and black side of the Tower. The row of Japanese flags that signified sinkings by the *Tigerfish* had grown. O'Brien nodded his head in approval. The *Tigerfish* had turned into a fighting ship. The crew had rounded into shape. They had performed well under the depth charging. There was fear, there was always fear during a depth charging. But it had been held in check. Give

ıe a little more time, he thought, just a little more time, and
ll have them whipped into shape, make real submariners out
f them.

"Those flags look pretty, don't they, Chief?" a seaman,
ɟaiting to take the mooring lines aboard when they came
ɫongside the pier, called out. "Those office commandos in
ʼearl see all those flags, they'll have to show us some respect,
ey, Chief?"

"You're missing a button on your shirt," Chief O'Brien
rowled. "Lay below and put on a shirt with all its buttons. On
he double!" The seaman looked down at his shirt, his mouth
ɪlling open, and then bolted for the open Forward Torpedo
ʇoom hatch. On the bridge Captain Hugh Foster turned to
ɔe Sibley with a smile.

"Never presume to get familiar with a Chief of the Boat
ɪnless you're wearing four gold stripes on your sleeve or
ou're his Commanding Officer, Joe."

"I know," Sibley said.

Admiral Nimitz led the welcoming party down to the deck of
ɦe *Tigerfish* as the seamen finished doubling up the mooring
ɪnes. He extended his hand to Captain Foster in greeting.

"Fine, aggressive patrol, Hugh."

"Thank you, Admiral."

"Something I wanted to ask you, Hugh. You'll be asked
ɓout it at the staff meeting, but I'd like to know now, if you
ɪave the information.

"Intelligence tells us they've intercepted messages advising
ɑpanese destroyers that they're being sent new pistols for
heir depth charges. The assumption we are making is that the
ɫepth-charge pistols have been modified so they can be set to
ɛxplode deeper than the norm. We know that when the war
tarted, their depth charges were much the same as ours; that
s, they could be set to explode no deeper than two hundred
ɪfty feet."

"They've done the modification," Captain Foster said. "I
ɲade a note of this in my patrol report. Their charges now
ɛxplode at roughly four hundred feet. I had to go down to four
ɦundred fifty feet and deeper. Once they triangulate on you
ɪnd find out you're down at four-fifty, they stop depth charging,
ɔut they keep their sonar search beams on you and wait until
you ease up a little."

"Our submarines aren't tested out for that depth," Admiral

Nimitz said thoughtfully. "How do you find the problem wit leaks?"

"Not too severe, sir. If you get down deep very quickly, an if you don't take any damage the leak problem isn't at all sever as deep as five hundred feet. But if you let them catch you an take some damage before you get that deep, then you have real problem."

Admiral Nimitz nodded slowly. "That's what we've got t know, Hugh. There's a reluctance on the part of the Captains go that deep and that may be why we're losing so many boats If you covered that in full in your patrol report, fine." H turned and looked down the deck and saw Chief O'Brien.

"A lot of people want to talk to you, Hugh. I'll see you agai this afternoon. There's an old shipmate of mine down the dec I want to say hello to. A very fine patrol, Captain." He shoo hands again and went down the deck to Chief O'Brien followed by his aides who were frowning at the Admiral obvious waste of his valuable time to talk with an enlisted man

The Chief of Staff, Captain Elmo Furst, grabbed Hug Foster by the hand.

"Damned good work, Hugh," he boomed, his red face spl in a wide smile. "Keep this up and we'll have to build a bigge Conning Tower so you'll have room for all your Jap flags. Now let's get down to business." He handed Captain Foster manila envelope.

"Lots of changes going on, Hugh. We're taking Joe Sible away from you. He's being sent to new construction, Eas Coast. His own boat. You said in your last patrol report he wa fully qualified for command, and God knows we need skipper with all the new boats we're building. You got anyone in you Wardroom you could move up to Exec? Be easier if I didn have to go through the fleet looking for an Executive Officer fo you. Lots easier to find you a new officer to train."

"I have a man I'd like to have as an Executive Officer, sir, Captain Foster said. "My Engineering Officer, Lieutenan Michael O'Connor. He's ready for the job in my opinion."

"He was a damned good football player at the Academy, Captain Furst said. "I like football players on submarines They're good team players. They carry the ball for thei Captains.

"Very well. Sibley's orders are here in the envelope. He's go another half-stripe and that should make him happy. Tel O'Connor if he doesn't measure up to your standards, I'll giv him command of a garbage scow in the harbor. You got your patrol report with you? Let me have it so I can go through it before the meeting this afternoon."

The two men moved away from the gangway and the relief-crew officers and Chief Petty Officers came aboard and fanned out over the deck, talking to the *Tigerfish* officers and Chiefs about needed repairs. The crew of the *Tigerfish* ignored them. They squatted or sat on the deck, reading their mail and eating cold-storage fresh fruit. Chief O'Brien gave them a half-hour to get through their mail and then ordered the crew to get into uniform of the day for the trip to the Royal Hawaiian Hotel.

After the relief-crew officers had left the ship, Captain Foster assembled his officers in the Wardroom. He handed a sealed envelope to Joe Sibley.

"Congratulations, Joe. You've got another half-stripe and you're going to have your own command. She's being built now on the East Coast. You leave in a week for your new ship. I'm very happy for you, I think you've earned command."

Sibley opened the envelope and glanced at the contents, his big, homely face flushing. "It's awfully nice of you to say that, Captain. I sort of hate to leave you and everyone else here but if it's for my own boat, I can't be too sorry."

"Didn't think you would be," Hugh Foster said. He nodded his head at Mike O'Connor. "Mike, you're moving up to take Joe's place. Make sure Joe doesn't take the ship's sextant with him. I'll give you the word on some reassignments of officers in a day or two. We'll be getting a George to be the new boy.

"The Chief of Staff said if you didn't do the job to my satisfaction, Mike, he'd give you your own command, a garbage scow in the harbor."

"Don't knock it, Mike," Sibley said. "You don't need a sextant and a copy of Bowditch to find out where you are in the harbor and you get liberty every night."

"Maybe Mike can find the entrance to Manila Bay easier than you did, Joe." Captain Foster had a faint smile on his cheerful face.

"Captain," Sibley said, trying to keep a straight face, "you know I go by the book. If my Captain has been to Manila before, during peacetime, and if he says that Sampaloc Point looks like the end of the Bataan Peninsula, I agree with my Captain. And when he asks me what the hell am I doing taking him up into Subic Bay instead of into Manila Harbor, I tell him that the war has changed a lot of things." He

lost his effort to keep a straight face as the other officers roared
with laughter and Captain Foster shook his head.

"Well, we did find Manila Harbor and we did sink some
ships, so everything came out all right," Captain Foster said.
He rose from the table. "I've got to go to lunch with Captain
Furst and his people and then to a meeting with the Admiral.
Mike, the buses will be here shortly to take the crew to the
hotel. I'll expect all of you to dine with me tonight at the hotel
if you haven't anything better to do."

Mike O'Connor sat at the Wardroom table after the other
officers had left to pack their suitcases for the two-week stay at
the Royal Hawaiian. Things move fast in a war, he thought. A
little more than a year ago he had been a happy Lieutenant,
junior grade, immersing himself in the intricacies of a big fleet
submarine, learning to be a Torpedo and Gunnery Officer.
Now he was the Executive Officer of a fleet submarine, its
navigator and his Captain's right arm.

Andy O'Connor found it difficult to talk to the Catholic
chaplain of the *Enterprise*. He was used to talking to priests.
They had been a large part of his life as he grew up on
Chicago's West Side. Priests and nuns had been his teachers in
elementary and high school. The long black cassocks the
Jesuits wore had been to Andy, as to the rest of the boys, the
ultimate sign of knowledge and authority. Even when the
priest who coached track came out to the field dressed in a
sweatshirt, shorts and track shoes, the cachet of the long black
Jesuit robe was there in Andy's mind.

The *Enterprise* carried several chaplains to minister to the
spiritual needs of the crew. Commander Peter Grass, a
grizzled veteran of twenty years of Navy service, was the
senior Catholic chaplain. Chaplain Emil Wofford headed the
Protestant chaplains, one of whom, by special dispensation
from the leaders of the Jewish faith, held services each week
for those in the crew who were of that faith. Like all the officers
and Chief Petty Officers, the chaplains dressed in khaki
uniforms except when they were performing sevices.

Commander Peter Grass sat in back of his gray metal desk in
a gray metal office smoking a pipe as Andy sat in front of him in
a gray metal chair that was bolted to the deck.

"I don't know what it is, Father," Andy said. "I'm finding it
very hard to talk to you. Maybe it's because you're in uniform,
the same as I am. I mean, sir, that I grew up with the Jesuits,

nd I sort of expect to see a priest in his robes. I know I'm
aying this badly, but I can't help it."

"I understand," Father Grass said. He relit his pipe with a
niny Zippo lighter and puffed reflectively. "If it would help,
ll go put on my cassock, or can you use your imagination and
aink of me as robed?"

"Let me try again," Andy said. He drew a deep breath. "I'm
orried, Father, about my wife in Pearl Harbor." The Com-
aander studied the pilot sitting across the desk from him. A
andsome young man, probably married to a very pretty
oung girl, and now he's far away at sea. He might have cause
or worry, the talk was that there were a thousand men in Pearl
Harbor for every woman.

"Go on, son," he said gently.

"We were both virgins when we got married," Andy said.
He saw the priest's eyebrows raise.

"I know that sounds odd, Father, but it's the truth. I was
aised in a strict Catholic family. My father is Irish, my mother
olish. I went to mass every day of my life when I was growing
p."

"I believe you. It's unusual, but it's refreshing to hear."

"We got married only a week or so before we sailed," Andy
ontinued. He lowered his head and stared at the gray metal
eck between his feet. "The first couple of nights were sort of
wkward and then everything went fine . . ."

"Go on," the Commander said in a soft voice.

"I don't like the word, Father, but it's the only one I know.
Carol became so passionate it scared me. It was, I don't know,
was as if I had broken a dam and I was being drowned in the
ood." He looked up, his face agonized.

The chaplain relit his pipe and puffed reflectively for a
noment. "The Church teaches us that physical love that is
ure and strong creates a very deep, very pure spiritual love,
ay son. I believe that because I have seen evidence of it
uring my life as a priest.

"The Church also teaches us that a man and a woman should
ome to each other in holy matrimony unsullied. Pure in heart
nd body. You are both blessed more than most couples if you
ntered your marriage in that state." He stopped and knocked
he dottle out of his pipe into an ashtray.

"I have seen much of what troubles you, Lieutenant. Permit
ne, as a priest, as a man who has lived for many years in

almost wholly male society, to make a guess about what
troubling you.

"I know what men talk about when they are at sea. You he
it because you cannot avoid hearing it. Men at sea talk abo
the women they have known carnally, women who, and I u
the vulgarities that I have heard, women with whom the
committed adultery because their husbands were at sea an
they had physical needs that they thought had to be satisfie

"Some of that talk, perhaps a small percentage, is true. Mo
of it is idle boasting. You say you are married to a woman wh
is passionate. You worry, then, that in marrying her you hav
opened a Pandora's box." He studied the pilot across from hi
and nodded his head slowly.

"Put your worries out of your mind, Lieutenant. If your lov
for each other is pure in God's eyes—and I am sure it is—on
good can come of that love. Does that help you at all?"

"Yes, sir," Andy said. He stood up. "Thank you for yo
time, Father, and your help." He went out of the chaplair
office, closing the door behind him. As he made his way towar
his quarters, he thought that the chaplain, good man thoug
he was, hadn't helped at all. He had jumped to a conclusio
that was wrong. He had not given Andy the opportunity to ta
about what was eating at his very soul, that Carol's passio
might be lust and that he was responsible for that feeling. Lu
was a sin. He went into his cabin. The ship's chaplain knew
great deal about men, about sailors. When he got back
Pearl, he'd find a Jesuit priest, someone who knew a lot abo
men and women and marriage. You could depend on th
Jesuits, they reasoned things out logically and came up wit
unassailable answers.

Mike O'Connor found a note waiting for him at the Roy
Hawaiian desk. He felt a surge of happiness as he recognize
Andy's handwriting on the envelope.

"You are invited to dine with Lieutenant Andrew
O'Connor and his lady at their home," the note read. "Pleas
call and confirm. Signed, Lieutenant and Mrs. A T. O'Conno

"P.S. Get over here and have some good chow, you big lu
Love, Andy." He held the note in his hand. Captain Foster ha
invited his officers to dinner. He reasoned that the Captai
would understand if he went to see Andy and his new sister-i
law.

Andy was waiting on the front porch of the Oster hom

when Mike rode up in a taxi. The two brothers threw their arms around each other.

"Easy, you grizzly bear," Andy yelped. "You'll break my ribs. Come on inside. Carol's cooking dinner." He led the way into the kitchen. Mike smiled at Carol and held out his hand.

"You can kiss her, dummy," Andy said. "She's one of the family." Carol wiped her hands on a dish towel and moved gracefully into Mike's arms and turned her face upward. Mike gently touched his lips to hers.

"Nice," he said, trying to keep his voice normal. "Very nice. You are a lovely lady, Carol." She shooed the two men out of her kitchen and they went into the front room and sat down.

"Her mother is staying with some friends while I'm in port," Andy said. "Did you bring your gear to stay over? There's no sense in going back to the hotel, we've got too much to talk about."

"In that little bag I dropped on deck in the hall," Mike said. "How's it going? You haven't been hurt or anything?"

"No," Andy said. "We flew air cover for the landings at Guadalcanal and then the Japs came after the fleet off the eastern Solomon Islands. That's why we're back in port. They hit the ship with two big bombs. Killed about seventy of our people and did a lot of damage that they couldn't repair at Noumea, so they sent us back here to the navy yard."

"You lose many planes?"

"Yes. Not as many as at Midway but too many."

"You shoot down any Japs, Andy?"

"Yes," Andy said. He looked away from his brother. "Five."

"What's the matter with you?" Mike said. "Five planes? That makes you an ace or something, doesn't it?"

"That's what everyone says." Andy turned and faced Mike. "We could always talk about things, Mike. We always did. I'll tell you what's bothering me.

"Dropping a bomb on a target didn't bother me. I was diving too fast, I had too many things to think about, to do, all at the same time, that all I thought about was keeping my point of aim, releasing the bomb at just the right second to get a hit and then getting out of the dive and away from danger.

"I didn't think about killing people. You can't see people when you're in a dive to drop a bomb. You don't look for them.

"I'm flying fighter planes now. Wildcats. The first plane I shot at in the battle we had in the eastern Solomons, I hit a Jap plane and I saw the pilot or the gunner, I don't know which

one, fly out of the plane. I could see he didn't have a parachute
on, he was that close to me. We were at twelve thousand feet.
If I didn't kill that man with the guns, Mike, I killed him
because he couldn't survive that fall. I killed other men. I saw
my gunfire go into their cockpits. I saw them throw their arms
around and then their planes either exploded or tipped over
and went down to crash in the sea."

Mike rubbed the side of his jaw with a finger the size of a
sausage. "Yeah. I think I can see what's bothering you. You
don't see the people on a ship before you torpedo it, so firing
the torpedo isn't a personal act. It's a group effort. Something
like what you went through could bother anyone. Maybe even
me but I was never as sensitive as you are." He stood up and
began to pace back and forth, his big frame dominating the
small room.

"It's something you'll just have to think through, Andy. We
didn't start this war. They did. I was here, at Pearl, that
morning. I saw the dead. I don't have any compunctions about
sinking Japanese ships and killing the people in them because
every time we've attacked the Jap ships, the escorting
destroyers have tried their damnest to kill us.

"Do you think the Jap pilots you fight against have any guilt
feelings about trying to kill you? You know goddam well they
don't."

"You don't have to take the Lord's name in vain, Mike,"
Andy said.

"Okay, I apologize. But answer my question."

"No, I don't think they have any guilt feelings. One shot up
my canopy just back of my head."

"Well, then," Mike said. The two men looked around as
Carol came in.

"Andy and I like our steaks medium well done," she said.

"Just light a match under the steer and singe him a little for
me," Mike said. "Rare, very rare, please." She made an
expression of mock disgust and went back into the kitchen.
Mike turned to Andy.

"Get it straight in your head, Andy. We didn't go into the
Academy to fight a war. We went there because there was the
Depression on and we agreed with the folks that a military
career was an honorable one. And it is.

"We've both been tested. Being a pilot must be a continual
test. So is being on a submarine. We passed those tests. We
were trained to serve this country and now we have to do that.

And the sooner you get it through your head that you don't have to worry about killing someone who's doing his damndest to kill you, the better you'll sleep and the better you'll do your job."

"I didn't know you'd turned philosopher," Andy said.

"I haven't," Mike said. "But when you've got the deck on the surface at night, you've got a lot of time to think. And I think."

"What about?"

"Some of the things you've just talked about. I've thought how, if we ever torpedo a Jap troop ship and there's no destroyers around, would I shoot the Japs in the water if the Old Man gave the order?"

His face hardened and he put his big hands on his knees. "I'd obey the orders. I'd shoot them in the water."

"Supposing it was you who had to give the order to shoot helpless men in the water. Could you give that order?"

"I've thought about that, too. They're not helpless men in the water. They're the enemy. Yes. I'd give the order."

"You've changed a lot, Mike. I remember the game when the quarterback told me you refused to run to the right because the defensive end on that side was limping and you didn't want to hurt him."

"Wrong," Mike said. "I didn't want to be accused of taking a cheap shot at a guy who couldn't use his wheels." He stood up and Carol came in.

The talk over dinner was mainly about the boyhood the two brothers had shared. Carol seemed to want to know everything Mike had done as a boy and a teenager. Mike obliged her and Andy chipped in with his own versions of Mike's stories. After dinner Andy and Mike cleared the table and did the dishes, and when everything was put away, the three moved to the porch and sat in wicker chairs. Mike pointed at Andy's shirtfront.

"That a gold star for a second Silver Star?"

Andy nodded. "I got the first one for not getting killed at the Battle of Midway. Got the second one for not getting killed in the Solomons. What did you get your Silver Star for?"

"Because the Old Man got a Navy Cross. All the officers in the Wardroom got a Silver Star."

"Navy Cross is awfully high, just below the Congressional Medal of Honor," Andy said. "Did he rate a Navy Cross?"

Mike nodded emphatically. "We attacked a convoy of four ships with two destroyers as escorts. He sank two of the merchant ships and the destroyers drove us down and held us down there for a long, long, time. We took a hellaceous depth charging for over eight hours. Did all sorts of damage to the ship.

"The Old Man realized we couldn't go on taking that sort of punishment, so he ordered a couple of mattresses ripped up and put into an empty torpedo tube. Then he eased upward in the water until the destroyers moved in to attack us again, and when they were depth charging—they can't hear anything with all that noise from the depth charges—he ordered the bilges pumped and the mattresses fired out of the torpedo tube.

"The Japs saw the oil from the bilges and the torn mattresses, and while they were yelling *Banzai*, he went on up to periscope depth and blew one of the destroyers in two. The other destroyer took off and left. He's a hell of a man, the Old Man."

"I take it you like him," Carol said.

"The proper way to say that is I hope he likes me after this next patrol."

"Why?" Andy asked.

"They moved me up to Executive Officer," Mike said. He smiled self-consciously. "On a submarine that means I'm the navigator. When we attack submerged, I run the attack problem and plot, and if we attack on the surface, I man the search periscope and give the Old Man the bearings and ranges of the targets, the angles on the bow of the tragets, that sort of thing. It's an awful big job."

"Exec!" Andy said. "That sure is a big job. We're proud to have had you to dinner, Executive Officer, sir."

"I suppose that you're flying around somewhere in the pack," Mike growled.

"I'm a squadron leader," Andy admitted. Carol smiled at the two men.

"You'll both be Admirals before the war is over," she said. Andy leaned over and touched her cheek with his hand.

"She keeps saying that to me," he said. "She keeps saying she's going to be the wife of an Admiral and the sister-in-law to another."

"You know why, don't you?" Mike said. "She's got it in for some Navy wives, and when she's an Admiral's lady, she can make them dance to her tune. That's why."

"That's not so," Carol said. "Almost every Navy wife I know

is a sweet girl or woman and they worry all the time about their men when they're at sea."

At midnight Mike yawned and Carol stood up. "You'll sleep in Mother's room, Mike," she said. "I put fresh linen on the bed this morning." Mike made his good nights and went to bed. He fell asleep almost at once.

An hour later he awoke suddenly, listening. He eased out of bed and knelt at the open window. The only sound he could hear was the rasping of coconut fronds in the night wind. As he rose to his feet, he heard the sound that had awakened him. It was Carol's voice, almost a wail. "Again, Andy! Don't stop now, for godsake! Andy! Andy! Andy!" He crawled back into bed as quietly as he could and put a pillow over his head and realized, with a rush of shame, that he was erect.

Mike looked at his watch as he finished his breakfast coffee. "I've got a car coming at zero nine hundred," he said. "I'd better get ready to leave. I'll give you a call tomorrow. I'd like to have you both and Mrs. Oster come to dinner at the hotel. The food is just wonderful. Okay?"

"You can't come over later, stay tonight?" Carol said in a wondering voice. "Was my cooking so terrible?"

"You cook just fine, honey," Mike said. "Andy can understand this. I'm a new boy as Exec. I've got a work load you wouldn't believe." He turned as a horn beeped outside in the street. He bent and kissed Carol on her forehead and reached an arm out and hugged Andy. He picked up his small overnight bag and trotted down the steps to the car.

Mike avoided going to see Andy and his wife at their house for the rest of the time the *Tigerfish* was in port. He took them to lunch every other day, pleading that the press of his work was too heavy to do any socializing, as much as he wanted to socialize. The day before the crew of the *Tigerfish* was due to return to the ship, the three of them lunched at the O-Club and Mike took Andy and Carol on a tour of the *Tigerfish*. Andy looked at the Spartan living conditions of the big submarine and shook his head.

"We've got people aboard the Big E who would desert if they couldn't have their movies every night on the hangar deck and if they couldn't buy an ice-cream sundae at the gedunk stands for a dime," he said. "This isn't living, Mike, it's penal servitude."

Mike looked at his brother quizzically. "I never thought of it that way. Everyone aboard has got his own bunk with a good mattress and a reading light and an air-conditioning outlet, right at the bunk. There's two showers for the crew and one for the officers and we can have a shower every third day. We go easy on water because we have to make our own and making it is a hot and dirty job. The food is wonderful and we all eat out of the same galley, officers and men eat the same chow."

"You mean you feed the whole crew out of that little bitty place with those four long hot plates and two small ovens?" Carol asked.

"The cooks feed seventy-two men out of the galley and the baker bakes bread and cakes and doughnuts and stuff at night. I never heard the cooks or the baker complain," Mike said.

As they walked into the Forward Torpedo Room to leave the ship, Andy touched a bunk rail. "I suppose the guy who has to pull this bunk out from under a torpedo doesn't complain?"

"No," Mike said. He grinned widely. "Maybe submariners are tougher people than you carrier people."

The *Tigerfish* went to sea a week later. As the big submarine moved slowly down the length of Pearl Harbor, the quartermaster on the bridge raised his binoculars.

"*Enterprise* is making a signal to us, Captain."

"Tell them to go ahead," Captain Foster said. The quartermaster raised a signal gun and pulled the trigger several times, telling the signalman on the bridge of the *Enterprise* to go ahead.

"Message reads, sir, 'To *Tigerfish*. Our best wishes for a successful war patrol. Signed, the pilots of the *Enterprise* and Andy O'Connor.' You want to answer, Captain, or just make a receipt?"

"Tell them we wish them safe landings and sign it *Tigerfish* and Mike O'Connor," Captain Foster said.

The *Tigerfish* blasted a good-bye with its whistle to the escorting destroyer outside the harbor entrance and turned its bullnose westward. Down in the Wardroom Mike O'Connor was laying out the course for Midway, where the submarine would top off its fuel tanks and then proceed to its war-patrol area—the shallow confines of the Yellow Sea where no American submarine had ever dared go.

Chapter Fourteen

THE *Enterprise* CLEARED the channel leading out of Pearl Harbor and stood out to sea. A string of signal flags burst from the carrier's yardarms. Answering signals flew from the yardarms of the escorting cruisers and destroyers and the escorting ships began to form their protective ring around the aircraft carrier as the small fleet set course for the Solomon Islands.

"Quite a sight, isn't it?" Orv Masters said to Andy O'Connor as they stood in the lee of the carrier's bridge structure. "I mean, the way the sun sparkles on the whitecaps, the ships. It's inspiring, like a recruiting poster." He glanced at O'Connor's brooding face. "What's the matter, boss? You find out you're gonna be a papa?"

"No," Andy snapped.

"You know what the ladies in my hometown in the hills of Kentucky say, don't you?" Masters said. "They say that if you keep trying, you'll find out how it's done." Andy turned his back on his wingman and walked away. Masters started to follow him and then stopped.

"Have to watch it, fella," he muttered to himself.

Andy O'Connor walked aft along the flight deck until he came to one of the five-inch gun batteries that were placed across the stern of the carrier. He went into a battery and sat down on an ammunition box, watching a lean destroyer rolling heavily as it cut across the carrier's foaming wake to take up its position in the formation. He sat, his hands in his lap, his mind going back to the morning after Mike had spent the night at Carol's house.

"Why do you suppose he left so soon?" Carol had asked. "He didn't say anything yesterday or last evening about having to

183

go back first thing this morning, did he? Did you know he had
a car coming for him?"

"I don't think he did," Andy said. "He was up before we
were, he had the coffee made. He must have called for
transportation then."

"But why? Did I do anything to offend him?"

Andy turned toward her, his face torn with the misery he
felt. "It was as much me as anything. Mike has always been a
light sleeper. He must have heard us during the night."

His wife faced him, her eyes blazing. "What you're saying is
that I embarrassed your brother, that I embarrass you because
I can't help making noises when we make love. Well, I just
can't help it. I love you and that's the way I am, and if you want
to know, you made me that way!" Her green eyes filled with
tears and she turned and ran into the house. Andy stood on the
porch for a long time and then he sighed and went into the
house and made a pot of fresh coffee. When it was ready, he
tapped softly on the closed door of their bedroom and called
out that the coffee was fresh.

She came out of the bedroom and sat at the kitchen table.
He poured a cup of coffee for her.

"I'm sorry," she said, wiping her eyes with a handkerchief. "I
don't know why I did that. I'm sorry."

"Maybe you're going to have a baby," he said. "I've read that
women who are going to have a baby often get upset for no
cause."

"I don't think so," she said.

"But you don't know," he said. She looked at him and saw
the eagerness in his face.

"No, I'm not absolutely sure."

"Maybe you, we, should go to a doctor," he suggested.

"Maybe that would be a good idea," she said. She smiled at
him and rose and went around the table and sat in his lap and
hugged him.

The doctor at the naval base was a gruff Commander with
very gentle hands. He stood in his office and looked at Andy
and Carol.

"Right now I'd say you aren't pregnant, Mrs. O'Connor," he
said. "But I'm hardly the last word in this area. I'm a GP and
on a major base like this it means that I treat just about
everything except things like this. I'd suggest you go over to
the naval hospital and let a gynecologist take a look at you.

Then you'd know for sure. I know how pressed for time you pilots are, Lieutenant, if you want me to, I can call a man over there and get you an appointment this morning." He walked to his desk and reached for the telephone as Andy nodded.

The gynecologist came out of the examining room and sat down behind his desk. "Your wife is getting dressed, she'll be out in a moment."

"Are we going to have a baby?" Andy asked.

"Your wife is not pregnant, Lieutenant."

"But she's okay, I mean, she could have a baby?"

"Of course," the physician said. "I gave her a pretty thorough physical. She's absolutely perfect, so far as child-bearing capability is concerned. She should have no trouble conceiving, should be able to bear children without difficulty."

"Then why isn't she pregnant?" Andy asked. "I mean," he lowered his head and blushed, "we haven't used any precautions, my religion doesn't allow that, sir."

"Any number of reasons," the doctor said. He leaned back in his chair and lit a cigarette. "You haven't been married long enough to really start worrying about it. And you are living a life of extreme stress. You're a fighter pilot, aren't you? That's a pretty tough existence. She probably worries a great deal about you. Worry could be one factor.

"Or," he looked at Andy O'Connor through a wavering cloud of cigarette smoke, "or it could be you."

"Me?" Andy said.

"You could have a low sperm count, Lieutenant. It's not uncommon. It's the first thing I recommend checking in cases where couples are worried about conceiving."

"I'm as healthy as a horse," Andy protested.

"That doesn't have anything to do with sperm count," the doctor said. "A low sperm count can come from a lot of causes. Stress is only one of them. Taking hot baths is another. Wearing a jock strap for several hours can cause a low sperm count. If you ever had rheumatic fever as a child, that could cause a low sperm count. Those are just a few of the reasons."

"I don't believe that is the case," Andy said stiffly.

The physician smiled slightly and stubbed out his cigarette in an ashtray. "Having a low sperm count doesn't make one less of a man, Lieutenant. It's just something that happens. We don't always know why. Sometimes a man is born with the deficiency."

"I'm not deficient, sir," Andy snapped.

"Of course you aren't," the doctor said. "You're a fighter pilot. But to set your mind at rest, I'd advise you to let me do a sperm count on you. That way you'd know and—". He raised one hand slightly as Andy opened his mouth.

"Let me finish, sir. If your sperm count is marginal, for example, you can inpregnate your wife. It would take some planning. She would have to keep records of her body temperature prior to, during and after ovulation. The data would indicate when her system would be most receptive to conception and you could try, then, to achieve the result you both seem to want so much." He stood up as a Navy nurse opened a door at the rear of the office and Carol came in. The nurse left the room, closing the door behind her.

"The nurse said you'd tell me the results of the examination, Doctor," Carol said.

"I've just told your husband that you're in wonderful physical condition," the doctor said with a smile. "You should have no trouble conceiving or in bearing children. To make absolutely sure of everything, I have suggested that your husband have a sperm count made, just to be certain."

Carol looked at Andy and saw the storm building in his eyes. "I'm sure Andy's in as fine a physical condition as I am, Doctor. Thank you so much for seeing us on such short notice."

The ride back to the house was made in silence. Andy parked Mrs. Oster's Ford in the driveway and then laid the table while Carol made lunch.

"The doctor said that one of the reasons you aren't pregnant is that maybe you're under stress, that you worry about me when I'm at sea," Andy said as Carol sat down at the table. "Do you worry a lot?"

She nodded her head. "Of course I worry when you're gone. But I don't worry to the point that I get upset. I pray for you each night. I think about you most of the time, wonder what you're doing. I don't think it causes me any stress. It's just normal worry, the same sort of worry all the girls have when their men are at sea." She reached for the coffee pot and poured.

"What was the doctor talking about when he said that you should have a sperm count made, dear?"

"He said that sometimes men have a low sperm count. He said it could be caused by taking too many hot baths, by wearing a jock strap or if I had had rheumatic fever when I was a kid. None of those things apply. I take showers. I haven't worn a jock strap since I was on the wrestling team at the Academy and I was never sick when I was a kid."

"Then we'll just have to keep on trying, won't we?" Her eyes were dancing. "We'll just have to keep on trying, over and over and over again!"

The next morning Andy told Carol that he had to go to the base on squadron business, that he would be back before noon. The doctor who had examined Carol the day before motioned Andy to a chair.

"You said I should have a sperm count," Andy said. "Can you do it? Will it take long? And how do you do it?"

The doctor nodded his head. "I think you're wise, Lieutenant. Yes, we can do it here. The count will take about an hour. All you have to do is go into the head with a little container and masturbate and catch the ejaculation in the container. The Chief Pharmacist's Mate will do the count for me."

Andy's face darkened. "Masturbation is a sin, Doctor."

"I know," the doctor said. "But this isn't self-abuse for the purpose of enjoyment, Lieutenant. It's a legitimate medical technique. If you wish, I can call the Catholic chaplain and have him reassure you that masturbation for this purpose is not a sin."

"That's not necessary, I guess," Andy said. He rose and followed the doctor into a small bathroom. The doctor gave him a small glass bottle with a wide neck and turned away as he saw the dark red flush creeping up Lieutenant O'Connor's neck and face.

The Chief Pharmacist's Mate knocked on the door of the doctor's office where Andy sat reading an old issue of *Life* magazine. The doctor took the report from the Chief and read it and looked up at Andy.

"I'm sorry," he said softly. "Your sperm count is so low that the Chief had trouble making any count at all."

"What's that mean?" Andy said harshly.

"It means that the odds are that you will never be a father," the doctor said.

"It means that I'm deficient and my wife isn't," Andy said.

"Not at all," the doctor said. "The fact that your body doesn't make sperm in sufficient quantity to impregnate your wife is not a deficiency. It's just an unfortunate fact. You're healthy, you're intelligent and by the ribbons you're wearing, you're efficient at your job. You have a long and useful life ahead of you. You and your wife can adopt a child or two and have a perfectly normal life. I would not say you're deficient, not in the meaning of that word."

Andy O'Connor climbed out of the five-inch gun battery and walked up the deck, threading his way between the parked dive bombers that were tied down at the after end of the carrier's deck. If only the doctor could have given him some hope. The trouble had started then, he reflected. His trouble. Not hers. She had turned to him that night in bed, her need for him as burning as always. He had responded mechanically, listening to her cries of exultation, half-revolted by her joy. The elderly priests in their weekly lectures to the boys in his class had stressed the sanctity of womanhood and taught that the purpose of cohabitation was for procreation. That was God's law.

She had made his favorite dinner the night before the *Enterprise* put to sea. Steak, a baked potato, peas and carrots and a fresh pineapple for dessert. He went into the living room after they had cleaned up the dirty dishes to read the paper. She came in a half-hour later dressed in a nightgown so sheer he could see through it. He could smell the perfume he had bought for her at the base.

"You have to leave early tomorrow morning, as soon as the curfew lifts," she said softly. She took him by the hand and led him into the bedroom. He had turned his back to her while he undressed. When he reached over to the chair beside the bed for his pajamas, they weren't there. He turned and saw her, lying nude on top of the sheet. He got into bed and she came to him. He kissed her gently and fumbled for the edge of the sheet under his back.

"I'm very tired," he said.

"I understand, dear," she said. She helped him free the sheet and draw it over him and got out of bed and put on her nightgown. She turned out the small lamp on the bed table on her side of the bed. He rolled over, his back to her.

He awoke out of a dream some time later. The dream disturbed him. The Jesuit priest who had taught family relations in his high school was lecturing the class on the sanctity of marital relations. He felt her slide out of bed and he heard a muffled sob as she went to the bathroom across the hall.

and closed the door. He got out of bed and tiptoed to the bathroom door and stood, listening.

Carol sat on the edge of the bathtub, holding a towel to her face so Andy wouldn't hear her crying. Andy heard her sobs and reached for the doorknob. Then he shook his head, pulled his hand back and tiptoed back to the bed. He lay down and pulled the sheet up around his shoulders and turned his back to her side of the bed.

The *Tigerfish* ran on the surface day and night until it was within aircraft search range of Kyushu, the southernmost island in the Japanese Empire. Mike O'Connor worked and reworked his navigation problems, making sure he was correct. Pete Savage, the leading quartermaster, who helped the navigator, gave his grudging approval of O'Connor as a navigator a week out of Pearl Harbor. The morning stars had been shot and the ship's position worked out. After the work was done, Savage went aft to the crew's mess for coffee and whatever the baker had prepared.

"Say one thing for that big Irishman," Savage said. "Sonofabitch goes about navigating this ship like he was building a watch. He's that careful. First time I see the sextant in those meat hooks he calls hands I figure he'd pop the adjusting screw off the arm minute he touched it. But he's got a nice touch. He can bring a star down to the horizon smooth as silk and get a readin', and you've got to hump to stay with him. When he starts the paper work, he's like he's got a set routine. Does it exactly the same way every damned time."

"I'm happy to know you approve of him," Chief O'Brien said from the coffee urn where he was drawing his first cup of the day. "Be tough on all of us if you didn't."

"Yeah," Savage said. "The real test is gonna come when we make the landfall. We're aimin' for that slot between the north end of the Ryukyu Islands and the southern end of Kyushu. Way he works, so careful, I'd almost be willin' to bet a fin that he makes it, right on the nose."

The *Tigerfish* hit the slot dead center and Mike O'Connor accepted the nod of congratulations from Captain Foster when periscope observations of the low island at the north end of the Ryukyu chain verified the ship's position.

"I want to pass this island called Cheju on my starboard hand, Mike," Captain Foster said as he stood with O'Connor at

the gyrocompass table in the Control Room, looking at the
chart. "Keep me well clear of the island. We don't know what
they might have stationed there, and I want to get to our patrol
area without being sighted." He looked again at the chart.

"The water is deep enough north of that island but it sure
shallows out when you get up the west coast of Korea."

"It's only sixty-five feet deep off the port of Inchon,"
O'Connor said. "When we get up north, off the Yalu River,
we'll have about a hundred twenty feet at the most, sir."

"Damned patrol area is nothing more than a wading pond,"
Hugh Foster said. "I'll be on the bridge the rest of the night.
We'll dive right after you do morning stars." He paused and
lowered his voice so only O'Connor could hear him.

"Hank's a good diving officer but he's still new at the job. See
to it you're here working out your morning stars when we
dive. I want to take her under as gently as we can. I don't want
to risk hitting the bottom."

"Will do, sir," O'Connor answered.

As the *Tigerfish* neared its patrol area at the northern end of
the Yellow Sea, the logbook began to fill with the sightings of
dozens of sampans and small junks. "Damned ocean is full of
small craft," Hank Copper grumbled. "They must be catching
enough fish to feed the whole Japanese Army."

The *Tigerfish* surfaced just past seven in the evening, easing
up slowly through the water to make as little disturbance as
possible. Standing on the bridge, Captain Foster could see the
tiny oil-lantern lights of the fishing boats.

"I doubt very much that any of those fishermen have
radios," he said to Wayne Raleigh, who had the Officer of the
Deck watch. "I don't want to get close to any of them if we can
avoid it. I do not, above all, want to run one of them down.
Keep your eyes peeled. Tell the lookouts to keep their voices
down when they report sightings of fishing boats. I'll be aft on
the cigarette deck. I don't want to know your every course
change to avoid contact with the fishing boats but if you get in a
bind, let me know at once." He touched Raleigh on the arm
and went aft to take up his all-night vigil. Shortly after
midnight a heavy fog set in and Captain Foster moved up into
the bridge area, straining his eyes to see the lights of the
fishing boats.

"I think we'd better get the hell out of here for a while," he
said. "Can't see much at all . . ." He jerked his head

suddenly to one side as a sobbing moan echoed through the thick fog.

"That's a ship's foghorn!" he said. "Must be something close by." As he spoke, the foghorn sounded again.

"Not the same foghorn," Raleigh said. "That first one was an F natural. The one we just heard was an A flat, sir."

"What are you talking about?" Captain Foster snapped.

"I majored in music, sir," Wayne Raleigh said. "Those were two different foghorns, sir." Another foghorn sounded and then there were several moaning blasts echoing through the fog.

"Four ships, Captain," Raleigh said. "An F natural, an A flat, a G sharp and a C sharp, sir. I make them to be off our port bow, Captain. I think they're moving aft down our port side. At least C sharp is farther forward than F natural."

Captain Foster looked at Raleigh and then turned and leaned down over the hatch down to the Conning Tower.

"Go to General Quarters. Don't sound the alarm. No running. No noise. Plotting Party stand by. Mr. O'Connor on the search periscope. Open all torpedo tubes. Set depth on all torpedoes at two feet. Make it fast and make it quiet!"

The foghorns wailed, muffled by the fog. Lieutenant (jg) Wayne Raleigh, USNR, stood listening, his head cocked to one side.

"F natural is leading, followed by G sharp and then A flat and C sharp. Coming down our port beam, Captain, and not too far away."

"Right full rudder," Captain Foster said into the bridge microphone.

"Right full rudder, aye, rudder is being put full right, Bridge," Chief O'Brien's voice came up through the hatch, muted from its usual bass roar. "Ship is at General Quarters, all torpedo-tube outer doors open. Depth set all torpedoes is two feet. Plotting Party standing by. Mr. O'Connor is in the Conning Tower."

The *Tigerfish* turned to the right in a big circle. The foghorns were blowing steadily, seeming to surround the submarine with their fog-blurred moaning. Wayne Raleigh stood in the center of the small bridge, his eyes closed, his face intent as he listened.

"F natural is off our starboard beam, Captain."

"How can you be sure? The damned things sound as if they're all around us."

"Harmonics, sir. The fog seems to make the sound diffuse but I can pick up the basic tones, Captain."

"Rudder amidships, meet her head right there," Captain Foster said into the bridge microphone. "Make turns for five knots. Stand by to go to all-ahead emergency on the double." The acknowledgment of the orders came back as the *Tigerfish* steadied on course and slowed down.

"Sound reports four sets of screws, all single screws, all turning slow. Bearing on the closest screw is zero-four-zero, Bridge."

"Very well," Captain Foster said. "Mike, see if you can pick up a masthead light through the search 'scope. Maybe you can get a reflection off the fog from that high up."

"Wind is picking up, Bridge," the starboard lookout said in a low voice. "Before there wasn't any wind, and now I can feel it on my face."

Captain Foster put his hands on the bridge rail and looked at the gray fog that surrounded his ship. Ahead of him, astern, all around him, the eerie moans of the foghorns sounded. He felt the sudden freshness of a breeze on his face.

"I've got a masthead light bearing zero-three-zero, Bridge," Mike O'Connor's voice echoed in the bridge space.

"Keep your voice down, Mike," Captain Foster said. He bent his face to the bridge microphone and spoke in a low voice.

"Plot, this is what we've got. The fog is still pretty heavy but a breeze seems to be trying to blow. I haven't seen the targets yet. As soon as I do, I'm going to shoot. I may have to eyeball it, so tell both torpedo rooms to stand by to shoot manually on my order." He straightened up from the microphone and stared into the fog.

"Like sailing down the inside of a peacoat sleeve," he grumbled.

"Wind's picking up, Bridge," the starboard lookout said suddenly. "I can see a ship! Bearing is one-two-zero, Bridge."

The fog was beginning to shred under the push of the light breeze. O'Connor's voice from the Conning Tower was sharp.

"Four ships in a line, Bridge. Bearing on the lead ship is one-one-seven. Range to that target is nine hundred yards. Angle on the bow is forty port."

"Right five degrees rudder. All engines on the line," Captain Foster ordered. He leaned on the bridge rail, trying to see through the thick shreds of fog ahead of his ship's bow. He heard the coughing roar of three diesel engines as they started.

"All four engines on the line, Bridge."

"Very well," Captain Foster said. The fog thinned ahead of the *Tigerfish* and he saw the dim bulk of a freighter.

"We have a shooting solution on the ship dead ahead, Bridge," O'Connor called up the hatch.

"FIRE ONE!" Captain Foster waited, counting down from seven to one.

"FIRE TWO! Shift target to that second ship. I can just see him!"

"Solution!" O'Conner yelled out.

"FIRE THREE!" As he counted down, a muffled explosion roared in the foggy night and he saw a sheet of flame reaching upward through the fog and heard a second explosion boom.

"HIT! Hit on the first target. HIT! Hit on the second target! All-back emergency! That third ship is turning to port! Fourth ship is behind it. Give me a setup on that third ship. Fast, dammit! All stop! All ahead one third. Hold her, meet her head right there!"

The *Tigerfish* shuddered in the water as the twin propellers went from all-back emergency to one-third ahead. The fog-horns were blaring now, and a siren on one of the ships was screaming in the night.

"Solution on the third ship, Bridge."

"FIRE FOUR!"

"FIRE FIVE! Dammit, that fourth ship is backing down! Left fifteen degrees rudder. All ahead two thirds." A booming explosion roared in the night and a gush of flame illuminated the third ship.

"HIT! Hit on the third target. All ahead full. Mike, I want to swing around and get a shot at that fourth ship from the After Room before he gets away!" Another explosion ripped the night apart.

"Bridge!" Mike O'Connor yelled out. "That fourth ship just blew up! I could see her whole stern blow off!"

"Make a periscope search for escorts," Captain Foster ordered. "They've got to be around somewhere and there's still a lot of fog close to the surface up here." He heard the search periscope turning above him.

"Negative on the search, Captain," O'Connor called out. "All I can see is a lot of fishing-boat lights, Bridge."

"Keep searching," Captain Foster ordered.

"I've got something, looks like the bottom of a ship, Bridge," the port lookout yelled out. "Bearing is two-seven-zero and close aboard, Bridge."

"Right five degrees rudder. Make turns for five knots," Captain Foster said.

"That might be F natural," Wayne Raleigh said as the *Tigerfish* eased by the overturned hull of a freighter. "She had a nice kind of foghorn. Melodious." A lifeboat appeared through a rift in one of the thick patches of fog clinging to the surface of the water. Voices were shouting from it.

"Negative on the periscope search, still searching, Bridge," O'Connor called up the hatch. "I've got one ship almost under bearing zero-nine-zero. Another target just went under. I saw four ships go down, Bridge."

"Relieve Mister O'Connor at the periscope, Wayne," Captain Foster said. "I want a constant search for escorts or anything else. Tell Mister O'Connor I want a course out of here to as deep a water as he can find in this damned wading pond before we dive."

The *Tigerfish* dove an hour later in 150 feet of water. Captain Foster ordered Chief O'Brien to take over the dive and assembled the officers in the Wardroom.

"I don't think the people who run torpedo-attack schools ever thought of making a surface attack on four ships in a heavy fog," he said with a wry grin. "If the Navy, in its infinite wisdom, hadn't sent us a Reserve Officer who majored in music as a replacement we might not have got off a shot before we were rammed by ships we couldn't see. Wayne sorted out the foghorns and was able to tell me where the ships were." Wayne Raleigh blushed and lowered his head.

"What sort of a plot did you get, Sullie?" He turned to Lieutenant Saul Silver.

"Kind of mixed up after the second target, sir. We had a good setup on Number Three but when Mike reported the fourth ship was hit and going down, it got confusing. You fired tubes Four and Five at the third target. The only thing I can figure out, I don't have any bearings for the fourth target, is that you missed with one of the torpedoes you fired at the third target and it ran on and hit the fourth target. Sounds weird, but that's the only thing I can think of, sir."

"I remember seeing the fourth ship, it was beyond the third

ship and I thought it was backing down." Captain Foster raised his wrist to his mouth and his teeth nipped off a hair.

"But it makes sense," he said slowly. "The third ship was broadside, almost a ninety-degree angle starboard. If I got her amidships with one fish and missed her with the other fish astern, that second fish could have kept on running and got the fourth ship when it was backing down. Blind luck."

"We'd just gone to all-back emergency and then all ahead one third," Mike O'Connor said. "That right, Sullie?" The Plotting Officer nodded.

"This ship lunges her bow to port when we go all-back emergency," Mike said. "I noticed that when we were doing operational drills, when I was the engineer. Could have been that our setup on the third ship was a little too quick, and the ship's bow lunging to port made one fish miss astern of the third target."

"Let's not confuse the people in Pearl Harbor with that theory," Captain Foster said with a grin. "I think you're probably right, Mike. We'll just say we eyeballed the fourth target and got the third and fourth targets with one fish each. I'm going to get some sleep. I want periscope observations on the quarter-hour." He left the Wardroom and went into his tiny cabin.

Hank Copper turned to Wayne Raleigh. "I didn't know you'd majored in music. What instrument did you play?"

"The harpsichord," Raleigh said, blushing.

The *Tigerfish* surfaced after dark, easing up cautiously through the murky water of the Yellow Sea. The radioman on watch sent off the contact report detailing the results of the previous night's action. The contact report noted the large number of small fishing boats in the area and the heavy fog that usually appeared after midnight.

No targets were seen for two days and nights after the *Tigerfish* returned to her patrol area. The fishing boats were out in large numbers despite the sinking of the four ships in the area. Just before dawn on the third night after the *Tigerfish* returned to the patrol area, the radio operator on watch heard his ship's call letters in his earphones. He typed furiously and then yelled for the messenger, who brought the message out to Mike O'Connor.

"Mister Raleigh is in the Wardroom," O'Connor said to the messenger. "Give him the message and ask him to decode it, please." He was absorbed in his plotting of the ship's position as the ship dove and Captain Foster slid down the ladder from the Conning Tower.

"Message came in a few minutes ago, Captain," O'Connor said. "I asked Wayne to decode it. He's in the Wardroom."

"Thank you," Hugh Foster said. "Come in and have coffee when you're done."

O'Connor thanked the Officer's Cook for the coffee and hot doughnuts placed before him at the Wardroom table. Captain Foster pushed the decoded message across the green baize cloth to O'Connor, who read it as he chewed.

"I think you ought to post this on the bulletin board in the crew's mess, sir," O'Connor said. That evening the crew members read the message.

"ComSubPac is pleased to give a sharpshooter's medal to Captain Hugh Foster. Sinking four ships with five torpedoes is not perfect but it's close. All four sinkings are confirmed by intelligence reports. Total tonnage is seventeen thousand and that is the highest single tonnage sunk in one attack on muliple targets to date.

"ComSubPac is pleased to hereafter refer to the Yellow Sea by Captain Foster's designation, that of quote wading pond unquote. ComSubPac congratulates Captain Foster, his Wardroom and his wading-pond crew on their tenacious attack. Keep up the good work."

"So that's what we are, wading-pond sailors," Dandy Don Miller said as he read the message. "I don't see nothin' in that message that says anything about how damned perfect my fish ran."

Far to the south of the *Tigerfish* Admiral Isoroku Yamamoto was planning his next moves against the American Navy. After the extraordinary success of the attack on Pearl Harbor, Admiral Yamamoto had promised his Emperor that he would run wild in the Pacific. His nose had been bloodied at Midway. The invasion of Guadalcanal had further shamed him. Every day the Americans remained on Guadalcanal was a blot on his personal record.

The Japanese Admiral had assembled a considerable force for his next move, a concerted effort to throw the Americans out of Guadalcanal, and in so doing, smash the American Navy's hold on the South Pacific forever. He had five battle-

ships, including the largest battleship in the world, the
Yamoto; four aircraft carriers, fourteen cruisers, forty-four
destroyers and twelve submarines, plus over two hundred
land-based planes at Rabaul. He stood at the chart table in the
Operations Room of the battleship *Yamoto,* anchored in Truk
Atoll, and studied the chart.

"We own this water," he growled, touching his finger to the
channel between Guadalcanal and Florida Island. "We tra-
verse it every night and the only opposition the Americans
offer is submarines and they don't hit anything. Where is the
American Battle Fleet? Where are their carriers? Where are
they hiding? Why don't they come out to fight?"

Admiral Yamamoto got his answer on October 19. An
intelligence officer approached him on the wing of the *Yamoto's*
bridge, bowed deeply and handed him a message. The
Japanese Admiral read the message and smiled.

"Ah," he said. "Admiral Nimitz has given command of all the
South Pacific forces to Admiral Halsey. Halsey! That man will
come out to fight! All we have to do is give him a reason, and
we'll do that!"

Chapter
Fifteen

ADMIRAL YAMAMOTO ISSUED his orders that afternoon. The battleships *Kongo* and *Haruna*, with an escorting force of cruisers and destroyers, would make nightly sallies down the "Slot," as the channel leading to Guadalcanal from the northwest was called, to bombard Henderson Air Field and the American shore installations with fourteen-inch shells. By day aircraft from Rabaul would carry out bombing raids. The army would reinforce its troops on Guadalcanal. As soon as the reinforcements were in place, an all-out assault against the American positions around Henderson Air Field would be mounted. Henderson Air Field would be recaptured by nightfall of October 22. Admiral Yamamoto ordered that the messages be sent in a code the Japanese knew the Americans had long ago broken. He wanted Admiral Halsey to know what he was doing, to come out and meet him in battle in the air and on the open sea. In another code he was sure had never been broken, Admiral Yamamoto ordered the bulk of his forces to steam southward to be ready to engage Halsey.

Radio messages intercepted later by Japanese intelligence told of the damage done by the air raids and the shelling by the battleships. Gasoline-storage dumps had been destroyed, buildings smashed, forty-eight of the ninety aircraft at the air field were destroyed. Food and medical supplies had been blown into rubble.

The American forces on Guadalcanal got ready for the assault they knew would come. They dug foxholes, cut fire lanes with bayonets through the seven-foot-high kunai grass and laid their guns to enfilade the approaches to their positions. On October 24, delayed by heavy jungle on his approach, General Maruyama launched a two-pronged attack at a place that would go down in military history—Bloody Ridge. The battle raged day and night for three days, until the Japanese, badly chewed up by the stubborn defense put up by the U.S. Marines and the U.S. Army's 164th Infantry Regiment, pulled back into the jungle.

As the battle for Henderson Air Field raged, the *Enterprise* and the battleship *South Dakota* rejoined Admiral Halsey's forces. The feisty Halsey knew perfectly well why Admiral Yamamoto had sent his orders in an old, almost unused code; he wanted to suck Halsey out into battle at a time and place of his own choosing. The American Admiral tallied up his own forces: two battleships, two carriers, ten cruisers and twenty destroyers, plus land-based dive bombers and high-level bombers and search planes. His forces were vastly inferior to the Japanese, but he had his own plans. He would smash Yamamoto's carriers with air attacks and avoid any pitched battle between the battleships. Halsey ordered the search planes into the air to find the Japanese main force. Hours later a PBY patrol plane sighted a Japanese carrier 450 miles northeast of Guadalcanal. More search planes found and identified other elements of the Japanese Combined Fleet.

Admiral Yamamoto, angered at the failure of his army to retake Henderson Air Field on the date decreed, issued a do-or-die order: the air field would be retaken by midnight of October 25. A naval liaison officer attached to General Maruyama sent a radio message to Admiral Yamamoto on the night of October 25—the air field had been recaptured. Hours later he sent another message that said the fighting was still going on but the issue was not in doubt.

The conflicting reports about the battle for Henderson Air Field, the absence of any naval opposition to the bombardment of the air field, worried Admiral Yamamoto. He knew Admiral Halsey was a cagey man, a worthy opponent. He hesitated, not sure what to do next.

Vice Admiral Halsey, in his headquarters at Noumea, did not hesitate. He divided his meager force into three striking units. Two carrier task forces and one battleship force. He looked at his charts and put his stubby forefinger on a string of four small volcano-tipped islands called the Santa Cruz Islands. The task forces would rendezvous there. He gave the order.

"Attack—repeat—attack!"

* * *

The Santa Cruz Islands lie 270 miles to the east and slightly south of Guadalcanal. The *Enterprise* and the *Hornet* swept past the eastern side of the islands and turned north and west to seek out the enemy fleet. A land-based search plane reported two Japanese carriers 360 miles northwest of the American carriers. Night fell as the two enemy forces, now aware of each other, maneuvered for position and prepared for battle.

The sun rose shortly after 0500 on October 26. The weather was fair, with a light breeze. The antiaircraft gunners in both fleets were edgy; huge cumulus clouds soared upward in the sky, merging into a solid cloud mass of stratocumulus high above the ocean, ideal cover for dive bombers. A lone Japanese Kate, dodging in and out of the clouds on a scouting mission, was sighted shortly after dawn. The *Enterprise* launched sixteen dive-bombers to search for and find the enemy carriers. The dive bombers spread out in a search pattern, two planes in each unit. The Japanese ships were sighted by one pair of dive bombers. Another pair sighted two Japanese carriers but had to take cover in the clouds to escape a swarm of Zekes that came after them. Still another pair of dive bombers had better luck; they sighted the Japanese carrier *Zuiho*, radioed information of the sighting and bored in for the attack, defying the Zeke fighter planes that raced to intercept them. One of the dive bombers scored a hit on the flight deck of the *Zuiho* with a five-hundred-pound bomb that penetrated the flight deck and started huge fires.

The skirmishing had begun. The *Enterprise*, the flagship of the carrier force, steamed at twenty-five knots toward the enemy. A tight circle of ships, the battleship *South Dakota*, a heavy cruiser, an antiaircraft cruiser and eight destroyers, surrounded the *Enterprise*. Ten miles to the southeast the carrier *Hornet* followed with its screen of two heavy cruisers, two light cruisers and seven destroyers. Overhead thirty-eight Wildcat fighters were stacked, waiting for the Japanese dive bombers and torpedo planes.

The Japanese Navy employed an unusual type of defense against carrier-plane attack. A screen of battleships and cruisers steamed fifty miles ahead of their carriers, ready to absorb the first blows of the American carrier planes and give them a heavy baptism of antiaircraft fire. Those planes that got by this first barrier would have to run the gauntlet of Zeke fighter planes. The Japanese depended greatly on the tactic of radical maneuver as a final defensive action when under air attack. Their ships, large and small, responded far more quickly to their rudders than did American ships.

When carriers engage carriers in battle, there are very few options. If one carrier force can launch its planes and find the enemy and bomb his flight decks before the enemy's planes can launch—victory is assured. If both sides launch before being attacked, the fortunes of war go to the side which can shoot down the other side's planes before they reach their targets. The enemy's carriers can then be destroyed at will. In the engagement that would go down in the history books as the Battle of Santa Cruz, the Japanese launched their dive bombers and torpedo planes a full half-hour before the Americans cleared their flight decks. The two enemy fleets of dive bombers and torpedo planes passed each other en route to their targets, the pilots undoubtedly wondering if they would have a ship to land on when they returned.

Alabama Jones's battle station was a gun tub with twin 20-mm machine guns. He checked his guns for the seventh or eighth time and looked up at the clouds. "Don't like those damned clouds," he muttered to his loaders. "Bastards can come right in on us and get close before we ever see 'em."

"The boss is upstairs," one of his loaders said. "Andy and his boys will pick 'em off before they get too close."

"Don't like the way he's actin'," Jones said. "The man has been as sour as a kosher pickle ever since we left Pearl. Can't figure him out."

"Seems okay to me," the loader said. "He bitched about his seat but I fixed it and he was nice as apple pie and ice cream."

"He's okay with the troops," Alabama Jones said. "He's different with me. I don't like his attitude. Half the time it seems he's off somewhere in his head. If he dopes off up there," he jerked his head upward where the Wildcat air cover for the carrier was circling, "he dopes off up there and we'll be gettin' a new plane and pilot."

"That'd be bad, huh?" the loader said.

"Fuckin' A it would be bad," Jones grumbled. "I took care of a lot of planes and pilots in my time, and this dude O'Connor is one of the best. A four-oh Joe. I just wish I knew what the fuck was eatin' on him. I ast Mister Masters and Mister Olsen if they knew, and they don't have a clue."

"Maybe his old lady give him a dose of clap when we got back to Pearl last time," the loader said.

"Shit!" Jones growled. "People like Mister O'Connor don't marry women who'd give them a dose." The bullhorn suddenly blared the order to stand by to repel air attack and Alabama Jones settled his bony fanny into the butt strap of the twin-20 and swung the twin muzzles upward.

"Here it comes," he said.

Andy O'Connor, circling high over the *Enterprise*, saw a flight of four Val dive bombers in a diamond formation just below him. He radioed the warning and tipped his fighter over in a dive and went rocketing down as the Vals broke their formation to line up to make their bombing dives. The faster Wildcats ate up the distance between the planes. O'Connor took dead aim at the trailing Val in the formation and touched his gun triggers. The incendiaries caught the Val just back of its canopy. The plane nosed over and went plunging down toward the sea. He saw Red Olsen take the next plane in the line and then Orv Masters sliced across and took the plane beyond that. Below and ahead of him a Wildcat, almost hanging by its propeller, poured a stream of incendiaries into the lead Val. The Val wobbled, burst into flame and plunged headlong into the Wildcat. The two planes, locked together in a bondage of twisted metal, cartwheeled downward.

The *Enterprise* was maneuvering at high speed to escape the dive-bomber attacks. A rain squall suddenly raced across the surface of the sea and the Captain of the big carrier steered his ship into the middle of the squall. The Japanese dive-bomber pilots, suddenly without a target, wheeled and concentrated on the *Hornet*, steaming a few miles away in bright sunlight. They descended on the *Hornet* like killer bees. A burst of flame and a column of smoke marked the first bomb hit on the *Hornet's* flight deck as huge water spouts erupted alongside her, near-misses that cracked the ship's hull. A Japanese plane, its pilot mortally wounded by antiaircraft fire, crashed his plane against the *Hornet's* bridge. His bombs, jarred loose by the impact, bounced across the carrier's deck and exploded. Two Kates, flying low and slow, sneaked in undetected and dropped their torpedoes. The *Hornet*, crippled, belching smoke and flames, stopped dead in the water as the Japanese dive-bomber pilots concentrated on their easy target. The gunners of the *Hornet,* valiant to the end, threw up a curtain of fire from their listing ship, but at least four of the dive bombers got through the fire and their bombs smashed through the flight deck to explode deep in the ship's vitals. In six minutes the attack was over and the surviving Japanese planes were streaking for home.

While the *Hornet* was receiving her death blows, her planes were winging toward the Japanese carriers. Smashing through a cloud of Zeke fighters, the *Hornet's* dive-bomber pilots dove on the carrier *Shokaku.* Four thousand-pound bombs landed on the *Shokaku's* flight deck and blew it into rubble, destroyed the hangar deck just below the flight deck and started immense fires. The second wave of *Hornet's* dive bombers found the cruiser *Chikuma* and scored a hit with a five-hundred-pound bomb that wrecked the ship's bridge and killed almost all of her officers.

The first stage of the battle was over and the issue was still in doubt. On the Japanese side two carriers, the *Zuiho* and the *Shokaku,* were crippled and out of action. The cruiser *Chikuma* was making all possible speed away from the fighting, signaling to its sister ships to supply officers to man the ship. The carriers *Zuikaku* and *Junyo* were untouched and launching their planes.

On the American side the *Hornet* was almost completely disabled. The ship was dead in the water and listing to starboard. The crew was busy fighting fires and trying to care for their wounded. Two of the ship's escorting destroyers pulled alongside, and their fire hoses helped bring the flames under control. Down in the engine rooms, shattered by torpedoes, the Black Gang was trying to accomplish miracles as they tried to get steam to the turbines so the ship could get underway as the cruiser *Northhampton* maneuvered ahead of the *Hornet* to pass a towing bridle to the crippled carrier.

The *Enterprise,* meanwhile, had run out of its covering rain squall. A Japanese submarine bored in and fired a spread of torpedoes. The deadly "Long Lance" torpedoes missed the maneuvering carrier but hit and sank a destroyer. As the entire task force, with the *Enterprise* in the center, maneuvered radically to avoid further submarine and air attacks, the battleship *South Dakota's* radar operators picked up a large number of planes at fifty miles range and closing. The gunners on the *Enterprise* braced themselves for the attack by the planes from the *Zuikaku* and the *Junyo* as the fighter screen above the carrier made ready to repulse the attack. The *South Dakota*, bristling with a new type of antiaircraft gun—the American version of the Swedish 40-mm AA gun mounted four to a nest and called a Bofors—left its station on the rim of the circle and closed to within a thousand yards of the *Enterprise* to give the carrier added antiaircraft protection.

The attack came with the Val dive bombers dropping down like hawks. The *South Dakota* gunners had a field day, shooting down thirty dive bombers in less than five minutes. But they couldn't shoot down all of the attacking planes. One bomb smashed into the flight deck of the *Enterprise* near the bow and blew parked planes over the side. Another smashed into the flight deck, penetrated down through the hangar deck and to the third deck before its delayed-action fuse exploded it, killing and wounding dozens of men.

Circling above the *Enterprise* under the command of the Flight Director, Andy O'Connor saw the first flight of Kate torpedo planes coming in from the south. He gave the warning and led his wingmen down in a long, shallow dive toward the slow torpedo bombers. He pulled out of his dive two hundred feet above the water and went racing toward the oncoming torpedo planes. In his earphones he could hear Red Olsen yelling and Orv Masters telling him to shut up. Then he was within range and he opened fire. The plane he shot at exploded and he instinctively ducked his head as his Wildcat flew through the burning debris.

The three Wildcats flashed through the formation of torpedo planes and turned and came back, now above the low-flying Japanese. O'Connor and his two wingmen downed three more of the Kates. Once again the three Wildcats, flying almost as one aircraft, soared upward and came down, guns blazing, on the remaining four Kates. O'Connor got one, Olsen shot down two and Masters splashed the remaining Kate. The three Wildcats climbed for position and O'Connor heard Olsen's voice in his earphones.

"Don't know what good I am, boss, I'm out of ammo."

"Me, too," Masters chimed in. "More of those bastards coming in up ahead."

The five-inch guns, their muzzles depressed, began to fire in volleys, their shells throwing up great water spouts. The *Enterprise* and the *South Dakota*, maneuvering almost as if they were a single ship, turned and dodged as the torpedoes raced toward them. One Kate pilot, apparently despairing of getting the *Enterprise*, crashed his plane with its torpedo into the bow of an escorting destroyer. The destroyer's Captain, peering through flames that were engulfing his ship almost back to the bridge, ordered his helmsman to steer the destroyer across the huge, tumbling wake of the *South Dakota*, and took seas aboard that helped douse the fires.

The flight director on the *Enterprise* was deluged with frantic requests from pilots from both the *Enterprise* and the *Hornet* to be allowed to land. Aboard the *Enterprise* damage crews were laboring to put out the fires and repair the holes caused by the two bombs that had struck the ship. All around the ship the clouds were lowering, ideal ambushes for attack by enemy dive bombers and torpedo planes. As the flight director gave orders for taking planes aboard, twenty planes from the carrier *Junyo* burst into view out of the cloud cover, flying low. The gunners in the task force went into action and drove off the planes, shooting down at least ten of the attackers.

The Japanese had been hit hard. They had lost two carriers and more than a hundred of their planes. But the Japanese commanders weren't through. At just past noon the *Junyo* sent off a flight of planes to sink the crippled *Hornet*. At 1500 hours the planes found the carrier being towed to safety by the cruiser *Northhampton*. As the torpedo planes began their run, the *Northhampton* dropped the towing bridle and began maneuvering to avoid torpedoes. The *Hornet* took a torpedo in her badly damaged engine spaces and began to list heavily to starboard. Two dive-bombing attacks scored hits. The order was given to abandon ship, and the escorting destroyers, ignoring the continual dive-bombing attacks, went alongside the crippled carrier to take off the crew. Later that day, after dark had fallen, the U.S.S. *Hornet,* the ship that had launched the Doolittle raid against Tokyo earlier in the war, slid downward toward the bottom, three miles below.

That night the Japanese forces regrouped and the commanders made plans for another carrier attack against the American Fleet at dawn. Just after midnight a PBY out of Espiritu found the Japanese force and launched a torpedo at the carrier *Zuikaku*. Another PBY got a torpedo hit in a destroyer. Admiral Yamamoto, a thousand miles to the north in Truk Atoll and deluged with contradictory reports of the disposition of

Vice Admiral Halsey's forces, summed up the results of the battle as best he could.

In tactical terms the Americans were the losers at this stage of the battle. They had lost one of their two carriers. In overall terms the Japanese had also lost. Two of their four carriers were out of action. They had lost scores of their aircraft and the cream of their naval pilot corps. Admiral Yamamoto decided to call the battle a Japanese victory and recalled his Combined Fleet from the battle area to await the next opportunity he would get to engage Vice Admiral Halsey. Until then the Japanese Army would have to do its best to hold the Americans on Guadalcanal at bay.

Meanwhile, Vice Admiral Halsey, in his headquarters nine hundred miles to the southeast of the battle zone, was equally frustrated. He had been Commander, South Pacific Forces, for only two weeks. His forces had managed to come to grips with Admiral Yamamoto's fleet, but the results were far short of what he had hoped for. He had lost the carrier *Hornet* and a destroyer and valuable pilots and planes. The *Enterprise* had been hit hard and was on her way to Noumea for repairs. Even worse, Guadalcanal was still threatened by Japanese shelling from the sea and bombing attacks from the air. Halsey and his staff studied the charts and made their decision; as soon as he could assemble the force he needed, he would bait Yamamoto into pitched battle on the high seas and smash him. The Battle of Santa Cruz had not been a victory, but neither had it been a defeat. It had accomplished one thing of value; it had bought the time needed to reinforce Guadalcanal, time to prepare for the next battle.

As the *Enterprise* steamed toward Noumea, Chaplain Peter Grass sat in his small office. Commander John Berry, the Air Group Commander of the *Enterprise*, sat across the desk from Chaplain Grass. The chaplain's yeoman brought in two mugs of steaming black coffee, set them down on the desk and went out, closing the door behind him. Commander Berry raised the cup to his lips, inhaled and then took a long sip.

"What did you lace this coffee with?"

"Just think of it as blessed coffee, John, and relax and enjoy." The pilot looked at the chaplain's bandaged right hand and arm.

"How's the hand?"

"It'll be all right. Hurts a little now and then. It's okay."

"The Damage Control Officer told me he saw you and all the other chaplains down in the wreckage and the fires after that bomb slammed through the hangar deck. Must have been pretty bad. Sure looked bad from up above."

The Catholic chaplain nodded slowly. "Very bad, John. It's always bad when men are killed and dying." The Air Group Commander sipped again at his coffee, relishing the fragrant steam rising from the cup.

"I'm not a Catholic, Padre, you know that. But I always wondered, when you're giving the last rites to men who are dying, do you or the other chaplains ask if the man is of your faith?"

The chaplain shook his head. "No, we just do what we are trained to do. I don't think it makes any difference to the Lord if the man is a Catholic or a Protestant or a Jew. We are all His souls."

"I've thought about that," Commander Berry said. "My grandfather was a Fundamentalist Baptist minister. After I heard about you and the other chaplains down there in the fires and explosions, I wondered if Grandfather would have asked if a man were a Baptist or not."

"I'm sure he wouldn't have done that," Chaplain Grass said. "My first parish was in the South, before I decided to enter the Navy. I knew a few Baptist ministers. Fine, fine men. I always envied them their absolute faith in the way they saw religion.

"I think any man who has given his life to the Lord's service would do what he could to give comfort to a dying man." He looked at Commander Berry, his face carefully devoid of expression.

"How did your people come through the attack? Did you lose many?"

"Too many," John Berry said slowly. "Not as many as the other side but one is one too many as far as I'm concerned."

"How are your people taking the losses?"

"They're sailors," Berry said. He took a long gulp from the coffee cup. "You ever have a dog, a female dog, Padre? You did. Well, you ever notice that if you gave away a pup from her litter, the rest of the pups didn't seem to mind?"

"That's a terrible analogy, John."

"I know," Berry growled. "It's the only thing I could think of quickly. What I'm trying to say is, they ignore the losses. They don't talk about the pilots who didn't get back. They put it out of their minds."

"All of them? They can all do that?"

"Well, not all of them. I've got maybe a dozen who are taking it pretty hard."

"Is Lieutenant O'Connor one of those?"

"What are you getting at, Padre?" There was an edge to Berry's voice.

"Nothing," Chaplain Grass said. "O'Connor is a devout Catholic. I wondered if he were affected."

Commander Berry put his cup on the desk. "O'Connor is my squadron leader. He's a leader in every respect, a fine pilot."

"So you need him, need him badly?"

"Yes," John Berry said. He sat back and studied the worn face of the chaplain across the desk.

"I get your point, Padre. O'Connor has changed. Something is bothering him. I noticed it before the battle. His wingmen told me something was bothering him. Do you know about this? Do you know what's wrong with him?"

Chaplain Grass nodded. "What he told me was privileged, John. It has nothing to do with his duties. It was purely personal. I'm not changing the subject but how long will we be in Noumea?"

"I don't know." Commander Berry rubbed his chin. "Three, maybe four weeks. We've got a plane elevator out and a lot of damage below decks."

"The people you say are feeling strain, John, would there be enough time for you to fly them back to Pear Harbor for a few days and then get them back again before we go back to sea?"

The Air Group Commander looked at the chaplain. "You aren't a Jesuit, are you, Padre?"

"No," Chaplain Grass said with a gentle smile.

"You thought about what a screaming and flail I'd face if I let some people go back to Pearl and kept most of them here?" He stood up. "Thanks for that blessed coffee, Padre. You want me to send O'Connor to see you before he goes back to Pearl?"

"That won't be necessary, John. And thank you. I'll say a prayer for you, if you don't mind."

"Mind? Every time I leave that flight deck, I hope that one of you chaplains is praying for me and my people. See you around, my friend."

"Distinguished Service Medal," Andy
posed to be planes." Mike said. "I'm proud
Japanese brother, his ev
"Boy!" Mike brother,
his younger Carol?"
home seeing Andy bega
"Mike, and in
growing up and I
things impo
"So impo
until to

210

ANDY O'CONNO
long circle arou
marines moored b
a little better. If M
Mike what was eati   ...der-
stand. He left the pl   ...ked to the
Operations Office.

"Can you tell me if   ...s in?" He asked a Chief
Yeoman. "My brother's   ...xec." The Chief looked at his
roster of ships in harbor.

"She came in last week, sir. The crew's at the Royal
Hawaiian. Do you want me to get the hotel on the phone?" He
saw the look on Andy O'Connor's face and dialed the number.

"Hey, there," Mike's deep voice boomed over the telephone. "I thought you were somewhere at sea. How come
you're in? You're not hurt or anything?"

"No, I'm okay," Andy said. "Mike, I've got to see you. Right
away."

"Where'll I meet you, at Carol's house?"

"No," Andy said. "I want to see you before I see her."

"I don't quite savvy that," Mike said. "But whatever you say.
Why don't you come out to the hotel? It's on your way home.
I'll be out at the gate."

"See you in an hour," Andy said. "And thanks, Mike."

The two brothers sat on a bench in back of a huge growth of
hibiscus in the hotel gardens. Mike leaned forward and
examined the new ribbon pinned below the gold pilot's wings
on Andy's chest.

"What's that one? I never saw that one before."

nswered. "I'm sup-
down more than ten

of you, brother." He looked at
s questioning. "Why aren't you

, "we were always close when we were
he Academy. We could talk things over, talk
ve to talk to you. It's awfully important."
tant you have to talk about it now? Can't it wait
orrow or the next day, after you've been home?"
, " Andy said.
Okay, talk," Mike said. He leaned forward, his elbows on
his knees, his face turned toward his brother. Andy spoke
slowly, his eyes on a palm tree across the pathway. When he
had finished, sweat was pouring down his face.

"The way I see it, Andy, is this. You married a girl who isn't a
Catholic. If you love her, I can't see much wrong with that. I
don't think the folks would see anything wrong with marrying
outside of the Church. Mother might hope she would join the
Church but I don't think either one of them would ever bring
it up. Have you talked to Carol about joining the Church?"

"Yes," Andy said. "She doesn't want to talk about it."

"Can't blame her," Mike said. "If she asked you to join her
church, you wouldn't want to talk about doing that."

"That's not a logical statement, Mike," Andy said. "Cathol-
icism is the only true religion, you know that."

"That's what the priests and nuns taught me," Mike said.
"Since I've been in the Navy, seen a few different countries,
different religions, I sometimes wonder about that. The people
in China think their religion is the only true religion. People in
Japan have a different religion and they believe theirs is the
only true religion. But let's not argue about that.

"Carol isn't a Catholic and that probably won't change, at
least not for a while. So let's talk about what else is bothering
you.

"Carol loves you and you love Carol. You say she's a
passionate woman. And because you say the doctor says you
can't make her pregnant, you think that her passion is lust and
her lust is sinful. Does that about cover it?"

"Just about," Andy said. "You don't put it very nicely but
that's about it."

Mike O'Connor studied his younger brother's face. "There's something else, something you haven't talked about. What is it?"

"I don't know what to do," Andy said. "That's why I wanted to talk to you, Mike. I've thought of a way out but I don't know," his voice trailed off.

"The priests used to teach us that the act of sex was for the purpose of making children. You thinking about celibacy?"

Andy nodded slowly, his face twisted. "For now. Until the war is over. Until I can get back home and talk to Father Joseph. He always knew all the answers."

"Raises a tough point, doesn't it?" Mike said.

"What point?"

"Carol is a passionate woman. That's what you say. It's one thing to be faithful to a husband who is out at sea and is coming home again. It might be something else if that husband doesn't intend to make love to a wife for maybe years to come."

"Yes," Andy said.

"But you haven't talked about that to her, have you? Thought not. Why don't you? See what she thinks. Better yet, before you spring something like this on her, why don't the two of you go to a priest here in town and then go to a minister of her church? She goes to church, doesn't she?"

"I guess so," Andy said. "Her mother belongs to a Lutheran church."

"Don't tell the priest that," Mike said. "Priests don't generally like Lutherans. But go to both of them. Get both sides, yours and hers. You owe her that, Andy. But get it over with while you're in port. Get it off your mind. If you don't, some damned Jap will shoot your ass off!"

"Thanks, Mike. It's good advice. Any chance of getting some chow in this fancy hotel? All I've had to eat in the last eighteen hours is some fruit on the courier plane."

"Sure," Mike said. "Come on up to the galley." The two men walked slowly through the gardens and into the hotel. An obliging cook fixed a plate of ham and eggs for Andy who took it to a corner table in the hotel dining room. Mike drew two glasses of milk from a dispenser and brought them to the table.

"When do you have to go back to the *Enterprise*?" he asked.

"Friday," Andy said. He looked up from his plate with a wry smile. "I'm supposed to be under a psychological strain."

"The Marines have a word for that," Mike said. "Combat fatigue."

"You have a good patrol?" Andy asked.

"North end of the Yellow Sea," Mike answered. "The Old Man called it a wading pond because it's so shallow. We got four ships. I didn't make any mistakes in my navigation and I ran the attack plot. But I didn't get a medal for that." He grinned.

"You'd better get with it, brother," Andy said as he mopped up the last of his egg yolk with a piece of bread. "We're going to make Admiral together, remember? They tell me medals count a lot when the promotion board sits to consider which four-stripe Captains will be turned into Admirals. You'd better do something to catch up to me or I'll beat you to the big gold stripe on the sleeve." He grinned at his brother and drained his glass of milk.

"I'll work on that," Mike said. He felt a sudden rush of relief. Andy was ribbing him, a sure sign that he was feeling good. The two men walked out into the hotel lobby.

"I owe you a big one, Mike," Andy said as they walked down the hotel steps. "Funny thing. I mentioned to Carol one day that you had always been the physical brother, the bull that goes charging through the china shop. She said you weren't just a bull, that you had a lot of depth. I'm beginning to think she was right. You've helped me a lot in this mess I'm in."

"It's not a mess," Mike said. "It's something you can work out between the two of you. It might not be a bad idea at all if you just go home and lay it all out like you laid it out to me and then tell Carol that the two of you should go to her minister and a priest."

"Don't mention anything to the folks when you write," Andy said.

"I won't," Mike said. "You have to leave on Friday and this is what, Tuesday? You haven't got a whole lot of time and you've got a lot to do. If you're too busy before you go back to break away, no sweat, I understand. But write me. We've got another week here in the hotel and then a week before we go to sea."

"We'll see how things go, Mike. If you do have some free time before you go to sea, take Carol and her mother to dinner. They both like you a lot."

"Will do," Mike said.

The following Sunday morning Mike telephoned the Oster home and invited Carol and her mother to dinner that afternoon at the hotel. After she accepted the invitation, Mike asked casually, "How's Andy?"

"He's fine," she said. "I had six, no, seven letters from him yesterday. He couldn't tell me where he was but he said he was well and working hard. I wrote to your mother last night and told her what he said."

"Letters?" Mike said in a low voice.

"Yes. Didn't you get any?"

"No," Mike answered. "Maybe my mail is back on the ship. I've got to go to the ship tomorrow, I'll check. See you at three thirty this afternoon? Good, I'm looking forward to it." He hung up and walked up and down his room, thinking.

He got back to the hotel barely in time to shower and put on fresh khakis before Carol and her mother arrived for dinner. The trip to the base had confirmed what he thought; Andy had spent three nights at the BOQ and had departed for his ship at 0400 on Friday. As Mike walked down to the lobby to wait for the women to arrive, he wondered if he had given Andy the right advice.

The *Tigerfish* put to sea ten days later, bound for the East China Sea. The patrol was uneventful. One small freighter was sighted, chased down and hit with one of the two torpedoes fired at it. A small coastal steamer blundered into view off Okinawa and Captain Foster decided to give his deck gun crew a workout. The gun crew, yelling with excitement, opened fire and missed with nine straight shots before a five-inch shell smashed into the steamer's engine room and brought it to a dead stop. A muffled explosion rolled across the water as the ship's boilers exploded and the ship broke in two.

"Secure from Battle Station Surface," Captain Foster ordered. When the last of the gun crew had gone below, Captain Foster turned to Mike O'Connor, who had been directing the gun fire from the bridge.

"Not very fancy shooting, Mike. Took ten rounds before we got a hit and nobody was shooting back at us. When we get back to Pearl, have Chief O'Brien round up five or six empty fifty-gallon oil drums and paint them red. We'll use them for target practice on the way out on the next patrol."

The patrol dragged on. The entries in the ship's log were the same, day after day. No ships sighted. The monotony began to get on the crew's nerves and Chief O'Brien began cautioning the leading petty officers in each compartment of the necessity of maintaining quiet control lest tempers frayed by the days and weeks of inaction should flare. Finally Hank Copper, the Engineering Officer, laid his fuel-oil report on the Wardroom table in front of Captain Foster.

"We've got enough fuel left to get back to Pearl Harbor with a ten percent margin for safety, Captain." Hugh Foster nodded and pushed the fuel report across the tablecloth to Mike O'Connor.

"Draft a report to ComSubPac and give them the status of our fuel. Get it off tonight, please." The message was sent and the following night the *Tigerfish* was ordered to return to Pearl Harbor. Four days out of Pearl Harbor Mike O'Connor stood on the bridge in the early morning, waiting for Pete Savage to sharpen the pencil he had just broken. As he waited, he wondered if he should call Carol when he got into port.

Two days after the crew had moved into the Royal Hawaiian, Mike O'Connor telephoned the Oster residence. Carol O'Connor answered the telephone.

"Mike O'Connor," he said. "We got in a couple of days ago. I know the *Enterprise* isn't in but is there any chance I could take you and your mother to dinner?"

"We'd be delighted," she said.

"Tomorrow okay? About sixteen-hundred? Here at the hotel?"

"You have the best food on the island at the hotel," she said. "We'll be there."

The dinner went smoothly, and as Mike was escorting Carol and her mother to their car, she slipped her hand into his. He felt the piece of paper in her hand and closed his fingers over it. He held the door for Mrs. Oster to get in and then walked around the car and held the door open so Carol could get in back of the wheel. As he walked back into the hotel, he opened the folded piece of paper.

"I must see you," the note read. "Alone, please. I'll meet you outside the hotel gate at noon tomorrow, if that's convenient. If not, leave word at the gate and I'll call you later that afternoon."

He tore the note into fragments and dropped them in a GI can in the lobby. Why did she want to meet him alone? He stopped suddenly as he walked through the lobby, smiling mechanically at one of his crew who was walking past him. She knew that Andy had been in port and hadn't gone home. That had to be it. Now what should he do? He remembered what his football coach at the Academy had preached. When in doubt, put your head down and run straight ahead.

The conversation over lunch was casual. Mike paid the check and they walked to the car. Carol got in back of the wheel and Mike closed her door and got into the seat beside her. She drove well, he noticed, shifting gears smoothly, handling the car with a subtle grace. She drove up into the foothills and followed a secondary road and then eased the car across a grassy area to a spot near some trees.

"I come here a lot," she said as she turned off the ignition. She half-turned in her seat to face him. "This is where Andy proposed to me. Right over there." She drew a full breath and let it out slowly.

"Why didn't you tell me Andy was in Pearl Harbor when you were here last time?"

He looked at her, his dark blue eyes pained.

"How do you know he was?"

"We know a couple, a Marine pilot and his wife. We were at their house after we were married. Her husband saw Andy at the BOQ. I checked the BOQ room record and Andy slept there for three nights. He left there two days before you took my mother and myself to dinner at the hotel on Sunday. You must have known he was there. Why didn't you tell me?"

"He asked me not to tell you," he said.

"Why?" she demanded.

"Andy's a tortured man," Mike said.

"Tortured is a subjective word," she said. "I'd like to know what you mean by that word. If you'll tell me."

Mike sat silent. He glanced at her and saw her eyes filling with tears. He squirmed around in his seat and got a clean white handkerchief out of his hip pocket and gently blotted the tears that were running down her cheeks.

"Let me try to explain," he said. "Maybe you won't understand but I owe it to both of you to try."

He began by going back to their high school days when the priests had lectured them on the sanctity of women, the holiness of marriage, the terrible punishment that would be visited upon a sinner, how seriously Andy had taken the teaching. He stared out of the windshield, avoiding her eyes, when he told her of the days at the Academy, the tongue-lashings Andy had given him for spending a night with a girl, how Andy had hounded him each time until he had gone to confession.

"I've always known that Andy took his religion very seriously," he said. "Until this came up, until he told me about it, I never realized how serious it is with him. He's, well, he's very religious."

"And you're not?"

"I'm religious, that is, I believe in God and I believe in a lot of things the Church taught me. But a lot of things the Church says are so I don't take very seriously." He fixed his eyes on Carol.

"That's the general background, Carol. Now I get to the hard part. Andy was here, yes. They flew him in for a few days' rest. They thought he was suffering from combat fatigue or something like that. He was suffering, but it wasn't from combat fatigue.

"We just happened to be in port when he got in and he called me as soon as he landed, he came here and left on a courier plane. I told him we'd be in the hotel for a few more days and then alongside the tender for another week and to give me a shout after he'd seen you and maybe we could all have lunch. He said he had to see me before he saw you, so I told him to stop by the hotel because it's on the way to your house; that is, it's not much out of the way." He lowered his head and in a low voice repeated everything Andy had said to him while they had sat on a bench in the gardens of the Royal Hawaiian Hotel.

"Oh my God!" she half-whispered. "He thinks he's sinning when we make love because I'm not pregnant yet? He thinks he's making me a sinner and I'll burn in hell? How could anyone, anyone, believe in things like that?"

"Andy does," he said.

"What did you say? What did you say when he told you all that?"

"I asked him what he intended to do about it. He said he'd thought about that a whole lot." He looked at her, his big face impassive. "He said he's considered celibacy until after the war or until he could get back to Chicago and talk to Father Joseph. He's a Jesuit priest who coached football and track at our high school. He and Andy were great friends. He thinks that maybe Father Joseph will be able to solve his problems."

"Do you think this Father Joseph could help?"

"No," Mike said, his voice gruff. "Father Joseph is awfully

smart about a lot of things, he's awfully good with kids growing
into manhood but I don't think he knows very much about
something like this."

"Did you tell Andy that?"

"No, I didn't. I did tell him that he should go straight home
to you and lay it out to you just as he'd laid it out for me. I told
him I thought you'd understand and that the two of you should
go to your minister and to a priest and get some advice and
counsel.

"He seemed to think that was a good idea. At least he said
so. He said he'd do that. He only had two full days left before
he went back, so I told him we'd get together next time, that I
knew he, the two of you, had a lot to talk about and a lot to do.

"I took him into the hotel and got him something to eat, he
hadn't had much on the plane on the way here, and he seemed
relaxed. He kidded me a lot about keeping up with him so we
could both make Admiral together. Oh, you probably don't
know unless he wrote you, he's won the Distinguished Service
Medal for bravery."

"He didn't tell me," she said.

"Well, he never was one for boasting. But before he left that
day, he suggested that I take you and your mother to lunch or
dinner before I went to sea. And that's why I called you that
Sunday, to invite you to dinner."

"I remember," she said. "You seemed a little upset and I
thought it was because I had some letters from him and you
said you didn't get any."

"When you said that, I had a suspicion he didn't go to you
after we talked," Mike said. "I went out to Ford Island and the
Operations Officer told me he'd left at zero four hundred hours
on Friday and that his phone number when he was in port was
the BOQ. I went over there and the yeoman told me he'd
stayed there."

"I can't understand someone who says he's in love with me
doing that," she said. "Can you? Can you!" Her voice broke.

"Andy is my brother," he said. The dark blue eyes under his
heavy black eyebrows were calm as he looked at Carol.

"He's my brother, so I can't be truly objective, can I? I can
only say I understand him because I want to understand him.
You objected to my use of the word tortured. Well, I think he
is tortured. He has to be awful damned worried about
committing a mortal sin and he must be even more worried
thinking that he has made you a sinner.

"I've said a lot of very personal things to you. I meant no disrespect. Andy meant no disrespect when he told me those things about the two of you. He knows I wouldn't think he was being disrespectful of your honor." She dabbed her eyes with his handkerchief and handed it back to him.

"You sound so, oh, old-fashioned. I know you mean no disrespect," she said. "I just remembered something. The morning you left after spending that one night at our house. I didn't know why you'd left and Andy told me that you were a light sleeper, that you'd probably heard us making love." She reached out and touched his hand as she saw the deep red flush creeping up his face.

"I told Andy it was just as much his fault as mine, that he made me do that. I guess that was the wrong thing to say."

"Perhaps," he said.

"Do you think love, physical love, is something that should only be indulged in for the purpose of having children? This is something I can't understand, Michael, I can't."

"I happen to think it's medieval," he said. "I guess Andy doesn't think the way I think. I've found out something else. I'm not very good at giving advice to anyone, let alone my brother. Or his wife."

"I think you are a very wise and understanding man," she said. She reached out and touched his leg above his knee and felt the heavy muscles beneath her fingers suddenly bunch.

"Have you ever been in love?" she asked suddenly. "I mean, in love with a girl?"

"No," he said.

"Neither was I until I met Andy. I thought I was completely in love, that I would always be in love with him. Now, I don't know, I just don't know." She bowed her head and he reached for his handkerchief again.

"Don't say that," he said gently. "It will work itself out. I know it will. When he comes back to port, you take the initiative. Make him sit down and talk himself out, as he did with me." She let him touch her face with his handkerchief.

"You are a dear and gentle man, Michael O'Connor, and I love you for that." She reached out with her hands and took his face between them and kissed him. He felt the pressure of her lips and returned it, gently, resisting the almost overwhelming urge he felt to hold her in his arms.

"I'll buy you an ice-cream sundae if you know some place that sells them," he said.

"I know a place," she answered.

Walking through the lobby of the hotel, O'Connor met Chief O'Brien. The Chief of the Boat's face was set in a heavy scowl.

"What's eating you, Chief?"

"*Sea Bass* is gone," O'Brien growled. "Two weeks overdue on patrol. Doesn't answer radio calls. Gone with all hands."

O'Connor felt his stomach muscles tighten and tasted the bile in his throat. "You're sure? It isn't scuttlebutt?"

"Straight dope, Mister O'Connor. All those good people gone. The Chief Yeoman who gave me the dope told me we've lost over twenty boats so far. That's a hell of a lot of boats, sir." He squared his shoulders. "The Old Man's in the lounge. Told me if I saw you that he'd like a word with you, sir."

Captain Foster laid aside the three-day-old copy of *The New York Times* he was reading. "Sit down, Mike. The staff has been shaking things up again.

"They've given me another half-stripe and they tell me I'm too senior to go to sea on a submarine. I'm being assigned as chief aide to the Chief of Staff."

"I have to say you've earned the promotion, Captain, and I mean it. Who gets the *Tigerfish*, sir?"

"Commander T. Prescott Salmon the Third," Captain Foster said. "I don't know him at all, he was two classes ahead of me at the Academy."

"Let me sort this out, Captain. You've just made full Commander and you've got too much rank to command a submarine. Your relief is a Commander and he's two classes senior to you and he's getting the *Tigerfish*. Doesn't make any sense. What boat is he coming from?"

"He's never made a war patrol. He served on R-boats and S-boats and he was the Executive Officer of the *Argonaut* for a time before the war. His present duty is Officer in Charge of the Base Commissary and Exchange."

"Sounds like he's got a good Chinaman," O'Connor said.

"Chinaman? That's a new word to me," Hugh Foster said.

"In Chicago, where I was born and raised, it means someone who watches over you, over your career, someone with influence. To me this means that Mister Salmon has got a friend or two higher up who want him to get in a couple of good war patrols so he can make Admiral."

"You could be right," Captain Foster said. "But now you know what a load you're going to have to carry this next patrol or two. I told the Chief of Staff that with you aboard as the Executive Officer, Captain Salmon had nothing to worry about. The Chief of Staff agreed with me. He has great faith in your ability." He reached in his pocket and pulled out a small white box.

"You've got another half-stripe as of today, Mike. You and your brother are now Lieutenant Commanders and I congratulate you." He handed the white box to Mike, who opened it and saw the two round gold leaves nestling in the cotton batting, the collar insignia of a Lieutenant Commander.

"You certainly run a hell of a course in how to be a Commanding Officer, Captain," he said in a low growl.

"I'm looking after my own interests," Hugh Foster said with a grin. "When you make Admiral and I'm still a four-stripe Captain, I might be working for you."

"If that ever happens, you'll be Chief of Naval Operations and I'll be happy as hell to be working for you," O'Connor said. "I suppose that we'll have a change-of-command ceremony?"

"The day we go back to the ship. Don't mention my leaving to anyone other than Chief O'Brien, so he'll be able to have everyone ready as soon as we go back aboard. Admiral Nimitz will be there, so I want everything shipshape."

Mike O'Connor found Chief O'Brien nursing a beer in the enlisted men's lounge off the lobby. The two men walked out into the gardens and Mike told the Chief about the change of Commanding Officers.

"I know T. Prescott Salmon the Third," O'Brien said. "Knew him in Panama."

"What sort of a man is he?" O'Connor asked, and then immediately regretted his question. He saw the barrier come down between himself and the Chief of the Boat, the almost invisible barrier that always dropped when an officer was unwise enough to ask an enlisted man about another officer.

"I never served with Mister Salmon, sir," O'Brien said. "I just know he was aboard R-boats and S-boats in Panama when I was there. I used to see him around the base, sir."

"I shouldn't have asked," O'Connor said. "Forget that I did. Between us we'll just have to make him a *Tigerfish* sailor."

"If you say so, sir," O'Brien said.

Chapter
Seventeen

THE CREW OF the *Tigerfish* stood in two rigid lines on the afterdeck in their spotless white uniforms, their white hats squared on their heads, their black uniform shoes gleaming in the bright sunlight. The Chief Petty Officers, in their khaki uniforms with jackets and black ties, stood at the head of the first rank of men. The officers of the *Tigerfish* stood in a row facing the crew. To one side of the assembly Admiral Chester Nimitz and his staff waited while a Chief Yeoman untied the ribbon around a large brown envelope. He took out a white envelope with a heavy wax seal holding the flap closed. He handed the envelope to the Chief of Staff, who turned and handed it to Commander T. Prescott Salmon III.

"Your orders, sir," Captain Furst intoned. "You will please read them to your command."

The ceremony of designating an officer to command a warship of the U.S. Navy is as old as the Navy itself. Commander Salmon accepted the envelope and carefully slid a finger under the flap and broke the wax seal. He took a sheet of paper out of the envelope, cleared his throat and faced the crew of the *Tigerfish* and read aloud the orders designating him as the Commanding Officer of the U.S.S. *Tigerfish*, fleet submarine.

Admiral Nimitz stepped forward and extended his hand. "Congratulations, Captain. You've got a fine ship and crew." The Admiral's staff lined up to shake hands with Captain Salmon. Commander Hugh Foster was the last man in the line.

"She's a fine ship and an excellent crew, Captain," Foster

said. "I know you'll make me proud that I once commanded the *Tigerfish*."

"Without any doubt, Commander," Captain Salmon said. "Without any doubt at all." He walked over and stood at the foot of the brow as the Admiral's staff left the ship. He turned and took position facing his crew.

The crew studied their new Captain. They saw a man of medium height with staring, belligerent eyes in a craggy face. Captain Salmon put his fists on his hips and stared at the crew.

"Captain Foster did a pretty good job with you people," he rasped. "I intend to do a better job. If you don't measure up, you'll be transferred as unfit for submarine duty. I'll see the officers of the ship in the Wardroom in five minutes. I'll see the Chief of the Boat when I'm finished with the officers. Mister O'Connor, take over. Dismiss the crew and inform Supply we're ready to take stores aboard."

"Real tough cookie," Chief Hahn said to Chief O'Brien as they waited for the crew to go below and change into dungarees. "I remember that dude from Panama. Word I got at that time was that his skipper transferred him because he got into an argument with another officer about two-thirds his size and when the other dude challenged him to go up to the gym and put on the gloves, Salmon chickened out, wouldn't go. We got ourselves a real fighting man for a Captain."

"Times change. Men change," O'Brien said. "Don't bad-mouth him to your people. Don't let them bad-mouth him."

The *Tigerfish* cleared the submarine net at the mouth of Pearl Harbor and turned her bullnose toward Midway, where she would top off her fuel tanks and head for her patrol area—Luzon Strait—the body of water between the southern end of Formosa and the northern tip of the Philippines. The strait, two hundred fifty miles wide with deep water, was the main route for shipping moving between Japan and the vital sources of oil, rubber and minerals it had conquered in Southeast Asia.

By agreement between the overall submarine command in Pearl Harbor and the submarine command in Australia, Luzon Strait was divided in half on an east to west axis. The southern half of the strait belonged to the submarines operating out of Brisbane and Fremantle in Australia. The northern half of the strait was the operating area of the submarines out of Pearl Harbor. When he drew in the boundaries of the patrol area on the chart, Mike O'Connor carefully drew a double red line

along the southern edge of Pearl Harbor's territory, mindful
that if his navigation allowed the *Tigerfish* to stray into the
southern half of the Luzon Strait, his ship could be the target
of an American submarine's torpedoes.

On the second day out of Pearl Harbor the crew changed
from dungarees and shirts to the accepted war-patrol uniform:
khaki shorts and submarine sandals, lightweight shoes that
fastened with a strap across the instep. The officers dressed in
khaki shorts, T-shirts and sandals.

Captain Salmon came out of his cabin at 0900 on the first day
outbound from Midway and summoned Chief Yeoman Harrington. "Get your notebook," he said. "I will inspect the ship
daily at zero nine hundred hours." He went up to the Forward
Torpedo Room, dark except for a single light over the torpedo
tubes where Dandy Don Miller sat on watch in a canvas-
backed folding chair.

"Light the compartment," Captain Salmon ordered. He
ignored the groans of protest from the night-watch standers
who were awakened by the lights, and began to inspect the
compartment. Chief Harrington dutifully wrote down each
discrepancy his Captain discovered. When Captain Salmon
left the compartment, heading aft, Dandy Don turned out the
lights and picked up the telephone and alerted the After
Torpedo Room to what was happening. He listened to the
grumbling coming from the bunks.

"You people better get used to a piss call at this hour every
day," he said cheerfully. "This Old Man's hot on inspections,
looks like. Have to see the Chief of the Boat and have him
straighten the Old Man out. This is the *Tigerfish*, not the
damned commissary on the base. Next thing I know, he'll be
orderin' me to fire a case of canned peas out of my torpedo
tubes."

Captain Salmon waited until the Wardroom table had been
cleared of the dishes of the noon meal. He pushed two sheets
of paper over to Mike O'Connor.

"This crew needs some tightening up, Mister O'Connor. See
to it these things I found on my morning inspection tour are
corrected at once.

"I want an order posted on the crew's bulletin board today.
There will be no more half-naked sailors on my ship. All hands
will wear T-shirts. I don't want to see any more bare feet in
sandals. The Navy issues socks. The men will wear them.

"Officers will wear long trousers, uniform shirts and ties and regulation shoes. Uniform hats will be worn when on bridge watch topside. Hats may be dispensed with when on watch submerged. Got it?"

"Sir," Mike O'Connor said, "if I may, I'd like to make an observation. Wearing T-shirts and socks will increase the amount of water needed for laundry, sir. As you know, making water is a hot and dirty job, and we try to conserve every way we can."

"Making fresh water is the job of the engineers and they're paid to do that job. Observation overruled. This is the United States Navy, mister, not some damned banana-republic navy. Post my orders and see to it they are obeyed to the letter." He rose and left the Wardroom. Hank Copper looked at O'Connor.

"If he's as hard on the Japs as he is on us, this is going to be one hell of a war patrol."

"I want to see him the first time some destroyer pins us down and we're rigged for silent running and the temperature gets up to about a hundred thirty and the humidity is one hundred percent and there isn't enough oxygen to keep a match burning," Wayne Raleigh said. "I want to see if he takes off his tie."

"Knock it off," O'Connor growled. "He's the Captain. He gives the orders. We obey his orders. That's the Navy way."

Running on the surface day and night at eighteen knots, the *Tigerfish* covered the four thousand miles between Midway and the Luzon Strait in less than ten days. The port lookout picked up the high bulk of the mountains on Bataan Island early one morning as Mike O'Connor was waiting on the bridge to take star sights. He grinned at Pete Savage.

"We hit her on the nose," he murmured, conscious of Captain Salmon patrolling the small cigarette deck aft of the bridge. He made his star sights and went below to work out the ship's position. Just before dawn the *Tigerfish* dove and O'Connor finished plotting the ship's position on the chart. He looked up as Captain Salmon stepped away from the ladder to the Conning Tower.

"We're right here, sir," O'Connor said, touching the points of a pair of dividers to a small triangle he had drawn in on the chart.

"You mean we're somewhere inside that triangle," Captain

Salmon said. "I've been meaning to speak to you about your navigation, mister. You've been using three stars to fix our position. I want five or more stars used. It makes the triangle that much smaller, lets me know exactly where I am, not approximately. That's how I navigated on the *Argonaut*. I always knew where the ship was within a half-mile. See to it." He turned and went forward to the Wardroom. O'Connor looked at Pete Savage, whose normally pleasant face was flushed with fury.

"Tomorrow morning we'll use seven stars," O'Connor said softly. "We'll give the man what he wants." He went aft to the crew's mess and drew a cup of coffee and sat down at a mess table, wondering if the baker had made doughnuts or sweet rolls during the night. The ship's cook came out of the galley.

"Sorry, Mister O'Connor," he said in a low voice so he wouldn't be overheard by three sailors sitting at a mess table in the far corner of the compartment. "Captain's orders are that all officers take their coffee in the Wardroom, sir." O'Connor nodded and went to the sink and poured his coffee down the drain. He rinsed the cup and put it back in the cup rack. As he passed through the Control Room on his way to the Wardroom, he heard the sudden scrape of feet in the Conning Tower. He paused, waiting.

"Contact!" Hank Copper's voice was sharp in the stillness. "Control! Tell the Captain I've got two destroyers in sight bearing two-one-zero. Range is four thousand yards."

Captain Salmon scrambled over the high hatch between the Forward Battery and the Control Room, cursing as he barked his shins on the edge of the hatch. He climbed the ladder to the Conning Tower as Mike O'Connor was putting the plotting chart and the maneuvering board on the gyrocompass table, ready for the action to come. The officers of the Plotting Party, alerted by the messenger's delivery of the contact to the Captain, assembled around the gyrocompass table.

"Bearing of the closest destroyer is two-one-zero. The second destroyer is following close behind the first one," Captain Salmon's harsh voice came down from the Conning Tower. "Range to the closest destroyer is four thousand yards. Angle on the bow on that destroyer is forty starboard."

"Enemy course is two-eight-two, Captain," Mike O'Connor called out. "If you can give me another bearing, we can get a speed for you, sir."

The bearing came down a moment later and O'Connor busied himself at his maneuvering board.

"Target's speed is fifteen knots, sir. We're twenty-two hundred fifty yards from the target's track. If we come left to course two-four-two and increase speed to six knots for five minutes and then slow to three knots, we can be in position to attack at a range of one thousand yards when the targets come by, sir." There was no reply from Captain Salmon.

"Shall I repeat the plot information, Captain?" O'Connor called out.

"I heard you," Captain Salmon said. O'Connor looked at his stopwatch, waiting for the course and speed changes to come down from the Conning Tower, making the minute adjustments necessary as the passage of time changed the torpedo problem. He could hear the hum of the periscope motor as the Captain raised and lowered the periscope. "What the hell is he waiting for?" O'Connor muttered under his breath. Wayne Raleigh nudged him and he saw Captain Salmon's khaki-clad legs coming down the ladder from the Conning Tower.

"Targets changed course radically to port," he said. "No chance to close with them. Secure the Plotting Party."

"Could you give me the bearing and angle on bow when they turned away, sir?" O'Connor asked. "For the plot, sir."

"I'll put those in when I do the finished plot from your rough," Captain Salmon said. He went forward to his cabin. O'Connor looked at the officers around the gyrocompass table and shrugged his shoulders. Chief O'Brien belched and O'Connor raised his head and looked at him.

"Sorry, sir," O'Brien said. "If I could have, I'da farted."

Hank Copper went back up into the Conning Tower and resumed his watch. He looked at Arnie Schwartz, the quartermaster of the watch, who shrugged his shoulders. Lieutenant Copper pushed the periscope UP button and the long, oiled periscope shaft slid upward. He put his eye to the big rubber eyepiece and began to turn the periscope around in a 360-degree sweep.

"Control!" he barked. "I have those two destroyers bearing zero-one-zero and close aboard. Range is two thousand yards!"

Captain Salmon came into the Control Room after Mike O'Connor had bellowed the report of the contact through the hatch to the Forward Battery.

"Right full rudder," he ordered. "Rig for depth charge. Rig

for silent running. Make your depth two hundred fifty feet. I want a constant search by sound."

Amos Stuckey, who had manned his battle station at the sound gear when the first sighting of the destroyers had been announced, bent his head, his eyes half-closed, his every nerve intent on what he was hearing through his big earphones.

"Two sets of twin screws. One ship bears one-six-zero. The other bears two-zero-zero. They're pinging, sir." As he gave the information, a loud ringing sound echoed throughout the hull of the *Tigerfish.*

"They've ranged on us, sir. Both screws picking up speed." He shoved the mufflike earphones off his ears and onto his temples so his eardrums wouldn't be damaged by the explosions he knew were coming.

"This is an attack run, Captain."

"Confine your remarks to giving me bearings, sailor. I don't need your opinions," Captain Salmon snapped. He jerked his head upward as the thunder of the destroyer's propellers filled the hull of the *Tigerfish* with shattering sound.

"We're at two hundred fifty feet, Captain. Rudder is still full right, sir," O'Connor said. Amos Stuckey looked around, opened his mouth as if to speak and then closed it. He turned back to his sound gear and waited for the depth charges he had just heard hitting the water to explode. A loud CRACK sounded through the thin hull of the submarine.

"Depth-charge pistol going off, Captain," O'Connor said in a calm voice. Captain Salmon drew a deep breath and glared at O'Connor and then went sprawling, rolling across the deck of the Control Room as the *Tigerfish* was smashed down and slideways by two gigantic explosions.

The machinist's mate at the high-pressure blow manifold lost his footing as Captain Salmon's rolling body slammed into his legs. He fell on top of his Captain, and as he rose, he happily ground a bony knee into Captain Salmon's kidney. He leaned down and extended his hand to the Captain, who ignored it and struggled to his feet as O'Connor ordered Stuckey to report when the second destroyer had dropped its charges.

"Suggest we put the rudder amidships and go down to four hundred feet, Captain," O'Connor said.

"Second destroyer has dropped!" Stuckey called out. "First destroyer bears zero-one-zero and he's picking up speed."

"He's picking up speed SIR," Captain Salmon snapped. "You say SIR to an officer when you make a report, sailor."

The second attack was expertly made. Four depth charges rolled off the racks on the destroyer's stern as two other depth charges arched out to either side of the destroyer from its Y-guns. The charges battered the *Tigerfish*, shaking the ship like a rat in the jaws of a terrier. The submarine rolled thirty degrees to port and shuddered violently as cork insulation rained down and every light bulb in the ship burst.

Mike O'Connor stared at Captain Salmon. "I suggest, sir, we go to four hundred or four hundred fifty feet and put the rudder amidships. We're turning in a circle and those people have got us bracketed. That ringing noise is their sonar search beam, Captain."

"I give the orders here," Captain Salmon said. He raised his head as the rumbling sound of a destroyer's propellers filled the ship. "Rudder amidships. Make depth three hundred fifty feet."

The depth charges seemed to burst alongside and above the *Tigerfish*. The submarine was crushed downward, rolling violently to starboard and then port and then laboring back to an even keel. A second barrage of depth charges burst above the *Tigerfish*, driving it deep down into the sea. The telephone talker began to call off reports of leaks in the various compartments. Mike O'Connor leaned over the gyrocompass table and strained his eyes to see the depth gauges in the dim light of the battle lanterns.

"We're at five hundred feet, Captain," he said. "I suggest we stay here. They don't drop charges once they've triangulated us and find we're this deep."

"We'll implode at this depth!" Captain Salmon said in a loud voice. "This ship's test depth is only three hundred feet."

"We've been this deep and deeper before, sir," O'Connor said, his voice stubborn. "We leak a little but nothing serious."

The two destroyers above the *Tigerfish* probed for the submarine with their sonar search beams and found her. Captain Salmon flinched as the tinny sounds of the sonar beams echoed through the Control Room.

"Now they'll hit us again," he said.

"I don't think so, sir," O'Connor said. "They know how deep we are. They won't drop anything if we're too deep for their depth charges to hurt us." He returned Captain Salmon's angry glare with his own impassive stare.

The destroyers followed the *Tigerfish* as it crept along at five hundred feet, and two hours later Amos Stuckey reported both sets of twin screws had picked up speed and were moving off. Captain Salmon ordered the *Tigerfish* to cruise at 250 feet until nightfall. He went into his cabin and Mike O'Connor went into the Wardroom to get a cup of coffee. The Officer's Cook shook his head slightly at O'Connor. "Captain said he wants to see you in his cabin, sir."

"Sit down, mister," Captain Salmon said. He waited until O'Connor had seated himself in the cabin's only chair and then he moved over and stood above the Executive Officer, his fists on his hips, glaring down at O'Connor.

"Let's get a few things straight, mister," Captain Salmon began. "I give the orders on this ship. I don't need your suggestions. I don't want you to give orders to the man on the sound gear. I don't want you to give orders to the men on the bow and stern planes. Is that clear?"

"Captain, with all due respect, Captain Foster trained us to work as a team. Any officer in the Control Room could and would give a necessary order."

"Every team has a Captain," Captain Salmon said, his voice grating. "I am the Captain of this team. I give the orders. Get that through your brain, if you have a brain after all that football you played. And send Copper in here. He had no business raising that periscope and giving our position away to those destroyers. You're dismissed, O'Connor. I'm a fair man and it's only fair to tell you that I'm going to make a note of your inefficiency in my patrol report. Count on that."

"I will, sir," O'Connor said, his face impassive. "I'll relieve Mister Copper and send him to you, sir."

There was only one topic of conversation among the enlisted men aboard the *Tigerfish* for the next week. The failure of the *Tigerfish* to attack the two destroyers, the way the Captain had acted during the depth charging. The Officer's Cook had faithfully relayed every word Captain Salmon had said to Mike O'Connor, the chewing-out he had administered to Hank Copper for alleged careless use of the periscope that caused the two Japanese destroyers to attack the *Tigerfish*.

In the Forward Torpedo Room Dandy Don Miller, who held

forth as the authority on all manner of things, kept one eye on
the hatch between the Forward Torpedo Room and the
Forward Battery where the Wardroom was located in case
Captain Salmon should come through the hatch to use the
officers' head that was located in the after starboard corner of
the torpedo room.

"Old Blood and Iron Foster would have eaten both them Jap
destroyers for breakfast, knocked them on their little yellow
asses before they knew what hit them," he said to his audience
of the people who lived in his torpedo room. "This dude we got
for an Old Man's got a yellow streak that runs from the crotch
of his skivvies right up his back to his neck."

"I can stand getting the hell kicked out of me if we sink
something," Amos Stuckey said. "We took ourselves one hell
of a beating and we didn't even shoot."

"Heard that the Old Man told you where to get off the bus,"
Miller said.

"He told me not to tell him anything except bearings on the
ships. Didn't want to know when the destroyers dropped
charges. Mister O'Connor told me to give him the dope, so I
said to myself, 'Fuck you, Captain,' and I gave the dope
anyway. Chief Harrington told me the Captain told him to put
a thing in my record that I don't know how to take orders. Next
time we get depth charged, I ain't gonna tell that fucker fuck-
all."

"Don't get so wise, kid," Miller said. "Me, I'm sitting up
here and I want to get back to port and get me some more
poon-tang. You listen to Irish Mike and do your damned job
the way you know how to do it."

"What do you think's gonna happen, Dandy?" Arnie
Schwartz asked.

"They's several things could happen," Miller said slowly.
"One of you people keep your eye on that hatch. If you see
anything looks like khaki comin' this way, give me the word so
I can start talkin' about something else.

"One thing could happen is we stay out here a long time and
not shoot one fish, stay out here until Hank Copper tells the
Old Man we're runnin' low on fuel and we got to shake our ass
for the barn.

"Another thing that could happen is that those Jap tin cans
could be tellin' every Jap tin-can skipper who wants a little
practice on droppin' depth charges to come on over where we

are and kick a little shit out of us. Or——" He put his hands back of his head, leaned back in his chair and grinned.

"Or this Old Man's gonna get that big Irishman we got for an Exec so pissed off that O'Connor will draw a forty-five from the gunner's mate and purely shoot the Old Man in the ass. And then O'Connor will take over."

"And you're full of shit, Dandy Don," Schwartz said.

"Well, I don't think Mike O'Connor would shoot the Old Man in the ass, but he could get pissed off enough to where he'd take over. He's mighty damned close to that point right now if I can read the man and I think I can. Last time we were in Pearl, I talked to a guy I know told me about one of the boats where the Exec and the Wardroom decided their Old Man was carrying about twenty degrees of left rudder and the Exec took over. They were ordered back to port, and when they got in, the doctors said the Old Man was nutty and the Exec got away with it. Could happen here."

"But it won't," Arnie Schwartz said. "O'Connor is all-Navy, and them all-Navy types will take anything from someone who's got rank on them."

Two weeks after the depth charging Mike O'Connor relieved Wayne Raleigh at the periscope for the noon meal. He looked at the day order book and at his watch and signaled to Arnie Schwartz to raise the periscope. He made a careful search out ahead of the *Tigerfish*, and as he turned the periscope around toward the stern, he saw smoke. He steadied the periscope and studied the smoke.

"Control," he called down the hatch, "notify the Captain that we have smoke on the horizon bearing one-seven-zero. The ships are still hull down but it's a definite smoke."

Captain Salmon elbowed O'Connor out of the way and put his eye to the periscope. He straightened up.

"I make it two columns of smoke. See if there's any change since you first saw it."

"Seem to be coming this way, Captain," O'Connor said as he studied the smoke columns. He stepped away from the periscope. "We could probably get a lot better look at them if we came up to decks awash, sir. Right now we've only got about two feet of the periscope out of the water, sir."

"That would make it easier for them to see us," Captain Salmon said. "Keep an eye on the contact. I'm going to finish my lunch. Call me if there's any change at all." He slid down the ladder and went forward to the Wardroom where Wayne Raleigh was finishing his lunch. Hank Copper was sitting at the end of the table signing engineering log books. He looked up, his eyes questioning.

"O'Connor saw the smoke from a couple of old coal-burning coastal steamers," Captain Salmon said. "He's an edgy man, have you noticed that, Copper?"

"I always thought he was a very stable, steady officer, sir," Copper said.

"One of your failings is you don't read character very well," Captain Salmon said. He accepted the cup of coffee the Officer's Cook put in front of him. "I shouldn't drink two cups for lunch," he said. "It will keep me awake all afternoon."

"That would be a shame, Captain," Wayne Raleigh said. He saw the glare in Captain Salmon's eyes. "I mean, sir, you spend all night every night on the bridge and you need your sleep."

"You're damned right I do," Captain Salmon said. He pushed the coffee cup away and left the Wardroom. Hank Copper looked at the young reserve officer with an amused glint in his eyes.

"One of these days he's going to catch on to the fact that you're ribbing him, and being able to play a harpsichord isn't going to help you at all."

An hour later Wayne Raleigh raised the periscope and steadied it and then leaned over the hatch and called out.

"Control, notify the Captain that we have at least four ships bearing one-seven-five."

Captain Salmon climbed the ladder to the Conning Tower, followed by Mike O'Connor. The Captain looked through the periscope and then motioned to O'Connor to take a look.

"You see what I saw?" he said to O'Connor.

"I saw two ships that look like freighters and two destroyers, sir. Coming right up our tail. The two freighters are smoking a lot. The destroyers appear to be running a search pattern out ahead of their sheep, sir." He moved to one side as Captain Salmon put his eye to the periscope.

"I can see a third destroyer coming up from astern," the Captain said. "Down periscope. Right ten degrees rudder. Steer course two-seven-five."

"Captain, that's taking us away from the targets." O'Connor's big Irish face was troubled. "Unless you're planning to take

them from the side. Do you want the crew sent to General
Quarters, sir?"

"I'll give that order when I think it's the right time, mister.
It's not our job to give battle to three destroyers. That's why
we've lost so many submarines this war, foolish attacks against
overwhelming odds."

"Steady on course two-seven-five," the helmsman reported.

"Make depth two hundred fifty feet, Mister O'Connor. I
want silence about the decks. I want a constant sonar search.
Call me if those destroyers seem to be coming after us." He
slid down the ladder to the Control Room. Arnie Schwartz, the
quartermaster of the watch, looked at Mike O'Connor.

"You figure the Old Man's carrying a little left rudder, sir?
Second time we've seen targets and turned away."

"Belay that talk, Arnie," O'Connor growled.

"Will do, sir. Only reason I spoke up is that I, I mean all of us
aboard, we figure we can talk to you and you don't take it
wrong. Whole crew figures this Old Man is yellow, sir." He saw
the frown forming on O'Connor's face. "You don't have to
believe me, sir. Talk to the Chief of the Boat. He'll tell you."

"I may do that," O'Connor said. "Meanwhile, my friend,
button your lip." He turned to Wayne Raleigh, who had been
standing in the after end of the Conning Tower.

"Wayne, take over the deck watch. Tell the sound watch to
give you continual reports on whatever he hears. And let's
have no more loose talk." He slid down the ladder to the
Control Room.

"Where's the Chief of the Boat?" he asked Chief Harrington,
who had the watch in the Control Room.

"Back aft, sir. After Room has got some trouble with a leaky
afterbody on a fish and he went back to lend a hand."
O'Connor nodded and went aft. He found Chief O'Brien at the
forward end of the After Room, supervising the work on the
torpedo. He motioned to the Chief and the two men walked aft
and stood in front of the torpedo tubes.

"Level with me, Chief," O'Connor said in a low voice. "I
hear talk the crew is upset because we didn't attack those two
destroyers two weeks ago."

"Some of them are talking about cold-cocking the Captain
when they clear the bridge some morning and leaving him
topside when we dive," O'Brien said.

"We can't have that kind of talk, Chief," O'Connor said. "If you can't stop it, I can."

"Mister O'Connor, sir," Chief O'Brien said. "You know damned well you can stop sailors from talking when you're around or when I'm around, but they won't stop talking when we're not around. I think what you'd better do is to tell this Captain to snap out of his hockey and stop his petty bullshit or you and me are going to be dealing with a mutiny."

"Wait a minute," O'Connor said. "That's pretty damned strong talk."

"Is it?" Chief O'Brien said. "We came aboard this ship, sir, when she was a damned pigpen. Captain Foster, you, the other officers and me, we made this crew into a submarine crew. We made them into proud people, Mister O'Connor. This Captain is cutting their pride into little pieces." He stopped and drew in a deep breath.

"Ain't but damned few officers I could ever talk to this way. Admiral Nimitz, before he made Admiral, and a few others. So listen close to me, sir.

"This crew knows what it is to be in the bar in the hotel and some guy asks them what ship they're off and they say *Tigerfish*. They know the look of respect they get from that other guy. The Captain is destroying their pride and they won't stand for it. Sailors can get back at a skipper who does that. They know how to do that.

"Me, I don't care a tiddley-damn about Captain Salmon, never have. But I care about my crew and my ship and my reputation. And yours, sir. Now if you'll excuse me, I got to take a look at that tacki-waxing job on that fish, sir." He turned and walked forward. Mike O'Connor studied the Chief of the Boat's broad back as he bent over the tail of the torpedo the After Room torpedomen were working on. As he walked forward, the torpedomen working on the exhaust valves of the torpedo looked at him, their faces impassive.

Chapter
Eighteen

FLEET ADMIRAL ISORUKU YAMAMOTO, the strategist who originated the plan of bombing Pearl Harbor, had a wide acquaintance among high-ranking U.S. Navy officers. They knew him as a brilliant tactician who had long advocated the role of the aircraft carrier as a striking force in its own right, rather than as part of the protective screen around a battleship strike force. The American naval officers also knew Yamamoto as a highly intelligent and aggressive officer who, prior to 1941, had been fond of playing poker, bridge or chess with them—games at which he was an acknowledged master.

In the rarefied atmosphere of the upper reaches of the Japanese military hierarchy, Admiral Yamamoto was regarded with caution. His brilliance could not be denied, nor was it. But his mingling with the common sailors of his command, his concern for their welfare, was not admired. It was his desire to make himself available to his men, to cheer them up and harden their resolve to fight harder by walking among them at their duties, and talking to the lowliest deckhand as if he were a man of great importance, that was to bring about his death at the age of fifty-nine.

Stung badly by their inability to recapture Guadalcanal, the Japanese High Command decided to make an all-out effort to turn the tide of war in the South Pacific. The American forces were now solidly entrenched on Guadalcanal and Tulagi at the eastern end of the Solomon Islands. General Douglas MacArthur had begun his move north and west from Australia. The Japanese knew if MacArthur was not stopped, their hold on the South Pacific would be broken. The High Command in

Tokyo decided the Americans must be stopped at the Bismarc
Archipelago—New Guinea must be held.

Fleet Admiral Yamamoto was the unanimous choice for th
job. He accepted it joyfully and set up his command headquar
ters at Rabaul, a Japanese stronghold on the northern tip o
New Britain, six hundred air miles from Guadalcanal. He the
called for his carrier forces and combed the Japanese Navy fo
the best pilots he could get hold of and had them assigned t
his carriers. With a strong naval force under his command
plus hundreds of land-based bombers and fighters, Yamamot
began a series of air raids, striking first at one American bas
and then another, exercising his brilliance as a tactician.

With his plans going well, the Japanese Admiral the
decided it was time to pay a personal visit to the uppe
Solomons to inspect and to bolster the morale of the Japanes
troops stationed there. His aides drew up a detailed schedul
of the trip. The Japanese Admiral and his staff would fly to th
various bases in two Mitsubishi Zero-I twin-engined Nav
medium bombers, a type of plane the Americans called
"Betty." Departure from Rabaul was scheduled for 0800, Apr
18, 1943. The first stop would be at Kahili Air Field at Buin,
base on the southeastern tip of Bougainville. The Admiral
itinerary was sent by radio to all the bases he would inspect
The radio messages were picked up by the cryptanalysts i
Pearl Harbor and the codes broken and read. The cryptana
lysts could not believe their vast good luck—in front of then
was the detailed schedule of the most valuable naval office
Japan had—and he would be vulnerable to ambush by air

The word was flashed to Washington and a debate began i
the higher echelons of the military establishment. If Admira
Yamamoto were to be ambushed and shot down, wouldn't thi
be an indication that the Americans had broken the top-secre
codes of the Japanese? Was Fleet Admiral Yamamoto suffi
ciently big game to take this risk?

The answer was—carry out the ambush, and Major John V
Mitchell of the Army Air Force's 339th Fighter Squadron wa
given the assignment. Mitchell prepared a timetable t
intercept Yamamoto as his planes came in for a landing at hi
first stop, Kahili Air Field at Buin, despite the fact that it wa
known that the area around Kahili was swarming with Zek
fighter planes.

Major Mitchell assigned eighteen P-38 "Lightning" fighte

planes to the operation. Fourteen of the planes would serve as
a fighter cover, while four others would make the attack on the
two Bettys carrying Yamamoto and his staff. At 0725 on the
morning of April 18, Major Mitchell led his flight off the runways of Henderson Air Field on Guadalcanal. Two of the
planes developed trouble almost at once: One blew a tire
during takeoff, the other's auxiliary fuel tank would not
function. The loss of the two planes was serious, 15 percent of
the total fighter cover was gone, but Major Mitchell decided to
carry through with the operation.

The flight of sixteen P-38s flew at thirty feet above the
surface of the sea, avoiding islands where Japanese watchers
might see them and report by radio. The 435-mile run was
covered in two hours and nine minutes. If all went well, the
intercept would occur at 0935, thirty-five miles from Kahili Air
Field.

At 0933 the radio silence that had been observed since
takeoff was broken by a pilot in the cover section. "Bogey. Ten
o'clock. High." The P-38s dropped their belly tanks in
preparation for the air battle they knew would begin in
moments. Major Mitchell saw two Bettys being escorted by a
half-dozen Zeke fighters and gave the order to carry out the
operation.

Captain Thomas G. Lanphier, the leader of the four-plane
attack section, roared in on the two Bettys. Three Zekes raced
to intercept him, their guns blazing as the two Bettys began to
take violent evasive action. Lanphier shot down one of the
Zekes. As it arched downward toward the sea, he rolled his
plane in a tight turn. His sharp eyes picked up the outline of a
Betty down below, just above the treetops. As he dove on the
Betty two Zekes attacked him. He ignored the attack and as
the Betty loomed in his gun sights he squeezed the trigger on
his joystick. The right engine of the Betty burst into flame and
the plane crashed into the jungle, exploding in a huge ball of
fire and smoke.

Vice Admiral Ugaki, Yamamoto's Chief of Staff, was riding in
the other Betty. He saw his Admiral's plane crash and burn and
prepared himself for death. Lieutenant Rex Barber caught the
surviving Betty over the jungle and chased it out over
the water. Barber's gunfire ripped through the interior of the
plane, killing many of its occupants. The Betty crashed in
the water at almost full speed, but Admiral Ugaki, badly in-

jured, survived. The P-38s raced away from the scene and
returned to their base on Guadalcanal. Only one plane and
pilot had been lost in the operation. Fleet Admiral Yamamoto,
the man who had promised his Emperor that he would "run
wild in the Pacific," was dead. With him went Japan's best
hope of achieving naval supremacy in the Pacific.

The word of Yamamoto's death was received with muted
cheers in the *Enterprise*. "We never did really whip that man
in a carrier battle," Orv Masters commented as he sat at lunch
with Red Olsen and Andy O'Connor. "Maybe the guy they'll
put in his place won't be as cagey. But I still feel pretty good
that they got him, don't you, boss?"

"I suppose so," Andy O'Connor said slowly. "One of the
twelve apostles, Saint James, said—'From whence come wars
and fightings among you? Come they not hence even of your
lusts that war in your members? Ye lust and have not; ye kill
and desire to have, and cannot obtain; ye fight and war yet ye
have not.'"

"I don't quite follow you," Red Olsen said.

"Lust," Andy O'Connor said. "Lust is a sin. We sin in the
name of war."

"Still don't get you," Red Olsen said. "I don't know anything
about the twelve apostles or much about the Bible, but I
always thought the Lord was on the side of those who were
right. We didn't start this war. They did. So we're the people
who are right and He should be on our side. I don't see what
lust has got to do with it."

"The Japanese are a have-not nation," Andy said. "They
wanted oil and rubber and tin and a lot of other things and they
knew we wouldn't let them take it from other nations. They
lusted for material gains and went to war to satisfy that lust.
The thing that interested me in that quotation from Saint
James is that the sin of lust, which most of think of only in the
physical sense between men and women, can be much
broader. It can reach from the physical lust of one person for
another to the lust of war between nations."

"I could do with some blonde exercising a little physical lust
for my fair white body," Olsen said. He grinned and then let
the grin fade as he saw O'Connor's face tighten.

"Before I forget it, Red," Andy said. "Those two new pilots

they flew out to us. Take them up this afternoon and teach them something about close-formation flying."

"Did that yesterday, boss," Olsen said. "They did pretty good."

"I was watching you from the ship's bridge," Andy said. "They didn't do pretty good. That man who was flying on your starboard hand kept sliding outboard when you went into a left turn. He's got to stick as tight as Masters does to me. Work on him."

"Yes, sir," Olsen said. "Did mail come in this morning? Good. Better go see if my heartthrob is lusting for me." He smiled broadly as O'Connor rose abruptly and left the table. Orv Masters waited until O'Connor was out of earshot and then leaned over the table.

"Down in Kentucky we'd say you ain't got the sense to come in out of a hailstorm," he said. "Dammit, can't you see that Andy's got something eating him? It isn't the job of Air Group Commander, he's carrying that load with no strain at all. Something else is chewing on him and chewing pretty damned good. I haven't seen him smile since he came back from that four days in Pearl."

"If they let me fly back to Pearl for four days and I had a wife back there looks like his wife does, I'd have a silly smile on my face for a month," Red Olsen said. "Okay, Orv. I see your point, old buddy. I'll lay off all my dirty sex talk and act like he's my Sunday school teacher I had when I was a young fella, although come to think of it, she was quite a dish."

Andy O'Connor closed the door to his cabin and sat down at the small desk that was built into the bulkhead. A stack of letters from Carol was piled neatly on one side. Three letters from his parents and one from Mike were in the center. He took a pocket knife out of his trousers and carefully slit open the letters from his parents and Mike. When he had finished reading his father's careful hand, his face had lost its grim expression. He pulled a pad of notepaper toward him and answered the letters from his parents. Then he picked up Mike's letter and weighed it in his hand. Light. Mike never wrote long letters. He read it.

Mike's submarine had a new Commanding Officer, and without much to go on, Mike had decided the man didn't measure up to Captain Foster. That was Mike. He made snap judgments. Mike had taken Carol and her mother to dinner.

He had enjoyed it and he thought the women had enjoyed the outing. Andy finished the short letter and wrote an equally short answer and put it in an envelope. He looked at the stack of letters from Carol and then at his watch. He decided to go topside and see if Red Olsen had taught anything to the new pilots. The work at hand was more important.

He returned to his cabin after the evening meal and shuffled the letters from Carol, looking for the numbers she always put below her return address. He put them in numerical order and, sighing, opened the first one.

He finished reading the stack of letters and sat back, thinking. Carol obviously didn't know he had been in Pearl Harbor. He could thank Mike for not telling her. The letters were cheerful, almost too cheerful, he decided. They were full of small talk: what she had done that day, what her mother had done, what his parents had said in their letters to her and what she had said to them. She was in good health. She missed him dreadfully. There was no mention of the soul-searing, dry-eyed parting that had taken place so many weeks ago. He put the letters away in a desk drawer. He'd answer them tomorrow or the next day.

The *Tigerfish* prowled the Luzon Strait, submerged by day, on the surface at night. Captain Salmon followed the routine almost all submarine Captains followed while on war patrol. He spent the nights on the cigarette deck aft of the bridge and slept during the day when the ship was submerged. As the days wore on with no sightings of enemy ships, Captain Salmon grew more and more irritable.

"They told me they'd given me a hot area," he grumbled at the evening meal. "All we've ever seen is smoke on the horizon, nothing close enough to overtake and attack."

"It might be a good idea to patrol the eastern end of the patrol area, Captain," Hank Copper suggested. "We've been keeping pretty steadily to the western end of the area and all the smoke we have seen is far to the east. It seems that most of the traffic is coming down the eastern side of Formosa, sir."

"If I were a Jap, and thank God I'm not," Captain Salmon said, "I'd use the channel between Formosa and China to go north and south, the western end of our area. We'll stay where we are." He sat back in his chair and glared at the officers around the table.

"I am not happy with the way this crew has shaped up under your tender attention, O'Connor. I want a regular Navy-style field day every Friday instead of this dab a little here, dab a little there they do every day. You've got to let sailors know you're an officer or they won't obey orders, won't keep the ship or themselves clean. See to it they snap out of it. And tell the Chief of the Boat that I expect the Chief Petty Officers to set an example. I saw Chief Hahn the other day with his foot up on the edge of the maneuvering board while he was on watch. I won't stand for that sort of sloppy watch standing. See to it."

"Aye, aye, sir," O'Connor said.

Shortly after the *Tigerfish* surfaced, two nights later, the radioman bent over his typewriter, his fingers hitting the keys in a furious rhythm. He ripped the coded message out of the typewriter and yelled for a messenger, who carried it to O'Connor. After he had decoded the message, he went to the Control Room and got out his charts. He worked for a few minutes and then passed the word to the Bridge to tell the Captain a message of enemy ship movements had come in and would the Captain please lay below and look at it?

Captain Salmon slid down the ladder, his face scowling. "It had better be important, mister," he growled at O'Connor. "I'll have to sit around for fifteen minutes in night-adaptation goggles before I can go back topside." He read the message and then read it aloud, slowly.

"'Four large tankers, eleven merchant ships, one light cruiser and two destroyers are proceeding from Nagasaki en route to Manila and points south. The convoy will join with four other destroyers off the northern tip of Formosa and proceed on course one-seven-eight, true. Convoy will clear the southern tip of Formosa at blah blah blah . . .' How the hell do they know what Japs are going to do? What's the rest of it say? This. 'To all submarines: Observe, report course and disposition of the ships and if possible attack and destroy.'"

"This is their course line, Captain," Mike O'Connor said, pointing at the chart. "They'll come through the eastern end of our patrol area. According to the schedule in the message, if they're on time, we can be in position to intercept by zero two hundred hours tomorrow morning. We'll have less than a quarter-moon, so we should have an advantage, sir."

"What's the disposition of the boats to the south of us, the Fremantle and Brisbane boats?" Captain Salmon asked.

"I don't know, I haven't plotted them in, sir."

"Do that now," Captain Salmon said. O'Connor reached for a clipboard on which he kept the positions of submarines after they filed their location reports each night and quickly marked them in on his chart.

"We've got six boats from the Southwest Pacific Submarine Command strung out along the convoy's route between the dividing line in Luzon Strait and Manila," he said. "The closest boat is about thirty miles south of the dividing line. Plenty of room for us to attack. They can have what we leave, sir."

Captain Salmon studied the convoy's course line. He put his finger on the chart a mile from the course line.

"Take me to that position. From there we should be able to carry out our orders to report the course and disposition of the enemy. If there are six destroyers with this group, the submarines to the south of us must be advised of the exact relationship of the destroyers to the convoy itself so they can avoid the destroyers. We'll take the initial risk of identifying the disposition of the destroyers."

There was a dead silence in the Control Room. Chief Yeoman Harrington, the Chief of the Watch, stared at Captain Salmon, the loathing clear in his eyes. Mike O'Connor cleared his throat.

"Sir, you do intend to attack after we get off the message reporting the disposition of the destroyers, don't you?"

"I intend to follow the orders in this message, mister. Observe and report the disposition of the enemy convoy. Set a course for the area I indicated."

"Captain, are you all right?" O'Connor's voice was clear, loud.

"Of course I'm all right!" Captain Salmon roared. "What do you infer, sir?" He thrust his face toward O'Connor, his eyes bulging below a thick vein that throbbed on his forehead.

"I think you're ill, sir," O'Connor said, his voice loud in the stillness of the Control Room. "I'll get the Pharmacist's Mate in here, sir."

Captain Salmon grabbed the edge of the gyrocompass table with both hands. His face darkened and he swayed back and forth. He looked around him and saw the Wardroom officers, who had been alerted by the loud voices, crowding into the Control Room. He swiveled his head around and looked toward the after end of the Control Room and saw the engine-room Chiefs standing looking at him. The Pharmacist's Mate came crowding between Chiefs Apple and Joy, his black bag in his hand.

"This is a damned plot, and it's your plot, O'Connor," the Captain said in a thick voice. "I'll see you hanged for a mutineer, damn your black Irish soul! You're relieved of all duties. You're confined to your cabin under arrest for the rest of this war patrol. The rest of you who aren't on watch—get out of my sight! Now!" His voice rose into a falsetto. Mike O'Connor walked around the gyrocompass table and his big hands gripped Captain Salmon's upper arms.

"The Captain is obviously ill," he said in clear tones. "Doc, will you give him something to relieve his pain and calm him down?" The Pharmacist's Mate slid a hypodermic needle through the fabric of the Captain's shirt and into his shoulder muscle as O'Connor held the Captain in a viselike grip. Salmon struggled against the overwhelming strength of O'Connor's hands and arms, and then, as the morphine took hold, he slumped, hanging limp in O'Connor's grasp.

"He'll be out for eight, ten hours, sir," the Pharmacist's Mate said to O'Connor.

"Some of you take him into his cabin, undress him and make him comfortable in his bunk," O'Connor said. He looked around the Control Room, seeing the sudden stifling of smiles on the faces of the people who had crowded into the compartment. He walked over to the bulkhead, picked up a telephone and turned the dial to the IMC circuit to talk to all the ship's compartments at one time.

"Now hear this," he said. "This is the Executive Officer speaking. Captain Salmon has been taken seriously ill. I am taking command.

"An enemy convoy is coming down the pike east of us. We will intercept and attack. I want all hands to be on their toes. We don't want to leave any good pickings for the Fremantle and Brisbane boats south of us." He put the telephone back on its hook and shook his head slightly as the faint sound of cheering sounded from the other compartments and reached into the Control Room.

"You want me to start a plot, Captain?" Hank Copper said from the gyrocompass table. "Plotting Party's all set to go, sir."

"Lay out a course to intercept, Hank," O'Connor said. "Have the quartermaster log the Captain's illness and have the

Pharmacist's Mate sign the log. Order the galley to start making sandwiches and coffee, lots of coffee. Tell the baker to produce whatever he can between now and the intercept time. If we make contact, it's liable to be a long while between meals."

In the Forward Torpedo Room Dandy Don Miller looked around at the people who lived in his room.

"Well, it happened. Maybe you people will listen to the Dandy Don when he gives out the straight dope," Miller said in a cheerful voice. "Didn't hear no pistol shot, so I guess Irish Mike didn't have to shoot the Old Man in the ass but he took over, just like I said he would."

Mike O'Connor stood in the Control Room, waiting for Hank Copper and his plotters to finish laying out the respective courses of the convoy and the *Tigerfish*.

"We should be there in plenty of time, Captain," Copper said, looking at O'Connor. He lowered his voice. "You know something, sir? Calling you Captain sounds perfectly natural."

"Doesn't seem natural to me," O'Connor muttered. "I don't know how in the hell I'm going to sort this mess out once we get past this attack but right now I don't give a damn." He looked at the chart. "How long before we should be in sight of the convoy?"

"I'd say about three hours, sir. If those are big ships, we should be able to pick them up before that with the search periscope. I'd put intercept time at zero one-forty-five at the latest. We're about a half-hour short of a full battery charge right now and I've allowed for getting that done. Once we've got the battery charged, we can barrel ahead on all four diesels, Captain."

"Very well," O'Connor said. "I'm going into the Wardroom. Find Chief O'Brien and bring him into the Wardroom, please."

As he walked into the Wardroom, the Officer's Cook drew a cup of hot coffee and put the cup and saucer down at the head of the table, at the Captain's place. The cook grinned at O'Connor and withdrew. O'Connor sat down in the chair, feeling a little strange. Hank Copper and Chief O'Brien came in and took places at the table.

"I don't ask either of you to pass judgment on what I did," he began. "I will be judged by the staff when we get back to port."

"I'd say you've got sixty-five witnesses that will back you up that Captain Salmon is a sick man, Captain," Chief O'Brien said. "Every man in the crew will swear on a stack of Bibles that you had to take the action you took, sir."

"The entire Wardroom shares that opinion, Captain," Hank Copper said quietly. "I've already sounded them out, sir."

"That isn't what I wanted to see you about but I thank you both," O'Connor said. "What I want to do is make a few changes before we sight that convoy. Hank, you'll take over as Exec and navigator. I want you to run the plot if we attack submerged. But if we attack on the surface, give the plot over to Wayne Raleigh and you take the search periscope. Raleigh will take over as Gunnery Officer. Chief, you can keep your eye on him. We'll move Lieutenant Saul Silver to Engineering Officer and Battle Stations Diving Officer. He's one smart dude and he can hack both jobs.

"Chief, I want you to take the midwatch as Officer of the Deck. I know you can handle the watch submerged and I'll be on the bridge at night if you need me. I want you to go through the ship when you leave here and make sure everyone is on their toes. This is the biggest damned convoy I've ever heard reported and I intend to by-God attack it and get as many ships as we can."

"What about Captain Salmon?" Hank Copper said in a low voice. "Doc said he'd wake up in eight or nine hours."

"I'll worry about that when he wakes up," O'Connor said. "Chief, I want all torpedo depths set at two feet. Tell both torpedo rooms that if we get into the middle of this convoy— and that's where I intend to go—that they will reload without my orders. Make sure they take all safety precautions, we might have to dive in a damned hurry and in the middle of a reload and I don't want a torpedo to get loose."

"They can do the job, Captain," Chief O'Brien said.

"Let's start the plot now, Hank. We've got to be letter-perfect in this attack." He smiled wryly. "This may be the last act of my naval career and I'd like it to be one I can remember."

Wayne Raleigh, manning the search periscope as the *Tigerfish* raced eastward, reported seeing the masts of ships at a little past 0100. O'Connor left the bridge and dropped down into the darkened Conning Tower and crouched at the hatch leading to the Control Room, closing his eyes so his night vision wouldn't be ruined by the Control Room lights.

"How long until we arrive on station?" he called down the hatch.

"Ten minutes, Captain," Hank Copper replied.

"Let's go to General Quarters," O'Connor said. "Tell Silver I want to flood down to decks awash as soon as we arrive on station. I don't want to give them any more silhouette than I have to. Remain on main-engine propulsion." He went back to the bridge and waited. Ten minutes later he heard the gentle sigh of the air in the ballast tanks escaping and saw the water creep up and eddy back and forth across the slotted deck of the *Tigerfish*. Chief O'Brien's voice floated up from the Control Room.

"All hands are at General Quarters. All torpedoes set for two feet depth, Captain."

"Very well," Mike O'Connor said. He raised his binoculars and saw the black bulk of ships on his port hand.

The *Tigerfish* and Captain Michael Turloch O'Connor waited.

Chapter
Nineteen

THE JAPANESE CONVOY MOVED southward through the night, three lines of ships steaming in formation. The center line was led by a large merchant ship followed at 750-yard intervals by four lumbering oil tankers. Out on each side of the center line of ships at a distance of 750 yards was a row of troop transports and supply ships, each keeping an interval of 750 yards from the ship ahead. A light cruiser led the formation, plowing along one thousand yards ahead of the center line of ships. Two destroyers ranged on either side of the convoy. Astern of the convoy a destroyer was alert for submarines. Out ahead of the cruiser still another big Fubuki destroyer crisscrossed back and forth in front of the convoy.

Hank Copper, manning the search periscope in the Conning Tower, focused on the ships coming toward the *Tigerfish* and let out a long, slow breath. "My God!" he half-whispered. Then, in a louder voice that could be heard in the Control Room, "Stand by for bearings."

"Destroyer. Let's call this DD Number One. He's crossing back and forth in front of the convoy. Now dead ahead of his sheep. His bearing is three-three-five, range is six thousand yards.

"Destroyer. DD Number Two. West of the convoy. Bearing is three-one-five. Range is six thousand yards.

"Destroyer. DD Number Three. West of the convoy. Bearing is two-nine-five. Range is seventy-eight hundred yards.

"Big ship out in front of the main body of the convoy. That's got to be the cruiser. Bearing is three-two-six. Range is sixty-seven hundred fifty yards.

"The convoy itself: There are three rows of ships. I'll give you a bearing on the row to the west. Lead ship. Bearing is three-two-zero. Range is sixty-eight hundred yards."

"Gotcha," Wayne Raleigh's voice came up through the hatch. "I'd like another bearing in two minutes so I can get a speed, sir."

Hank Copper sent down the bearings two minutes later and Wayne Raleigh busied himself at the plotting board.

"Speed of the convoy proper is fifteen knots, Bridge. Distance to the track of the targets is five thousand yards. At our present speed we'll be a thousand yards from the target's track in five minutes. That lead destroyer, DD Number One, should be past us in two minutes. The big ship you identify as the cruiser should be dead ahead in six and one-half minutes. Suggest we run at this speed for four minutes and then slow to fifteen knots, sir."

"You hear all that, Captain?" Hank Copper called up the hatch to the bridge. "Or do you want a repeat?"

"I got it all, Hank," Mike O'Connor called down. "Put the low-pressure blowers on the ballast tanks and get us up to cruising trim." He waited until the blowers had stopped.

"Make turns for fifteen knots," O'Connor called down the hatch. "Hank, here's what I'm going to do.

"I can see the destroyer out ahead of the convoy. He's running back and forth like a hunting dog. I'm going to let him go by and take the cruiser first. I want to shoot at the cruiser from under a thousand yards if possible.

"Then I'll go past his stern and take the first ship in the outboard row. That will probably be the last chance we have for a regular setup on a target. Once I get into the middle of the convoy, it's going to be eyeball and shoot. Alert the torpedo rooms to that situation and tell them to stand by to shoot on my orders. Once we take a crack at the second target, Hank, I want you to keep an eye on those damned destroyers. All that clear to you people down below?"

"Yes, sir," Hank Copper said in a strangled voice.

"All clear, Bridge," Wayne Raleigh's voice came up the hatch.

"Destroyer Number One is on a leg to the east and dead ahead, Bridge," Hank Copper called out from the search periscope. "We've got a constant solution running on the cruiser. Do you want to send a contact report?"

"After we attack," O'Connor said. "Write out the message and send it after we've fired."

"Cruiser will be in range in three minutes, Bridge," Wayne Raleigh said.

"Very well," O'Connor said. He leaned his elbows on the bridge rail and steadied the rubber eyepieces of his binoculars against his eyes. He had never seen so many enemy ships at one time. As he swung the binoculars to the left, he saw a distant bow wave curling. The destroyer that was riding herd on the convoy's starboard side was turning and reversing course. He grinned to himself.

"Plot," he called out. "Destroyer Number Two has reversed course. We'll take the cruiser and then I'll try to get at the leading ship in the center column if I can. Might as well take advantage of the tin can putting himself out of the action for a few minutes." He heard the acknowledgment from down below. He let his binoculars hang from the leather strap around his neck and bowed his head.

"Lord," he said in a whisper, "if I am truly doing Your work, help me to do it well." He raised his head and drew a deep breath.

"Clear the bridge!"

The lookouts thudded down from their stations in the periscope shears and went below. The last man down turned away from the ladder in the Control Room.

"Jeeezus!" he said. "There's ships all over up there!"

O'Connor looked around the empty bridge. He leveled his binoculars at his first target, seeing the oddly shaped superstructure of the ship. "You have to be a cruiser," he muttered. He fidgeted, waiting for word from Wayne Raleigh that he was within a thousand yards of his target.

"Range is one thousand yards to the first target, Captain," Raleigh's voice came up through the hatches from the Control Room.

"We have a constant solution on the TDC," Hank Copper called out.

"Stand by!" O'Connor took a quick look around.

"Nine hundred yards and closing, Captain!"

"FIRE ONE!" He counted down slowly.

"FIRE TWO!"

"Torpedoes running hot, straight and normal," Amos Stuckey reported.

O'Connor stared at his target. He heard a whistle suddenly blast in the night and saw the cruiser begin a slow turn toward him as the cruiser's Officer of the Deck, alerted by a lookout's sighting of torpedo wakes, tried to present the ship's bow to the onrushing torpedoes. A sudden burst of flame showed at the cruiser's midsection and a booming roar echoed across the water, followed by another burst of flame and a blasting explosion that twisted the cruiser to one side, steam erupting in a white geyser from the ship's midsection.

"Two hits on the cruiser!" O'Connor yelled. "Fifteen degrees left rudder. Pour on the coal! Give me all the speed you've got!"

"Rudder is fifteen left. Making turns for all-ahead emergency," Chief O'Brien's voice boomed up from the Control Room.

"Meet her head right there," O'Connor yelled. He looked around, his eyes searching for the convoy's destroyers. He saw his next target out ahead of him. To his right the cruiser was listing badly to starboard, steam boiling out of the ship in big white clouds.

"Solution is constant on the next target, Captain," Hank Copper called out from the Conning Tower. "Range is twelve hundred yards and closing, sir."

"Stand by," O'Connor replied. He let his binoculars hang by the strap and gripped the bridge rail with his hands. He felt strangely calm. His target was beginning a turn away from him, presenting more of the broad side of the ship to the submarine.

"Nine hundred yards!" Copper yelled.

"FIRE THREE!"

"FIRE FOUR!"

In the Forward Torpedo Room an incredible ballet of strength, coordination and agility had begun as Dandy Don Miller started to reload the torpedo tubes that had been fired. He grabbed a big Y-wrench from a reload-crew member and slammed it on the outer door stud for Number One tube and spun it with all the strength of his long, sinewy arms. The outer door slammed shut with a muted clang and Miller opened the tube drain valve and twisted open a valve that put air pressure in the tube to make it drain faster. He leaped back between the torpedo tubes as the telephone talker relayed the order to fire Number Two tube, his fingers pushing the manual firing key down a split-second after the tube fired electrically from the Conning Tower. He jumped out from between the tubes and shut the air valve putting pressure in Number One tube, opened the tube vent, grabbed the wrench that opened the tube's inner door and rotated the bayonet joint that opened the inner door. He ducked out of the way as the inner tube door slammed open.

"Pull that fucker inna tube!" he yelled at the reload crew. The reload crew hauled on the block and tackle and the three-thousand-pound torpedo began to slide along its skid and onto the rollers in the torpedo tube. Miller jumped back between the tubes as the talker yelled to stand by and then ducked out again after tubes Three and Four had been fired, dodging out of the way of Big John Sanders, the number-two torpedoman in the Forward Room, who was busy reloading Number Two tube. Miller raised his right arm as the tail of the reload torpedo for Number One tube neared the breech of the tube. He unhooked the block and tackle, yanked the propeller lock off the torpedo's propellers, and bracing his back against the torpedo roller stand, he eased the torpedo home into the tube with brute strength. He dropped to his knees and opened a valve to recharge the impulse firing tank for the tube while a reload man closed the inner door and opened the outer door. He closed the impulse charging valve and turned to the telephone talker.

"Number One tube reloaded. Depth set two feet. Depth spindle disengaged." As the talker relayed the information, Big John Sanders slapped the talker on the shoulder and reported Number Two tube reloaded and ready. As the talker relayed the information, Miller and Sanders were busy reloading tubes Three and Four.

Mike O'Connor saw his second target suddenly slow, and as the sound of the torpedo exploding against the ship echoed across the black water, he saw the target's bow suddenly dip downward.

"Hit on the second target!" O'Connor yelled. "He's down by the bow. Left fifteen degrees rudder. I'll take this next one . . . he's turning . . . stop turning, you sonofabitch! Stand by . . .

"FIRE FIVE!"

"FIRE SIX! What tubes do I have, Control? Dammit, tell me!"

"You've got One, Two, Three and Four forward," Chief

O'Brien's deep bass shout came up the hatches. "Repeat. One, Two, Three, Four forward. All tubes aft."

"Very well," O'Connor said.

"Destroyer outboard to port is coming in after us!" Hank Copper reported from the search periscope in the Conning Tower. "Wait . . . Oh, good Christ!" The tanker O'Connor had fired at exploded in a bellowing column of fire that soared upward. The destroyer sheered away from the burning ship.

"Hit on a tanker!" O'Connor yelled. "Ease your rudder . . . meet her head right there . . . I need more speed if you've got it . . ." He looked around.

The ocean seemed to be choked with ships. Astern of him the cruiser, his first target, was showing flashes of fire in the steam still belching out of the crippled ship. In the bright light of the burning tanker he could see his second target, its bow deep under the sea, its big single screw still turning as its stern stuck out of the water. Ahead of him a merchant ship, its whistle screaming steadily, was cutting across his bow.

"Stand by Forward," O'Connor yelled. "Steady on course right there . . . stand by . . . oh, you bastard, I've got you . . . FIRE ONE! . . . FIRE TWO!" He ran over to the starboard side of the bridge.

"Right twenty degrees on the rudder . . ." He shielded his face from the heat with his forearm as the *Tigerfish* turned toward the burning tanker. "Meet your helm there! Steady on that course! My God, it's hot up here!" He jumped as an enormous explosion sounded astern. He whirled and saw the ship he had just fired at explode in a tremendous cataclysm of red, blue, yellow, orange and white flame. One explosion followed another as the ship burst apart, huge streamers of fire arcing high in the air.

"Hit in the last target! Ammunition ship!" O'Connor yelled. "Left fifteen degrees rudder there's a destroyer back there . . . stand by Aft . . . FIRE SEVEN! . . . FIRE EIGHT! . . . oh, don't turn you bastard! Got you!" O'Connor screamed the last words as he saw his second torpedo slam into the stern of the destroyer. The destroyer's depth charges exploded and the entire after end of the ship disappeared. "Hit on a destroyer!" O'Connor yelled. "His whole stern blew off." He trotted from one side of the bridge to the other, maneuvering the *Tigerfish* between the burning ships, trying to stay out of sight of the destroyers that were now in among the convoy and experiencing difficulty to avoid being rammed by the panicky merchant captains who were maneuvering their ships in every direction. As the *Tigerfish* ran by the stern of a merchant ship, a gun crew on the ship's stern opened fire on the submarine, the shells screaming above the submarine.

"What tubes do I have?" O'Connor bellowed.

"You've got all tubes. Repeat. All tubes," O'Brien yelled back.

O'Connor heard a sudden clanging in the periscope shears above him and he half-turned, looking upward. He felt his uniform hat suddenly whip off as a hot iron seared the back of his head. He staggered and then shook himself. He put his hand to the back of his head and winced with pain. He looked at the palm of his hand and saw the dark stain of blood.

"Stand by Forward," he shouted. "These people are shooting at us . . . stand by . . . FIRE ONE! . . . FIRE TWO! . . . Left full rudder." He saw the gush of flame in the stern of the ship he had just fired at and saw the ship stop dead in the water and begin to go down by the stern.

"Hit in that last target!" he yelled. He ran to the other side of the bridge and saw a destroyer beyond a merchant ship. His seaman's eyes calculated the sea room he had between the ship he had just hit, the oil tanker that was burning fiercely on his starboard hand and another tanker that was coming straight at him.

"Right full rudder," he yelled. "Give me every turn you can! Control . . . stand by to go under when I give the word. It's getting too hot up here. Close torpedo-tube outer doors . . . house your 'scope." He turned his head and saw a destroyer that had come into the melee of the convoy after him. The destroyer was turning away to avoid a collision with a tanker that was running wild through the convoy. He saw the flares of light on the destroyer's stern area and heard shells going by overhead. His meaty hand jammed the diving alarm and he dropped through the hatch, pulling it closed above his head.

O'Connor's feet hit the deck of the Control Room with a thud as he slid down the ladder from the Conning Tower.

"Let's get down fast, Sullie," he said to Saul Silver. "Make it three hundred fifty feet. As soon as we pass two hundred feet, come right to a course ninety degrees from our heading now. Rig for depth charge. Rig for silent running."

Wayne Raleigh looked up from his plot. "I know this plot is a mess, Captain, we didn't have any bearings except what Hank could get once in a while when you were shooting, but if I'm right, we'll be heading back at the tanker you hit when we come right."

"That's right," O'Connor said. "That tanker's a big ship and he's gonna burn for a long while and there's a lot of destroyers up there that want our ass fried and on toast."

The telephone talker in the Control Room, his eyes wide as he looked at the back of his Captain's head, spoke into his telephone. "Pharmacist's Mate to the Control Room on the double. Captain's bleeding like a stuck pig." O'Connor half-turned as he heard the talker and then he put his hand to the back of his head and winced.

"Sonofabitch on one of those ships shot my hat right off my head," he said.

"Two hundred feet, ten-degree down angle. Rudder is right twenty degrees, sir," Lieutenant Silver said. He straightened his lanky frame and stared at the depth gauges in front of the bow and stern planesmen.

"Very well," O'Connor said. He stood patiently as the Pharmacist's Mate dabbed at the back of his head.

"You must have an iron skull, Captain," the Pharmacist's Mate said. "You got a deep crease back here, but the bone looks nice and solid. White. You better grab onto something, sir. I'm gonna slop on some iodine and it will hurt."

"Go ahead," O'Connor said. His eyes flicked sideways as he saw Amos Stuckey suddenly stiffen on his stool in front of the sound gear.

"I've got a set of twin screws bearing zero-one-zero, Captain," Stuckey said.

"Rudder amidships," O'Connor ordered. He tensed his neck and shoulder muscles as the iodine bit into the raw flesh on the back of his head.

"I'll put a compress on the wound and wrap a bandage around your head, Captain," the Pharmacist's Mate said. "I know you haven't got time to let me shave your head and put in sutures, so this'll stop the bleeding." He swiftly wrapped several windings of bandage around Captain O'Connor's head and taped it down. O'Connor touched the thick bandage that covered his forehead.

"You're a hell of a doctor, Doc," he said. "Thanks. Amos, get your ears to working. Wayne, start a plot of the sound bearings."

Amos Stuckey closed his eyes and concentrated on the sounds that were coming into his earphones.

"The single-screw ships are moving away, Captain. I can hear three or four twin-screws up there, all of them moving fast. One twin screw bears zero-one-zero. Another one bears zero-seven-zero. Got another one at one-seven-zero, sir. One more twin screw bearing two-five-zero with the single screws, sir."

"One of the tin cans is herding the sheep out of the way," O'Connor grunted. "Once they get what we left out of that convoy out of the way, they'll come after us. Stay at this depth, Sullie, until we see what they're going to do." He walked over to the ladder that led to the Conning Tower.

"Hank, clear the Conning Tower and close the hatch after you. No sense in anyone being up there in that drum when they begin depth charging." Hank Copper and Pete Savage came down the ladder. O'Connor walked over and looked at the plot.

"Pretty good box score," Copper said. "I can confirm every one of them by observation through the periscope. One cruiser, one destroyer, three pretty big merchant ships and one oil tanker."

"We fired twelve fish and got seven hits," Wayne Raleigh said.

"Good God, that many ships down? Six?" O'Connor said.

"Not too bad," Copper said. He looked at the plot. "You fired at the cruiser at zero one-fifty. We dove at zero two-fifty. You were in the middle of the convoy for about fifty-five minutes, Captain."

"Seemed like fifty-five days," O'Connor said. He turned as Amos Stuckey spoke up.

"The single-screw ships are quite a way away, sir. One twin-screw ships still with them. I've got four sets of twin screws near to us. Bearings are zero-two-zero . . . one-six-zero . . . two-zero-zero and two-eight-zero. All four ships are echo-ranging, sir."

O'Connor watched as Wayne Raleigh swiftly plotted the positions of the destroyers up above. "Look," he said to Raleigh. "They're maneuvering, taking position to get us in a box. Whichever way we turn, we run into one of them. Pass the word that the music will start any minute now." He looked

at the temperature and humidity gauges. The temperature was
98 degrees, the humidity read 97 percent. He walked around
the gyrocompass table and peered at the bathythermograph.
The slender stylus had marked an even arc on the smoked
card, an indication there was no colder layer of salt water in
the vicinity of the submarine that it could take shelter under.

"Put a fresh card in the bathythermograph, John," Captain
O'Connor said to John Ribbon. "Keep a close eye on it, son.
Let me know if that stylus jiggles either way. I'm depending on
you, my friend."

John Ribbon, his thin body tense, nodded. "Yes, sir. Will do,
Captain."

On the surface four big Fubuki destroyers maneuvered,
circling, their sonar search beams probing for the submarine
below them. On the bridge of the Fubuki leader Commander
Shigatero Izumani, the Squadron Commander, paced back and
forth, his olive face grim. A junior officer approached him and
stood, nervously shifting from one foot to another.

"No contact as yet, sir," he said.

"Keep trying," Commander Izumani said. "The plot shows
that the submarine, or submarines, there may be two or three
of them, should be within our circle. Set all rack depth charges
for three hundred fifty feet. Set Y-gun charges for two hundred
fifty feet." He spun around as a sound rating yelled.

"Contact!"

The Squadron Commander leaned over the shoulder of his
plotting officer. "Ah, we were right," he said. "We've got at
least one of them down there. Triangulate him, get his depth.
Once we have that, we begin the attack."

Amos Stuckey opened his mouth and then closed it as the
ringing sound of a sonar search beam echoed through the hull
of the *Tigerfish*. In the Forward Torpedo Room Dandy Don
Miller stood in front of the torpedo tubes and stretched out his
arms, gripping the door handles of Numbers One and Two
tubes in his hands.

"The music the crazy Irishman said was going to start is
coming right now," he said. "All hands except those on the
sound heads and me and Big John get in the bunks and hold
on." He grinned crookedly. "Woman once told me if you
screwed enough women, you stood to get a dose of clap. I

guess if you sink enough ships, you stand to get the shit kicked
out of you."

"Contact bearing one-seven-zero is picking up speed, Captain," Stuckey said. "He's coming fast."

"Four hundred feet, Sullie," Captain O'Connor ordered. He
gripped the edge of the gyrocompass table as the *Tigerfish*
slanted downward. The thunder of a destroyer's propellers
hammered through the hull of the *Tigerfish*, shaking the ship
slightly.

"He's dropped!" Stuckey half-whispered.

"Three hundred seventy five . . . three hundred eighty-
five . . . ease your bubble, men," Saul Silver said quietly.
"Coming to four hundred feet, Captain."

Loud cracking sounds hammered at the hull of the submarine, the depth-charge pistols exploding, and then the
depth charges went off with shattering roars. The *Tigerfish*
staggered and rolled heavily to port, her hull creaking in the
enormous vortex of water that enveloped her.

"Four hundred fifty feet, Sullie," Captain O'Connor ordered. "All compartments report damage."

"Contact bearing zero-two-zero is picking up speed, sir,"
Stuckey said. "Coming fast."

"All stop," O'Connor ordered. He looked at Copper.
"Maybe they'll overshoot us." He fought back the impulse to
look upward as he heard several depth-charge pistols go off
almost as one. The explosions battered the submarine, breaking all the light bulbs in their sockets, tearing loose the
insulation in the ship's overhead. In the After Torpedo Room a
half-dozen streams of pencil-thin water shot out from between
the torpedo tubes. Jerry McGovern, the torpedoman in charge
of the After Room, reached outboard of the torpedo on the
port side of the room and grabbed a big orange canvas sack.

"Don't nobody get in front of that water," he warned. "That
stuff will slice into you like a hot knife into butter." He tapped
the telephone talker on the shoulder.

"Tell the Control Room the grease fittings on the after
bulkhead are blowing out and I'll plug 'em up. Tell Control I
think we got a ruptured After Trim tank, is what I think. Only
thing that could make them grease fittings blow out is sea
pressure and we're fucking deep." He dropped down on his
belly and began to crawl aft between the two lower torpedo
tubes, dragging the canvas bag behind him, keeping below the
streams of water, fully aware that with the sea pressure outside

the hull at two hundred pounds to the square inch, the streams of water would pierce his flesh like a dagger.

"Compensate for a flooded After Trim, Sullie," Mike O'Connor said. "Shift water when they come back and drop charges, they won't hear us then."

The telephone talker in the Forward Torpedo Room relayed the information of what had happened in the After Room to Dandy Don Miller.

"Ask the Chief of the Boat does Jerry need any help," Miller said.

"Negative," the talker said. "Chief says Jerry can hack it."

Jerry McGovern reached the bulkhead and rolled over onto his back. He fumbled in the orange sack and pulled out a short-handled sledge and laid it on his stomach. He reached in the bag again and pulled out a tapered wooden plug made of hard oak. He positioned himself under the streams of water.

"Somebody back there watch me and give me the word when I get close to the bottom stream of water," he called out. "And don't get hit by the fucking water."

He inched the plug upward, holding it with both hands, keeping the point of the plug touching the bulkhead. A torpedoman crouching to one side of the streams of water aimed the beam of a battle lantern at the bulkhead.

"Little to starboard . . . little more . . . you're right under it now . . . about an inch or two," he called out. McGovern took a deep breath and pushed the plug upward, feeling for the hole where the grease fitting had blown out. He felt the sharp point of the plug sink in a little and he arched his back, shoving the plug into the hole with all his strength. He cautiously dropped one hand and groped for the handle of the sledge hammer. He tapped the large end of the plug once, gently, then harder. He hit the plug twice more and tentatively relaxed his grip. The plug was holding. He took the sledge in both hands, and lying on his back, he smashed at the plug as hard as he could. He hit the plug again and again and then dropped his arms and took a deep breath.

"That's one of the fuckers," he said. "Only five more to go." He laid the sledge hammer on his chest and reached in the bag for another plug.

Ten miles to the south of the dividing line in Luzon Strait, the U.S.S. *Angelfish*, thirty-four days out of Fremantle in western Australia, cruised on the surface. Her Captain stood in the bridge with the Officer of the Deck, listening to the distant thunder of depth-charge explosions.

"Any word yet from Fremantle on whether we can cross the dividing line and help him out?" the OOD asked.

"Not yet. I sent the message addressed to Pearl and Fremantle two hours ago. Told them that whoever was just north of the line was putting on the damndest show I ever saw, that I know he hit at least one tanker and I thought he hit an ammo ship.

"You and I both know Fremantle won't say anything until Pearl gives them the word." He squinted at his watch. "It's close to zero eight hundred hours in Pearl now. They should have the word. Maybe we'll know in an hour or two."

"First light is in an hour, Captain, hour and fifteen minutes."

"I know," the Captain of the *Angelfish* said. "We'll stay topside as long we can. If they send a message that lets us go help him out, I want to be able to receive it. We've got ten fish left, and if the Jap is concentrating on that poor bastard getting that hammering, we might be able to sneak in and knock off a couple of them."

The Japanese destroyers above the *Tigerfish* moved in an ordered pattern, searching for the submarine, and when they found it at four hundred fifty feet or shallower, moving to the attack with skilled savagery. When their triangulation showed the submarine to be below four hundred fifty feet, they were content to keep their sonar search beams hammering at the submarine to let the men inside their target know they weren't going to get away.

Captain Izumani stood in his ship's bridge chart room and studied the plot. "He hasn't done anything radical or different," he said. "He doesn't seem to like it much down below four hundred fifty feet. He keeps going down to that depth and then after a while he comes up to four hundred feet."

"Maybe we've hurt him and he's leaking," the plotting officer said. "At below four hundred fifty feet the leaks, if he has them, would be impossible to control."

"That's one possibility," Captain Izumani said. He looked out the wide glass window of the chart room. "Morning light is in an hour or so. What's the status of the cruiser?"

"The fires are out. Her engine rooms are flooded and they're trying to pump those areas now but they don't think they can, sir. She's badly holed astern. As soon as daylight comes, the

Kazami will put a towing bridle on her, sir." The Plotting Officer looked at his Captain.

"This submarine man is a good shot, sir."

"Not so good," the Fubuki Captain said. "Where he was in the middle of the convoy with those stupid merchant captains panicking, all he had to do was to keep firing torpedoes. He would have hit something with every other shot."

"He hit enough as it was," the Communications Officer said. "I sent off the message detailing the losses, sir."

Captain Izumani nodded irritably. "I don't like this order from Tokyo that we must report all losses at once. If we get the submarine we report it but after we have told what he got, and that makes killing the submarine anticlimactic." He looked around as his Sonar Officer approached.

"The target is at four hundred feet, sir."

"Commence an attack run, all ships in turn," Captain Izumani ordered.

"No layers, sir," John Ribbon reported from the bathythermograph.

"Thank you, John," Captain O'Connor said. He turned to Lieutenant Saul Silver. "How's your Trim, Sullie?"

"It isn't," Silver said. "After Trim is definitely flooded. No doubt of it. Best I can do is to hold her with a three-degree up bubble."

"Just don't lose her, kid," Mike O'Connor said.

"Here they come again," Stuckey said. He pushed his earphones up on his temples as the thunder of the destroyer's propellers filled the *Tigerfish*.

The attack was nicely coordinated as each of the four Fubukis wheeled into position and then raced down the track of the *Tigerfish* and released depth charges from the racks on their sterns and fired others from their Y-guns. Down below the attackers, the *Tigerfish* was twisted and wracked, her welds straining, water gushing into the ship in thin streams from a hundred different explosion-tortured valve fittings.

The interior of the *Tigerfish* was humid to the point of saturation. Water condensed in the 130-degree temperature and formed pools on every level surface. The men in the crew not needed for duty lay in their bunks, gasping for air in the fetid heat. Dandy Don Miller looked at a page in a soggy notebook he had put on the skid rest.

"I count eighty-six depth charges so far and for chrissake it's only zero-six-thirty. Them fuckers will have us all day long if they don't run out of depth charges."

"Five hundred feet, Sullie," Mike O'Connor ordered. "Let's see if we can find a layer down there." He stepped over and added his brawn to Chief Harrington's panting effort to tilt the bow planes to hard dive. Saul Silver, his wide, muscular shoulders straining, was helping out the man on the stern planes. The *Tigerfish* slid deeper into the sea.

"All compartments report leaks," Hank Copper ordered.

"Forward Torpedo Room says the packing gland of the anchor is leaking heavily," the telephone talker said. "Leaks in the two engine rooms are bad. Chief Apple says he can stand this depth for about ten minutes and then he's going to have to pump bilges or wade, sir. After Room is replacing the plugs in the bulkhead that blew out again, sir."

"Very well," Captain O'Connor said. He moved over and stood beside John Ribbon, watching the stylus scratch the smoked card of the bathythermograph. He turned and went back to the gyrocompass table and studied the plot, wiping away the sweat that was streaming down his face with a soiled towel.

"Here they come again," Amos Stuckey said, his voice almost a moan.

"Tell the engine rooms to put their bilges on the line," Saul Silver ordered. "I'll start pumping as soon as they start dropping."

Mike O'Connor turned as he heard the securing dogs on the watertight door that led from the Control Room to the Forward Battery Compartment moving. The watertight door swung open and Captain Salmon stepped through it into the Control Room.

"What the hell are you doing?" Captain Salmon rasped. He grabbed at the edge of the gyrocompass table as two depth charges slammed the *Tigerfish* sideways.

"You're under arrest, O'Connor! Get to your cabin or I'll shoot you down like a damned dog!" He pulled a .45 automatic out of his trouser pocket and leveled it at Mike O'Connor's chest.

"Move, you mutinous sonofabitch!"

Chapter
Twenty

THE ONLY MAN MOVING in the tableau in the Control Room was the machinist's mate at the trim manifold. He listened to the thundering of the depth charges, and as the noise of the explosions began to die down, he shut down the trim pump that was pumping the engine-room bilges and spun closed the discharge valve. He turned to report and his jaw dropped in surprise as he saw Captain Salmon steadying a .45 automatic on the gyrocompass table, its muzzle pointed at Mike O'Connor on the other side of the table.

"You're guilty of mutiny, O'Connor," Captain Salmon grated. "You're under arrest. Get to your cabin and I'll try to save this ship from being destroyed." His thumb slid upward and curled around the gun's hammer. John Ribbon, standing in front of the bathythermograph at the corner of the gyrocompass table, began to ease silently toward Captain Salmon in a smooth, fluid motion. Suddenly his hands reached out and clutched the weapon.

Chief O'Brien reacted. He took a long step from his battle station at the main hydraulic manifold, his powerful right arm swinging like an axe, his fist smashing down on to the muscle on the top of Captain Salmon's forearm. The officer cried out in pain and doubled over, his left hand clutching at his right forearm. John Ribbon's eyes widened in horror as he looked at the cocked automatic he was holding. He half-turned and Hank Copper reached over the table and gently took the gun from his hands. He carefully let the hammer down and pressed the magazine release. A loaded clip slid out of the gun's butt. He worked the slide and a cartridge popped out and landed on the gyro table and rolled in a half-circle.

"Sonofabitch had one up the spout," he said in an awed tone of voice.

Captain Salmon straightened up and charged at Chief O'Brien, screaming curses, his left hand clawing at the big Chief Petty Officer's eyes. O'Brien slapped the hand to one side and wrapped his arms around the screaming officer. He spread his feet and began to squeeze.

"Get the Pharmacist's Mate in here on the double with his bag," Mike O'Connor ordered. He turned and looked at Chief O'Brien, who was growling murderously as he squeezed Captain Salmon.

"Don't hurt the man, Chief," O'Connor cautioned.

"Captain," O'Brien grunted as he jerked his head to one side. "This man is biting my neck!" Chief Harrington rose from his bench in front of the bow planes and reached over and got a double handful of Captain Salmon's hair and yanked his head back savagely.

"That better, Chief?" he asked genially.

The Pharmacist's Mate appeared. He took one look at the two struggling men and put his bag on the gyrocompass table and opened it. He took out a hypodermic syringe and fitted a needle through the rubber top of a small bottle. He pulled the plunger all the way out and moved toward the two men.

"Grab him by the shoulders, sir," he half-whispered to Hank Copper. "I'll get him in the big back muscle." Hank Copper clutched at Captain Salmon's shoulders as the Pharmacist's Mate poised the needle like a harpooner. His hand swooped down and he pushed the plunger all the way home and then whipped out the needle.

"Hold him, Chief," he said in a professional tone. "It'll take effect right quick like." Captain Salmon's struggles grew weaker, and as Harrington let go of his hair, his head rolled over to one side, a long string of spittle dangling from his chin.

"Put him in his bunk," Mike O'Connor ordered. "Get some handcuffs from the gunner's mate and handcuff one of his wrists to the bunk rail. He might wake up in another hour."

"He might never wake up, Captain," the Pharmacist's Mate said in a doleful voice, "I really loaded him this time, sir. I got a guy with a broken arm in the After Engine Room and another one with a broken nose. Nothing to worry about, sir, I can take care of it."

Mike O'Connor looked at John Ribbon, who was shaking violently.

"I owe you a big one, John," O'Connor said. "I'll owe you two if you can find a layer for us." Ribbon ground his teeth together and took a long, shaky breath.

"Aye, aye, Captain," he said.

"Here they come again," Stuckey said.

With daylight the Japanese destroyers maneuvered more precisely, coordinating their attacks with greater efficiency than in the black of night. The *Tigerfish*, creeping southward, was battered by a succession of attacks. In each of the sealed-off compartments of the submarine, the crew members did their best to stop the leaks. Chief Machinist's Mate Apple, his chest heaving as he gasped for air in the humid, oxygen-depleted interior of the submarine, patrolled the Forward Engine Room. He couldn't stop the score of leaks that were pouring streams of water into the compartment. The best he could do was to slow them down. From time to time he talked on the telephone with Chief Joy in the After Room, who was facing the same problems.

Lieutenant Saul Silver had his own problems. The ruptured After Trim Tank, filled with sea water, added almost five tons of dead weight to the *Tigerfish*. A submerged submarine is kept in balance, or "trim," by distributing various weights of water to the variable ballast tanks built into the ship for that purpose. The problem of achieving trim is not unlike that of balancing a yardstick on the edge of a razor blade. Weights added to the yardstick that are near the balance point of the razor edge have less effect on the balance than a similar weight added to the far end of the yardstick. The flooded After Trim Tank, located at the after end of the ship, presented a major problem in achieving trim because no similar weight could be added to the forward end of the ship. Ten torpedoes had been fired out of the Forward Torpedo Room. The Forward Trim Tank and the Water Round Torpedo Tank had already been filled to compensate for the loss of fifteen tons of torpedoes. Meanwhile, Lieutenant Silver performed feats of mathematical acrobatics in his head as he transferred water from one tank to the other, flooded and pumped while depth charges slammed the *Tigerfish*, rolling it violently from side to side.

Mike O'Connor wiped the sweat from his face and neck with the towel draped around his neck and looked around the

Control Room. The only sound between attacks was the gasping of men fighting for breath. Hank Copper was standing, his hands braced on the top of the gyrocompass table, his chest heaving as he fought for oxygen. The bow and stern planesmen were huddled on their benches in front of their big hand-wheels, obviously near the end of their endurance. Amos Stuckey was slumped on his small stool in front of the sound gear. From time to time he made a listless swipe with a towel at the pool of water on the deck between his feet.

Mike O'Connor peered at his wristwatch in the dim gloom of the Control Room. "Eleven hundred," he muttered. "Eight hours of this crap." He wondered if the men in the rest of the ship were suffering as much as the men around him in the Control Room, knowing they were.

Captain Izumani paced the bridge of his destroyer, staring out at the small white caps that dotted the ocean surface. He came to a halt as his Executive Officer approached him and bowed and then stood at attention.

"Sir," the Executive Officer said, "I must report that almost half of our store of depth charges has been expended. The other ships report the same expenditure, sir."

"That's a lot of depth charges and no results we know of," Captain Izumani snapped.

"After it got light, we saw some oil, sir. Maybe we've hurt him."

"Possibly," the destroyer squadron leader said. "We've probably damaged him. The attacks we made were excellent. If he's damaged, he may be leaking a lot, and when we attack, he pumps his bilges to keep up with the leaks." He whirled as he heard a lookout's shout.

"Submarine! On the surface bearing zero-seven-five!"

Captain Izumani ran to the starboard wing of his ship's bridge and leveled his binoculars on the bearing the lookout had given. He could see the pencil-thin outline of a submarine's periscope and the small bulk of its bridge.

"I knew there was more than one of them," he said. He stood in the wing of the bridge, thinking, and then he turned to his Executive Officer.

"The one down below us is hurt a little. He won't go anywhere. This other submarine out there has come back to help his friend. We'll take him under attack, and once we've pinned him down we'll divide the force and carry out attacks on both submarines until we kill them.

"Make the signal. All ships. Attack the submarine bearing zero-six-zero from us. Right full rudder. All-ahead flank speed. Gun crews stand by to engage the enemy!" The big Fubuki heeled over in a turn and its high, knifelike bow reared as the ship's powerful engines went to high speed. The other three Fubukis followed their squadron leader.

"Range to the target is eight thousand yards, sir," the Gunnery Officer reported.

"Stand by to open fire," Captain Izumani snapped. He stood in the wing of the bridge, his binoculars at his eyes. The image of the surfaced submarine grew larger in the lens of the binoculars.

"We are within easy range, Captain," the Gunnery Officer said.

"Commence firing!" the Fubuki squadron leader ordered.

The five-inch guns of the big destroyer began to bark, the shells reaching out toward the U.S.S. *Angelfish*. On the submarine a lookout yelled a warning and then jumped downward from his lookout stand as the ship's Captain ordered the bridge cleared. The *Angelfish* plunged beneath the sea as a pair of shells bracketed her. The destroyers rushed toward her, their gunnery ratings standing by their depth-charge racks and Y-guns.

Amos Stuckey raised his sagging head and with a visible effort turned to Captain O'Connor.

"All four sets of twin screws are turning up very fast revolutions, sir," he gasped. "They're moving away from us very fast."

"What's their bearing, Amos?"

"They bear, the four of them, bear three-five-zero, sir. They're really making speed, going as fast as they do when they make an attack run."

"I wonder what the hell is up?" O'Connor muttered. "Keep listening, Amos." Stuckey nodded and turned back to his sound gear. The minutes crept by.

"I can hardly hear them, Captain. They stayed steady on that bearing, sir, they're way off now." He suddenly straightened on his stool, his back stiffening.

"I can hear depth charges! Lots of depth charges, Captain! Way off but those are depth charges, sir."

"You sure?" O'Connor came over and stood beside Stuckey.

"Absolutely sure, Captain. I can't hear their screws anymore but those explosions are coming from the last bearing I had on their screws, sir."

O'Connor tapped the telephone talker on the shoulder. "Pass the word to all hands; for some reason or other the destroyers have moved away from us and we think we can hear them depth charging off to the south. They might have another one of our submarines under attack.

"We're going up and take a look. I want all hands to sharpen up. I know it's bad but we're all in the same condition. I want torpedo-tube outer doors opened when we pass ninety feet. Set torpedo depth at two feet. Shift to hydraulic power on the bow and stern planes, helm and sound gear. If we get a chance, men, we're going to sink one or two of those bastards who've been working us over.

"Sullie, bring me up to periscope depth. Do it damned carefully, I don't want to stick ten feet of our bow out of water with our ass end down at two hundred fifty feet."

"Stand by to put the low-pressure blowers on the after balance tanks," Saul Silver ordered. "We'll take it easy, Captain, float you right up there nice and gentle."

The *Tigerfish* moved upward through the water, Saul Silver watching the bubble in front of the bow and stern planesmen, keeping the upward slant of the ship at no more than three degrees. Mike O'Connor climbed up into the Conning Tower, his legs trembling with the effort of raising his body up each rung of the ladder. Pete Savage followed him and moved to the TDC at the after end of the Conning Tower. O'Connor looked at him, his eyebrows raising.

"I was on the TDC when you were firing at the convoy, Captain," Savage said. "I know how to run it, sir."

"Okay," O'Connor said.

"All torpedo-tube outer doors open. Depth set two feet all torpedoes. Coming to periscope depth, Captain," Chief O'Brien's heavy voice came up the hatch. Pete Savage punched the UP button on the periscope control box and O'Connor squatted on the deck. He grabbed the handles of the battle periscope and snapped them outward as the periscope cleared the deck well and let the rising periscope pull him erect as he put his eye to the lens. He swiveled the periscope to the last bearing Stuckey had given him of the depth-charging noises. There they were, the slender masts of several ships a long way distant.

"I can still hear depth charges, Captain," Stuckey called out. "I've got a new bearing on a very slow twin screw. Bearing is one-five-five, sir. I haven't heard that one before, sir."

O'Connor turned the periscope to the bearing and the people in the Control Room could hear him gasp.

"Plot! Target bears one-five-two!" He twisted the range-finder knob with his right hand.

"Range is fifteen hundred yards. Angle on the bow is ninety port. The target is that damned cruiser we hit last night! He's way down by the stern and a destroyer has got him under tow. Maybe we can get both of the bastards. We'll shoot from the After Room . . . stand by . . . stand by . . ."

"You have a solution, Captain," Pete Savage said. He raised his hand, his index finger poised over the electrical firing buttons for the After Torpedo Room.

"I'll shot tubes Seven and Eight at the cruiser and then we'll try to get that damned destroyer towing her," O'Connor called out.

"Constant solution, sir," Savage said. "Range is now sixteen hundred yards, sir."

"FIRE SEVEN!"

"FIRE EIGHT!"

"Torpedoes running hot, straight and normal, Captain," Stuckey called out.

O'Connor watched through the periscope. He saw a geyser of water rise near the bow of the cruiser, followed by a huge blast of flame. As he drew his breath to announce the hit, another explosion ripped apart the midsection of the cruiser.

"Two hits in that sonofabitch!" he yelled. He swung the periscope around and focused on the destroyer.

"Bearing on the destroyer is one-five-two. Range is seventeen hundred yards. Angle on the bow is . . . he's dropped his towing bridle . . . stand by Aft . . . FIRE NINE! Right full rudder. Stand by Forward . . . ah, hell, he's taking off, the sonofabitch! I missed him! Rudder amidships." He swung the periscope around, searching for the cruiser.

"Hank," he yelled. "Get up here and confirm this. He's rolling over!" He turned and reached down and grabbed Hank

Copper's arm, lifting him bodily up through the hatch and pushing him toward the periscope.

"By God, he is rolling over! There's his bottom!" Copper said. He stepped back so O'Connor could see. He turned the periscope in a 360-degree circle.

"Nothing coming this way," he said. "Let's take a chance, Hank." He moved over and bent his head to talk to the Control Room.

"Sullie, I want you to bring me up to decks awash. As soon as I open the hatch and get it latched, I'll give you the word. As soon as I do, open all watertight doors and start the main engines in the After Engine Room. We'll take a suction from amidships at least, clear out some of that damned heat and humidity. Stand by to shut down the engines and take us back under if anything comes this way. Hank, I want you to keep an eye on the last bearing of those destroyers through the search 'scope." He climbed up a few rungs on the ladder that led to the bridge and waited for Saul Silver to give him the word that the decks were awash.

"You can open the hatch, Captain," Saul Silver called out. O'Connor spun the dogging wheel and pushed the hatch open, wincing as the residual seawater in the bridge gushed over his head and soaked the bandage. He scrambled out into the bridge and raised his binoculars and began a search.

"Destroyers are still way off, bearing one-six-zero, Captain," Hank Copper said.

"What the hell," O'Connor said. "Might as well be hung for a sheep as a lamb, as my father used to say. Sullie, bring us all the way up and tell the Forward Torpedo Room to stand by to open their deck hatch. Open the watertight doors forward. Might as well sweeten the whole ship. Hank, keep searching."

The *Tigerfish*, its fetid interior cleansed by the fresh sea air, submerged fifteen minutes later, Saul Silver easing the submarine down carefully, mindful of the enormous weight of water in the after end of the ship. Mike O'Connor watched his new Battle-Stations Diving Officer, nodding his head in approval.

"Make it one hundred feet, Sullie," O'Connor said. "Get as decent a trim as you can. Get damage reports from all compartments, Hank. Sullie, as soon as you've got the best trim you can get, turn the dive over to Chief O'Brien and we'll have a meeting in the Wardroom." He went forward and sat down in the chair at the head of the table and braced his elbows on the cloth, holding his head in his hands. The Officer's Cook slid a cup and saucer in front of him.

"Fresh coffee, Captain," he said in a low voice.

The *Tigerfish* officers assembled in the Wardroom fifteen minutes later. O'Connor looked around the table at the sweaty officers and grinned.

"Fine bunch of smart-looking officers you are," he said. "You look like someone doused you with a fire hose.

"I want to thank all of you for doing one hell of a job. Now all we have to do is sort out what we do next. The first thing on the agenda is a contact report. We've got to let Pearl Harbor know what we attacked when we go up tonight.

"Then we have to figure out what to do about Captain Salmon." He looked at Lieutenant Saul Silver.

"Sullie, you were a lawyer in civilian life. You got any suggestions?"

"I've been thinking about this, Captain," Saul Silver said slowly. "First off, I think you should have Hank make out the contact report. That way, a third person doing it, you can't be accused of self-interest. Have Hank sign the contact report. Then you attach a codicil to the report stating your reasons for taking command and you sign the codicil and we can all sign as witnesses. It might not be a bad idea for all the Chief Petty Officers to sign the codicil as well."

"Sounds reasonable," Mike O'Connor said. "All we have to do is figure out how to word that codicil. That could be touchy. Beyond that, what do we do with Captain Salmon after he wakes up? We can't keep him under morphine. I don't know what that would do to his health, probably ruin it."

"Threatening to shoot you at a time when we were under attack, his physical attack on Chief O'Brien after the Chief had struck his arm to make him release the gun, constitutes, I would think in legal sense, indicates at least temporary insanity on the part of Captain Salmon," Lieutenant Silver said slowly. "I think that if we say that our opinion does not have the weight of medical verification but that it is an opinion shared by the officers and the Chief Petty Officers, we could be on solid ground, sir."

"Could be," O'Connor said slowly. "Then we come to the problem of advising Pearl what we're going to do with Captain Salmon until we get back to port." He looked at Saul Silver.

"If we state that we believe he is mentally unbalanced," Silver said, "we might as well go whole hog, if you'll forgive the expression from one of my faith, and advise Pearl Harbor that we have handcuffed and confined Captain Salmon to his bunk until we can return to port and that he is being given every possible consideration for his well-being."

"I honestly think something's wrong with him," Mike O'Connor said. "I mean, not wanting to attack the enemy. My God, that's what we're out here for. And then pointing a loaded gun at me. If it hadn't been for that kid John Ribbon and the Chief of the Boat, I might have been dead, some of you might have been dead."

"I'm not a doctor," Saul Silver said, "but I could make a strong case in a courtroom that Captain Salmon was temporarily insane, not only at the time of the incident but before that, that he was under a stress that robbed him of his normal ability to make judgments. I'd strongly suggest that if you agree with that diagnosis, if you will, sir, that if you agree you keep him confined with a man on watch in the passageway outside his cabin. Do everything we can to make him comfortable, bring his food to him, escort him to the head and shower but don't ever relax those measures. Once you've decided that he is not right mentally, you have to go all the way to make it stick."

"I agree," Mike O'Connor said. He looked around the table, seeing each man nod his head in turn. "Very well. We'd better start by agreeing on the contact report. I think Sullie's right in suggesting you make out the contact report and sign it, Hank. I'll help all I can with that, because I did most of the work by eyeball, there isn't much of a plot to go by. Hank, what was the final box score?"

"We fired fifteen torpedoes, Captain. You got nine hits. You sank a cruiser. The message that alerted us said it was a light cruiser, so we can say that. You got a destroyer, a big one. On the merchant side you got three freighters and an oil tanker. All of them looked pretty big to me but I don't have any idea of what tonnages they would be, have you?"

O'Connor shook his head. "Haven't the slightest idea. I think they were big, maybe nine, ten thousand tons each. But I don't know. Put in the contact report that I didn't have time to properly judge tonnages of the ships I was shooting at because of the circumstances. And get to work on the contact report right now. Sullie, will you work on the codicil you mentioned? Don't put it in legal language, but be sure that you don't involve anyone in the decision to take over from Captain Salmon but myself. If they come out with a bucket of hot tar and feathers when we dock at Pearl I don't want any of the tar on you people. I did it. I'll take the blame for it.

"Sullie, have you got a list of materiel damage?" Saul Silver pushed his notebook across the table to Captain O'Connor.

"My God," Mike O'Connor said. "They'll never let us stay out here with all this damage. Hank, just mention the major stuff like the ruptured After Trim Tank and minimize the rest. Sullie seems to have worked out a way to keep a halfway decent trim, and mention that and maybe we can stick around a couple of more weeks. Might find something to shoot at in that time." He grinned at the men around the table.

"I don't know about you people, but I could eat a steer if someone would hold onto his tail so he couldn't get away. Hank, ask the cooks to serve steaks for evening chow and ask them to pick out two big, juicy ones for me."

The Communications Officer on duty in Pearl Harbor decoded the long message from the *Tigerfish*, read it through a second time and pursed his lips in a soundless whistle. He dialed the BOQ and asked that Commander Foster's phone be rung at once and kept ringing until he awoke and answered it. He waited until he heard the Chief of Staff's aide grunt and clear his throat. And then he slowly read the entire message from the *Tigerfish*.

"I'll be there in twenty minutes," Captain Foster said. "Lieutenant, this is a direct order: That message you just read to me is strictly confidential. Is that clear?" He hung up and searched through a small directory of telephone numbers not listed in the base telephone book. He found the number of the cryptanalysts' office and dialed it. The man who answered the telephone did not identify himself. He merely said "yes?" and waited. Commander Foster recited his full name, rank, service number and job and then summarized the content of the message he had just had read to him over the telephone. The man on the other end of the telephone thanked him.

"One more thing, sir," Commander Foster said. "I'll be in my office in about a half-hour. If you have any confirmation of what I've told you, I would appreciate very much receiving it before zero eight hundred hours. Thank you."

By the time the staff had assembled for its daily 0830 meeting, Hugh Foster had worked out his plan of action. Captain Elmo Furst, the Chief of Staff, could be a difficult man. He couldn't be pushed an inch, but Hugh Foster had learned that he could be led if he wasn't conscious of being led. Captain Furst was always explosively appreciative of aggressive action by one of his submarine Captains. He was also, Hugh Foster reflected, an old friend of Commander T. Prescott Salmon III.

The staff settled down to work and Hugh Foster disposed of a half-dozen routine matters. Then he opened a large manila envelope lying on the table in front of him and looked around at the staff.

"At approximately zero two hundred hours, Zone Twenty time yesterday, the *Tigerfish* intercepted the convoy the cryptanalysts had warned us was moving from Nagasaki toward Manila. It was a large convoy escorted by a light cruiser and six Fubuki destroyers, those are what we would call destroyer leaders, as we all know. Very large, heavily armed, very fast.

"*Tigerfish* attacked at night on the surface. From what I deduce in the message *Tigerfish* transmitted to Pearl early this morning—I will pass around copies of the dispatch in a moment—from what I can deduce, *Tigerfish* ran wild on the surface through the convoy. Fifteen torpedoes were fired and six ships were sunk, including the light cruiser and one Fubuki destroyer. The sinkings have been confirmed."

"So soon?" Captain Furst said. "Confirmation usually takes several days, Hugh. Has in the past, anyway."

"The cryptanalysts told me that the Japanese are now reporting their losses to Tokyo as soon as they happen. Commander Rochefort's cryptanalysts confirm that *Tigerfish* sank the light cruiser and the Fubuki—we have the names of those ships but I haven't as yet looked up their tonnages. *Tigerfish* also sank an ammunition ship, tonnage six thousand; an oil tanker, tonnage seven thousand, and two other merchant ships. Total tonnage of those two merchant ships is eleven thousand five hundred.

"In sum, *Tigerfish* downed a light cruiser, a big Fubuki destroyer and twenty-four thousand five hundred tons of merchant shipping in less than one hour."

"My God!" Captain Furst said, awe in his voice. "That's the biggest bag any submarine skipper has ever got in this war!

And to think that old T. Prescott Salmon the Third did it! I can hardly believe it!"

"I regret, sir, that it isn't quite that way," Hugh Foster said quietly. "Apparently Captain Salmon was taken ill before the action started. The information is outlined in a report appended to the action report. Here are copies, gentlemen." He passed the copies of the contact report around the table and sipped at his coffee while the other officers read the report.

"The acting Executive Officer says that in his opinion, in the opinion of the whole damned Wardroom, Captain Salmon went bonkers," Captain Furst said.

"I believe the words he used were temporary insanity, sir," Foster said.

"Temporary insanity, bonkers, it's all the same," Captain Furst growled. "In any case, it's loose talk. They're not doctors."

"Mr. Copper made that point, sir."

"Handcuffing him to his bunk, that's shocking!" Captain Furst went on doggedly. "They'll have to answer for that to a Board of Inquiry."

"Yes, sir," Hugh Foster said. "I presume you want *Tigerfish* ordered back to port?"

"They've got to come back," the Staff Engineering Officer broke in. "With a ruptured After Trim? They can't stay out with that. Be damned lucky to get home, in my opinion."

"Order *Tigerfish* home, Hugh," Captain Furst said. "Make the usual advisory to all ships of her return route." He looked again at the messsage.

"Says here that Lieutenant Commander Michael O'Connor—oh, he's the football player, isn't he?" He looked around the table. "Football players make damned good submariners and don't you forget it. Says here that he was alone on the bridge all during the action on the surface. That's when he got wounded.

"God almighty! Can't you see that crazy football player alone on the bridge, the *Tigerfish* running wild through a big convoy? Eyeballing his torpedo shots and getting hits. Ships blowing up all over. My God, he must have thought he had a football and he was in an open field and he straight-armed every damned tackler that came his way! Nobody has ever got a box score like this one. Captain O'Connor is one hell of a fighting man!"

Hugh Foster felt his tensed stomach muscles relax. Captain
Furst called Mike "Captain O'Connor," he thought to himself.
He's already made the transference of command in his mind.
He looked around the table.

"I suggest, Captain," he said, "I think you'd make Admiral
Nimitz a mighty happy man if you were to send the report of
the Tigerfish over to him."

"I'll take it myself," Captain Furst said, rising. "Right now.
And Hugh, have the Chief Yeoman make out the papers for a
Congressional Medal of Honor. We've been the Silent Service
too long. This is one submarine attack that the American
people should have a chance to cheer about. I know Admiral
Nimitz will agree with me."

"Yes, sir," Hugh Foster said. "What name do you want on
the Medal of Honor recommendation, sir?"

"What name? Why, Captain O'Connor. Who else?" He
smiled broadly. "He won't be the first man to win the Medal of
Honor after getting shot in the head. In the Marine Corps
that's the first requirement for a Medal of Honor—get shot in
the head. Captain O'Connor qualifies."

Chapter
Twenty-one

THE *Tigerfish,* HER STERN sagging and a huge dent in one side of her Conning Tower, her decks ripped and torn by depth charges, moved slowly through Pearl Harbor. As she passed other ships, those ships' crews lined up at attention and the ships' whistles blared in salute. Mike O'Connor stood in the bridge of the *Tigerfish* as the ship approached the submarine piers.

"My God!" Hank Copper said, "look at all the gold braid on the pier. And they've got a band there, hear them?" He turned to Captain O'Connor, his voice low. "Captain, Doc just passed the word to me that Captain Salmon isn't going to come topside. He wants the Chief of Staff to see him handcuffed to his bunk."

Captain O'Connor leaned over the bridge rail as Chief O'Brien's seamen doubled up the mooring lines. He turned to Hank Copper.

"I gave Chief O'Brien orders to go below and bring Captain Salmon topside after we had tied up, and if I know Chief O'Brien, he'll bring Captain Salmon topside." He walked back to the cigarette deck and watched while a group of carpenters placed a sheet of metal over a gaping hole in the ship's afterdeck. He swung down to the deck and walked to the end of the gangway and waited.

Admiral Nimitz came down the gangway, followed by his staff. The Admiral walked up to O'Connor, his hand outstretched.

"Congratulations, Captain, on the most aggressive war patrol ever conducted by a submarine. I'm proud to be in the same Navy with you. I've read your contact report and I think 'll give you command of a heavy cruiser and assign you to Vice Admiral Halsey, he could use a man like you." He saw the stricken look on Mike O'Connor's face.

"Just kidding, Captain. I don't get many chances to make jokes these days. I'm a little pushed for time." He turned to one of his aides. "What time does the crew go to the hotel?"

"Eleven hundred hours, Admiral."

"I'll be back here at that time," Admiral Nimitz said. "I want to talk to your crew and tell them how proud the United States, how proud we are, of the job they did." He turned to his aide again.

"Captain O'Connor and his Wardroom are to report to your headquarters at fourteen hundred hours, Admiral."

"I'll see you later, Captain," Admiral Nimitz said. He turned and left.

Captain Furst bulled his way through the cluster of officers that had formed around Mike O'Connor after the Admiral had left the ship.

"Dammitall, Captain, what have you done to your ship? Look at it. Damned thing looks like that garbage scow I was going to give you as your first command!" He threw his heavy arm around Mike O'Connor's shoulders. O'Connor opened his mouth to speak and stopped as a scream echoed from below decks. The officers standing on the deck turned, frozen, as Captain Salmon burst out of the crew's mess compartment hatch, a .45 automatic in his hand.

"Where is that mutinous sonofabitch!" Captain Salmon yelled. He glared around the deck as the officers near him shrank back.

"There you are, you bastard!" He leveled the automatic at O'Connor and pulled the trigger. There was a sharp snap of the hammer striking the firing pin. Captain Salmon looked at the gun and grabbed at the slide to pull it back.

"I'll take that, sir," Chief O'Brien said from behind Captain Salmon, his big right hand reaching around the Captain and clamping around the gun and the Captain's hand. He forced the hand and gun upward until the muzzle was pointing at the sky and then his left arm went around Captain Salmon's neck and O'Brien leaned back, lifting the officer until only his toes touched the deck. Standing on the pier, Commander Hugh Foster nodded his head and four hospital corpsmen jumped out of a panel truck and trotted down the gangway, one of them

unfolding a straitjacket. Chief O'Brien released his grip around
Captain Salmon as the corpsmen surrounded the deranged
man.

"Easy, now, sir," one of the corpsmen said as he buckled the
straps of the straitjacket. The four corpsmen gently shep-
herded Captain Salmon up the gangway and into the panel
truck and drove off.

Captain Furst, his ruddy face ashen, walked over to Chief
O'Brien, who held out the gun.

"He forgot to pull back the slide to put a cartridge in the
chamber, sir," Chief O'Brien said.

"Damned good thing for Captain O'Connor that he did.
Damned good thing you were on hand, Chief." Captain Furst
reached for the gun and clip. "I'd better take these, Chief.
There'll be a hearing and they'll be evidence." He turned and
went back to Mike O'Connor.

"My God, what a terrible thing to happen. Thank God the
Admiral wasn't here. Terrible. I'll see you later, Captain." He
turned and walked toward the gangway, muttering, "That poor
man. That poor, sick, man." Hugh Foster came down the
gangway.

"Thank God Chief O'Brien was there," he said to O'Connor.
"Word to the wise, Captain. Wear your best uniform when you
go to the Admiral's headquarters this afternoon. Same goes for
the officers." He put his arm around O'Connor's shoulders.
"Fine patrol, wonderful patrol, Mike. You make me proud
once commanded this ship." He turned and left.

Captain O'Connor jerked his head at Chief O'Brien and the
two men walked down the deck away from the officers who
were clustered in groups, talking excitedly about Captain
Salmon.

"Where did he get that gun?" O'Connor said in a low voice.

"Can't rightly say, Captain," O'Brien said. "I can tell you one
thing, though." He handed an empty .45 clip to Mike
O'Connor. "The loaded clip was in my hip pocket until they
were taking him away, sir." Mike O'Connor stared into the
Chief of the Boat's guileless eyes.

"Chief Petty Officers take care of their Captains," O'Brien
said softly. "It's always been that way, sir."

A Chief Yeoman came out of Admiral Nimitz's office and
snapped off a salute to Mike O'Connor and his officers.

"The Admiral will see you alone, Captain," the chief said.
Go through the door and bear left into his office. The rest of
our officers will please follow me." He led the *Tigerfish*
fficers down the passageway and through a door. Mike
)'Connor walked into the Admiral's office and stood at
ttention.

"I followed your football career at the Academy, Captain,"
.dmiral Nimitz said. "You were not only a great football
layer, you were a great team player. I mention that because I
m asking you to take part in what I call a team effort.

"We are winning this war, Captain. I know that. The
.merican people need to know it. So I'm asking you as a team
layer to allow us to make an example of you." A warm smile
pread across the Admiral's flinty face.

"Whatever you say, Admiral," Mike O'Connor said. The
dmiral gathered up a sheaf of papers from his desk and rose.

"Follow me, Captain. And brace yourself. Remember, it's a
:am effort." He walked across the Chief Yeoman's office and
pened a door. Through the door Mike O'Connor could see a
arge room filled with people, most of them civilians. He saw
is own officers standing in a group at one side of the room.

"Attention!" Captain Furst bellowed as Admiral Nimitz
ntered the room.

"At ease," Admiral Nimitz said. "I want to personally thank
ur guests for coming here on such short notice. I am sure my
:aff has given each of you a copy of the story we are releasing
)day." He turned and faced Mike O'Connor. He began to read
om a paper he held in his hand.

"At an area and on a date which must remain classified for
:curity reasons, the fleet submarine *Tigerfish* intercepted a
arge Japanese convoy of merchant ships and oil tankers
uarded by a light cruiser and six large destroyers.

"The U.S.S. *Tigerfish*, under command of Captain Michael
. O'Connor, attacked the convoy in a night surface attack. In
hat we can say was an attack unprecedented in our Navy's
istory, Captain O'Connor torpedoed and sank the light
:uiser and then maneuvered his submarine through the
onvoy, avoiding the destroyers, and torpedoed and sank three
arge merchant ships, one oil tanker and a Japanese destroyer.

"During fifty-five minutes of action on the surface among the
onvoy, Captain O'Connor was wounded by enemy shrapnel

but he remained alone on the bridge of his submarine, attacking the enemy.

"The retaliation by the Japanese destroyers was savage and prolonged. The *Tigerfish* was heavily damaged by depth-charge attacks. Captain O'Connor brought his ship safely through the depth-charging attacks—which lasted more than eight hours—and then brought his ship safely home." He stopped and Captain Furst stepped forward, a polished wooden case in his hand. He opened the box and Admiral Nimitz took out a medal, a five-pointed star suspended from an anchor on a pale blue ribbon studded with small white stars.

"For courage above and beyond the call of duty in time of war, the President of the United States is pleased and honored to award the Congressional Medal of Honor to Lieutenant Commander Michael Turloch O'Connor." He carefully spread the ribbon wide and lifted it over Mike O'Connor's bowed head and draped it around his neck. He stepped back two paces and brought his hand to the brim of his uniform cap in a salute.

"Courage is a word often misused, Captain O'Connor. I have always believed that courage, as I know it, is the result of discipline, of fidelity to one's sworn duty to flag and country. You have demonstrated that sort of courage. It is a privilege to be allowed to give you this award, sir." He shook O'Connor's hand as photographers scuttled around the two men, snapping their pictures.

"And now, if you will, Captain Furst," Admiral Nimitz said.

"*Tigerfish* officers front and center," Captain Furst ordered. "Fall in beside Captain O'Connor." The officers took their places. An aide holding a stack of dark blue boxes moved in beside Admiral Nimitz.

"No ship's Captain can accomplish great deeds without the help of dedicated and efficient officers and an equally dedicated and efficient crew," Admiral Nimitz said. "The President of the United States is pleased and honored to award a Navy Cross to each of the officers of the U.S.S. *Tigerfish*, a Silver Star to each of the Chief Petty Officers and a Bronze Star with a V for Valor to each crew member of the *Tigerfish*. The awards to the crew members will be made aboard ship when the crew return from the Royal Hawaiian Hotel in two weeks." He moved down the line of *Tigerfish* officers, pinning a medal on the uniform jacket of each man, shaking hands with them.

"And now, Captain O'Connor, a further test of your courage is about to begin," Admiral Nimitz said. "The people here in civilian clothes are from the press. They have an account of the night surface attack you conducted and I now turn you over to them."

It was almost 1630 when the reporters finished their interviews. When the last photograph had been taken, O'Connor mopped his face with a handkerchief and turned to Captain Furst.

"Sir," he said, "I'd just soon not to have to go through that again."

"Glad it was you and not me," Captain Furst said. "But you carried the ball well, you did fine. Now, if it's not inconvenient for you, my staff and I would like to have you and Hank Copper as our guests for lunch tomorrow. Good. Why don't the two of you drop by my office at about twelve hundred thirty hours tomorrow? See you then."

Captain Furst settled himself in the backseat of a staff car and waited until Hugh Foster had seated himself beside him and closed the door. "The doctors at the hospital called me just before the medal ceremony," Captain Furst said. "Poor Salmon is in bad shape. Gone bonkers for sure. He's the third skipper to go off the rails like that. Whose idea was it to have those damned corpsmen with that straitjacket on hand? Not that it wasn't needed," he added hastily. "That poor man might have shot two or three people if Chief O'Brien, is that his name? Yes. He saved several people from getting shot and he saved Captain Salmon from being court-martialed on a charge of murder or attempted murder. I want a letter of special commendation put in the Chief's record. I'll sign it after you've written it." He turned his head and studied Hugh Foster's calm face. "I take it you ordered the corpsmen to be on hand?"

"I thought it wise to issue that order, sir," Hugh Foster said. "Mike O'Connor and Hank Copper served under me, as you know. I know them both to be honest, level-headed officers. I reasoned that if Captain Salmon had to be handcuffed to his bunk and put under guard, he must have acted in a violent manner. We know now that he had tried to shoot O'Connor once before and that Chief O'Brien and a seaman named John Ribbon stopped that from happening. I presume you want a letter of commendation put in Ribbon's record as well?"

"Do that," Captain Furst said. "I'd forgotten about Ribbon.

Looking at him, he's so skinny and young, you wouldn't think he had that sort of guts. One more thing, Hugh..Put your mind to work on what we're going to do about getting a new Commanding Officer for the *Tigerfish*. I want to have that business all settled before lunch tomorrow."

The telephone jangled insistently in Mike O'Connor's room at the Royal Hawaiian. He padded out of the bathroom, a bath towel hitched around his waist, wiping lather from the unshaved side of his face with a hand towel.

"O'Connor here," he growled into the mouthpiece.

"Captain O'Connor, your big ugly face is all over the front page of the morning paper. What the hell have you been doing?" Andy O'Connor's voice broke into an excited yell. "You big lunk! A Congressional Medal of Honor! A Purple Heart Medal! Why didn't you call me when you got in?"

"I wanted to, Andy, but from the time we tied up until late last night, I haven't had a minute to myself. I was going to call you this morning."

"How about me coming over for breakfast if you haven't eaten?"

"I'd like that more than anything," Mike O'Connor said. "Truth is, I'm halfway through shaving—what time is it? Eight-thirtyish? I've got to have breakfast with some people from *Time* and *Life* magazines and their photographers at zero nine hundred hours. I tried to get out of that, they were at the ceremony yesterday, but the Chief of Staff gave me orders to give them something they call an exclusive story."

"Then I've got to get squared away for lunch with the Chief of Staff and his people at twelve-thirty. I should be back here by fifteen hundred hours at the latest. Why don't you bring Carol and her mother and have dinner with me at the hotel?"

"Okay," Andy said. "Dinner will be fine. One thing I can't understand, though. Last time I saw you, you were going out on patrol as a brand-new Executive Officer. Now you're the Captain of the *Tigerfish*. How did that happen?"

"I can't talk about that on the phone, Andy. I'll tell you about it at dinner."

Commander Hugh Foster walked into Captain Furst's office at 1145 and sat down in a chair at one side of the Captain's cluttered desk.

"I've met with the staff, sir," he said. "We considered the matter of a new Commanding Officer for the *Tigerfish*. As you know, there are about twenty officers who are qualified for command now assigned to shore duty here at Pearl.

"All of those officers are senior to O'Connor. I pulled the records of all those officers yesterday afternoon and we, the staff, spent all evening going over each officer's record. We considered each officer's qualifications very carefully.

"This morning I went out to the hotel and talked to the officers of the *Tigerfish*. I talked to the Chief of the Boat and his Chiefs and to those senior Petty Officers who were available at that hour, sir."

"Who were sober, you mean," Captain Furst said with a grin. "I heard the *Tigerfish* crew had a party to end all parties at the hotel last night."

"I believe that was the case," Hugh Foster said. "At any rate, the consensus of opinion of the Wardroom, the Chief Petty Officers and the crew is that they will sail into hell and attack the devil himself if Captain O'Connor is on the bridge, sir." He looked at the clipboard he had brought with him.

"The word is out that there's at least one vacancy in the *Tigerfish* Wardroom, sir. As of a half-hour ago I had requests from more than a dozen junior officers asking to be assigned to serve with Captain O'Connor." He turned a page on the pad on the clipboard.

"The consensus of opinion of your staff, sir, is that Lieutenant Commander Michael T. O'Connor has demonstrated beyond doubt that he is a leader of men, he is an able ship-handler, he has demonstrated his skill at shooting torpedoes. In short, sir, the staff believes that Lieutenant Commander O'Connor is qualified for command."

Captain Furst leaned back in his chair and put his hands behind his head. "Have you thought what a storm will blow up if we jump him over officers senior to him?"

"Yes, sir," Foster said. "Some of those officers deserve command. Some have had their chances and flubbed them. But none of them—for that matter, no other living submariner—has a Medal of Honor. I think that's the answer to whatever protests are made. Further, sir, if some other officer is given command of the *Tigerfish*, we'll be faced with a mass request for transfer from every man aboard."

"Wouldn't blame them, either," Captain Furst growled. "I

concur with the recommendation of the staff. I suppose you want to keep Hank Copper as Exec? Thought you would, he's a good man. You deserve a lot of credit for those two, Hugh, you trained them.

"Well, that's settled. We'll break the news to them at lunch."

Mike O'Connor left the luncheon and got into the backseat of the car Captain Furst had provided to deliver them to the hotel. Hank Copper climbed in and sat down. Conscious of the enlisted driver and the Marine Sergeant sitting beside him, they confined their conversation to the events of the previous evening, the noisy party the *Tigerfish* crew had put on. The car turned into the gate at the hotel and went up the winding drive to the hotel entrance. The Marine Sergeant got out of the car and opened the back door for the two officers. As Mike O'Connor got out of the car, he saw the distinctive pale blue ribbon studded with stars above a row of campaign ribbons that included a Purple Heart ribbon with two small bronze stars on it on the Sergeant's crisp khaki shirt. The Sergeant saw O'Connor's eyes stare at the medal ribbon.

"Welcome to the club, Captain. I'm First Sergeant James C. Jones, sir."

"Where?" Mike O'Connor asked.

"Guadalcanal. Bloody Ridge, sir."

O'Connor nodded. "That puts me in pretty select company, Sergeant. Stay well, friend."

O'Connor and Copper walked slowly through the hotel lobby. "I can't get over one thing," O'Connor said. "They never once mentioned Captain Salmon at lunch. It's as if he didn't exist."

"He doesn't, officially," Hank Copper said. "Commander Furst told me that when he gets out of the hospital—and no one knows when that will be—they'll decide what to do with him."

"His career is ruined," O'Connor said slowly. "No one can come back from something like that."

"I wonder where he got that gun?" Copper said.

"I don't know," O'Connor said. He looked at his watch. "I've got to shower again. I sweat buckets at lunch before they told us they were leaving the two of us aboard. My brother, his wife and mother-in-law are coming over for dinner. One more thing, Hank.

"We've got to rearrange the Wardroom assignments. We'll

be getting a new officer aboard to fill out the roster. Mr. Foster told me he has a stack of requests from junior officers who want to be transferred to *Tigerfish*. I want you to get together with him and go over the records of those people, pick the best man. Check back with me in, oh, three days, and I'll make the decision on whom we take. I want all the paper work done before we leave the hotel so the man can be in place when we go back to the ship."

"Will do, Captain," Hank Copper said.

Chapter
Twenty-two

ANDY O'CONNOR knocked on the door of his brother's room and walked in when he heard the door was unlocked. Mike turned from the window and the two brothers hugged each other gleefully.

"Where's Carol and her mother, down in the lobby?" Mike asked.

"I told her that I wanted some time alone with you," Andy said. "She understands. We'll get together tomorrow." Mike waved his brother to a chair and stretched out on the bed, pulling the two pillows back of his shoulders so he could face Andy. He unfolded the newspaper Andy had brought with him and looked at the picture of Admiral Nimitz draping the Metal of Honor around his neck. He began to read the paper and then sat upright, his face horrified.

"My God, this is just awful!" he spluttered.

"What's awful?" Andy asked.

"Why, this story here about our attack on the convoy. Where did they get this stuff? 'Captain Michael O'Connor, blood pouring from his wounds, raged through the enemy convoy firing torpedoes from both ends of his submarine, his voice roaring Gaelic curses as his torpedoes exploded one ship after another.' That's awful, Andy, it wasn't like that at all."

"What was it like, Mike? Tell me." Andy settled himself in a chair near the bed, his eyes on his older brother. "Start with how you became the Captain."

Mike lay back against the pillows, his eyes half-closed, and dispassionately recounted the events that led to his taking command of the *Tigerfish* from Captain Salmon, the attack on the convoy, the depth charging and Captain Salmon's attempt

286

to shoot him and the actions of Captain Salmon after the *Tigerfish* had tied up to the pier. Andy got out of the chair, walked to the foot of the bed and stood looking at his brother.

"I was always proud to be your brother," he said slowly. "Now I don't know how I feel. As if I were brother to a cardinal or the Pope or something."

"Come off it," Mike growled. "If Dad heard you say something as silly as that, he'd kick your butt for you and you know it." He half-rolled and sat up on the edge of the bed. "I hope you didn't send the folks a copy of this stupid newspaper story."

"No," Andy said. "When I read the story, I did want to get a dozen or so copies, so I called the newspaper office to ask how I went about doing that and I told them my name, that you were my brother, and the girl in the newspaper office put some fellow on the line who said he worked for the *Chicago Tribune* and since we're from Chicago could he come out and talk to me? I said okay.

"He's a really nice guy. Name is Bob Cromie and he's a war correspondent. Very low-key man. The kind of guy you want to trust, he's so decent. He asked all the right sort of questions about you and the folks and growing up in Chicago. He agreed with me that the story in the local paper was pretty awful. I think he'll do a much better story and he told me it would be in the *Tribune* tomorrow with pictures, so the folks will read his story and not this one. He asked me if I could set up an appointment with you for something he called a follow-up."

"If he's as decent a man as you say he is, tell him to call me here at the hotel," Mike said. He stood up and stretched. "How's Carol?"

"Fine," Andy said. "I want to thank you for not telling her I was in Pearl that time. She found out, though. A friend of hers is married to a Marine pilot and he saw me at the BOQ and told his wife and Carol found out."

"She give you a hard time?"

"No, she said she understood, and I don't understand that."

"Did the two of you go to see a priest and a minister, as I suggested?"

Andy began to pace up and down the room. "I can go to see a priest, Mike, but I can't ask a Protestant minister for counsel. That would be the same as saying I doubted what the priest told me, that I doubted everything I believe in."

"How did she react to that?" Mike asked. He walked over to the window and looked out at the beach.

"She didn't like it very much. But I did go to a priest and I told her what he suggested."

"Which was?"

Andy leaned his back against the wall of the room, his face bleak.

"He wasn't much help. He's old. He suggested that Carol take instruction and join the Church and then she'll understand."

Mike turned from the window. "What about now, what about the time until the war is over, what did he suggest doing about your present problems?"

"He suggested we practice celibacy," Andy said. "I know, you know, lust is a sin."

"He suggested that all by himself, or did you suggest it to him?"

"We came to a meeting of minds," Andy said stiffly.

"I don't see how anyone, priest or minister or rabbi, could call love for a wife or husband lust," Mike said. "I know you well enough, you're my only brother, to know you wouldn't marry her unless you loved her. From what I've seen of her, I don't think she'd marry anyone unless she really loved him. From where I stand, she loves you. That's not lust."

"You make the same argument she makes," Andy said. "It's a fallacious argument. The purpose of copulation is procreation. That's what I was taught."

Mike looked at his brother and shook his head. "I don't know about you, Andy. Sometimes I wonder why we're so different. I don't question our being different. I just wonder about it."

"We're different, all right." There was acid in Andy's voice. He walked over and looked out the window.

"Tell me something, Mike," he said. He stared out the window. "Tell me the truth. Weren't you in some sort of mess when you were in submarine school? Something about you being all messed up in a paternity suit? Did you get some girl pregnant?"

"I was called up in front of the Skipper," Mike said. "Yes. There was a girl who was pregnant, had a baby. She said I was responsible."

"Were you?"

"I could have been, I guess," Mike said. "The Navy lawyers

proved that about twenty different guys, enlisted men and some officers, could have been responsible. They threw the case out of court."

"Did they do any tests on you, blood types or sperm counts?"

"Yeah," Mike said. "I was a different blood type than the woman's baby."

"How about the sperm count?"

"What the hell are you getting at?" Mike growled.

Andy turned from the window, his face twisted. "I flunked my sperm-count test. We went to the doctor, Carol and myself. She's normal. She can have babies. I went back the next day to see the doctor. I'm deficient. My sperm count is so low that she can never have a baby." He stared at his brother.

"I'm deficient, Mike. I'm not a man. I can't father a child!"

"Oh, bullshit," Mike growled. "If fathering a kid is what it takes to be a man, then any damned native in some place like Africa who's got a dozen kids is a better man than you are and you know that isn't so." He looked at his brother, his eyes narrowing.

"Does Carol know this? I mean, you did tell her?"

"No," Andy said. "I didn't tell her."

"You fool!" Mike snapped. "Good God, man, you owe it to her to tell her. You're making her suffer, can't you see that? I don't know for beans about being a husband but I know enough to share something like this with my wife, if I had one. Looks to me like the only person around Carol she can confide in or trust is her mother."

"Let's not talk about her," Andy said.

"You got mother-in-law trouble, too?" Mike asked. He forced a grin.

"It's nothing to laugh about, Mike. When I get into port she goes to a friend's house, a widow's house, to stay until the day I leave. We see each other, go out to dinner, that sort of thing.

"I asked Carol to call her mother the other day and we'd all have dinner and Carol told me she was busy, that she had a gentleman friend. I thought that was sort of odd, she's a widow, so I asked Carol who he was and she said he was a civilian engineer who's out here working in the navy yard and she's staying at his house. She's sleeping with this guy, Mike!"

"I don't see too much wrong with that," Mike said. "Mrs. Oster is what, somewhere in her early fifties? She's got appetites, I guess. If she loves the guy, they might be making each other happy, you ever think of that?"

"She's sinning in the sight of God!" Andy hissed.

"Oh bullshit!" Mike said. "Next thing you'll be telling me that like mother, like daughter. The trouble with you, brother is you think too much like a priest. Let's change the subject, how long will you be in port?"

Andy glared at his brother. Then his face softened. "I know I think I'm the guardian of everyone's morals. Red Olsen, my wingman, told me that not long ago when I chewed him out for telling a dirty joke to our crew chief."

"I hope your wingman told you to butt out, to mind your own damned business."

"He did," Andy said. "He let me have it with both barrels. How long are we in port? We leave in three weeks, more or less. Back to the South Pacific. General MacArthur is playing leapfrog, jumping from one island to the other, and the word we get is that the Japanese are coming out to stop us."

"You pray much when you're at sea, Andy?"

"Of course, don't you?"

"Oh, yeah. But lately, when we've been getting the hell depth charged out of us, I wonder if the guys doing the depth charging are praying to God also and whose side He'll favor."

"The Japs aren't Christians, you'd better see a priest yourself. You're beginning to talk like an atheist."

"Or a Protestant?" Mike asked, struggling to keep from grinning.

"You're putting me on, you big lug!" Andy suddenly threw his arms around his brother. His voice, muffled against Mike's big chest, was faint.

"I get so mixed up, Mike, that I just don't know what to do."

"Everything will work out, Andy," Mike said softly. He pushed Andy away and touched his campaign and medal ribbons.

"The DSM and two Silver Stars," he said. "Awfully damned good for a fly-boy. But not good enough. If we're going to make Admiral together, you're going to have to hump it to catch up with me. You've got to get at least a Navy Cross or the Big One, you savvy?"

The day after the *Enterprise* sailed, Carol called the *Tigerfish* and asked for Captain O'Connor. "I was afraid you'd gone to sea," she said.

"Day after tomorrow," he told her.

"Are you too busy to see me, Mike? I want to talk to you if I can."

"I'm never too busy to see you, Carol. If you can hustle a little, I can meet you at the main gate and we could go to lunch somewhere. Thirty minutes is fine with me. See you."

She kept the conversation casual during lunch, chiding him for not spending much time with Andy and herself. After lunch, at Mike's suggestion, she drove them to the Royal Hawaiian Hotel and parked the car. They walked through the gardens until they found a bench in an isolated area. She sat on the bench, her knees touching each other, her feet tucked under the bench.

"When you talked with Andy, when you saw him alone after you got in, did he mention anything about us? I think he did, because he was upset when he came home."

Mike nodded slowly. "We had quite a session in my room. It wasn't easy for him." He reached over and took her slender hand in his.

"I've done an awful lot of thinking since that day. I guess I never really understood my own brother. Maybe I don't now. But at least I understand more about him than I did before. He's my brother, so I have to try and understand him."

"What did he tell you about us, what did he say?"

"He told me the two of you went to a doctor."

"Did he tell you what the doctor said?" Her eyes were boring into his.

Mike nodded. "He said the doctor gave you a clean bill of health, that you were perfectly normal, that you could have babies. And he told me what he had said before, that because there weren't, wasn't, a baby on the way, he was sinning and he's making you a sinner."

"What do you think of that?" she asked.

"I think it's all a crock of sh—" he caught himself. "I think it's crazy." He squeezed her hand gently.

"I've found out a lot of things about my brother that I didn't know before," he said slowly. "You have to understand something; we grew up together. I was always bigger than he was. He was always smarter than I was in school. We were competitive.

"I could do some things he couldn't. Play football was one thing. But he made up for it in his own way. At the Academy he wrestled and ran cross-country. He was as good at those things as I was in football. He went to flying school when we graduated, I went to submarine school. We always shared everything with each other. Sharing was something our parents taught us. They share everything with each other."

"You think there's something he's not sharing with me?" she said. "Something that he's told you and you think he should have told me?"

"My mother used to say that women are intuitive," he growled. "She was right." His dark blue eyes met hers.

"Did he tell you he went back to see the doctor the next day after you had your exam?"

"No," she half-whispered.

His voice was dogged. "He did. He had a sperm count. The doctor told him he would never be a father. He thinks he's deficient, that he's not a man."

"Oh, my God!" she said. The tears began to stream down her face, and Mike, instinctively, folded her into his arms. He held her for a few minutes and then released her. She dried her eyes with a wisp of lace she took out of her pocketbook.

"That's why he wanted us to be celibate," she said. "Is that it?"

He nodded. "I guess so. He's living with a devil, Carol. God, what a burden this has put on you." He drew a long breath and let it out slowly.

"What are you going to do, Carol?"

"Stay married to him," she said. "That's what he wants."

"You love him that much," he said in a gentle voice.

"I love him but I don't know what kind of love it is," she said. "I've thought a lot about that. I loved him from the first time I saw him and I loved him after we got married. I think I still love him but it's not the same kind of feeling as it was. I don't want him in what he calls the 'carnal' way.

"I never had a brother, I'm an only child, but I think I love him more as a brother than as a lover or a husband." She looked at him, tears beginning to form in the corners of her eyes. "Is that a sin, too, in your church?"

"No," he said in his deep rumble. "I think it's just maturity."

"Andy told me once that he prays for your soul every night because you are weak and a sinner. Does that bother you, that he thinks you're a sinner?"

He reached out and gently wiped away the tears on her face

with his handkerchief. "No. Andy's not a judge. He's just a man." He stood up, balancing his 225 pounds on his toes and then rocking back on his heels.

"Maybe when the war is over, when he's had time to think about things, to realize how lucky he is to have you, maybe he'll recognize that everything in this world isn't black and white. God knows, I'll do all I can to hammer some sense into his thick head. Just keep your chin up, Lady Carol." She rose and they walked back to the car. Mike returned the salute of the Marine sentry at the gate and she drove the car down to the head of the submarine pier where the *Tigerfish* was moored. She waited until a working party sweeping the street had passed and then turned in the seat and took Mike's face in her two hands and kissed him.

"I don't know what I would do without you, Michael." He reached up and took her two hands in his and grinned at her.

"As they say in this man's Navy," he said, "deep-six your troubles and two-block your hopes. I'll call you when we get back to port." He got out of the car and walked down the pier toward his ship.

The lagoon at Majuro in the Marshall Islands was crowded with the ships of Task Force 58. Andy O'Connor stood on the flight deck of the *Enterprise* watching Alabama Jones finish stenciling a small Japanese flag beneath a row of similar flags under the edge of his plane's cockpit.

"Makes seventeen, sir," the crew chief said. "Makes us the hottest pilot on this carrier. How d'ya like this Hellcat compared to the Wildcat?"

"More guns," Andy said with a smile. "When they don't jam, that is."

"These Fifties can get crappy, once in a while," Alabama Jones said. "The armorer thinks he's figured out what makes them jam. Those metal belts that carry the bullets can kink if they feed into the breech at too sharp an angle. I got him to fix your plane and Mr. Olsen's and Mr. Masters's planes so that won't happen. He welded a round piece of metal on the gun breech so the belt has to come up over it and feeds in straighter. He says it will work, he fixed up a gun and tried it out off the stern last week when he got the idea." He looked around the crowded lagoon.

"Got ever' damned ship in the whole Navy out here," he

said. "Hell of a place to be. Nothin' to do but work and go on
the beach every third day and drink your two cans of beer and
come back. Hotter'n a pistol all the time. How much longer we
gonna swing around the anchor, sir?"

"I'm going to an intelligence briefing in a half-hour, Chief. If
I hear anything I'll let you know."

O'Connor enjoyed the intelligence briefings. The briefing
officer, Lieutenant Commander Ernest "Rip" Ripper, was a
repressed comedian. One day he would give the briefing in a
broad German accent, strutting up and down in front of the
pilots. The next day he would be British, with a swagger stick
under his arm. His accents were perfect.

"I wonder who Rip will be today?" Andy said to Red Olsen.

"I hope he's Betty Grable," Orv Masters said as he sat down
next to the other two.

"He hasn't got the legs," Olsen said.

The briefing officer was being Rip Ripper on this day. He set
up his folding easel and arranged his charts and faced the pilots
sprawled in their chairs.

"Gentlemen," he said. "here is the latest and straightest
from the moles who work somewhere underground in Pearl
breaking the codes of the Japanese. We all know that when our
brothers in arms in the Army Air Force shot down Admiral
Yamamoto they did all of us a big favor. Old YamYam was quite
a man.

"The fellow they picked to take his place was no slouch.
Admiral named Koga. God helped us with him. He was lost a
few weeks ago when his plane ran into a thundercloud over the
Philippines during a storm."

"Chalk one up for God," a pilot in the rear of the briefing
room said.

"Yes," Rip Ripper said. He consulted his notes. "The
resourceful Jap has looked in his Admiral locker and come up
with another tough man. His name is Admiral Toyodo. Known
as a brilliant tactician and one of Yamamoto's disciples in the
school of thought that aircraft carriers are the primary ships of
war over the battleships.

"The moles in intelligence tell us that Admiral Toyodo's
primary task is to engage the American Navy in an all-out
carrier battle that will destroy our capability to control the
South Pacific and thus enable the Japanese Army to recapture
Guadalcanal and drive General MacArthur back to Brisbane.

"To carry out this small chore, he has to coax us out of this garden spot where we now languish in solitude and luxury."

"He could try putting a few broads on a raft," a pilot said. Andy O'Connor stood up and faced his men.

"That will be enough, gentlemen. You're here to pay attention."

"Ah, thank you, Mr. O'Connor," Mr. Ripper said. "Now to business once again.

"Operation Forager, the invasion of Saipan, began a few days ago. It is the opinion of our best military thinkers that Japan cannot afford to lose Saipan and thus risk losing Tinian and Guam shortly thereafter. The thinking is that Operation Forager will bring Admiral Toyodo out fighting.

"This opinion has been upheld by a sighting by one of our submarines on patrol in the Philippines." He looked at his notes. "The submarine *Redfin* sighted major heavy elements of the Japanese Battle Fleet leaving Tawi Tawi and heading northeast. The submarine, unfortunately, was unable to close with the Japanese Battle Fleet and attack it."

"Lucky submarine," a voice from the rear said.

"In sum," the briefing officer said, "get lots of sleep and eat well. If Operation Forager sucks the Japanese Battle Fleet out into the open sea, we will beat to quarters, run out the cannon and all become heroes in short order. That's all, gentlemen."

The invasion of Saipan caused Tokyo's military strategists to meet in emergency sessions. The decision was made: Saipan must be held. If Saipan went, Tinian would be next in line, then Guam. Admiral Toyodo faced two major problems. One was fuel. American submarines had sent twenty-one oil tankers to the bottom during the first five months of 1944. The Japanese Tanker Fleet was running out of ships. Fuel supplies were dangerously low in Japan itself. Admiral Toyodo thought he could solve that problem. His ships could fuel in Borneo. The oil pumped out of the Borneo oil fields at Balikapapan and Tarakan was pure enough to be used without refining. There was a certain danger in this practice; there were volatiles in the raw fuel oil that could explode easily. The Admiral reasoned that he could run that risk.

His second problem was sheer numbers. Japanese intelligence reports backed up by the sightings by long-range search planes had identified the composition of Task Force 58 in the

Marshall Islands. Admiral Toyodo knew that he was out-gunned. Task Force 58 consisted of seven big carriers to his five; eight light carriers to his four; seven battleships to his five—although two of his battleships were the monsters *Yamoto* and *Musashi;* eight heavy cruisers to his eleven; thirteen light cruisers to his two; and sixty-nine destroyers to his twenty-eight. In terms of carrier aircraft, the Americans had a margin of 891 to Toyodo's 436.

Despite the numerical imbalance of forces, Admiral Toyodo was sure he could win a major battle. He had several advantages that he would utilize. One was that if Task Force 58 left the Marshalls and sailed west to meet him in battle, the task force would come within bombing range of more than 540 Japanese land-based aircraft.

His search planes, because of their lack of armor and the lesser weight of their nonsealing gasoline tanks, had a much longer range than did American search planes. The late Admiral Yamamoto had learned his lesson at Midway; if you don't know the location of the enemy carriers, you are doomed. Toyodo's search planes would allow him to know where the American carriers were long before the Americans knew where his carriers were. The Japanese Admiral reasoned that if the Americans came out to fight, his search planes could pinpoint the enemy carriers and then his land-based aircraft could smash the enemy carriers into smoking rubble.

Finally Admiral Toyodo planned to engage the Americans in a pitched sea battle between battleships at night. The Japanese gunners and torpedomen had already demonstrated their superiority in night fighting over the Americans in several battles.

All Admiral Toyodo needed now was a man to carry out his orders. His choice was Vice Admiral Jisaburo Ozawa, a lynx-eyed man with a receding hairline who was noted for his cool aggressiveness and his proven skill in night fighting. Admiral Toyodo designated his battle plan as "Operation A-GO" and ordered Admiral Ozawa to entice Task Force 58 into range of the land-based aircraft and then engage what was left of the task force in night battle. He assembled his Battle Fleet in the Philippines and took them south to Borneo to refuel and to load his fleet oil tankers and set a course for Saipan. A copy of Admiral Toyodo's order was sent to the Commanding Officer of each ship: "Seek out the enemy and destroy him." The battle for supremacy of the air and sea which historians would call the Battle of the Philippine Sea was about to be joined.

At 0330 on the morning of June 19, 1944, four days after the U.S. Marines had stormed ashore at Saipan, the two Battle Fleets were steaming in formation, 320 miles from each other. Admiral Ozawa was steaming eastward in the hope of luring Task Force 58 into coming after him and under attack from his land-based aircraft.

Ozawa had split his Battle Fleet into two sections. In the van, under the command of Vice Admiral Kurita, he put three carriers, four of his five battleships, nine of his eleven heavy cruisers and seven of his small force of twenty-eight destroyers. Approximately one hundred kilometers astern of the van, Admiral Ozawa flew his flag in the super carrier *Taibu* in company with five other carriers, his remaining cruisers, two heavies and two lights, the battleship *Nagato* and the rest of his destroyers.

At that hour a frustrated and angry Vice Admiral Marc A. Mitscher, flying his flag in the carrier *Lexington,* was leading Task Force 58 to the east, away from Admiral Ozawa. Admiral Mitscher had his orders from Admiral Raymond A. Spruance, and the doughty little carrier Admiral didn't like those orders. Admiral Spruance had decreed that Task Force 58's priority mission was to protect the landings at Saipan, and only if engaged would Task Force 58 turn to meet the enemy.

Admiral Spruance, trained in battleships and not at ease in command of a fast carrier attack force, was doing exactly what Admiral Ozawa had anticipated he would do. Spruance was intent on protecting the Saipan landings. Ozawa changed course and headed directly for Saipan, confident that he had his enemy caught in the jaws of a vise. His land-based force of more than five hundred aircraft would strike the American Battle Fleet first and destroy its carrier capability and do whatever damage could be done to the rest of the American Battle Force. And then he would swoop down on Saipan at night and finish the job of destruction. At just past 0500 on June 19, Admiral Ozawa ordered his battleships and cruisers in the van to launch search planes and find the enemy.

Task Force 58 was divided into five separate units. Three of those units cruised in a line abreast, twelve miles apart. Each of these units had as its core four aircraft carriers screened by cruisers and destroyers. Fifteen miles astern of the center unit of the three carrier units, seven battleships and their escorting cruisers and destroyers made up the battleship strike force. Just to the left side of that strike force were the remaining three carriers and their escorts. None of the almost one hundred thousand men in Task Force 58 knew exactly where the Japanese Battle Force was located or what it was doing. Admiral Mitscher, a carrier man from his brown shoes up, knew one thing; he had a powerful seaborne enemy somewhere to the west, and behind him were land-based enemy aircraft. He requested and received permission to attack the Japanese air fields. He launched planes at dawn.

Andy O'Connor lifted his Hellcat fighter off the *Enterprise* and headed for Orote Air Field on Guam, ninety miles distant. As he neared his target, the flight director on the Big E advised that a large flight of enemy planes was approaching Guam from the northeast. Moments later Red Olsen, flying on O'Connor's left wing, yelled, "Bogeys! Six o'clock and high!" O'Connor whipped his plane around in a steep climbing turn and raced head-on toward a cluster of Zeke fighters. The nose of a Zeke loomed in his gunsight and he pressed his gun triggers and six streams of .50-caliber incendiaries poured out. The Zeke exploded in a shower of debris, and O'Connor, instinctively ducking his head as the burning debris splattered against his canopy, saw a Zeke turning to one side ahead of him. He fired a short burst and the wing of the Zeke burst open in a huge ball of fire. He horsed his plane into a sharp turn and saw Orv Masters pursuing a Zeke with another Zeke on his tail. As he shouted a warning into his microphone, he saw Red Olsen slide in behind the second Zeke and chew half of the Zeke's right wing off with a long burst from his guns. The Zeke went down in a twisting, graveyard spiral that ended in a splash and a spreading oil stain in the water. O'Connor saw a lone Zeke off to his left and whipped over in pursuit. The Jap pilot made no effort to attack. Instead, he went into an instruction-book exhibition of acrobatics, doing wingovers, half-loops, snap rolls, slow rolls and sudden loops. O'Connor, puzzled, chased the Zeke down close to the water, and as the Zeke hesitated slightly as its pilot tried to zoom upward, O'Connor hit it with a burst that drove the Zeke into the sea. O'Connor pointed the nose of his Hellcat upward, calling for his wingmen to reform on him. Orv Masters came sliding around the edge of a fluffy cloud and took position on his right wing. Red Olsen was nowhere to be seen. O'Connor looked around, searching for Olsen, and saw the distinctive shape of a Hellcat following a line of Jill torpedo bombers that were on their landing leg to put down at Orote Air Field. He saw the last plane in the line burst into flames and go down. Then the Hellcat shot down the next three Jills before soaring upward, and Red Olsen's exultant voice was yelling over the radio, "Got four of those bastards!"

Just before 1000 the radar operators in Task Force 58 picked up a large number of blips coming in from the west. Admiral Mitscher, sure now that an all-out carrier battle was imminent, was in his element. He prepared for the battle. The fighter planes were recalled, refueled and rearmed, and sent back into the air to wait for the enemy planes. The dive bombers and torpedo bombers also rode off to wait for directions to the enemy carriers.

The Battle of the Philippine Sea was about to begin.

Chapter
Twenty-three

THE REPORT FROM the Captain of the U.S.S. *Redfin* that he had sighted major elements of the Japanese Battle Fleet leaving Tawi Tawi in the southern Philippines sent Vice Admiral Charles A. Lockwood, Commander Submarines Pacific Fleet, to his chartroom where, in company with his staff, he studied a large chart of the Southwest Pacific.

Admiral Lockwood, who was affectionately called "Uncle Charlie" by his submariners, knew where Task Force 58 was located. Intelligence reports showed that Admiral Ozawa had been ordered to smash the American effort to take and hold Saipan—an invasion that was meeting with extremely stubborn resistance by the Japanese defenders. Admiral Lockwood had no reason to doubt the ability of Task Force 58 to give a good accounting of itself, but he saw no reason why the Japanese force should arrive for combat with all its ships intact. He had submarines available; he would use them.

He bent over the chart and traced the probable course Admiral Ozawa would take to reach Saipan. The difficult problem was in ascertaining just where Ozawa would begin launching his aircraft to attack Task Force 58. He studied the chart, bringing to bear everything he knew about Japanese strategy, everything he knew about Admiral Ozawa, a man he respected as a naval strategist and tactician. Finally he put his forefinger on the chart 350 miles west and slightly south of the southern end of Guam.

"There," he said flatly. "He will launch his main carrier attacks from this area. His search planes have long-range capability. They will have found Admiral Spruance by the time he reaches this area."

"That's a pretty long range for air attacks, Admiral," one of his staff protested. "Their turn-around spot would be reached before they got to Task Force Fifty-eight." He stopped as Admiral Lockwood put his finger on Guam and then Rota. "Yes," the staff officer said. "I see. They wouldn't have to return to their carriers. They could land at their air fields on Guam and Rota, refuel, rearm and then take another crack at the task force on their way home."

Admiral Lockwood picked up a pencil and drew in a rough rectangle that covered the possible courses that Admiral Ozawa could follow to reach the launch point. "Pull the four submarines closest to this area away from their patrol areas and station one at each corner of the rectangle. I want each submarine to patrol in a thirty-mile radius, using the corners of the rectangle as the centers of their patrol areas. I want contact reports made before an attack is launched if that's at all possible. Don't make it imperative, I don't want to deny any Captain the chance to attack big targets."

The *Tigerfish* was ordered away from its patrol area twelve miles off the southeast entrance to Truk Atoll on June 14. It had been a sterile area for a patrol. Air strikes by B-24s from the Central and South Pacific against Truk had started in February and were followed in March and April by heavy attacks by fast carrier groups. By June the few aircraft still able to fly at Truk had been shifted to Orote Air Field on Guam, and no surface ships were left in the huge lagoon. The *Tigerfish* had cruised up and down for two weeks with no targets.

The order for a new patrol area in the Philippine Sea was welcome. Mike O'Connor studied the decoded message as he sat at the Wardroom table. "Says here that the sighting of any major elements of the enemy will be vital information and must be transmitted at once if it is not possible to attack those units." He looked at Hank Copper and Saul Silver. "Uncle Charlie must expect something awfully big to be coming through that area."

"I've drawn in our patrol area, Captain," Hank Copper said. "We're going to have to be damned careful with our navigation. A thirty-mile radius around that point on the chart is a damned small area, and we've got the *Cavalla*, the *Stingray* and the *Finback* out here with us and none of us are very far apart."

"I've got faith in you, old buddy," Mike O'Connor said. "Once we get where we're supposed to be, we'll sail straight out for thirty miles and then we'll just start sailing in a circle."

"Provided there's no current, no wind," Hank Copper grunted.

The *Tigerfish* arrived on station just past midnight on June 19. Hank Copper spent an hour taking star sights before *Tigerfish* dove just before dawn. When he had finished his navigation, he went into the Wardroom, where Mike O'Connor was eating powdered eggs and canned bacon.

"We're dead smack where we should be, Captain," he said "I've put us on a course away from the *Cavalla's* position and by the time we surface this evening we should be out at the end of our thirty-mile radius. Then we can begin a long circle around the basic position."

"Good," Captain O'Connor said. "If Uncle Charlie knows what he's doing, and he almost always does, we might see something in a day or two."

Admiral Lockwood's canny assessment of what course Admiral Ozawa would follow as he headed for Saipan was on the nose. At a little after 0800 Wayne Raleigh swiveled the periscope around in a routine search and sang out the words that galvanized a submarine crew on war patrol into instant action.

"Contact! Call the Captain."

Captain O'Connor's shoulder muscles bunched under his thin khaki shirt as he looked through the periscope.

"Quartermaster," he said, "make this entry in the log. I have two carriers in sight. One is very large. I can see two cruisers. They look like heavies. I can see three destroyers. I can see the topmasts of a number of other ships." He rattled off the bearings to the quartermaster.

"Sound General Quarters," Captain O'Connor said. "Open all torpedo-tube outer doors. Set depth ten feet on all torpedoes in the Forward Room. Set depth two feet on all torpedoes in the After Room. Down periscope." He turned and squatted at the hatch and looked down into the Control Room where Hank Copper and his plotting crew were standing at the gyrocompass table.

"Hank, write out a plain-language message giving the position of those carriers I just saw. Range was ten thousand yards, angle on the bow of the lead carrier, that's one big bastard that one, was ten starboard. Work out their course and our position and include that in the message. We'll transmit the message when we're shooting. Got it?"

"Will do, Captain," Copper said. Captain O'Connor rose and nodded at Pete Savage to raise the periscope.

"Crew is at General Quarters. Depth set at ten feet on all torpedoes forward. Depth set two feet all torpedoes aft. Outer doors on all tubes are open. Radioman is standing by to transmit when you begin to shoot, Captain," Chief O'Brien's voice boomed up the hatch.

"Very well," Captain O'Connor said. He looked through the periscope lens. "Here we go, Plot. First bearing will be on that big carrier, and I mean that ship is big! Bearing is . . . Mark!" He took a bearing on each of the ships he could see and Pete Savage read the azimuth circle of the periscope and relayed the bearings down to Hank Copper. The last bearing he gave was a second bearing on the big carrier.

"Carrier's speed is twenty-six knots, Captain," Hank Copper called up the hatch. "If he holds course, we'll have a torpedo track of twenty-three hundred yards, sir."

"Down 'scope," Captain O'Connor ordered. "Sound. There's a destroyer bearing three-five-zero. Get on him and keep track of him. Hank, I want to get closer than twenty-three hundred yards if I can. I want to be sure of this bastard."

"Destroyer is passing ahead of us, Captain," Amos Stuckey said. "His screw beat is steady. Sounds like he's going too fast to do any listening."

"Very well," Captain O'Connor said. He motioned to Savage to raise the periscope and rode it upward, clinging to the handles, his eyes at the lens as it broke water.

"Request another set of bearings, Captain," Hank Copper called out.

"The sonofabitch is turning to port!" O'Connor yelled. "Raise the radio mast. Transmit the sighting report. I'm going to have to eyeball this. Forward Room . . . fire all tubes manually . . . five-second intervals . . . FIRE ONE!"

In the Forward Torpedo Room Dandy Don Miller jammed his fingers down on the firing key for Number One tube, waited as he counted down from five to one and then fired Number Two tube. As he continued to fire the six torpedo tubes, Big John Sanders was handling the poppet valves that gulped the bubbles of firing air back into the ship so the

bubbles couldn't rise and break on the surface and give away
the sub's position. The telephone talker in the Forward Room,
his face intent as he watched Miller, reported as each torpedo
left the tube. As Miller came out from between the tubes and
began to help Big John close the outer-tube doors, the
telephone talker relayed the information that Stuckey had
reported all torpedoes were running hot, straight and normal.

"Natch," Miller panted as he whirled a Y-wrench to close
Number Five tube outer door. "Report all outer-tube doors
closed. We'll drain the tubes and stand by for word to reload."

"Take me deep!" Captain O'Connor yelled. "Down 'scope.
Close outer-tube doors. Three destroyers coming this way!
Make it four hundred feet, Sullie, and make it fast. Rig ship for
silent running. Rig ship for depth charge." He slid down the
ladder to the Control Room as a distant explosion shook the
Tigerfish slightly. Hank Copper looked up from the stopwatch
he was holding.

"That times out as a hit with the first torpedo we fired,
Captain."

Amos Stuckey half-turned on his stool. "Three sets of twin
screws, sir. Bear three-one-zero, zero-two-five and zero-eight-
zero, sir. I can still hear torpedoes running."

"Right fifteen degrees rudder," Captain O'Connor said.
"Can't run from the bastards, so we'll go under them."

"Coming to four hundred feet, Captain," Saul Silver reported.

"Now we'll see how good those people up there are,"
O'Connor said. He shook his head in disgust. "Biggest damned
ship I ever saw and I get one possible hit! If that isn't a crock."
He looked around as the distinctive sound of a depth-charge
pistol going off sounded through the hull of the Tigerfish.

Admiral Ozawa stood in the flight-director room on the
bridge of the giant carrier Taihu, watching his combat flight
officer plot the position of the enemy as reports from scouting
planes came in by radio. He turned, his narrowed eyes
questioning as the Taihu staggered slightly and rolled a few
degrees to port. A few minutes later a junior officer answered
the telephone and then turned to his Admiral.

"A torpedo hit the starboard side near the bow, sir. Damage
is not serious. The forward elevator is jammed but can be
repaired. There are no fires. Damage Control reports the ship

:an maintain speed. The submarine that fired the torpedo is
now being attacked and sunk, sir." Admiral Ozawa nodded and
turned back to the plotting charts. The *Taihu* had been built to
take heavy punishment. Its designers and builders had given
assurance that the big ship could absorb many torpedo hits.
He put the matter from his mind and concentrated on the
plotting charts. One of the Plotting Officers priced off the
distance between the American Battle Fleet and the position
of the Japanese Battle Force. He was within attack range of the
Americans. His planes could make the attack and then land at
Guam or Rota, refuel and rearm and then make a second attack
as they returned. His eyebrows raised slightly as his Plotting
Officer looked at him.

"No, Admiral," the officer said, knowing instinctively the
question Admiral Ozawa was asking. "We have sighted no
American search planes."

"Launch Raid One," Admiral Ozawa ordered.

Raid One was launched from the carriers in the van, one
hundred kilometers out ahead of Admiral Ozawa's flagship. It
was a small raid, sixty-one Zeke fighters, forty-five of them
carrying bombs, and eight Jill torpedo planes. They were
picked up on radar when they were still 150 miles from Task
Force 58. Admiral Mitscher ordered his carriers to turn into
the wind and launch fighters to repel the attack. Only one of
the Japanese planes managed to fight its way through the
swarm of Hellcats and into the center of Task Force 58. That
plane dropped its bomb and hit the battleship *South Dakota*,
killing twenty-seven men. Thirty-four of the Japanese attackers were shot down by Hellcats or antiaircraft fire; the
remaining thirty-five managed to reach Orote Air Field on
Guam, where American raids had earlier smashed all communications facilities and set the fuel tanks on fire.

Admiral Ozawa's Raid Two was launched from his carrier
Taihu. Raid Two was a major strike force; fifty-three Judy dive
bombers, forty-eight Zeke fighters and twenty-seven Jill
torpedo planes left the *Taihu* and arrowed toward the American Fleet.

Andy O'Connor, leading his fighters from the *Enterprise*,
was vectored into the incoming Japanese planes when they
were still sixty miles from their targets. He sighted the first
group of Judy dive bombers and made a head-on attack with
his fighter planes following him. His first target blew up in a

gush of flame and he dove downward to get beneath the dive
bomber formation and out of range of the rear-seat gunners in
the Judys. He zoomed upward underneath the tail-end
Charlie in the formation and fired a short burst that missed
He whipped his plane around and saw Red Olsen flame a dive
bomber and then close in behind another Judy and explode it
with a short burst into the dive bomber's wing root. He skewed
his plane violently to the left in response to Orv Masters's yell
in his earphones and saw a Zeke slide by him with Masters on
its tail, his guns chewing away at the Zeke's tail surfaces.

The battle lasted six minutes. Seventy of the 128 Japanese
planes of Raid Two were shot down. Twenty of the planes of
Raid Two got as far as the ships of Task Force 58. They did little
damage. Only 31 of the 128 planes that had flown off the *Taihu*
flight deck managed to survive. Raid Three, launched from the
carriers in Ozawa's van, was luckier. Its planes did no damage
but forty of the forty-seven that took to the air in Raid Three
managed to get back to their carriers.

Shortly before noon Admiral Ozawa gave the order to
launch Raid Four—eighty-one planes. Most of the planes in
this raid failed to find Task Force 58 and headed for Orote Air
Field on Guam to refuel. The Hellcats from a half-dozen of the
carriers in Task Force 58 were waiting for them. Seventy of the
eighty-one planes were destroyed before they could land.

By 1300 Admiral Ozawa realized he was riding a tiger and he
didn't dare get off. More than half of his aircraft had failed to
return to their carriers, and because communications from
Guam and Rota were not working, he didn't know how many of
the missing planes had landed safely and were refueling and
rearming for another attack. He hesitated, not knowing quite
what to do, and disaster struck.

The carrier *Shokaku* of his carrier force had turned into the
wind in preparation to receive planes returning from Raid
Three. As Admiral Ozawa and his staff watched the big carrier
maneuver, they saw a burst of flame soar upward from along
the carrier's side and then the big carrier staggered and began
to slow and drop out of the formation, mortally wounded by
three torpedoes fired by the U.S.S. *Cavalla*. An hour later the
fires started by the torpedoes reached the *Shokaku*'s bomb
storage areas and the ship was ripped apart.

Meanwhile, an inexperienced damage-control officer in the
Taihu, worried about the concentration of fuel-oil fumes in the

forward elevator that had been damaged by the single torpedo from the *Tigerfish*, ordered all ventilation ducts opened and the ventilation fans turned up to high to dissipate the fumes.

The fumes, heavy with the unrefined volatiles of the Borneo oil, surged throughout the ship and finally reached an open flame. The *Taihu*, the mightiest carrier in the Imperial Japanese Navy, exploded like a giant firecracker. The armored flight deck split open from bow to stern. The sides of the great hull bulged outward and holes were blown in the ship's bottom. In a matter of minutes the carrier was engulfed in flames. Thanks to the superb seamanship of a lifeboat coxswain from a nearby destroyer, Admiral Ozawa and his staff (with a junior officer carrying the ship's portrait of the Emperor) were able to abandon ship safely and were taken to the cruiser *Naguro*. More than seventeen hundred crewmen of the carrier *Taihu* died in the explosions and fires.

Admiral Ozawa showed no signs of dismay as he assembled his staff in the cruiser's fighting bridge. He had lost two of his biggest carriers, but most of their planes had been in the air and, Ozawa reasoned, could land on the other carriers when they returned. So far as he was concerned, the loss of the two carriers would have no effect on his eventual victory. He ordered a message sent to Admiral Kakuta, the land-based air commander at Taiwan, requesting that he report the exact positions of the American Battle Force and what actions the ground-based aircraft were taking against the enemy. The cruiser's communications systems were not sophisticated enough for the requirements of a Fleet Admiral, and the message took some time to get through.

Admiral Kakuta finally reported back. A large number of Admiral Ozawa's carrier planes had landed at Guam and Rota. But what he did not say—either because he did not know or because of the faulty communications—was that almost all of those aircraft had been badly shot up after they landed and were out of service.

Andy O'Connor climbed down out of his Hellcat fighter and took the mug of hot coffee Alabama Jones handed to him.

"How many, boss?" Jones asked in a low voice.

"Six."

"Guns all okay?"

"Fine. Thank that gunner for me. Better yet, when this is

over, I want to see the man. He deserves some recognition."
He looked around as a pilot's voice, high and excited, could be
heard above the noise on the flight deck.

"Hit 'em anywhere in the wings except the wing tips and
they burn! They BURN! Never saw anything like it! They were
blowing up in my face!"

"Jap planes don't have self-sealing gas tanks," Chief Jones
said. "Guess you found that out?"

"I didn't know what it was," Andy O'Connor said, "but it's
true, if you hit them anywhere amidships in the wings they
explode."

"Damned Navy is never gonna change," Chief Jones
growled. "They never get the word out to the people who have
to know it. They told us a long time ago to load the ammo belts
with incendiaries because the Japs don't have self-sealing gas
tanks. I thought they told you, too, which is why I didn't say
anything to you, sir. Here come Mr. Olsen and Mr. Masters.
We'll have all of you refueled and the ammo belts replaced in
about twenty minutes. You used the pee bottle, do I need to
empty it?" Andy shook his head and passed his coffee cup to
Olsen, who took a drink and passed it to Orv Masters.

"Can't figure it out, boss," Olsen said. "These aren't the
same sort of pilots we used to fight. The Zekes don't cover their
dive bombers or their torpedo planes, they jink away from
them as soon as you begin an attack. I chased one of those
damned monkeys all over the sky while he did every exercise
in acrobatics I ever saw and some I never heard of. When he
finally ran out of things to do, he flat-out tried to ram me."

"I had one of those during a raid on Guam," O'Connor said.
"I followed him while he did everything I ever saw a plane do
and then he got down close to the deck and when he tried to
give his plane full power, she stalled and I had time to get in a
burst."

"You notice the ocean when we were flying back?" Orv
Masters said. "I was looking down and all you can see for miles
is big circles of oil or gasoline on the water. God only knows
how many Japs went down today. Must be close to a hundred,
maybe more. I don't know how many carriers they've got out
there, but they must be short of planes and pilots by now."

"They had nine carriers before this thing started," Chief
Jones said as he came up to the three pilots. He was carrying

cardboard tray piled with thick ham sandwiches and cartons of milk. Red Olsen reached for a sandwich and milk.

"Mr. O'Connor makes me a Chief, which I deserved," he grumped, "and I wind up doing mess-cook duty." He handed the tray to a gunner's mate, who stuffed a sandwich under his arm and carried the tray over to another group of pilots.

"I heard from a Chif Yeoman been up on the bridge they have five big carriers and four small ones," Jones said. "One thing I want to know, Mr. O'Connor, is when in the hell are we gonna stop runnin' away from the Japs and turn around and go the hell after them? We got all the damned battleships in the world and a lot more carriers than they've got."

"Meaning what?" O'Connor said.

"We're headin' east again, sir. Far as I know, the Japs are out west."

"He's right," Red Olsen said. "Look at the sun, it's almost aft of us."

"The Admiral must have a good reason," O'Connor said. The bullhorn roared from the bridge structure.

"Pilots report to ready rooms on the double!"

Lieutenant Commander "Rip" Ripper finished interrogating the pilots and did his sums in a small notebook.

"If none of you are guilty of fibbing, if all the pilots on the other carriers are telling the bone-honest truth, then our not-so-honorable enemy has lost over three hundred planes today."

"How many did we lose?" Andy O'Connor's voice was somber.

"As of last report, forty planes," Ripper said. "But a number of destroyers have reported picking up pilots so that figure isn't exact so far as pilots are concerned."

"When are we going after their ships?" Red Olsen said as he lit a cigar.

"The word I have is that Admiral Spruance wants to keep us close enough to Saipan to protect the landings there until we have some positive information on the location of their fleet," Ripper said. "I would suggest that all of you get a lot of sleep, because tomorrow is liable to be a very busy day. The flight-deck people and the armorers will be up all night, and that should answer your question, Mr. Olsen."

* * *

Aboard the *Naguro* Admiral Ozawa was busy making his plans for the next day. He issued orders for all his ships to change course to the north and to stand by to refuel at dawn on the twentieth. Despite the loss of his two big carriers, he was confident he could engage the American Fleet the next day with air strikes from his planes that were overnighting at Guam and Rota. On the twentieth he could tighten the jaws of his vise on Admiral Spruance with raids against Task Force 58 from Guam and Rota and simultaneous strikes from his remaining carriers. His confidence was bolstered by reports from those pilots who had returned that at least six American carriers were afire and sinking and that more than four hundred American planes had been shot down.

He planned to fence with the Americans, keep them off-balance with air attacks during the daylight hours while he maneuvered the heavy elements of his Battle Fleet into position. Once dusk fell, he would launch the attack with his surface ships. Admiral Ozawa knew he was outnumbered in terms of ships, but he was confident; he had the two mightiest battleships in the world in his task force, the *Yamoto* and the *Musashi*, battleships so huge, so heavily armed, that no enemy force could stand up to them. His cruiser force and his destroyer squadrons were still intact, and he owned, he thought, the supreme advantage over the Americans—his gunners and torpedomen were experienced and deadly in night battle.

As the hours wore on, it was apparent that Admiral Ozawa's order to his ships to get into position to refuel was not being carried out. Exasperated at his inability to contact the ships in his two forces and the land-based aircraft commanders with the cruiser's crude communications system, Admiral Ozawa transferred his flag to the carrier *Zuikaka*—and there learned the shattering news that his carrier air force had lost 330 of its 436 planes and the truth from Admiral Kakuta on Tinian—that the carrier planes that had made it to Guam and Rota had been destroyed as they grouped to land or on the ground after they had landed.

The Japanese Admiral wanted to fight, and as long as Tokyo had not told him to withdraw, he was going to fight. From his new flagship he issued orders for all ships to refuel at dawn and be prepared to strike the enemy in full force on the twenty-first. Shortly after the orders had been issued, one of his cruisers reported intercepting a message from an American search plane giving the location of the Japanese Force. Admiral Ozawa rescinded his order to refuel and made plans to sail east and engage the enemy that night.

Admiral Marc Mitscher received the word of the sighting of the Japanese Force shortly before four in the afternoon. Standing in the middle of his silent staff, the doughty little carrier Admiral had to make a decision no one else could make; a decision that might cost the lives of thousands of men.

Admiral Mitscher knew the Japanese preferred to fight their sea battles at night. He knew, as well, that the Japanese pilots were highly trained in night bombing and night carrier landings. His own pilots were not so trained.

The Japanese were far to the west, almost at the limit of the effective range of his aircraft. The sun would set at seven that evening, making it necessary, if he launched planes now, for his pilots to return after dark. The pilots would be exhausted after hours in the air; some might be wounded, planes would be low on fuel and some would probably be damaged. To make matters worse, the wind was out of the east and would be steady all evening and night, making it necessary for the carriers to turn and steam away at high speed from the returning planes in order to take planes aboard.

Admiral Mitscher weighed all the factors, and at ten minutes after four he gave the order.

"Get their carriers!"

Andy O'Connor raced across the deck of the *Enterprise*, his oxygen mask bobbing against his chest, a heavy pistol on his belt banging against his thigh. He climbed up the boarding ladder, his navigation clipboard tucked under one arm, and Chief Alabama Jones scrambled up the ladder after him and leaned into the cockpit to help him fasten his parachute harness and safety belts.

The crew Chief backed down the boarding ladder muttering under his breath the words he considered Andy O'Connor's good luck charm, the words he had said the first time he had sent his pilot out to do air battle, "Y'all come back safe." He unhooked the boarding ladder and moved away from the plane, seeing O'Connor's gloved fist rise above the edge of the cockpit in a thumbs-up salute. The bullhorn bellowed from the bridge area and O'Connor started his plane's engine and taxied

into position. At twenty minutes past four in the afternoon the
carriers of Task Force 58 turned directly into the east wind and
launched a full strike—eighty-five fighters, seventy-seven dive
bombers and fifty-four torpedo planes. The planes sortied
briefly over the task force and then turned and headed west.

Two hours later Andy O'Connor saw the enemy fleet far out
ahead of him, strung out in three groups heading away from
the oncoming American planes. He calmly worked out his
navigation and radioed the longitude, latitude and course of
the enemy ships.

The casual interplane chatter of the pilots was stilled as they
double-checked O'Connor's navigation and the realization sank
in that they were now so far west of their home carriers that
getting back to the carriers was going to be a major problem.
The enemy fleet was at least sixty miles farther to the west than
the report from the search plane had indicated, and headed
west at twenty knots. The information of Ozawa's position and
course gave Admiral Mitscher pause; he decided to hold his
second launch until the following day.

Admiral Ozawa, alerted by a scouting plane's sighting of the
oncoming American planes, reacted. He had one hundred
planes on his carrier flight decks—Zeke fighters and Hamps,
Mitsubishi Zero-2 fighters—and he launched them to intercept. His ships clustered into small groups to make their
antiaircraft fire more effective. The last phase of the Battle of
the Philippine Sea was about to begin against a backdrop of a
tropical sunset.

Flying as protective cover above the dive bombers and
torpedo planes, Andy O'Connor saw four Avenger torpedo
bombers slice through a cloud above a Japanese carrier and
then begin their approach, turning 180 degrees to put the
setting sun at their backs. They leveled out down near the
water and began their attack. The lead Avenger was hit by the
carrier's antiaircraft fire. The midsection of the plane gushed
fire and the radioman and the gunner bailed out. The wounded
pilot of the Avenger, his cockpit torn by shrapnel, pressed
home his attack, dropped his torpedo and somehow managed
to pull his plane up and over the carrier's deck and made his
escape. The carrier staggered under the impact of the torpedo
and then stopped dead in the water as a second torpedo from
an Avenger slammed home into the carrier's engine rooms.

"Here they come," Orv Masters yelled into his microphone,

and O'Connor tipped his plane over into a dive to meet a cluster of Hamps swarming up after the circling dive bombers. O'Connor and his two wingmen smashed through the oncoming Hamps. O'Connor's first target evaded him and he yanked his plane around and up and saw a Hamp spew a long stream of fire into Orv Masters's plane. He saw Masters's head snap back and his goggles fly off and then Masters's Hellcat went into a steep dive and disappeared. As the Hamp pulled up, O'Connor's six .50-caliber guns poured a solid stream of incendiaries into the other plane and it exploded in a burst of flame and followed Masters's plane down into the sea. O'Connor saw the body of the Hamp's pilot turning over and over in the air, and for a brief second he was possessed by an insane desire to shoot the pilot if he could get him in his sights.

Lacking the fuel to circle for very long to pick the most desirable targets and make coordinated attacks, the American dive bombers went after the ships closest to them. The Japanese fighter planes, outnumbered and outfought by the Hellcats, offered only token opposition as the dive bombers unloaded on their targets.

The battle in the skies over the Japanese Fleet lasted twenty minutes, and then the American planes turned for home. The damage they had done was significant. The carrier *Hiyo*, torpedoed by two Avengers, was afire and sinking. The carrier *Zuikako* had taken several bomb hits on her flight deck and was afire and badly damaged. The carrier *Chiyuda* took only one bomb hit, but that completely wrecked its flight deck and caused fires below decks. Two of the fleet's big oil tankers had been hit by the dive bombers and were burning and sinking.

The damage to Admiral Ozawa's carrier-plane force was catastrophic. When Raid One was launched, Ozawa had 436 planes operational. As the sun went down in a blaze of tropical glory on June 19, the air battle which American pilots would later call the Marianas Turkey Shoot had claimed 401 Japanese aircraft, their pilots, gunners and radiomen.

Despite these staggering losses, Admiral Ozawa issued an order to his battleships and cruisers to reverse course and close with the American Fleet and engage. The commanders of the battleships and cruisers dutifully turned their ships and began to steam east as their crews prepared for an all-out night battle with a superior force. They continued to sail toward the east as twenty-four knots for two hours until Admiral Ozawa came to the realization that the odds against him were too heavy; he had no air cover, he did not know exactly where the American Battle Force was at that moment and he recognized that the closer he got to the American Battle Force, the greater the risk he ran of suffering another devastating attack from the American planes. Two hours before midnight Admiral Ozawa reluctantly gave the order to cancel the effort to find and engage the Americans and turned what was left of the striking force of Operation A-GO toward Okinawa.

Meanwhile, the American carrier pilots flying eastward were in total darkness. The black sky and an equally black sea offered no visible horizon. Far to the east lightning bolts were shooting out of thunderheads. Fuel was low so the pilots leaned their fuel-air mixtures and set their throttles to minimum speed for the two-and-a-half-hour flight back to the carriers and safety. Many of the planes had been damaged and would not make it all the way. Some of the pilots had been wounded and a few of them would not survive the trip. The nerve shock and fatigue of the long flight to the battle area, the excitement of the battle itself, now set in. With no visible horizon, vertigo became an insidious enemy. The pilots, so skilled in battle such a short time ago, now wandered almost aimlessly as they tried to fly a straight course, their eyes constantly looking at the fuel gauges. On the radio intercom pilots were asking for help, offering to bunch up and fly together so that if they had to ditch their planes, they could tie their life rafts together.

Aboard the ships of Task Force 58 the radio operators had listened and copied down the excited voices of their pilots as they fought the brief battle over Ozawa's force. Now they listened—and typed out—the conversations of the pilots as they tried to get home to the carriers.

An hour and a half later the first planes began to fall out of the sky. Here and there along the course that led toward the American Battle Fleet, a patch of phosphorescence would suddenly bloom on the black surface of the sea, marking the spot where a plane out of fuel, a plane with a wounded pilot or a plane whose pilot was so overcome by fatigue and vertigo he could no longer fly, dropped out and down into the sea.

Aboard his flagship, the carrier *Lexington*, Admiral Mitscher knew what his pilots were going through, the confusion they would feel when they finally reached the Battle Force. He ordered his carrier forces to open their intervals from twelve to fifteen miles so there would be ample room for maneuvering. He ordered the radio beacons turned on to help his pilots find their way.

The storm building far to the east occasionally lit the black bulks of the ships of Task Force 58 with giant bolts of lightning as the Battle Fleet steamed at flank speed to the west toward its incoming pilots. At just past 2100 hours the radar operators picked up the first incoming planes some seventy miles to the east. Admiral Mitscher ordered his carriers and their escorts to reverse course to the east, into the wind, and to make twenty-two knots in preparation for taking the planes aboard.

Standing in the bridge of his carrier, Admiral Mitscher suddenly turned to a Communications Officer and said, "Order all destroyers and cruisers to swing out lifeboats and man them with crews." The order would save many lives in the hours to come.

At 2130 the first incoming planes appeared over the carrier force and it was immediately apparent to the anxious men on the ships that the pilots were confused, disoriented. In the total darkness below them they could not distinguish the bulk of a battleship or a cruiser from that of a carrier. Admiral Mitscher snapped out the order that would forever endear him to all naval pilots.

"Turn on all the lights!"

The Battle Fleet lit up like a giant cluster of Christmas trees. Running lights showed red and green against the blackness. Red masthead lights went on. The carriers turned on their deck lights and on each carrier a searchlight beam was aimed vertically into the sky. Destroyers and cruisers fired star shells to give the incoming pilots vision. But despite the lighting of the fleet, something that had never been done in war, planes began to crash as pilots, untrained in night carrier landings, misjudged distances. Other pilots, suffering extreme vertigo after the long flight with no visible horizon and confused by the sudden blaze of lights all over the ocean surface, simply flew their planes into the water. The lifeboat crews, standing by in response to Admiral Mitscher's order, did yeoman work, pulling exhausted and wounded pilots out of their sinking planes, scooping them out of their one-man rafts. One observer aboard a carrier later said, "The surface of the ocean

during that time looked like a huge field of flowers with the
little flashlights the pilots carried winking as the pilots tried to
attract lifeboats to them."

When the last of the planes had arrived, shortly after 2200
hours, seventeen fighter planes, forty-two dive bombers and
twenty-three torpedo planes had either ditched in the water
among the ships of the fleet or had crash-landed on carrier
decks, their pilots pulled out of the planes, and the planes
themselves, too badly damaged to repair, pushed over the
side.

As the last planes landed in the water and the last of the
pilots had been picked up, Admiral Mitscher, every inch as
much a fighter as his opponent, Admiral Ozawa, requested
permission from Admiral Spruance to launch a second raid
against Ozawa's fleet. He also suggested that Admiral Lee's
force of seven battleships and their escorts be released from
Task Force 58 to steam west and engage Ozawa's battleships in
a surface battle the next day, a suggestion Admiral Lee heartily
approved of. Admiral Spruance denied the request, but did
order the fleet to reorganize into its original battle formation
and proceed west at economical speed. Shortly after midnight
the *Enterprise* launched two search planes manned by pilots
experienced in night flying and night carrier landings. The
pilots of the search planes found Admiral Ozawa's fleet 360
miles to the west and making high speed. Ozawa had gained
the edge he needed, his ships were beyond effective striking
range of the American carrier planes. Admiral Spruance,
hoping to overtake some of Ozawa's ships that might have been
crippled and unable to make full speed, ordered his flagship,
the cruiser *Indianapolis,* to join up with Admiral Lee's
battleship force and make all possible speed in pursuit. The
carrier force, with its destroyer force zigging and zagging back
and forth over the course the carrier pilots had flown on their
way home earlier that night, proceeded at a much slower pace
as the destroyers found and rescued pilots floating in their
small life rafts. By noon of the next day Admiral Spruance
decided that Admiral Ozawa had made good his escape. He
ordered Task Force 58 to reverse course and proceed at slow
speed toward Saipan and continue the search for pilots who
had ditched their planes the night before.

At about the time Admiral Spruance ordered his ships to
reverse course, Admiral Ozawa was sitting in his cabin aboard

the damaged carrier *Zuikaka* dictating his letter of resignation. The offer to resign was sent by radio that afternoon to Tokyo. Admiral Toyodo refused to accept the resignation and kept Admiral Ozawa in command of all the Imperial Japanese Navy's carrier forces, a decision that in the postwar analyses came in for criticism. Admiral Halsey would later soundly defeat Admiral Ozawa in the Battle of Cape Engano and send most of the carriers Admiral Ozawa commanded to the bottom of the sea.

In the eyes of dispassionate naval strategists, the Battle of the Philippine Sea was inconclusive. The American Battle Force was vastly superior to the Japanese forces in terms of capital ships, carriers and numbers of planes. The Japanese Fleet had escaped with the loss of two of its largest carriers and one smaller carrier, and severe damage to two other carriers, but the rest of Admiral Ozawa's fleet had escaped. The Japanese had, however, suffered a catastrophic blow to their carrier-plane force. Admiral Ozawa had lost all but 35 of his 436 carrier aircraft, their pilots, gunners and radiomen. Another fifty land-based aircraft operating out of Guam and Rota had been destroyed. The American Fleet had lost 130 aircraft, but thanks to the rescue efforts of the destroyer lifeboat crews, only 76 pilots, gunners and radiomen had been lost.

The victory—and it was a victory of sorts—had insured the doom of the Japanese forces holding Saipan, Tinian and Guam.

Chapter
Twenty-four

THE THREE DESTROYERS that raced for the *Tigerfish* when a Japanese pilot reported torpedoes had been fired at the carrier *Taihu* delivered three attacks each, dropped a total of thirty-six depth charges and then went off at high speed toward the *Taihu*, reporting the American submarine had been smashed and sunk. Ten minutes after Amos Stuckey reported he had lost all contact with the destroyers, Captain Mike O'Connor ordered the *Tigerfish* to periscope depth. He studied the eastern horizon through the periscope and saw dozens of aircraft.

"Did you get a receipt of that contact report you sent?" he called down the hatch.

"Negative, Captain," Hank Copper replied.

"Run the radio mast up and send it again and put the time you sent the original message in the text and mention those planes I just saw. We'll stay up here until we get a receipt. Sullie, bring me up another ten feet so we make sure we get the message off." The receipt came ten minutes later and the *Tigerfish* went down to periscope depth.

"Secure from General Quarters. Set regular sea detail. Reload the Forward Room torpedo tubes," Captain O'Connor ordered. He waited until Wayne Raleigh climbed to the Conning Tower and took over the OOD watch and then went below to the Control Room. He looked at the plot.

"One damned hit," he said in a disgusted voice. "With a target that big, I should have got at least three fish into her."

"Captain, look at the plot," Hank Copper said patiently. "The target was making a lot of speed, twenty-six knots when we first saw her, and she was making a lot of speed when she

318

turned left. She turned just before we got a solution on the TDC and I think you did damned well to get even one hit, shooting from the hip."

"Did you say anything about the hit, about a possible damage to the target?"

"Yes, sir, I added that to the second contact report we sent a few minutes ago. I think we can take credit for damaging the carrier."

"Damaging isn't sinking, dammit," O'Connor muttered. "A target that big can probably absorb one torpedo with about as much trouble as a mosquito gives to us."

"Depends on where you hit the target, Captain," Saul Silver said. "If you got a fish into her engine rooms, she's hurt."

"Not much chance of that," O'Connor said. "She's not in sight, nothing's in sight except those aircraft I reported for the second sighting report." He went forward to the Forward Torpedo Room where Dandy Don Miller was supervising the reloading of all six torpedo tubes.

"You people up here did a damned fine job," he said to Miller. "Sorry I had to shoot from the hip like that, but what happened was we had a big carrier, there were two big carriers in sight, real big ships. I was setting up on the biggest one of the two and we were within a thin red hair of having a solution and she turned ninety degrees to port. She was going awfully fast, twenty-six knots when we first saw her, so I had to start shooting as soon as I saw her turning away from us.

"We got one timed hit. I missed with the other five and that's not the fault of you people. Dandy Don, you got those fish off every five seconds on the nose, exactly. Damned good work."

"If we hit him with one torpedo, the sonofabitch'll sink, Captain," Miller said. "What we shoot at we hit and what we hit we sink."

Big John Sanders secured the inner door of Number Three torpedo tube and turned to Captain O'Connor.

"What's going on, Captain?" he asked.

"I don't know, John," O'Connor said. "The only thing I can think of, and it's purely a guess, is that the Jap Navy might be on its way to try and throw the Marines off Saipan. We invaded a few days ago, it was in the fleet news we got over the radio the other night."

"If they were on their way to do that, why did they have all those planes in the air that you saw a little while ago through the periscope?" Miller asked.

"The telephone talkers don't miss much, do they?" Captain O'Connor said with a grin. "Come to think of it, there's no reason for those planes being in the air except," he rubbed the side of his jaw with a thick finger, "we were about four hundred miles from Saipan, that's a rough guess, when we fired at the carrier. She turned to port, to the east, and she was pouring on the coal. We came up to periscope depth two hours later and I could see planes. So the carrier should be about three hundred sixty miles from Saipan by that time, maybe a little closer. Maybe our carriers are near Saipan, to the west of the island, and maybe the Jap carrier planes were getting ready to hit at our carriers. If they're going to go head-to-head with our carriers, maybe we'll get orders to chase after them and we could get another shot at that damned carrier I missed."

"It's sunk by now, Captain," Dandy Don Miller said. "We hit it with one of my fish, it's sunk. Hey, don't you have a brother flying dive bombers? He could be dive bombing the other Jap ships. If we get over there, we could call it the Battle of the O'Connors, Captain."

"He's on the *Enterprise*, but he's flying fighter planes now. He's the Air Group Commander for all the *Enterprise* fighters," Captain O'Connor said. "Yeah, the Battle of the O'Connors. Soon as we surface this evening, I'll get off a message and ask permission to leave this area and chase after those ships."

He left the torpedo room and went into the Wardroom. After his big frame had cleared the hatch between the two compartments, Dandy Don Miller looked around at his reload crew.

"Any of you people ever get any ideas about getting gold braid and want to be a Captain, just study that big Irishman. That's the best damned submarine skipper this Navy ever had."

The message from the *Tigerfish* requesting permission to leave its patrol area and set out in pursuit of the ships it had reported seeing was ignored. The submarines assigned by Vice Admiral Lockwood to intercept Admiral Ozawa's Battle Force were forgotten as the two carrier fleets clashed in battle. Four days after the battle ended, the *Tigerfish* received a message congratulating her on the sighting and the accurate position report of the enemy and ordering the *Tigerfish* to take station twenty miles west of Saipan and patrol on a north-south line until further orders were received. Hank Copper set the course for the new patrol area, and for three weeks the *Tigerfish* ran north and south on its patrol line, submerged by day and on the surface at night, without seeing an enemy ship. Then orders came for the *Tigerfish* to proceed to Pearl Harbor.

Captain Elmo Furst, the Chief of Staff, and Commander Hugh Foster headed the welcoming delegation as the *Tigerfish* tied up at the submarine pier in Pearl Harbor. Captain Furst thundered down the gangway, his hand outstretched.

"Damned fine work, Captain," he boomed. "Damned fine patrol."

"Nice of you to say that, sir," Mike O'Connor said, "but we didn't sink a single ship."

"You're getting credit for a successful war patrol," Captain Furst said. "That sighting you made of the Jap carrier fleet and the second report you sent let the fly-boy Admirals know what was going on and they poured it to the Japs. And now I've got some good and some bad news for you.

"The good news is that intelligence intercepted some Jap radio traffic. The torpedoes you fired at that carrier—you got one hit. The carrier sank about six, seven hours later.

"The bad news is we can't give you credit for sinking the *Taihu*, thirty-one thousand tons. The radio messages our intelligence people intercepted and read said that some goofball of a damage officer opened all the ventilation ducts and turned up the vent fans to get rid of the oil fumes that were in the area where you hit the carrier, somewhere up near the bow.

"The carrier's oil tanks were full of Borneo oil and the fumes exploded and the damned carrier busted up like a tin can and went down. They lost almost two thousand men aboard her. Biggest carrier they had. But you don't get credit for putting her down. You get credit for severely damaging her and partial credit for her sinking."

"I don't think that's fair, Captain," Mike O'Connor said.

"Of course it isn't fair," Captain Furst said. "But I don't make the rules. Dammit, if a defensive end hurries a quarterback and he throws an interception and the guy who intercepts the pass goes for a touchdown, the six points count. I think you should get credit and I'm going to keep arguing about it. The Japs lost one other big carrier, the *Shokaku*, thirty thousand tons. Herman Kossler in *Cavella* hit her with three fish and she went down just a couple of hours before your carrier blew up." He looked at his watch. "I'd like to see you in my office at fourteen hundred hours and we'll go from there to see Admiral Nimitz, he wants to talk with you. Okay?" He left the ship, and Commander Hugh Foster put his arm around Mike O'Connor.

"Nothing's going to change old Elmo," he said. "He does everything in a hurry. I think he sleeps in a hurry, but he's a damned good Chief of Staff. Now let's get down to business. The buses will be here at eleven hundred hours to take the crew to the hotel. They'll have their noon meal at the hotel.

"We're going to put the *Tigerfish* in drydock tomorrow afternoon. They'll install some new sound heads and some brand-new radar gear, real fancy stuff." He opened a notebook and the two men discussed the work that had to be done on the *Tigerfish*, one ship's Captain talking to a man who had been a ship's Captain and who would, in time, command ships again. When Hugh Foster had left the ship, Captain O'Connor found Chief O'Brien and told him to have the crew ready for the buses at 1100. He walked back up the deck, and Amos Stuckey, who had the deck watch, raised his hand to stop him.

"That Lieutenant Commander up on the pier has been waiting to see you, Captain."

"Come aboard, sir," Captain O'Connor called out. The Lieutenant Commander came down the gangway, walking carefully, favoring his left leg. He saluted the quarterdeck and the flag and turned to Captain O'Connor.

"My name is Oscar Olsen, sir, people usually call me Red. I'd like to talk to you in private, if I could, Captain." Mike O'Connor's eyes took in the gold pilot's wings pinned above a row of medal and campaign ribbons on the Lieutenant Commander's khaki shirt.

"We can go below to my cabin, Mister Olsen. Please follow me." He led the way down the Forward Torpedo Room hatch and waited at the bottom of the ladder until Red Olsen had stiff-legged it down the vertical ladder. In his tiny cabin he pulled the chair out from behind the desk and walked over and sat on the edge of his bunk.

"It's about my brother, about Andy?" he said in a low voice.

"Yes, sir," Red Olsen said. "I'm not very good at this sort of thing, Captain, but I think Andy would have wanted someone who knew him pretty good to tell you. I was his port wingman; that is, I flew on his port hand ever since the Battle of Midway."

"You used the past tense, Mister Olsen," Mike O'Connor said slowly. "He's gone?"

Red Olsen nodded and watched the big man on the edge of the bunk suddenly seem to draw in on himself, his head lowering, his massive hands gripping his knees. He saw the tears falling between Mike O'Connor's feet, heard the single tortured sob. He felt his own eyes filling and he reached for a handkerchief and wiped his eyes and then refolded the handkerchief and reached out and very gently put it on the back of Mike O'Connor's left hand. After a minute or two O'Connor wiped his eyes and handed back the handkerchief.

"Do you know how it happened?" O'Connor said.

"I don't know the details. I didn't see it, no one saw it, Captain. Do you know about the Marianas Turkey Shoot, the Battle of the Philippine Sea when we tangled with the Jap carrier fleet last month?"

O'Connor nodded. "We get a news report on radio at night when we surface. They mentioned something about that, but they didn't give many details."

"The big air battle was on the nineteenth of last month," Olsen said. "Before that, Orv Masters, he was Andy's starboard wingman, and myself and Andy flew a lot of missions against Guam and Rota air fields. The morning of the big battle we flew four sorties against Guam. Andy got eight planes. That brought his total to twenty-five planes shot down. He led the ship in that category."

He smiled gently, remembering. "He chewed me out for fair, that day. I disobeyed him. His orders were that we never get separated from each other. I saw a line of Jap dive bombers on their final leg, their final approach leg to land at the air field on Guam and I couldn't resist falling in behind them as if I were part of the landing. I shot four of them down and when we got back to the carrier, Andy read me off something fierce for breaking away. He was right, I shouldn't have done it but it seemed like a good idea at the time."

"How was he then, I mean, how did he seem to you?" Mike asked in a low voice.

"I don't quite know what you mean, sir," Olsen said.

"I mean, was he as he always was? Or was he worried or preoccupied, had he changed at all? You said you had been with him a long time."

"Well, yes," Red Olsen said. "He was always a very strict

officer when it came to duty stuff. Nobody minds that, you expect it of a good man." He sat back in the chair, his eyes distant.

"I think all of us, Orv Masters and myself and our crew Chief, Alabama Jones, noticed a change in him after the last time we were in Pearl getting some bomb hits we had taken fixed up.

"Andy was always determined to be the best fighter pilot in the Navy. I think he was. But to be a really good fighter pilot you have to be very sensitive; sensitive to everything around you. I don't know how it is in a ship like this but in the air you have to be so alert, so sensitive to conditions that are changing every second, that it sort of carries over into everything else you do. Does that make sense to you, sir?"

Mike nodded. "I think I can understand that. You move at high speeds up there. The enemy is moving at high speed. Yes. I understand."

"We had a good team. Andy was the leader and Orv and I followed. The Chief who took care of our planes and his crew, they were part of the team. We worked together as a team. We were awfully close.

"We flew a lot of missions before the last big battle. Truk, places like that. After every mission we'd be debriefed by intelligence and then Andy would get us off together, Orv and me and the crew Chief, and we'd go over every little detail. Things like why did I slide out to the left so far when we pulled up out of a dive over Truk or something like that. Why did Andy's engine show like ten degrees over the normal heat? He wanted answers to every damned little thing.

"Sometimes it got a little bit too much, if you know what I mean. I remember on the morning of the big battle, we'd flown four missions against Guam and they weren't any piece of cake. We came back and we were waiting to be refueled and rearmed and I patted Andy on the back and told him he'd done a hell of a job, because he had.

"He turned and stared at me and said something about he hadn't done as well as he should have because he was deficient. That's the word he used, deficient. I thought he was being stupid because he'd done a hell of a job. For one thing, he took a Zeke off my tail that was about to chew me up. Deficient my ass. Andy was the least deficient man I ever knew."

Mike nodded, his face grim. "No, he wasn't deficient, Mr. Olsen. Please go on."

"They sent us out about sixteen hundred twenty hours that afternoon to find the Jap Fleet. Andy flew the point, out in front of all of us. He was the flight leader and he was the best navigator. If we found the Japs our carriers could depend on the position he'd radio back. We found them and then we went in for the attack.

"It's pretty hard to make much sense of this sort of thing for someone who's never flown aircraft. I don't suppose I could understand much about your branch of the service, although Andy told us a lot about it. We were all pretty tired. We'd been flying and fighting all morning and up until about fourteen hundred hours that day. The Jap Fleet was a long way off, just about as far as we could go, stooge around for fifteen minutes or so and then have enough gas to get back home.

"I saw Andy get two Hamps, they're a new Jap fighter plane, and I got three. I think Orv Masters got a couple. I was flying on Andy's left wing and I looked across his plane and saw Orv get it from a Hamp. Andy saw it, too, and he went after the Hamp and got it. He flamed it, blew it up. And then things got hot and heavy. There were an awful lot of Japs around and we were there to protect the dive bombers and we got separated." He stopped, his pale face with its freckles standing out in sharp contrast, somber.

"The only other time we ever got separated was when I was a smart-ass and ducked down to get into the landing formation of those dive bombers over Guam," he said slowly. "I kept looking for him but every time I broke loose from some Japs, another bunch would jump me. I got hit in the left leg and it was bleeding pretty bad and I knew that if I didn't get started for home I'd never make it. When I got rid of the last Jap that was trying to get me, I looked at my fuel gauge and I knew it was going to be damned close to being empty before I ever got back. I was trying to put a tourniquet on my leg, and when I got that done I started for home."

"Then what happened?" Mike O'Connor asked.

"I made it back. I think I landed with the engine burning memories instead of gasoline," Olsen said. "Andy didn't make it back." He lowered his head and stared at the deck. "If it would be any comfort to you, the whole squadron, all the radiomen on the carriers, the battleships, all the task force, heard his last words."

"If everyone heard them I'd like to hear them," Mike O'Connor said.

"The last thing they heard from Andy, sir, was . . . 'I've got four of them down and I've got fifteen more cornered.'" He raised his head, the tears streaming down his cheeks. "One of the people in the paint locker made some signs with those words on them. The signs hang in the bridge and in the pilot ready rooms, sir."

"Do your people copy, I mean, do they type up things that come in over the radio?"

"Yes, sir," Olsen said. He took a thick envelope out of his trouser pocket. "I brought you a copy of the radio traffic of the last fifteen minutes of the battle, Captain." He handed the envelope to O'Connor.

"Thank you, Mister Olsen," Mike O'Connor said. "My father will treasure this. And I thank you for taking it on yourself to carry out such a painful duty." He turned away and Red Olsen backed out of the small cabin into the narrow passageway and bumped into someone. He turned his head and saw a craggy face beneath a Chief Petty Officer's cap.

"Follow me, sir," Chief O'Brien said. He led Red Olsen to the ladder in the Forward Torpedo Room.

"You did what you had to do very damned well, Commander," O'Brien said in a low rumble. "We'll take care of the Captain now." He followed Red Olsen up the ladder, and after the pilot had left the ship, O'Brien went up on the dock to a telephone. He dialed Commander Hugh Foster's office and told his former Captain what he had overheard while he was standing near Captain O'Connor's cabin.

"He's got to see Admiral Nimitz at fourteen hundred thirty hours," Hugh Foster said. "I think he can get through that, he's a strong man. I'll stay with him after that, Chief, bring him back to the ship to get his gear and then bring him out to the hotel and if I can I'll stay with him all evening."

"Might be a good idea to get him blind-eyed drunk, sir," Chief O'Brien said. "Wouldn't expect you to sit through that but I can organize the other Chiefs and the Wardroom to handle that."

"That might help, even though he isn't a drinking man," Hugh Foster said slowly. "Get the word to Mister Copper and have him round up the other officers, and if you don't mind, I'll be there. It will be a relief to tie one on and forget some of the rotten things that happen in this war."

"Leave it to me, sir," Chief O'Brien said.

"I intended to do just that, Chief," Hugh Foster said.

Mike O'Connor woke the next morning with an aching head and a sick stomach. He rolled over in bed and sat up and grabbed his head in his hands. He heard a noise in the room and forced his eyes open, wincing at the light streaming in the window. He saw Chief O'Brien get out of a chair and watched, squinting, as his Chief of the Boat did something at a table across the room. He heard the clink of ice and O'Brien turned and came toward him holding a glass filled with thick yellow liquid.

"What's that stuff?" O'Connor groaned.

"It's some kind of a Dutch drink, Captain," O'Brien said in his gruff voice. "Never mind what it looks like or what it tastes like, just drink it down. The whole glass. Without stopping. It'll make you feel a lot better, sir."

O'Connor took the glass in both hands and raised it to his lips. His nose wrinkled at the slightly sweet smell, but he finished the tall glass of liquid, gulping it down, fighting back the urge to throw up.

"Now just sit quiet, Captain," O'Brien said. "In about two, three minutes, your belly will quiet down and your head will stop aching." He went into the bathroom and rinsed out the glass and dried it, and put it back on the table.

"Have you been here all night, Chief?" O'Connor asked.

"I drew the duty, Captain," O'Brien said. "How you feeling, sir?"

Mike O'Connor sat up straight on the edge of the bed. "My God," he said in an awed voice. "It's working, whatever the hell it is. I feel pretty good!"

"Wait another two, three minutes, Captain, and then hit the shower." While O'Connor showered, O'Brien rummaged through his suitcase and laid out fresh underwear, socks and a clean uniform. He laid the clothes on the bed and went to the window and stood there, looking out at the beach and the sea, while his Commanding Officer got dressed. He turned around.

"Best thing you can do now, Captain, is eat some breakfast. I made arrangements with the galley to send it up." He reached for the telephone. "Just tell me what you want, sir."

"I think maybe you're right, Chief," O'Connor said. "Let me try about four eggs, over easy, some bacon and buttered toast and about a quart of hot coffee. And while you're ordering, get something for yourself. I hate to eat alone."

The two men finished eating and Chief O'Brien piled the dirty dishes on a tray and put it outside the door of the room. "Just for the record, Chief," Captain O'Connor said, "what was that yellow stuff you made me drink? I never thought anything could make me feel halfway decent after what I drank last night."

"It's some Dutch drink," O'Brien answered. "Now that you've eaten and feel pretty good I can tell you what's in it. Far as I know it's a mixture of egg yolks, heavy cream and a little touch of brandy. I don't know why it works but it does. Before the war when I was in San Diego we used to mix the stuff with a lot of cherry brandy, whip it up real foamy and fluffy and then feed it to some gal who was willing to talk but not put out, if you know what I mean." He grinned.

"She'd drink it down, get a couple of glasses down, and all of a sudden she'd discover that she didn't give a damn what happened and that made things kind of nice all around. Before the war I bought a case of it and I still had a couple of bottles stashed in the ship's locker on the base, sir. I know that's against regulations but I'm glad I had it handy. You aren't what I'd call a regular sort of drinker, sir."

"I know," Captain O'Connor said. "About last night, I didn't do anything I might not like to know about?"

"No, sir. You just tied on a regulation coming-in-off-a-war-patrol drunk, Captain. Nothing unusual."

"If it wasn't unusual why were you sitting here in the room when I woke up? If I remember, you said something about drawing the duty."

"Captain, you must have had more to drink than I figured. I was just passing by and I thought the Dutch stuff would be needed. If it's okay I'll shove off. You said something about calling your sister-in-law last night so I wrote her phone number on the pad there so you won't forget. Appreciate the breakfast, sir." He left, closing the door of the room behind him. O'Connor went to the window and looked out. The waves were breaking gently on the beach and a group of sailors were playing volleyball in the sand. You people weren't out drinking last night, he said to himself. He turned and walked over to the desk and sat down at the telephone and looked at the pad with Carol's telephone number on it.

Chief Petty Officers, he thought to himself. When I graduated from Sub School, the Commanding Officer told us that when we get to flag rank we can depend on a good staff to cover our mistakes and make us look good, but until we get that high we had better damned well depend on the Chief Petty Officers of this Navy. He drew a deep breath and asked the switchboard operator to connect him with the number on the pad.

He got into her car outside of the main gate of the hotel. "We can go to the house if you don't mind," she said. "I'm living there alone now. Oh, you wouldn't know, Mother got married to the engineer she'd been going with. He came out here to help raise the battleships and then they wanted him to stay on and work as an engineer in the navy yard. They went back to the mainland a month ago for their honeymoon, and as far as I know, they'll come back here to sell the house and then they'll be living in New York."

"Is he a nice man?" Mike asked.

"He's a dear," she said. "He's a little older than Mother, but I like him a lot."

"You didn't mind her getting married?"

"Of course not," Carol said. "She has a right to be loved, to love someone. She loved my father, I know she loved him a great deal, but that doesn't mean she can't love someone else if he's the right man for her."

She pulled the car into the driveway of the house and got out. Mike walked behind her, admiring against his will the sweet curve of her back and the long, clean lines of her legs. She went into the kitchen and made coffee and brought it into the living room.

"You've heard about Andy," she said.

"Yes. A Lieutenant Commander named Olsen came to see me yesterday, right after we got in."

"Red Olsen," Carol said. "A very sweet man."

"Are you all right, Carol?" Mike said suddenly, and then regretted the banality of his question.

"All right? Yes. I'm all right. It's been over a month since the chaplain from the base came out and told me that Andy was missing in action and presumed dead.

"It was hard at first, hard to realize that he was gone. He was so vital, but . . ." She looked away from Mike's eyes and then took her coffee cup in both hands and drank from it.

"But what?" Mike said.

She faced him, her green eyes clear and level. "I expected

the chaplain to come and tell me he was gone, Michael. I expected it from the last day he was here in Pearl Harbor."

"Why? I mean, if you want to tell me. You don't have to."

"Because of our trouble," she said. "He thought there was no way out of what was between us. I thought there was a chance, a small chance, that he could accept it, that he could accept my love for what it was, just love and not lust or anything sinful. But after he left I knew, down deep I knew, there wasn't a chance." She drew a deep breath.

"I've thought about it a lot. I don't think he deliberately went out and committed suicide in battle because committing suicide is a sin in his religion, isn't it?" Mike nodded.

"I think that he just didn't care anymore, that he took too many chances. Red Olsen told me he'd shot down more enemy planes than any pilot on the ship. I keep thinking that in that last big battle he just didn't care."

"How much do you know about that battle?" Mike asked.

"Only what the newspapers said, what Red Olsen told me. The newspapers said that the Japanese lost hundreds of planes. That means that hundreds of Japanese pilots died, but no one says anything about them. They did say that only about seventy-six Americans pilots died.

"They told me that Andy had shot down more than thirty planes. It seems to me that someone as good as Andy was wouldn't have been killed unless he didn't care what happened to him."

Mike O'Connor put his coffee cup on the table and stood up and began to pace up and down the room, his face grim.

"Let me tell you what I know about that battle," he said. He talked slowly, picking his words with care, telling her what Red Olsen had told him about Andy chewing out Olsen for leaving their three-plane formation.

"Andy had lots of chances to do what you said. He could have done what Red Olsen did, leave the formation, make a suicide attack on the Jap planes on the airfield. He could have dived his plane into the gasoline tanks, the aviation fuel tanks at the airfield on Guam. That would have made him a hell of a big hero, because as long as the Japs had planes and fuel on Guam, they could attack our ships.

"He didn't have to wait until that big air battle. Before that the *Enterprise* was making air raids on Truk, that's a big Japanese stronghold out in the Pacific. He could have done something stupid and very brave and it wouldn't have looked like suicide and to him it wouldn't have been suicide." He stopped and looked down at the slim girl sitting in front of him.

"I know my brother, Carol. I grew up with him. I can't tell you how many fights I got into because he was always taking on two or three guys bigger than he was. Andy was a fighter. He wasn't a quitter. Sure, you both had a big problem. It tore him up inside. But he wouldn't have quit! He would have faced it when he got back to port. I won't accept what you say. I won't accept it because it isn't true." He pulled the envelope Red Olsen had given him out of his shirt pocket.

"Did the chaplain or Olsen tell you what his last words were?"

"No," she said in a small voice.

"Well, read this," he said. He dropped the envelope in her lap and turned away and stared out the window for a long time. He heard her sob and felt her hands on his shoulders and turned and took her into his arms, her head against his chest, her body shaking as she cried. He held her until she had stopped crying and then he gently wiped her eyes with his handkerchief.

"Those aren't the words of a quitter," he said in a gentle voice. "Those were the words of a fighter taking on all comers. Maybe that's hard for you to understand. Whatever trouble you had between you had nothing to do with why he died." He paused and held her out at arm's length.

"I didn't tell you yet, I had a letter from the folks when I got in. They want you to come and stay with them for a while. I think it would be the right thing to do. You'll like my parents."

She walked over to the mantel and took down a polished wooden box and gave it to him. He recognized the box, he had one. He opened it, a dread seeping through him as he did so, and saw the twin of his own Medal of Honor.

"Oh, my God!" he said to himself. "He killed himself trying to get this damned medal because I had one and he didn't!" He looked up, his face agonized, and Carol went to him and held him.

Chapter
Twenty-five

THE COURIER PLANE LANDED at Midway Airport in Chicago and taxied down to a military hangar at the far end of the airfield. A Chief Yeoman waited until the stairs were dropped from the DC-3 and then trotted up into the plane. He found Mike O'Connor and sat down beside him as the other military passengers gathered up their hand luggage and began to leave the plane.

"I'm Chief Miller, Captain," the Chief Yeoman said. "The Admiral at Great Lakes thought you'd like to get home to your folks' house with as little confusion as possible, sir. He's laid on a car and driver to take you to Evanston. That's where your folks live? Day after tomorrow the Admiral would like to have you come out to Great Lakes Naval Training Station for a press conference and maybe talk to the recruits, if you don't mind."

"Whatever the Admiral wants," Mike O'Connor said.

"I'll call you about ten o'clock, day after tomorrow, sir. The Admiral will send a car and driver to pick you up. This your bag? I'll carry it, sir."

"I don't understand all this stuff going on," O'Connor grumbled.

"We never had anyone with the big medal from Chicago, Captain," the Chief said with a grin. "Just relax and let it come to you, it won't hurt a bit. There's your driver, Bos'n's Mate First Drobowski. He'll get you home in time for breakfast, sir."

"I'm afraid I don't know where they live," Mike O'Connor said to the driver as the car crossed Howard Street and headed into Evanston. "My folks bought their house up here since I had my last leave, before the war started."

"I know where you live, sir," the driver said. "I brought the

Admiral out here once to see your folks. Your mother and I had a lot of fun, she speaks better Polish than I do." He made a left turn on Central Street. "Your folks live on Park Place, like in the Monopoly game, sir."

He turned into the street, and Mike, peering through the windshield, could see the lean, erect figure of his father standing on the porch of a house in the middle of the block. Beside him was the buxom, equally erect figure of his mother, her arm around Carol. The car stopped and he got out and trotted up the sidewalk while the driver got his suitcases out of the car's trunk. He engulfed his mother in a hug, reaching past her to grab his father's hand.

"I have a strudel I baked last night," his mother said as she led the way into the house. "And fresh coffee."

"She baked the strudel at four this morning," his father growled. "She was so restless because you were coming this morning that I kicked her out of bed and told her to do something useful." They trooped into the kitchen and sat down around a table.

"How long can you stay?" his mother asked from the sideboard where she was pouring coffee.

"Ten days," Mike said. "I've got a new ship, a new submarine. She's being built at New London, in Connecticut. Doesn't even have a name yet, just a number. We won't be ready for sea for five or six months, maybe a little longer."

"Does that mean you can come back again once or twice?" his mother asked.

"If you'll promise to make another strudel," Mike said. He turned to Carol. "Mom's strudel was a big treat when we were growing up. We usually got one on every holy day."

"And whenever your father declared it to be a holy day," Sophia O'Connor said. "Now that you've had your dessert, how do you want your eggs, same as always?"

After breakfast Mike's father led him into the living room while the women cleared away the dishes and washed up. He motioned his son to a chair at one side of the fireplace and sat down in a matching chair across from him.

"You've noticed we didn't speak of your brother," his father said. "It was not an oversight. We honor his memory. His loss took a part of our hearts, your mother's and mine." He stopped and his face twisted in pain.

"The Irish and the Poles are proud people," he said after a

moment. "Andrew died in a cause that our forefathers died for, the right to be free."

"How did Mother take it?" Mike asked in a low voice.

"Your mother is a thoroughbred," his father said. He looked into the fireplace and then he turned to his son, his dark blue eyes misting with tears.

"She held me when my grief became too much for me. But if she cried I did not see it." He pulled out a handkerchief and blew his nose.

"Your sending Carol to us was the medicine we both needed. She's such a lovely colleen. These five months she's been here with us have have been a little bit of heaven for your mother. And for me." He listened with an experienced ear to the sounds coming from the kitchen.

"Your mother is a neatnik. So is Carol, bless her soul. They can clean things up so fast you'd never know anything had been dirty. So I'll say one more thing before they come in with another pot of coffee.

"Your mother wants some time alone with you. I don't have to go back to the office until you've left, so sometime in the next few days I'll take Carol off with me to the store or something."

"Aye, aye, sir," Mike said. He looked up with a grin as his mother and Carol came into the living room with a tray loaded with coffee, cups, sugar and cream. He took the cup of coffee Carol had poured for him and sat back.

"Will you be going out to fight again, Michael?" His mother's face was drawn, worried.

"I don't think so," Mike said. "The war is winding down. The Japanese are defeated. We know it and they know it. I think it will be all over before Labor Day this year." His mother crossed herself and murmured, "Thank the Lord."

The next few days were hectic as the senior O'Connors and Carol took Mike on a round of visits to neighbors, to the local stores to shake hands with the store owners and their clerks. On the fourth day Mike's father rose from the kithchen table and nodded his head at Carol. She slid out of her seat and went to the front-room coat closet and got her coat and left with him.

Sophia O'Connor waited until she heard the car leave the garage and then she cleared the table and poured two cups of coffee.

"You're a grown man, my son," she said. "I want to talk to you as a grown woman to a man, not as mother to son. Can we do that?"

"Of course," Mike said.

"I want to talk to you about Carol and Andrew. I want to know what you know about their marriage, knowing ahead of time that I love this girl as much as if I had borne her."

"What about their marriage?" her son asked.

"What was wrong with their marriage? And don't look across your coffee cup at me with your father's eyes as he always does when I ask him something important."

He put down his cup. "What makes you think something was wrong?"

"His letters changed after he got married. That's one thing. There was something wrong when he was writing. I could feel that. Then Carol came here and I have lived with that lovely girl for the past five months." She paused and looked at her son across the table.

"I am a complete woman, Michael, a whole woman as your father would tell you if he spoke of such things and thank God he does not.

"Nor does Carol speak of such things. But I know. She is a whole woman, the sort of woman I was when I was her age. She will be a full-blooded woman when she is my age, as I am. Do you know what I am talking about?"

"I think I do," Mike O'Connor said.

"Then tell me."

Mike O'Connor put his hand on the scrubbed white wooden kitchen table and began to talk. He told his mother what Andy had told him, what advice he had given to Andy. He spoke, his voice very low, of what Carol had told him. When he had finished, his mother put her hands on top of his.

"I've never heard of this thing you mention," Sophia O'Connor said. "But if you say it's not uncommon..." Her voice trailed off and her eyes looked past her son.

"The poor, dear girl," she said softly. "What a pity that Andrew was not more like his father."

"What do you mean?" Mike asked. His mother looked at him with her steady eyes.

"I will tell you something that you will not repeat to your father. I was brought up on the Church teachings and I obeyed them. Your father had lived a rougher life in Ireland and when he first came to this country, but he never spoke of what he had done to me.

"I was a virgin when we were married. Your father's love awakened a passion in me I had never imagined was there. It did not dismay him. You came along to bless our love and then Andy came. But the passion was still there in both of us. We decided that the Church was sincere in its teachings, but its priests, celibate men, could not know everything about the human heart and soul. We have been happy, my son, very happy." Her hands tightened on his.

"Andrew was always one for hanging around the good fathers. You were not so much that way, as I remember. Maybe Carol's pain is something I will have to answer for when I am judged, because I bear some of the blame for that pain.

"I taught the two of you about what used to be called the facts of life, but I never told you about how two people can feel toward each other, how physical passion, love, can be the greatest thing in the lives of two people. I just assumed that because you were both boys that you would be like your father."

Mike turned his hands over and engulfed hers in his. "No, no," he said in a soft voice. "You bear no blame, none at all. You raised us and you did a good job. No two sons could have had better parents.

"Andy and I were different in ways you didn't know. He told me that he realized that he was always thinking that he was my moral guardian, the moral guardian of everyone else close to him. It started a long time ago, in high school." He sat back in his chair.

"I tried to convince Andy that, well, let me put it this way. I could understand how he felt about not being able to be a father. He knew I understood that. What I don't think I did was to convince him that it shouldn't make a difference to him, to Carol, that they could have a good life, a full life.

"Andy was convinced that the priests were right when they taught us that it was sinful to, ah—" He felt the flush crawling up his face and his mother's hands tightened on his.

"I know," she said in a soft voice. "He hurt himself. He hurt a lovely girl and he thought he was doing the right thing."

"She told me she was going to stay married to him, no matter what, as long as he wanted it that way," Mike said.

"I believe that," his mother said. "As your father is fond of

saying, she's a thoroughbred. She would defy the devil himself
if she thought what she was doing was right."

"Will you tell Dad what we've talked about, what I told
you?"

"Of course," his mother said. "Your father is part of my
heart. But I won't tell him until after you've gone and after
Carol has left." She saw his thick black eyebrows raise.

"Your father has what is called clout in this city, if you
remember what the word means. He says he has never been a
politician but he's a better politician than those who make a
profession of it. He's respected by the leaders of both parties in
the city, county and the state. And when he asks for something
he gets it.

"A month or so ago he sat down with Carol and they talked.
She agreed with him that she was a young woman, that she had
her own life to live. So he talked to some people he knows and
she's been offered a very good job in Washington, with the
Navy. She's happy about the job. If she tells you, act surprised.
I wouldn't want her to know that I've told you, because I think
she's looking forward to telling you herself."

She rose from her chair in a graceful, fluid movement. "Your
father will be back soon and he'll have bags of groceries I don't
need. Letting that man loose in a grocery store or meat market
is like turning a burglar loose in a bank. He grabs everything in
sight." She walked around the table and stood behind Mike
O'Connor and put her arms around his broad back and laid her
head on his.

"Thank you for telling me. I knew something was wrong, but
I didn't know what. And do me one more favor; the only time
Carol has been out at all is with us. She needs to go out with
someone younger. Take her to dinner or the movies or
something."

The waiter at the Blackhawk Restaurant brought the coffee
and Mike sat back in his chair. "I've eaten in restaurants in
China and the Philippines and a lot of other places, but I've
never found any place that can fix Lake Michigan whitefish the
way they do here."

"I know," Carol said. "I've eaten here with the folks three or
four times. Your father is very fond of whitefish. I like it, too."
She smiled across the table at him. "What do you think of my
new job?"

"I think it's great," Mike said. "Washington isn't far from New London. Maybe I could run down and take you to dinner."

"I'd like that," she said. "I'd like that very much."

"How about finding a place to live?" he asked. "Aren't apartments hard to find these days?"

"I know some people who were stationed in Pearl Harbor before the war, Captain Anders and his wife. They've found me an apartment, it's furnished and it's close enough to where I'll be working so I can walk to work. I love to walk, so that's no bother. I won't need a car, not that you can buy one these days without paying with both arms and legs."

"If you need any money," he said quickly, "I mean, I've been piling it up since the war started."

She put her hand on his. "No. I don't need any money. I have the pension and I'll have my salary. What I really needed you gave to me, and then your dad and mother gave me even more. They gave me their love."

He closed the garage doors and they walked up the sidewalk toward the back door of his father's house. He held her arm so she wouldn't slip on the ice.

"It's been a lovely evening, Michael," she said. She turned to him and raised her face. He bent and kissed her. His lips clung to hers for a long moment and he smelled again the sweet aroma of her skin, tasted the fragrance of her lips and then he hunched his shoulders in his heavy uniform overcoat.

"It's cold," he said. "Let's go in."

Captain O'Connor's first three weeks at New London were hectic. He was satisfied with the officers who had been assigned to the new submarine. His Executive Officer was a dour Lieutenant who had made four war patrols. Three other officers had each made two war patrols, and when the construction of the ship was further along, he would get two junior officers from submarine school to fill out the Wardroom.

The Chief Petty Officers and most of the leading petty officers had arrived, and Mike O'Connor was pleased with them. The Chief of the Boat was an old hand with sixteen years in the submarine navy, plus five war patrols under his belt. Captain O'Connor spent his days with his officers and enlisted men, scrambling through the cluttered interior of the submarine, watching as the navy yard artificers installed and connected the air, hydraulic oil and water lines that are the arteries of a submarine, tracing the intricate electrical networks that would be the nervous system of the ship, learning each of the thousands of details of the machinery within the sleek hull of this most modern of underwater fighting ships. He checked in at the construction shack after work late one afternoon before going to his quarters and found a message asking him to call a number in Washington. He plodded up to his quarters, stripped off his filthy working khaki uniform and showered. Wrapped in a robe, he sat in the combination sitting room-bedroom of his quarters and dialed the number.

"Isn't it about time you kept your promise to take me to dinner?" Carol's voice asked.

"I think it is," he said. "What's today, Thursday? How about Saturday? I looked up the train schedules when I first got here. I can be there by about two o'clock. That okay? Look, would you do the honors and pick out a restaurant and make the reservations? I don't know anything about Washington. And if you would, get me a reservation for a room at the BOQ for Saturday night, if you don't mind. I won't have to leave until about three o'clock Sunday."

The taxicab let him off in front of an apartment house and he found her name beside a black button in the lobby. The door buzzer echoed sharply in the small vestibule and he went to the elevator and rode up to the fourth floor. Carol was standing outside her apartment door, her face radiant. She closed the door behind her and took his overcoat and hung it up and then kissed him.

"Coffee will be ready in a minute," she said, "and I made a strudel. Your mother gave me her recipe. I tried it out last week and it tasted all right to me. I'll be back in a minute."

He sat down and looked around the apartment. He noticed a small picture of Andy on the mantel over the fake fireplace. She came out of the kitchen with coffee and a platter of sliced strudel. He picked up a slice and bit into it.

"By golly, you've made it just as good as Mom does," he said.

"Thank goodness," she said fervently. He finished the slice while she poured the coffee and then he reached for another slice.

They talked away the rest of the afternoon. From time to time she'd leave the room and go into the kitchen. Each time she did so, a tantalizing aroma floated into the small living room.

"Smells like we're not going to a restaurant, that we're going to eat here, that right?" he asked.

"Pot roast with baby carrots, onions, celery, potatoes and lots of thick gravy," she said.

"Did you make a trial run on that, too?"

"A week ago last Sunday. I had the Captain and his wife who found this apartment for me here for dinner. It turned out all right, I think, he ate three helpings. Just cross your fingers it will be all right this time."

The pot roast was delicious. Mike went back for seconds and then, with an apologetic grin, he put two pieces of bread on his plate and ladled the thick, savory gravy over them.

"Your mother told me you used to do that with bread and gravy when you were a kid," she said.

"You cook mighty well, Lady Carol," he said. "Very tender gravy, no bones." He finished and helped her clear the table, and against her protests he took off his uniform jacket, loosened his tie and rolled up his sleeves and washed the dishes while she dried. When the kitchen was cleaned up, they went into the living room.

"I don't think I told you," she said. "I gave Andy's Medal of Honor to the folks to keep."

"That's very generous of you," he said. "It would mean an awful lot to Dad." He looked at her, his eyes questioning. "You're over the guilt feelings you had, that's all back of you now?"

"Yes," she said. "After you left to go to New London, your mother and I had a very long talk. I didn't know she had sensed that there was something wrong between Andy and myself. She's a very sensitive woman."

"Poles are dreamers, idealists," he said. "The Irish and Poles have fought hard, bled and died to be free. You have to be a dreamer, an idealist, to fight against the odds they have fought against."

"Your mother told me about herself and your father," Carol said. She rose and pulled the chain of a lamp to offset the gloom of the darkness outside.

"She told me how it was with her and your father when they got married. They are two very fortunate people, your parents. They were strong enough to trust to their love for each other. She told me she had told you about that."

He nodded. "She told me. I guess I should have been embarrassed, my mother telling me things like that, but I wasn't. I envy the two of them. They give each other love. They never hid that when we were kids.

"What bothers me was that in your case it was almost a case of history repeating itself, only Andy wasn't as smart as his father. She said as much to me."

"And to me," Carol said. "I'm glad she told me, because it made me feel better, as if everything were finally over and done with. What happened between Andy and myself wasn't his fault and it wasn't my fault. It was just something very sad that happened. I guess I'll always love him, in a different sort of way than I used to feel. But I know now that he didn't die to solve our problems."

"I know how you felt," Mike said slowly. "I don't want to make you feel badly, but I know, from my own experience, that you don't think about your brother or your parents or your wife, if you've got one, when you're in combat and someone is trying their damndest to kill you.

"You think about only one thing. How to beat the other guy. How to kill him, if you'll excuse the use of that word. You think about living. You don't have the time, the luxury, to think about anything else but surviving."

"Dad said as much to me in different words," Carol said. "I don't have any guilt feelings anymore. When are you going to get rid of yours?"

He looked up, startled. "You're as fey as my mother," he said. He stood up, his face somber in the light of the lamp.

"I don't know, Carol. We, Andy and I, we had a thing going between ourselves ever since we entered the Academy. We were going to make Admiral together. The Admirals O'Connor, we used to say. When he won the Distinguished Service Cross, he kidded me a lot, wrote me a lot of letters and told me I had to win a Navy Cross so I could catch up with him, because a DSM is a lot more important medal than the Silver Star I had." He stopped and slowly shook his head.

"Medals won in a war are so damned important for promotion to Admiral. The bigger your medals the better the chance you've got to step up out of the crowd.

"When I got the Medal of Honor I really ribbed him. I kept

riding him. Wrote him letters and told him to get off his butt, win the Medal of Honor or a Navy Cross or I'd make Admiral before he did." He turned and walked to the window and stood staring out into the darkness.

"Sometimes I wake up at night and wonder if maybe I rode him too hard, if maybe he made a mistake because he was trying to catch up with me."

She rose and went to him and put her arms around him, her head resting against his broad back.

"No," she said. "No!" He turned in her arms and stared down at her face. Then he bent his head and their lips met. She pressed herself against him, her lips opening to his mouth. They clung together. A long minute later he pulled his mouth free and looked down at her.

"Carol!" he breathed. She raised her face, her lips opening, and he met them with his own lips, feeling the steady pressure of her hips against him. They separated and he looked at his wristwatch.

"I'd better go," he said in a choked voice.

She walked across the living room and into the small hall that led to the front door of the apartment. The apartment's single bedroom opened off the hall and she stopped at the door of the bedroom. She walked in and Mike O'Connor stopped outside. She turned in the dimly lit bedroom and faced him, her eyes serene.

"Your father told me that he thought the ability to give love and to receive love was a gift from God," she said. "He said that once you had that gift, you always had it, but that you must use it to make yourself and someone you love happy." She looked at him and smiled.

"You have a choice, Michael Turloch O'Connor, whom I love. If you stay, it will be forever."

He looked at her for a long moment from the doorway. He smiled gently and walked into the room and her arms.

ABOUT THE AUTHOR

Author HARRY HOMEWOOD was a qualified submariner before he was seventeen years old—having lied about his age to the Navy—serving in a little "S"-boat in the Asiatic fleet. After Pearl Harbor he reenlisted and made eleven war patrols in the Southwest Pacific. He was also a qualified four-engine pilot. He later became Chicago bureau chief for *Newsweek*, chief editorial writer for the *Chicago Sun-Times*, and for eleven years had his own weekly news program syndicated to thirty-two PBS television stations.